Benjamin Franklin ★ N
Mark Twain ★ Ar
Edith Wharton ★ 1
Sinclair Lewis ★ Will Rog... ★ Dorothy Parker
★ James Thurber ★ Langston Hughes ★
Russell Baker ★ Calvin Trillin ★ Molly Ivins ★
and a host of other brilliantly barbed talents

What good American writer would attack war, politics, patriotism, religion, marriage, even motherhood?

Only the best.

The writers in this volume were not out to make friends. They were aiming to destroy enemies, and their enemies were formidable. But so were these writers' weapons, whether they used prose or verse, fiction or parody, reportage or criticism. This superb collection provides over three hundred years of deliciously deadly wit and cutting social commentary that is at once serious, informative, and very entertaining.

American Satire

AN ANTHOLOGY OF WRITINGS FROM COLONIAL TIMES TO THE PRESENT

Nicholas Bakalar is a writer and editor with numerous books to his credit. He lives with his wife in New York City.

American Satire

AN ANTHOLOGY OF WRITINGS FROM COLONIAL TIMES TO THE PRESENT

Edited by Nicholas Bakalar

Introduction by Stephen Koch
Columbia University

A MERIDIAN BOOK

MERIDIAN
Published by the Penguin Group
Penguin Books USA Inc., 375 Hudson Street,
New York, New York 10014, U.S.A.
Penguin Books Ltd, 27 Wrights Lane, London W8 5TZ, England
Penguin Books Australia Ltd, Ringwood, Victoria, Australia
Penguin Books Canada Ltd, 10 Alcorn Avenue,
Toronto, Ontario, Canada M4V 3B2
Penguin Books (N.Z.) Ltd, 182–190 Wairau Road,
Auckland 10, New Zealand

Penguin Books Ltd, Registered Offices: Harmondsworth, Middlesex, England

First published by Meridian, an imprint of Dutton Signet,
a division of Penguin Books USA Inc.

First Printing, April, 1997
10 9 8 7 6 5 4 3 2

Ⓜ REGISTERED TRADEMARK—MARCA REGISTRADA

LIBRARY OF CONGRESS CATALOGING-IN-PUBLICATION DATA:
American satire : an anthology of writings from Colonial times to the
present / edited by Nicholas Bakalar ; introduction by Stephen Koch.
          p.   cm.
          ISBN 0-452-01174-4
1. Satire, American.   2. American literature.   3. United States—
          Civilization—Humor.   I. Bakalar, Nick.
          PN6231.S2A47   1997
817.008—dc20
                                                      96-44144
                                                          CIP

Printed in the United States of America
Set in New Baskerville
Designed by Eve L. Kirch

BOOKS ARE AVAILABLE AT QUANTITY DISCOUNTS WHEN USED TO PROMOTE
PRODUCTS OR SERVICES. FOR INFORMATION PLEASE WRITE TO PREMIUM MAR-
KETING DIVISION, PENGUIN BOOKS USA INC., 375 HUDSON STREET, NEW YORK,
NEW YORK 10014.

For Libby, whose idea it was.

CONTENTS

PREFACE

This collection is meant to be serious without being dull. The pieces chosen have literary merit of one kind or another—a choice easy to make for earlier selections, since satire without some literary value in general does not survive. For the modern selections, the task is somewhat more difficult, and involves more in the way of subjective judgment. But satire, in its most powerful form, is at once funny and deadly serious, and I have tried to choose pieces that are both of those things. Twain, Mencken, Vidal, Vonnegut, Buchwald, even Parker and Thurber (allowances made for the subjects they choose), are serious about their satire, so they all find a place in this collection. Of course, what is seriously funny is very much a matter of opinion, and my opinion will not be shared by all.

From colonial days to the present, the form has attracted the country's best writers—some famous primarily for their satire like Twain or Ambrose Bierce, and others perhaps better known for other work but whose satires continue to provoke a smile and a knowing nod: Francis Hopkinson, a signer of the Declaration of Independence, was among several who participated in a flourishing of political satire around the time of the Revolution; Washington Irving gently satirized the literary life; Nathaniel Hawthorne turned his pen on the Transcendentalists. And, at least sometimes, the satirist's humor reached even the halls of power where folly has its most serious consequences: Lincoln himself is said to have read Artemus Ward before presenting the Emancipation Proclamation to his cabinet, and later Theodore Roosevelt, a victim of the satire of Finley Peter Dunne (but nevertheless always a consummate politician), invited the author to visit him in Washington. President McKinley was also an avid reader of Dunne's Mr. Dooley stories.

I have demonstrated the long history of American satire by including examples from the earliest days up to the present. This creates a problem: The older a satire is, the more obscure the allusions, and the less understandable to modern readers. So the earliest pieces here may require more historical knowledge than some readers have, and more effort at understanding than others are willing to invest. At the same time, some early pieces—I am thinking here particularly of the selection from Washington Irving's *Tales of a Traveler*—seem entirely modern, perfectly understandable to today's reader without explanation or special knowledge of any kind. And some satire is eternal: Mark Twain's "War Prayer" is as pointed today as it was when it was written almost one hundred years ago.

I have tried occasionally to show how the preoccupations of today's satirists are not all that different from those of earlier eras. Benjamin Franklin thought to satirize letters of recommendation; so did Mark Twain, and we might wonder whether Twain had ever seen Franklin's parody. P. J. O'Rourke makes the comparison with Twain explicit in the essay included here. From Franklin to Twain to P. J. O'Rourke, whatever their varying talents and interests, a direct line of American satirical writing can easily be traced.

NICHOLAS BAKALAR

INTRODUCTION

Stephen Koch
Columbia University

Insult, derision, scorn: These may spell the downfall of decent manners, but they are the basis of satire, and their insolent energy sparks one of the highest, and funniest, forms of comedy. There is a little bit of satire in almost all humor; comedy is never wholly unconnected to the ridiculous, and some of the satiric spirit can be found lying around wherever people are laughing. Almost every time you make a wisecrack, almost every time you crack a joke, a little spark from the force field of ridicule has been caught, shaped, and tossed back at something. The satiric mode takes a thousand irreverent shapes, and it does so in every medium: In television and film; on stage and in print—every spoof, lampoon, cartoon, and takeoff is plugged into the mode. The style can be high or low. It may assume the airs of refined disdain, or it may be a crude raspberry in words. Satire's purpose is always the same: To break the solemn spell of pomposity, to laugh down whatever refuses to be laughed at. It may be political; it may be personal —no matter. Satire is always a weapon, and as a weapon, it is always pointed at some target. True, the satiric slingshot may be shooting puffballs filled with confetti, but it can also be armed with lethal ammunition—and so it matters who is pointing the weapon at whom. There is a little bit of cruelty coiled inside every satire, and unfortunately, not every satire is a weapon aimed by a good person at something bad.

The writing in *American Satire* has been collected to show how Americans have used the satiric mode from before the founding of the republic until the end of the twentieth century, and how it has been used at every phase of American history to make the country and its culture what they are.

Let's begin with the eighteenth century. The humor of that admirable epoch stands out as a great age of satire, and satire in turn is bound to the eighteenth century as a catalyst for the great achievements in both politics and in thought that brought about, among other signal events, the birth of the American republic. Satire, revolution, the republic—these three are linked, and the force that links them is the Enlightenment, that wave of rationalist, humanitarian, liberal, scientific thought which, following the emergence of a new science in the seventeenth century, transformed Western life. It was the Enlightenment that supplied the ideology for the French Revolution; and the same Enlightenment shaped the thinking of the American founding fathers.

Satire has come down to us as the most memorable form of Enlightenment humor. In fact, the satiric spirit was an essential element of Enlightenment thinking, one of the forces driving its most serious enterprises. Consider, for example, that great philosophe and wit, Voltaire (1694–1778). Virtually every portrait of Voltaire in existence shows the French sage smiling, and Voltaire's smile is a very special one. It is a smile of mockery, a gently sneering smile; thin, and if not exactly cruel, still relentlessly, habitually amused; a smile like a weapon. Here is one of the greatest of the philosophes—one of those eighteenth-century men of ideas who led the intellectual life of their age. The sound of a century's laughter can still be heard echoing around Voltaire, not merely laughter over his satiric tales like *Candide* (1759), but over the mockery and wit that run through volume after volume of his prose.

Voltaire and the philosophes had friends in England, but they had true heirs in America, where the colonial legatees of the Enlightenment met their destiny founding a government that would transform the world. England gave Voltaire the thinker a kind of model for political reason, while providing Voltaire the man with tremendous colleagues in the arts of ridicule. Satire was vital to the political transformations of the age—though in England satire took a less obviously political path than it did in France, or in America either for that matter. The greatest British satire—the satire of Jonathan Swift (1667–1745) and Alexander Pope (1688–1744)—had powerful political motives but took as its target human folly in general. The ideal example is Swift's *Gulliver's Travels* (1726). Among the angry colonists in America, on the other hand, the cutting edge of the Enlightenment took the form of more obviously political ridicule, as we see here in selections from Alexander Hamilton (Hamilton the writer, not the more famous secretary of the treasury under George Washington and fighter of duels), Francis Hopkinson, and above all Benjamin Franklin. Voltaire's British friends included the greatest satirists of the age—he knew both Swift and Pope—the major figures who lived and wrote in the generation immediately preceding these Americans.

America had its own philosophes, of whom the two most illustrious were Thomas Jefferson (1743–1826) and Benjamin Franklin (1706–1790). Franklin's cutting satiric attacks on British policy toward the American colonies—above all his "Rules by Which a Great Empire May Be Reduced to a Small One"—have much the same sound as Swift's mordant, chilling "Modest Proposal" (1729) in which Swift suggests that the solution to the problem of overpopulation in Ireland would be for the rich to simply kill, and then dine on, Irish babies.

Three years after "Rules by Which a Great Empire May Be Reduced to a Small One" Thomas Jefferson transposed many of the abuses listed in Franklin's inventory of ridicule into another list of abuses, writing not satirically but in the most elevated political discourse of the age: the Declaration of Independence. If the Declaration is America's greatest piece of Enlightenment prose, Franklin's Swiftian raillery captures something essential to all the philosophes: In it we hear the laughter of minds setting themselves free.

If the eighteenth century was a great age of satire, the nineteenth brought changes that took the wind out of the sails of the satiric spirit. It is not that satire vanished in 1800, of course, but the new century did transform it. Romanticism became the dominant movement, and with the rise of the Romantic novel, the age of the philosophes began to fade. Satire did not die, but it took new forms.

Consider Charles Dickens and the art of caricature, of which

Dickens was perhaps the century's greatest literary practitioner. Caricature is in essence a satiric art, and though a certain number of Dickens's caricatures are more lovable than cruel, Dickens did level the weapon of caricature in full fury against all kinds of frauds and abuses too. Yet is it right to call Dickens a satirist? Not quite. The spirit somehow is wrong, except, I fear, when Dickens writes about America, as he does in his genuinely satiric novel *Martin Chuzzlewit* (1843).

Satire is the comedy of outrage, and perhaps one reason satire changed is that the nineteenth century, in its romanticism, moved into a new relation to moral outrage, and with it to humor. If satire is, as the great literary critic Northrop Frye put it, "irony militant," then one would suppose that some of the most grievous ironies of nineteenth-century American life cried out for satiric treatment. By far the most outrageous of these national incongruities was that the American experiment in democracy also tolerated, defended, and exploited human slavery based in racism. In the eighteenth century that great English conservative Samuel Johnson growled at American hypocrisies: "How is it that we hear the loudest yelps for liberty among the drivers of Negroes?" Here was a case, if ever there was one, that called for "irony militant."

Yet there is strangely little American satire directed against slavery. There is some, however. For example, James Russell Lowell (1819–1890) in 1848 wrote an anti-slavery tirade in dialect, *The Biglow Papers*. But the most important nineteenth-century attacks on slavery were not satiric at all. By far the most influential piece of writing against slavery of the entire century was Harriet Beecher Stowe's novel *Uncle Tom's Cabin, or Life Among the Lowly* (1851–1852). When Stowe was presented to Abraham Lincoln at the White House, he said, "So this is the little lady who made this big war." Voltaire and Franklin had wanted their readers to laugh at wickedness. Mrs. Stowe did not. She wanted them to weep, to pound the table in anger, clutch their fevered brows in outrage. She was a romantic moralist; she was driven by a love for what she saw as the good and by fury against the bad; she was fiery with a moral vision in which satire and irony played no role—except posthumously, in the twentieth century, when new generations, laughing at Uncle Toms, would brush aside her lost sentimental certainties.

The high style of the eighteenth century could not survive in a romantic age. Satire did survive, of course. Some new American satire, such as Washington Irving's *Bracebridge Hall* (1822) and Nathaniel Hawthorne's "The Celestial Railroad" (1843) and *The Blithedale Romance* (1852) remained American versions of European models.

After the Civil War, however, a newly influential kind of low satire began to pop up all over American writing. It was a satire that was distinctly American for the simple reason that it spoke with a distinctly American accent. I am referring to the illiterate chuckling drawl of the American yokel: the hick, the backwoods country oaf. With this new kind of character, there emerged an enduring stereotype that has survived the decades in many forms. The great cliché of the stupid, uncouth American took shape. He and his descendants have been a standard feature of American culture both in art and life.

Every country has its bumpkins and fools, and while America may or may not have more than its share, real-life models for this essentially literary creation were easy to find. All through the nineteenth century, America was being populated by waves of none-too-highly-educated immigrants, the settlers who were the targets of Dickens's satire in *Martin Chuzzlewit*. But after the Civil War, the American oaf slowly ceased to be merely the *object* of satire. He—for the oaf was usually male—began to serve as satire's vehicle, its voice. Satire began to speak as a kind of hick wisdom; we began to be edified by the ironies of a bunch of bumpkin Candides. The idea was that from the mouths of the ignorant a kind of wisdom might flow that was uncluttered with the deformations of learning; in the country of the common man, this ironic, often satiric voice would be the sound of the common man's wisdom. For good and ill, this fantasy became a durable part of the culture.

And some was indeed for ill. For example, some of the most malevolent, racist, and anti-Union satire during the Civil War took the form of the now mercifully almost forgotten, almost incomprehensible jabbering of a sadistic, racist backwoods yokel named "Sut Lovingood," the creation of a journalist called George Washington Harris, whose hate-filled diatribes had a real following between 1854 and 1869. Here is a clear example of the satiric weapon used to evil ends. On the other hand, the new style could sometimes rise to wonderful things. Though it is always a little tainted by the sentimentalism of crudity of its premise, it did find, in Mark Twain (1835–1910), a great writer to advance it, and in 1884, a masterpiece to preserve it: *The Adventures of Huckleberry Finn.*

With the twentieth century, American satire acquired a new cutting edge and a new confidence, helped by the modernist impulse to shed the Romantic moralizing of the Victorian age and assisted, no doubt, by the emergence of America as a great power. Yet perhaps the greatest single force behind the flourishing of American wit in the new century was the proliferation of media. By the end of the nineteenth century, American theater, in the work of such playwrights as George Ade, was a real force. In the early part of the twentieth century, the lightning emergence of film as a cultural form opened vast new possibilities; satire was soon alive even in silent film. Then came broadcasting. Wit flourished in these new hothouses of the image and word. The new growth naturally caused changes in the culture. For example, some of the richest and funniest varieties of American parody and satire first sprouted into sight in the immigrant entertainment parading through the vaudeville houses that began to appear in the big cities around 1881, and ending when the Palace Theater in New York closed in 1932. The satire of vaudeville may have been low-down and vulgar, but it was satire nonetheless: Skits, send-ups, lampoons, roasts of everything that made the life of the big-city immigrant hard. Vaudeville was a great and vital form of comedy, and it did not die when the Palace closed its doors. It was rescued by radio, and the comedy of newcomers and outcasts found a mass audience on the airwaves. Twenty years later, with the arrival of television, that same comedy acquired an even more vivid new life and was taken up by new generations, while vaudeville also moved into film, as the genius of the Marx Brothers makes clear.

In literature, the new schools for satire were magazines. By far the most famous and influential of these was *The New Yorker* (founded 1925), originally a magazine largely devoted to satire. Which leads us to the round table. Many of the original writers of that publication used to gather for lunch and malice around a large round corner table in the Algonquin Hotel, near *The New Yorker*'s offices. The coterie came to be known as the wits of the round table. The masthead of *The New Yorker* featured the cartoon of an imaginary nineteenth-century highbrow, a high-hatted Manhattanite named Eustace Tilley, gazing through his monocle at a butterfly. The image caught the tone. *The New Yorker* gave a comic spin to the grand language people imagined a social registrant like Edith Wharton must have used—the same Edith Wharton who, as we see in this collection, had satiric moments of her own. In the Algonquin wits, the haughty aspirations of an era got a stylish but laughable spin. As Dorothy Parker said, "I was following in the exquisite footsteps of Edna St. Vincent Millay, unhappily in my own horrible sneakers." The Algonquin round table mixed high and low, and opened the way into other media: Many of its members, including Mrs. Parker herself, moved on to Hollywood, while one of the habitués at the Algonquin was Harpo Marx. And he talked!

Where next? The satiric spirit is an essential part of human comedy, and where it will move with the turn of a new century must be left to satirists to guess. We may be sure ridicule will follow its own ludicrous path into the new age. Wherever the fog of humorlessness darkens the scene, we may hope that somebody will have the wit to laugh.

Thomas Morton

(ca. 1590–ca. 1647)

Thomas Morton came to America from England as a business-man in 1624, and immediately fell into conflict with his Puritan neighbors. He took charge of a colony at the site of modern Quincy, Massachusetts, named it Merry Mount, and set about justifying the community's name by erecting a maypole, encouraging convivial merrymaking, poking fun at Puritans, and writing bawdy verse. For his trouble he was exiled from the colony, made his way back to England, and then two years later returned, only to be arrested and banished to England again. By 1643, he was back in Massachusetts, where he was quickly jailed and then exiled to Maine.

Morton became the model anti-Puritan. Hawthorne used him as a character in his short story "The Maypole of Merrymount," and he appears in two novels by John Lothrop Motley, *Morton's Hope* (1839) and *Merry Mount* (1849). He also turns up in a 1934 opera, *Merry Mount*, by the composer Howard Hanson. We reprint here an excerpt from his account of life in the colonies, *New English Canaan*.

New English Canaan

CHAP. VI.

Of the Indians apparrell.

The Indians in these parts do make their apparrell of the skinnes of severall sortes of beastes, and commonly of those that doe frequent those partes where they doe live; yet some of them, for variety, will have the skinnes of such beasts that frequent the partes of their neighbors, which they purchase of them by Commerce and Trade.

The Indians make good lether.

These skinnes they convert into very good lether, making the same plume and soft. Some of these skinnes they dresse with the haire on, and some with the haire off; the hairy side in winter time they weare next their bodies, and in warme weather they weare the haire outwardes: they make likewise some Coates of the Feathers of Turkies, which they weave together with twine of their owne makinge, very prittily: these garments they weare like mantels knit over their shoulders, and put under their arme: they have likewise another sort of mantels, made of Mose skinnes, which beast is a great large Deere so bigge as a horse; these skinnes they commonly dresse bare, and make them wondrous white, and stripe them with size round about the borders, in forme like lace set on by a Taylor, and some they stripe with size in workes of severall fashions very curious, according to the sev-

Indians ingenious workemen for their garments.

erall fantasies of the workemen, wherein they strive to excell one another: And Mantels made of Beares skinnes is an usuall wearinge, among the Natives that live where the Beares doe haunt: they make shooes of Mose skinnes, which is the principall leather used to that purpose; and for want of such lether (which is the strongest) they make shooes of Deeres skinnes, very handsomly and commodious; and, of such deeres skinnes as they dresse bare, they make stockings that comes within their shooes, like a stirrop stockinge, and is fastned above at their belt, which is about their middell; Every male, after hee attaines unto the age which they call Pubes, wereth a belt about his middell, and a broad peece of lether that goeth betweene his leggs and is tuckt up both before and behinde under that belt; and this they weare to hide their secreats of nature, which by no meanes they will suffer to be seene, so much modesty they use in that particular; those garments they allwayes put on, when they goe a huntinge, to keepe their skinnes from the brush of the Shrubbs: and when they have their Apparrell one they looke like Irish in their trouses, the Stockinges joyne so to their breeches. A good well growne deere skin is of great account with them, and it must have the tale on, or else they account it defaced; the tale being three times as long as the tales of our English Deere, yea foure times so longe, this when they travell is raped round about their body, and, with a girdle of their making, bound round about their middles, to which girdle is fastned a bagg, in which his instruments be with which hee can strike fire upon any occasion.

The modesty of the Indian men.

Indians travaille with materials to strike fire at all times.

Thus with their bow in their left hand, and their quiuer of Arrowes at their back, hanging one their left shoulder with the lower end of it in their right hand, they will runne away a dogg trot untill they come to their journey end; and, in this kinde of ornament, they doe seeme to me to be hansomer than when they are in English apparrell, their gesture being answerable to their one habit and not unto ours.

Their women have shooes and stockinges to weare like-wise when they please, such as the men have, but the mantle they use to cover their nakednesse with is much longer then that which the men use; for, as the men have one Deeres skinn, the women have two soed together at the full lenght, and it is so lardge that it trailes after them like a great Ladies trane; and in time I thinke they may have their Pages to beare them up; and where the men use but one Beares skinn for a Mantle, the women have two soed together; and if any of their women would at any time shift one, they take that which they intend to make use of, and cast it over them round, before they shifte away the other, for modesty, being unwilling to be

seene to discover their nakednesse; and the one being so cast over, they slip the other from under them in a decent manner, which is to be noted in people uncivilized; therein they seeme to have as much modesty as civilized people, and deserve to be applauded for it.

CHAP. VII.

Of their Child-bearing, and delivery, and what manner of persons they are.

The women of this Country are not suffered to be used for procreation untill the ripenesse of their age, at which time they weare a redd cap made of lether, in forme like to our flat caps, and this they weare for the space of 12 moneths, for all men to take notice of them that have any minde to a wife; and then it is the custome of some of their Sachems or Lords of the territories, to have the first say or maidenhead of the females. Very apt they are to be with childe, and

The women big with child very laborious.

very laborious when they beare children; yea, when they are as great as they can be: yet in that case they neither forbeare laboure, nor travaile; I have seene them in that plight with burthens at their backs enough to load a horse; yet doe they not miscarry, but have a faire delivery, and a quick: their women are very good midwifes, and the women very lusty after delivery, and in a day or two will travell or trudge about. Their infants are borne with haire on their heads, and are of complexion white as our nation;

but their mothers in their infancy make a bath of
Wallnut leaves, huskes of Walnuts, and such things as
will staine their skinne for ever, wherein they dip and
washe them to make them tawny; the coloure of their
haire is black, and their eyes black. These infants are
carried at their mothers backs by the help of a cradle
made of a board forket at both ends, whereon the
childe is fast bound and wrapped in furres; his knees
thrust up towards his bellie, because they may be the
more usefull for them when he sitteth, which is as a
dogge does on his bumme: and this cradle surely
preserues them better then the cradles of our nation,
for as much as we finde them well proportioned, not
any of them crooked backed or wry legged: and to
give their charracter in a worde, they are as proper
men and women for feature and limbes as can be
found, for flesh and bloud as active: longe handed
they are, (I never sawe a clunchfisted Salvadg
amongst them all in my time.) The colour of their
eies being so generally black made a Salvage, that had
a younge infant whose eies were gray, shewed him to
us, and said they were English mens eies; I tould the
Father that his sonne was *nan weeteo,* which is a bastard; hee replied *titta Cheshetue squaa,* which is, hee
could not tell, his wife might play the whore; and this
childe the father desired might have an English
name, because of the litenesse of his eies, which his
father had in admiration because of novelty amongst
their nation.

*Children
bathed to
staine the
skinne.*

Chap. VIII.

Of their Reverence, and respect to age.

It is a thing to be admired, and indeede made a president, that a Nation yet uncivilizied should more respect age then some nations civilized, since there are
so many precepts both of divine and humane writers

*Age
honoured
among the
Indians.*

extant to instruct more Civill Nations: in that particular, wherein they excell, the younger are allwayes
obedient unto the elder people, and at their com-
maunds in every respect without grummbling; in all
councels, (as therein they are circumspect to do their
acciones by advise and councell, and not rashly or
inconsiderately,) the younger mens opinion shall be
heard, but the old mens opinion and councell im-
braced and followed: besides, as the elder feede and
provide for the younger in infancy, so doe the
younger, after being growne to yeares of manhood,
provide for those that be aged: and in distribution of
Acctes the elder men are first served by their dispen-
sator; and their counsels (especially if they be powahs) are esteemed as oracles amongst the younger
Natives.

The consideration of these things, mee thinkes,
should reduce some of our irregular young people of
civilized Nations, when this story shall come to their
knowledge, to better manners, and make them
ashamed of their former error in this kinde, and to
become hereafter more duetyfull; which I, as a friend,
(by observation having found,) have herein recorded
for that purpose.

CHAP. IX.

Of their pretty conjuring tricks.

If we doe not judge amisse of these Salvages in ac-
counting them witches, yet out of all question we may
be bould to conclude them to be but weake witches,
such of them as wee call by the names of Powahs:
some correspondency they have with the Devil out of
al doubt, as by some of their accions, in which they
glory, is manifested. Papasiquineo, that Sachem or
Sagamore, is a Powah of greate estimation amongst
all kinde of Salvages there: hee is at their Revels

(which is the time when a great company of Salvages
meete from severall parts of the Country, in amity
with their neighbours) hath advaunced his honor in
his feats or jugling tricks (as I may right tearme them)
to the admiration of the spectators, whome hee en-
devoured to perswade that he would goe under water
to the further side of a river, to broade for any man
to undertake with a breath, which thing hee performed by swimming over, and deluding the company with casting a mist before their eies that see him
enter in and come out, but no part of the way hee
has bin seene: likewise by our English, in the heat of
all summer to make Ice appeare in a bowle of faire
water; first, having the water set before him, hee hath
begunne his incantation according to their usuall ac-
custome, and before the same has bin ended a thick
Clowde has darkned the aire and, on a sodane, a
thunder clap hath bin heard that has amazed the natives; in an instant hee hath shewed a firme peece of
Ice to flote in the middest of the bowle in the presence of the vulgar people, which doubtles was done
by the agility of Satan, his consort.

And by meanes of these sleights, and such like trivial things as these, they gaine such estimation
amongst the rest of the Salvages that it is thought a
very impious matter for any man to derogate from
the words of these Powahs. In so much as hee that
should slight them, is thought to commit a crime no
lesse hainous amongst them as sacriledge is with us,
as may appeare by this one passage, which I wil set
forth for an instance.

A neighbour of mine that had entertain'd a Salvage
into his service, to be his factor for the beaver trade
amongst his countrymen, delivered unto him divers
parcells of commodities fit for them to trade with;
amongst the rest there was one coate of more es-
teeme then any of the other, and with this his new
entertained marchant man travels amonst his countrymen to truck them away for beaver: as our custome

A Salvage enter-tained a factor.

hath bin, the Salvage went up into the Country amongst his neighbours for beaver, and returned with some, but not enough answerable to his Masteers expectation, but being called to an accompt, and especially for that one Coate of speciall note, made answer that he had given that coate to Tantoquineo, a Powah: to which his master in a rage cryed, what have I to doe with Tantoquineo? The Salvage, very angry at the matter, cryed, what you speake? you are not a very good man; wil you not give Tantoq. a coat? whats this? as if he had offered *Tantoquineo* the greatest indignity that could be devised: so great is the estimation and reverence that these people have of these Iugling Powahs, who are usually sent for when any person is sicke and ill at ease to recover them, for which they receive rewards as doe our Chirgeons and Phisitions; and they doe make a trade of it, and boast of their skill where they come: One amongst the rest did undertake to cure an Englishman of a swelling of his hand for a parcell of biskett, which being delivered him hee tooke the party greived into the woods aside from company, and with the helpe of the devill, (as may be conjectured,) quickly recovered him of that swelling, and sent him about his worke againe.

An English-man cured of a swelling.

Ebenezer Cook

(fl. 1708)

Nothing definite is known of the life of Ebenezer Cook, and his work may in fact not strictly be a part of American literature, since—although he lived for a time in Maryland—he claimed he was an Englishman. Cook was probably the author of *Sotweed Redivivus*, a serious verse treatise on the overproduction of tobacco, and of burlesque poems including "The History of Colonel Nathaniel Bacon's Rebellion." His *The Sot-Weed Factor* is a satirical poem about life in Maryland in the early eighteenth century—a poem perhaps better known as the inspiration for John Barth's 1951 novel of the same name than for itself. Whether Cook considered himself American or not, the poem can arguably be called the first American satire, so it finds a place in this collection.

The Sot-Weed Factor; Or, a Voyage to Maryland, &c.

Condemn'd by Fate to way-ward Curse,
Of Friends unkind, and empty Purse;
Plagues worse than fill'd *Pandora's* Box,
I took my leave of *Albion's* Rocks:
With heavy Heart, concerned that I
Was forc'd my Native Soil to fly,
And the *Old World* must bid good-buy

But Heav'n ordain'd it should be so,
And to repine is vain we know:
Freighted with Fools from *Plymouth* found
To *Mary-Land* our Ship was bound,
Where we arrived in dreadful Pain,
Shock'd by the Terrours of the Main;
For full three Months, our wavering Boat,
Did thro' the surley Ocean float,
And furious Storms and threat'ning Blasts,
Both tore our Sails and sprung our Masts;
Wearied, yet pleas'd we did escape
Such Ills, we anchor'd at the (a) *Cape*,
But weighing soon, we plough'd the *Bay*,
To (b) Cove it in (c) *Piscato-way*,
Intending there to open Store,
I put myself and Goods a-shoar:
Where soon repair'd a numerous Crew,
In Shirts and Drawers of (d) *Scotch-cloth* Blue
With neither Stockings, Hat nor Shooe.
These *Sot-weed* Planters Crowd the Shoar,
In hue as tawny as a Moor:
Figures so strange, no God design'd,
To be a part of Humane kind:
But wanton Nature, void of Rest,
Moulded the brittle Clay in Jest.
At last a Fancy very odd
Took me, this was the Land of *Nod*;
Planted at first, when Vagrant *Cain*,
His Brother had unjustly slain;
Then Conscious of the Crime he'd done
From Vengeance dire, he hither run,
And in a hut supinely dwelt,

(a) By the Cape is meant the *Capes* of *Virginea*, the first Land on the Coast of *Virginia* and *Mary-Land*.

(b) To *Cove* is to lie at Anchor safe in Harbour.

(c) The Bay of *Piscato-way*, the usual place where our Ships come to an Anchor in *Mary-Land*.

(d) The Planters generally wear *Blue Linnen*.

The first in *Furs* and *Sot-weed* dealt.
And ever since his Time, the Place,
Has harbour'd a detested Race;
Who when they cou'd not live at Home,
For refuge to these Worlds did roam;
In hopes by Flight they might prevent,
The Devil and his fell intent;
Obtain from Tripple-Tree reprieve,
And Heav'n and Hell alike deceive;
But e're their Manners I display,
I think it fit I open lay
My Entertainment by the way:
That Strangers well may be aware on,
What homely Diet they must fare on.
To touch that Shoar where no good Sense is found,
But Conversation's lost, and Manners drown'd.
I cros't unto the other side,
A River whose impetuous Tide,
The Savage Borders does divide;
In such a shining odd invention,
I scarce can give its due Dimention.
The *Indians* call this watry Waggon
(e) *Canoo*, a Vessel none can brag on;
Cut from a *Popular-Tree* or *Pine*,
And fashion'd like a Trough for Swine:
In this most noble Fishing-Boat,
I boldly put myself afloat;
Standing erect, with Legs stretch'd wide,
We paddled to the other side:
Where being Landed safe by hap,
As *Sol* fell into *Thetis'* Lap.
A ravenous Gang bent on the stroul,
Of (f) Wolves for Prey, began to howl;
This put me in a pannick Fright,
Least I should be devoured quite:
But as I there a musing stood,

(e) A *Canoo* is an *Indian* Boat, cut out of the body of a Popular-Tree.
(f) Wolves are very numerous in *Mary-Land*.

And quite benighted in a Wood,
A Female Voice pierc'd thro' my Ears,
Crying, *You Rogue drive home the Steirs.*
I listen'd to th' attractive sound,
And straight a Herd of Cattel found
Drove by a Youth, and homeward bound;
Cheer'd with the sight, I straight thought fit,
To ask where I a Bed might get.
The surley Peasant bid me stay,
And ask'd from whom (g) I'de run away.
Surprized at such a saucy Word,
I instantly lugg'd out my Sword;
Swearing I was no Fugitive,
But from *Great-Britain* did arrive,
In hopes I better there might Thrive.
To which he mildly made reply,
I beg your Pardon, Sir, *that I*
Should talk to you Unmannerly;
But if you please to go with me,
To yonder House, you'll welcome be.
Encountring soon the smoaky Seat,
The Planter old did thus me greet:
"Whether you come from Goal or Colledge,
"You're welcome to my certain Knowledge;
"And if you please all Night to stay,
"My Son shall put you in the way."
Which offer I most kindly took,
And for a Seat did round me look;
When presently amongst the rest,
He plac'd his unknown *English* Guest,
Who found them drinking for a whet,
A Cask of (h) Syder on the Fret,
Till Supper came upon the Table,
On which I fed whilst I was able.

(g) 'Tis supposed by the Planters that all unknown Persons run away from some Master.

(h) Syder-pap is a sort of Food made of Syder and small Homine, like our Oatmeal.

So after hearty Entertainment,
Of Drink and Victuals without Payment;
For Planters Tables, you must know,
Are free for all that come and go.
While (i) Pon and Milk, with (k) Mush well stoar'd,
In Wooden Dishes grac'd the Board;
With (l) Homine and Syder-pap,
(Which scarce a hungry dog wou'd lap)
Well stuff'd with Fat from Bacon fry'd,
Or with *Mollossus* dulcify'd.
Then out our Landlord pulls a Pouch,
As greasy as the Leather Couch
On which he sat, and straight begun
To load with Weed his *Indian* Gun;
In length, scarce longer than one's Finger.
His Pipe smoak'd out with aweful Grace,
With aspect grave and solemn pace;
The reverend Sire walks to a Chest,
Of all his Furniture the best,
Closely confined within a Room,
Which seldom felt the weight of Broom;
From thence he lugs a Cag of Rum,
And nodding to me, thus begun:
I find, says he, you don't much care
For this our *Indian* Country Fare;
But let me tell you, Friend of mine,
You may be glad of it in time,
Tho' now your Stomach is so fine;
And if within this Land you stay,
You'll find it true what I do say.
This said, the Rundlet up he threw,
And bending backwards strongly drew:
I pluck'd as stoutly for my part,
Altho' it made me sick at Heart,

(i) Pon is Bread made of *Indian-Corn*.

(k) Mush is a sort of hasty-pudding made with water and *Indian* Flower.

(l) Homine is a dish that is made of boiled *Indian* Wheat, eaten with Mollossus, or Bacon-Fat.

And got so soon into my Head
I scarce cou'd find my way to Bed;
Where I was instantly convey'd
By one who pass'd for Chamber-Maid,
Tho' by her loose and sluttish Dress,
She rather seemed a *Bedlam-Bess*:
Curious to know from whence she came,
I prest her to declare her Name.
She Blushing, seem'd to hide her Eyes,
And thus in Civil Terms replies;
In better Times, e'er to this Land,
I was unhappily Trapann'd;
Perchance as well I did appear,
As any Lord or Lady here,
Not then a Slave for twice two[a] Year.
My Cloaths were fashionably new,
Nor were my Shifts of Linnen Blue;
But things are changed, now at the Hoe,
I daily work, and Bare-foot go,
In weeding Corn or feeding Swine,
I spend my melancholy Time.
Kidnap'd and Fool'd, I hither fled,
To shun a hated Nuptial[b] Bed,
And to my cost already find,
Worse Plagues than those I left behind.
Whate'er the Wanderer did profess,
Good-faith I cou'd not chuse but guess
The Cause which brought her to this place,
Was supping e'er the Priest said Grace.
Quick as my Thoughts, the Slave was fled,
(Her Candle left to shew my Bed)
Which made of Feathers soft and good,
Close in the[c] Chimney-corner stood;

(a) 'Tis the Custom for Servants to be obliged for four Years to very servile
Work; after which time they have their Freedom.

(b) These are the general Excuses made by *English* Women, which are sold,
or sell themselves to *Mary-Land*.

(c) Beds stand in the Chimney-corner in this Country.

I threw me down expecting Rest,
To be in golden Slumbers blest:
But soon a noise disturb'd my quiet,
And plagu'd me with nocturnal Riot;
A Puss which in the ashes lay,
With grunting Pig began a Fray;
And prudent Dog, that feuds might cease,
Most strongly bark'd to keep the Peace.
This Quarrel scarcely was decided,
By stick that ready lay provided;
But *Reynard*, arch and cunning Loon,
Broke into my Appartment soon:
In hot pursuit of Ducks and Geese,
With fell intent the same to seize:
Their Cackling Plaints with strange surprize,
Chac'd Sleep's thick Vapours from my Eyes;
Raging I jump'd upon the Floar,
And like a Drunken Saylor Swore;
With Sword I fiercely laid about,
And soon dispers'd the Feather'd Rout:
The Poultry out of Window flew,
And *Reynard* cautiously withdrew:
The Dogs who this Encounter heard,
Fiercely themselves to aid me rear'd,
And to the Place of Combat run,
Exactly as the Field was won.
Fretting and hot as roasting Capon,
And greasy as a Flitch of Bacon;
I to the Orchard did repair,
To Breathe the cool and open Air;
Expecting there the rising Day,
Extended on a Bank I lay;
But Fortune here, that saucy Whore,
Disturb'd me worse and plagu'd me more,
Than she had done the night before:
Hoarse croaking[(d)] Frogs did 'bout me ring,

(d) Frogs are called *Virginea* Bells and make (both in that country and *Mary-Land*) during the Night, a very hoarse ungrateful Noise.

Such Peals the Dead to Life wou'd bring,
A Noise might move their Wooden King.
I stuffed my Ears with Cotten white,
For fear of being deaf out-right,
And curst the melancholy Night;
But soon my Vows I did recant,
And Hearing as a Blessing grant;
When a confounded Rattle-Snake,
With hissing made my Heart to ake:
Not knowing how to fly the Foe,
Or whither in the Dark to go;
By strange good Luck, I took a Tree,
Prepar'd by Fate to set me free;
Where riding on a Limb a stride,
Night and the Branches did me hide,
And I the Devil and Snake defy'd.
Not yet from Plagues exempted quite,
The curst Muskitoes did me bite;
Till rising Morn' and blushing Day,
Drove both my Fears and Ills away;
And from Night's Errors set me free.
Discharg'd from hospitable Tree;
I did to Planter's Booth repair,
And there at Breakfast nobly Fare
On rashier broil'd of infant Bear:
I thought the Cub delicious Meat,
Which ne'er did ought but Chesnuts eat;
Nor was young Orsin's flesh the worse,
Because he sucked a Pagan Nurse.
Our Breakfast done, my Landlord stout,
Handed a Glass of Rum about;
Pleas'd with the Treatment I did find,
I took my leave of Oast so kind;
Who to oblige me, did provide,
His eldest son to be my Guide,
And lent me Horses of his own,
A skittish Colt, and aged Rhoan,
The four-leg'd prop of his Wife *Joan*:
Steering our Barks in Trot or Pace,
We sail'd directly for a place

In *Mary-Land*, of high renown,
Known by the Name of Battle-Town.
To view the Crowds did there resort,
Which Justice made, and Law their sport,
In that sagacious County Court:
Scarce had we enter'd on the way,
Which thro' thick Woods and Marshes lay;
But *Indians* strange did soon appear,
In hot persuit of wounded Deer;
No mortal Creature can express,
His wild fantastick Air and Dress;
His painted Skin in Colours dy'd,
His sable hair in Satchel ty'd,
Shew'd Savages not free from Pride;
His tawny Thighs, and Bosom bare,
Disdain'd a useless Coat to wear,
Scorn'd Summer's Heat, and Winter's Air;
His manly shoulders such as please
Widows and Wives, were bathed in grease,
Of Cub and Bear, whose supple Oil
Prepar'd his Limbs 'gainst Heat or Toil.
Thus naked Pict in Battel fought,
Or undisguis'd his Mistress sought;
And knowing well his Ware was good,
Refus'd to screen it with a Hood;
His visage dun, and chin that ne'er
Did Raizor feel or Scissers bare,
Or knew the Ornament of Hair,
Look'd sternly Grim, surprized with Fear,
I spur'd my Horse as he drew near:
But Rhoan who better knew than I,
The little Cause I had to fly;
Seem'd by his solemn steps and pace,
Resolv'd I shou'd the Specter face,
Nor faster mov'd, tho' spur'd and lick'd,
Than *Balaam's* Ass by Prophet kick'd.
Kekicknitop[a] the Heathen cry'd;

(a) *Kekicknitop* is an *Indian* Expression, and signifies no more than this, *How do you do?*

How is it, *Tom*, my Friend reply'd,
Judging from thence the Brute was civil,
I boldly fac'd the Courteous Devil;
And lugging out a Dram of Rum,
I gave his Tawny worship some:
Who in his language as I guess,
(My Guide informing me no less,)
Implored the[b] Devil, me to bless.
I thank'd him for his good Intent,
And forwards on my Journey went,
Discoursing as along I rode,
Whether this Race was framed by God,
Or whether some Malignant pow'r,
Contriv'd them in an evil hour,
And from his own Infernal Look,
Their Dusky form and Image took:
From hence we fell to Argument
Whence Peopled was this Continent.
My Friend suppos'd *Tartarians* wild,
Or *Chinese* from their Home exiled,
Wandering thro' Mountains hid with Snow
And Rills did in the Vallies flow
Far to the South of *Mexico*:
Broke thro' the Barrs which Nature cast
And wide unbeaten Regions past,
Till near those Streams the humane deludge roll'd,
Which sparkling shin'd with glittering Sands of Gold

(b) These *Indians* worship the Devil, and pray to him as we do to God Almighty. 'Tis suppos'd, that *America* was peopled from *Scythia* or *Tartaria*, which Borders on *China*, by reason the *Tartarians* and *Americans*, very much agree in their Manners, Arms and Government. Other persons are of Opinion, that the *Chinese* first peopled the *West-Indies*; imagining *China* and the Southern part of *America* to be contiguous. Others believe that the Phœnicians who were very skilful Mariners, first planted a Colony in the Isles of *America*, and supply'd the Persons left to inhabit there with Women and all other Necessaries; till either the Death or Shipwreck of the first Discoverers, or some other Misfortune, occasioned the loss of the Discovery, which had been purchased by the Peril of the first Adventurers.

And fetch'd[d] *Pizarro* from the[e] *Iberian* Shoar,
To rob the Natives of their fatal Stoar.
I smil'd to hear my young Logician
Thus reason like a Politician;
Who ne're by Father's Pains and Earning
Had got at Mother *Cambridge* Learning;
Where Lubber youth just free from birch
Most stoutly drink to prop the Church;
Nor with[f] *Grey Groat* had taken Pains
To purge his Head and Cleanse his Reines:
And in obedience to the Colledge,
Had pleas'd himself with carnal knowledge:
And tho' I lik'd the youngster's Wit,
I judg'd the Truth he had not hit;
And could not chuse but smile to think
What they could do for Meat and Drink,
Who o'er so many Desarts ran
With Brats and Wives in *Caravan*;
Unless perchance they'd got the Trick,
To eat no more than Porker sick;
Or could with well contented Maws
Quarter like[g] Bears upon their Paws.
Thinking his Reasons to confute,
I gravely thus commenc'd Dispute,
And urged that tho' a *Chinese* Host,
Might penetrate this *Indian* Coast,
Yet this was certainly most true,
They never cou'd the Isles subdue;
For knowing not to steer a Boat,
They could not on the Ocean float,
Or plant their Sunburnt Colonies,

(d) Pizarro was the Person that conquer'd Peru; a Man of a most bloody Disposition, base, treacherous, covetous and revengeful.

(e) *Spanish* Shoar.

(f) There is a very bad Custom in some Colledges, of giving the Students *A Groat ad purgandas Rhenes,* which is usually employ'd to the use of the *Donor.*

(g) Bears are said to live by sucking of their *Paws,* according to the Notion of some Learned Authors.

In Regions parted by the Seas;
I thence inferr'd[h] *Phœnicians* old,
Discover'd first with Vessels bold
These Western Shoars, and planted here,
Returning once or twice a Year,
With *Naval Stoars* and Lasses kind,
To comfort those were left behind;
Till by the Winds and Tempest toar,
From their intended Golden Shoar,
They suffer'd Ship-wreck, or were drown'd,
And lost the World so newly found.
But after long and learn'd Contention,
We could not finish our dissention;
And when that both had talk'd their fill,
We had the self same Notion still.
Thus Parson grave well read and Sage,
Does in dispute with Priest engage;
The one protests they are not Wise,
Who judge by[i] Sense and trust their Eyes;
And vows he'd burn for it at Stake,
That Man may God his Maker make;
The other smiles at his Religion,
And vows he's but a learned Widgeon:
And when they have empty'd all their Stoar
From Books or Fathers, are not more
Convinc'd or wiser than before.
  Scarce had we finish'd serious Story,
But I espy'd the Town before me,
And roaring Planters on the ground,
Drinking of Healths in Circle round:
Dismounting Steed with friendly Guide,

(h) The *Phœnicians* were the best and boldest Saylors of Antiquity, and indeed the only Persons, in former Ages, who durst venture themselves on the Main Sea.

(i) The *Priests* argue, That our Senses in point of *Transubstantiation* ought not to be believed, for tho' the Consecrated Bread has all the accidents of Bread, yet they affirm, 'tis the Body of Christ, and not of Bread but Flesh and Bones.

Our Horses to a Tree we ty'd,
And forwards pass'd among the Rout,
To chuse convenient *Quarters* out:
But being none were to be found,
We sat like others on the ground
Carousing Punch in open Air,
Till Cryer did the Court declare;
The planting Rabble being met
Their Drunken Worships likewise set;
Cryer proclaims that Noise shou'd cease
And streight the Lawyers broke the Peace:
Wrangling for Plantiff and Defendant,
I thought they ne'er wou'd make an end on't:
With nonsense, stuff and false quotations,
With brazen Lyes and Allegations;
And in the splitting of the Cause,
They used such Motions with their Paws,
As shew'd their Zeal was strongly bent,
In Blows to end the Argument.
A reverend Judge, who to the shame
Of all the Bench, cou'd write his[k] his Name;
At Petty-fogger took offence,
And wonder'd at his Impudence.
My Neighbour *Dash* with scorn replies,
And in the Face of Justice flies;
The Bench in fury streight divide,
And Scribble's take or Judge's side;
The Jury, Lawyers and their Clyents,
Contending fight like earth-born Gyants;
But Sheriff wily lay perdue,
Hoping Indictments wou'd ensue,
And when————
A Hat or Wig fell in the way,
He seized them for the *Queen* as stray:
The Court adjourn'd in usual manner
In Battle Blood and fractious Clamour;

(k) In the County-Court of Mary-Land, very few of the Justices of the Peace
can write or read.

I thought it proper to provide,
A Lodging for myself and Guide,
So to our Inn we march'd away,
Which at a little distance lay;
Where all things were in such Confusion,
I thought the World at its conclusion;
A Herd of Planters on the ground,
O'er-whelm'd with Punch, dead drunk, we found;
Others were fighting and contending,
Some burnt their Cloaths to save the mending.
A few whose Heads by frequent use,
Could better bare the potent Juice,
Gravely debated State Affairs.
Whilst I most nimbly trip'd up Stairs;
Leaving my Friend discoursing oddly,
And mixing things Prophane and Godly;
Just then beginning to be Drunk,
As from the Company I slunk,
To every Room and Nook I crept,
In hopes I might have somewhere slept;
But all the bedding was possest
By one or other drunken Guest:
But after looking long about,
I found an antient Corn-loft out,
Glad that I might in quiet sleep,
And there my bones unfractur'd keep.
I lay'd me down secure from Fray,
And soundly snoar'd till break of Day;
When waking fresh I sat upright,
And found my Shooes were vanished quite;
Hat, Wig, and Stockings, all were fled
From this extended *Indian* Bed;
Vext at the Loss of Goods and Chattel,
I swore I'd give the Rascal battel,
Who had abus'd me in this sort,
And Merchant Stranger made his Sport.
I furiously descended Ladder;
No Hare in *March* was ever madder;
In vain I search'd for my Apparel,

And did with Oast and Servants Quarrel;
For one whose Mind did much aspire
To[a] Mischief, threw them in the Fire;
Equipt with neither Hat nor Shooe,
I did my coming hither rue,
And doubtful thought what I should do:
Then looking round, I saw my Friend
Lie naked on a Table's end;
A sight so dismal to behold,
One wou'd have judg'd him dead and cold,
When wringing of his bloody Nose,
By fighting got we may suppose;
I found him not so fast asleep,
Might give his friends a cause to weep:
Rise[b] *Oronooko*, rise said I,
And from this *Hell* and *Bedlam* fly.
My Guide starts up, and in amaze,
With blood-shot Eyes did round him gaze;
At length with many a sigh and groan,
He went in search of aged Rhoan;
But Rhoan, tho' seldom us'd to faulter,
Had fairly this time slipt his Halter;
And not content all Night to stay
Ty'd up from Fodder, ran away:
After my Guide to ketch him ran,
And so I lost both Horse and Man:
Which Disappointment tho' so great,
Did only Mirth and Jests create:
Till one more Civil than the rest,
In Conversation for the best,
Observing that for want of Rhoan,
I should be left to walk alone;
Most readily did me intreat,
To take a Bottle at his Seat;

(a) 'Tis the Custom of the Planters to throw their own, or any other Person's Hat, Wig, Shooes or Stockings in the Fire.

(b) Planters are usually call'd by the Name of *Oronooko*, from their Planting *Oronooko-Tobacco*.

A Favour at that time so great,
I blest my kind propitious Fate;
And finding soon a fresh supply,
Of Cloaths from Stoar-house kept hard by,
I mounted streight on such a Steed,
Did rather curb, than whipping need;
And straining at the usual rate,
With spur of Punch which lay in Pate,
E'er long we lighted at the Gate:
Where in an antient *Cedar* House,
Dwelt my new Friend a[a] Cockerouse;
Whose Fabrick tho' 'twas built of Wood,
Had many Springs and Winters stood;
When sturdy Oaks, and lofty Pines
Were level'd with[b] Musmillion Vines,
And Plants eradicated were,
By Hurricanes into the air;
There with good Punch and Apple Juice,
We spent our Hours without abuse;
Till Midnight in her sable Vest,
Persuaded Gods and Men to rest;
And with a pleasing kind surprize,
Indulg'd soft Slumbers to my Eyes.
Fierce[c] *Æthon* courser of the Sun,
Had half his Race exactly run;
And breath'd on me a fiery Ray,
Darting hot Beams the following Day,
When snug in Blanket white I lay:
But Heat and[d] Chinces rais'd the Sinner,
Most opportunely to his Dinner;
Wild Fowl and Fish delicious Meats,
As good as *Neptune's* doxy eats,
Began our Hospitable Treat;
Fat Venson follow'd in the Rear,

(a) Cockerouse, is a Man of Quality.
(b) Musmilleon Vines are what we call Musk milleon Plants.
(c) *Æthon* is one of the Poetical Horses of the Sun.
(d) *Chinces* are a sort of Vermin like our *Bugs* in *England*.

And Turkies wild[f] Luxurious Chear:
But what the Feast did most commend,
Was hearty welcom from my Friend.
Thus having made a noble Feast,
And eat as well as pamper'd Priest,
Madera strong in flowing Bowls,
Fill'd with extream delight our Souls;
Till wearied with a purple Flood,
Of generous Wine (the Giant's blood,
As Poets feign) away I made,
For some refreshing verdant Shade;
Where musing on my Rambles strange,
And Fortune which so oft did change;
In midst of various Contemplations
Of Fancies odd, and Meditations,
I slumbered long————
Till hazy Night with noxious Dews
Did sleep's unwholsom Fetters lose;
With Vapors chil'd, and misty air,
To fire-side I did repair;
Near which a jolly Female Crew,
Were deep engag'd at *Lanctre-Looe*;
In Night-rails white, with dirty Mein,
Such Sights are scarce in *England* seen:
I thought them first some Witches bent,
On Black Designs in dire Convent.
Till one who with affected air,
Had nicely learn'd to Curse and Swear;
Cry'd Dealing's lost is but a Flam,
And vow'd by G—d she'd keep her *Pam*.
When dealing through the board had run,
They ask'd me kindly to make one;
Not staying often to be bid,
I sat me down as others did;
We scarce had play'd a Round about,
But that these *Indian* Froes fell out.
D—m you, says one, tho' now so brave,

(f) Wild Turkies are very good Meat, and prodigiously large in *Mary-Land.*

I knew you late a Four-Years Slave;
What if for Planter's Wife you go,
Nature designed you for the Hoe.
Rot you replies the other streight,
The Captain kiss'd you for his Freight;
And if the Truth was known aright,
And how you walk'd the Streets by night
You'd blush (if one cou'd blush) for shame,
Who from *Bridewell* or *New gate* came:
From Words they fairly fell to Blows,
And being loath to interpose,
Or meddle in the Wars of Punk,
Away to Bed in hast I slunk.
Waking next day, with aking Head,
And Thirst, that made me quit my Bed;
I rigg'd myself, and soon got up,
To cool my Liver with a Cup
Of[a] *Succahana* fresh and clear,
Not half so good as *English* Beer;
Which ready stood in Kitchin Pail,
And was in fact but *Adam's* Ale;
For Planter's Cellars you must know,
Seldom with good *October* flow,
But Perry Quince and Apple Juice,
Spout from the Tap like any Sluce;
Untill the Cask's grown low and stale,
They're forc'd again to[b] Goud and Pail:
The soathing drought scarce down my Throat,
Enough to put a ship afloat,
With Cockerouse as I was sitting,
I felt a Feaver Intermitting;
A fiery Pulse beat in my Veins,
From Cold I felt resembling Pains:
This cursed seasoning I remember,
Lasted from *March* to cold *December*;

(a) Succahana is Water.

(b) A Goud grows upon an *Indian* Vine, resembling a Bottle, when ripe it is hollow; this the Planters make use of to drink water out of.

Nor would it then its *Quarters* shift
Until by *Cardus* turn'd adrift,
And had my Doctress wanted skill,
Or Kitchin Physick at her will,
My Father's Son had lost his Lands,
And never seen the *Goodwin Sands*:
But thanks to Fortune and a Nurse
Whose Care depended on my Purse,
I saw myself in good Condition,
Without the help of a Physitian:
At length the shivering ill relieved,
Which long my Head and Heart had grieved;
I then began to think with Care,
How I might sell my *British* Ware,
That with my Freight I might comply,
Did on my Charter party lie:
To this intent, with Guide before,
I tript it to the Eastern Shoar;
While riding near a Sandy Bay,
I met a *Quaker, Yea* and *Nay*;
A Pious Consientious Rogue,
As e'er woar Bonnet or a Brogue,
Who neither Swore nor kept his Word
But cheated in the Fear of God;
And when his Debts he would not pay,
By Light within he ran away.
With this sly Zealot soon I struck
A Bargain for my *English* Truck
Agreeing for ten thousand weight,
Of *Sot-weed* good and fit for freight,
Broad Oronooko bright and sound,
The growth and product of his ground;
In Cask that should contain compleat,
Five hundred of Tobacco neat.
The Contract thus betwixt us made,
Not well acquainted with the Trade,
My Goods I trusted to the Cheat,
Whose crop was then aboard the Fleet;
And going to receive my own,

I found the Bird was newly flown;
Cursing this execrable Slave,
This damn'd pretended Godly Knave;
On dire Revenge and Justice bent,
I instantly to Counsel went,
Unto an ambodexter[c] *Quack,*
Who learnedly had got the Knack
Of giving Glisters, making Pills,
Of filling Bonds, and forging Wills;
And with a stock of Impudence,
Supply'd his want of Wit and Sense;
With Looks demure, amazing People,
No wiser than a Daw in Steeple;
My Anger flushing in my Face,
I stated the preceeding Case:
And of my Money was so lavish,
That he'd have poyson'd half the Parish,
And hang'd his Father on a Tree
For such another tempting Fee;
Smiling, said he, the Cause is clear,
I'll manage him you need not fear;
The Case is judg'd, good Sir, but look
In *Galen,* No—in my Lord *Cook,*
I vow to God I was mistook:
I'll take out a Provincial Writ,
And trounce him for his Knavish Wit;
Upon my Life we'll win the Cause,
With all the ease I cure the[d] Yaws:
Resolv'd to plague the holy Brother,
I set one Rogue to catch another;
To try the cause then fully bent,
Up to[e] *Annapolis* I went,
A City Situate on a Plain,
Where scarce a House will keep out Rain;
The Buildings framed with Cyprus rare,

(c) This Fellow was an Apothecary, and turned an Attorney at Law.
(d) The *Yaws* is the *Pox.*
(e) The chief of *Mary-Land* containing about twenty-four *Houses.*

Resembles much our *Southwark* Fair:
But Stranger here will scarcely meet
With Market-place, Exchange, or Street;
And if the Truth I may report,
'Tis not so large as *Tottenham Court.*
St *Mary's* once was in repute,
Now here the Judges try the Suit
And Lawyers twice a year dispute.
As oft the Bench most gravely meet,
Some to get Drunk, and some to eat
A swinging share of Country Treat.
But as for Justice right or wrong,
Not one amongst the numerous throng,
Knows what they mean, or has the Heart,
To give his Verdict on a Stranger's part:
Now Court being call'd by beat of Drum,
The Judges left their Punch and Rum,
When Pettifogger Docter draws,
His Paper forth, and opens Cause;
And least I shou'd the better get,
Brib'd *Quack* supprest his knavish Wit.
So Maid upon the Downy Field
Pretends a Force, and Fights to yield:
The Byast Court without delay,
Adjudg'd my Debt in Country Pay;
In^(f) Pipe staves, Corn or Flesh of Boar,
Rare Cargo for the *English* Shoar;
Raging with Grief, full speed I ran
To joyn the Fleet at^(g) *Kicketan*;
Embarqu'd and waiting for a Wind
I left this dreadful Curse behind.

May Canniballs transported o'er the Sea
Prey on these Slaves, as they have done on me;
May never Merchant's trading Sails explore

(f) There is a Law in this Country, the Plantiff may pay his Debt in Country pay, which consists in the produce of his Plantation.

(g) The home ward bound fleet meets here.

This Cruel, this inhospitable Shoar;
But left abandon'd by the World to starve,
May they sustain the Fate they well deserve;
May they turn Savage, or as *Indians* Wild,
From Trade, Converse and Happiness exil'd;
Recreant to Heaven, may they adore the Sun,
And into Pagan Superstitions run
For Vengence ripe————
May Wrath Divine then lay those Regions wast
Where no Man's(*) Faithful, nor a Woman Chast.

F I N I S .

(*) The Author does not intend by this any of the *English* Gentlemen res-
ident there.

Francis Hopkinson

(1737–1791)

Hopkinson was born in Philadelphia and became the first graduate of the College of Philadelphia. He then studied law, became director of customs, and in 1776, was elected to serve in the Continental Congress. Politics was not his only career. He was an accomplished harpsichordist and composer, a poet of some skill, an essayist, a humorist, and a satirist. And he still had time to be a signer of the Declaration of Independence, chairman of the Continental Navy Board, treasurer of loans, and a judge of admiralty for Pennsylvania. He also had skills as an artist and designer, creating various seals for departments of the new government and drawing designs for coins and paper money.

Hopkinson's political satires were among his most popular works, beginning with the "Letter Written by a Foreigner on the Character of the English Nation," in which he satirized the mores of the mother country. "A Pretty Story," printed here, was published in 1774, and concerns the deteriorating relationship between England and the American colonies that would lead to the formation of the Continental Congress. The story is in the form of an allegory: A farmer's family has built a prosperous life for itself in a foreign land, and now finds that prosperity threatened by the greed of a wicked stepmother and her lover. The farmer is the American colonies, the stepmother (called a mother-in-law in those times) is the Crown, and her sly lover is the British House of Parliament. Heavy-handed though this may seem to modern eyes, it was, when published, at once sharp satire and radical propaganda.

A Pretty Story

PREFACE

A book without a Preface is like a Face without a Nose. Let the other Features be ever so agreeable and well proportioned, it is looked on with Detestation and Horror if this material Ornament be wanting.

Or rather, a Book is like a House: The grand Portico is the Dedication; the flagged Pavement is an humble Address to the Reader, in Order to pave the Way for a kind Reception of the Work; the Front Door with its fluted Pillars, Pediment, Trigliffs and Modillons are the Title Page with its Motto, Author's Name and Titles, Date of the Year, &c. The Entry is the Preface (often-times of a tedious Length) and the several Apartments and Closets are the Chapters and Sections of the Work itself.

As I am but a clumsy Carpenter at best, I shall not attempt to decorate my little Cottage with any *out of Door* Ornaments; but as it would be inconvenient and uncomfortable to have my Front Door open immediately into the Apartments of my House, I have made this Preface by Way of Entry.

And now, gentle Reader, if you should think my Entry too plain and simple you may set your Imagination to work, and furnish it with a grand Staircase, with Cornices, Stucco and Paintings. That is, you may suppose that I entered very unwillingly upon this Work, being compelled to it by a Chain of unforeseen Circumstances: That it was written in the Midst of a great Hurry of other Business, and under particular Disadvantages of Time and Place, and that it was only intended for the Inspection of a few Friends, without any Expectations of ever seeing it in the Press.

You may, kind Reader, go on to suppose that when my Friends perused my Work, they were struck with the Energy of my Genius, and insisted that the Public ought not to be deprived of such a Fund of Amusement and Improvement through my obstinate Modesty; and that after many Solicitations and powerful Persuasions I had been prevailed upon to bless Mankind with the Fruits of my Labour.

Or, if you like not this, you may suppose that the following

Sheets were found in the cabinet of some deceased Gentleman; or that they were dug out of an ancient Ruins, or discovered in a Hermit's Cave, or dropped from the Clouds in a Hail Storm. In short you may suppose just what you please. And when by the Help of Imagination, you have seasoned the Preface to your Palate, you may turn over this Leaf, and feast upon the Body of the Work itself.

CHAPTER I

Once upon a Time, a great While ago, there lived a certain Nobleman, who had long possessed a very valuable Farm, and had a great Number of Children and Grandchildren.

Besides the annual Profits of his Land, which were very considerable, he kept a large Shop of Goods; and being very successful in Trade, he became, in Process of Time, exceeding rich and powerful; insomuch that all his Neighbours feared and respected him.

With Respect to the Management of his Family, it was thought he had adopted the most perfect Mode that could be devised, for he had been at the Pains to examine the Œconomy of all his Neighbours, and had selected from their Plans all such Parts as appeared to be equitable and beneficial, and omitted those which from Experience were found to be inconvenient. Or rather, by blending their several Constitutions together he had so ingeniously counterbalanced the Evils of one Mode of Government with the Benefits of another, that the Advantages were richly enjoyed, and the Inconveniencies scarcely felt. In short, his Family was thought to be the best ordered of any in his Neighbourhood.

He never exercised any undue Authority over his Children or Servants; neither indeed could he oppress them if he was so disposed; for it was particularly covenanted in his Marriage Articles that he should not at any Time impose any Tasks or Hardships whatever upon his Children without the free Consent of his Wife.

Now the Custom in his Family was this, that at the End of every seven Years his Marriage became of Course null and void; at which Time his Children and Grandchildren met together and chose another Wife for him, whom the old Gentleman was obliged to marry under the same Articles and Restrictions as before. If his late Wife had conducted herself, during her seven Year's Marriage, with Mildness, Discretion and Integrity, she was re-elected; if otherwise, deposed: By which Means the Children had always a great Interest in their Mother in Law; and through her, a reasonable Check upon their Father's Temper. For besides that he could do nothing material respecting his Children without her Approbation, she was sole Mistress of the Purse Strings; and gave him out, from Time to Time, such Sums of Money as she thought necessary for the Expences of his Family.

Being one Day in a very extraordinary good Humour, he gave his Children a Writing under his Hand and Seal, by which he released them from many Badges of Dependance, and confirmed to them several very important Privileges. The chief were the two following, viz. that none of his Children should be punished for any Offence, or supposed Offence, until his Brethren had first declared him worthy of such Punishment; and secondly, he gave fresh Assurances that he would impose no Hardships upon them without the Consent of their Mother in Law.

This Writing, on Account of its singular Importance, was called *The Great Paper.* After it was executed with the utmost Solemnity, he caused his Chaplain to publish a dire *Anathema* against all who should attempt to violate the Articles of the *Great Paper,* in the Words following.

"In the Name of the *Father, Son* and *Holy Ghost,* AMEN! Whereas our Lord and Master, to the Honour of God and for the common Profit of this Farm hath granted, for him and his Heirs forever, these Articles above written: I, his Chaplain and spiritual Pastor of all this Farm, do admonish the People of the Farm *Once, Twice,* and *Thrice:* Because that Shortness will not suffer so much Delay as to give Knowledge to the People of these Presents in Writing; I therefore enjoyn all Persons, of what Estate soever they be, that they and every of them, as much as in them is, shall uphold and maintain these Articles granted by our Lord and Master in all Points. And all those that in any Point do resist, or break, or in any Manner hereafter procure, counsel or any Ways assent to resist or break these Ordinances, or go about it by Word or Deed, openly or privately, by any Manner of Pretence or Colour: I the aforesaid Chaplain, by my Authority, do *excommunicate* and *accurse,* and from the Body of our Lord *Jesus Christ,* and from all the *Company of Heaven,* and from all the *Sacraments* of holy Church do *sequester* and *exclude.*''

CHAPTER II

Now it came to pass that this Nobleman had, by some Means or other, obtained a Right to an immense Tract of wild uncultivated Country at a vast Distance from his Mansion House. But he set little Store by this Acquisition, as it yielded him no Profit; nor was it likely to do so, being not only difficult of Access on Account of the Distance, but was also overrun with innumerable wild Beasts very fierce and savage; so that it would be extremely dangerous to attempt taking Possession of it.

In Process of Time, however, some of his Children, more stout and enterprising than the rest, requested Leave of their Father to go and settle on this distant Tract of Land. Leave was readily obtained; but before they set out certain Agreements were stipulated between them—the principal were—The old Gentleman, on his Part, engaged to protect and defend the Adventurers in their new Settlements; to assist them in chacing away the wild Beasts, and to extend to them all the Benefits of the Government under which they were born: Assuring them that although they should be removed so far from his Presence they should nevertheless be considered as the Children of his Family, and treated accordingly. At the same Time he gave each of them a Bond for the faithful Performance of these Promises; in which, among other Things, it was covenanted that they should, each of them in their several Families, have a Liberty of making such Rules and Regulations for their own good Government as they should find convenient; provided these Rules and Regulations should not contradict or be inconsistent with the general standing Orders established in his Farm.

In return for these Favours he insisted that they, on their Parts, should at all Times acknowledge him to be their Father; that they should not deal with their Neighbours without his Leave, but send to his Shop only for such Merchandize as they should want. But in Order to enable them to pay for such Goods as they should purchase, they were permitted to sell the Produce of their Lands to certain of his Neighbours.

These Preliminaries being duly adjusted, our Adventurers bid Adieu to the Comforts and Conveniencies of their Father's House, and set off on their Journey—Many and great were the Difficulties they encountered on their Way: but many more and much greater had they to combat on their Arrival in the new Country. Here they found Nothing but wild Nature, Mountains over-grown with inaccessible Foliage, and Plains steeped in stagnated Waters. Their Ears are no longer attentive to the repeated Strokes of industrious Labour and the busy Hum of Men, instead of these, the roaring Tempest and incessant Howlings of Beasts of Prey fill their Minds with Ho[r]ror and Dismay. The needful Comforts of Life are no longer in their Power—no friendly Roof to shelter them from inclement Skies; no Fortress to protect them from surrounding Dangers. Unaccustomed as they were to Hardships like these, some were cut off by Sickness and Disease, and others snatched away by the Hands of Barbarity. They began however, with great Perseverance, to clear the Land of encumbering Rubbish, and the Woods resound with the Strokes of Labour; they drain the Waters from the sedged Morass, and pour the Sun Beams on the reeking Soil; they are forced to exercise all the Powers of Industry and Œconomy for bare Subsistence, and like their first Parent, when driven from Paradise, to earn their Bread with the Sweat of their Brows. In this Work they were frequently interrupted by the Incursions of the wild Beasts, against whom they defended themselves with heroic Prowess and Magnanimity.

After some Time, however, by Dint of indefatigable Perseverance, they found themselves comfortably settled in this new Farm; and had the delightful Prospect of vast Tracts of Land waving with luxuriant Harvests, and perfuming the Air with delicious Fruits, which before had been a dreary Wilderness, unfit for the Habitation of Men.

In the mean Time they kept up a constant Correspondence with their Father's Family, and at a great Expence provided Waggons, Horses and Drivers to bring from his Shop such Goods and Merchandize as they wanted, for which they paid out of the Produce of their Lands.

CHAPTER III

Now the new Settlers had adopted a Mode of Government in their several Families similar to that their Father had established in the old Farm; in taking a new Wife at the End of certain Periods of Time; which Wife was chosen for them by their Children, and without whose Consent they could do nothing material in the Conduct of their Affairs. Under these Circumstances they thrived exceedingly, and became very numerous; living in great Harmony amongst themselves, and in constitutional Obedience to their Father and his Wife.

Notwithstanding their successful Progress, however, they were frequently annoyed by the wild Beasts, which were not yet expelled the Country; and were moreover troubled by some of their Neighbours who wanted to drive them off the Land, and take Possession of it themselves.

To assist them in these Difficulties, and protect them from Danger, the old Nobleman sent over several of his Servants, who with the Help of the new Settlers drove away their Enemies. But then he required that they should reimburse him for the Expence and Trouble he was at in their Behalf; this they did with great Cheerfulness, by applying from Time to Time to their respective Wives, who always commanded their Cash.

Thus did Matters go on for a considerable Time, to their mutual Happiness and Benefit. But now the Nobleman's Wife began to cast an avaricious Eye upon the new Settlers; saying to herself, if by the natural Consequence of their Intercourse with us my Wealth and Power are so much increased, how much more would they accumulate if I can persuade them that all they have belonged to us, and therefore I may at any Time demand from them such Part of their Earnings as I please. At the same Time she was fully sensible of the Promises and Agreements her Husband had made when they left the old Farm, and of the Tenor and Purport of the *Great Paper*. She therefore thought it necessary to proceed with great Caution and Art, and endeavoured to gain her Point by imperceptible Steps.

In Order to do this, she first issued an Edict setting forth, That whereas the Tailors of her Family were greatly injured by the People of the new Farm, inasmuch as they presumed to make their own Clothes whereby the said Tailors were deprived of the Benefit of their Custom; it was therefore ordained that for the future the new Settlers should not be permitted to have amongst them any Shears or Scissars larger than a certain fixed size. In Consequence of this, our Adventurers were compelled to have their Clothes made by their Father's Tailors: But out of Regard to the old Gentleman, they patiently submitted to this Grievance.

Encouraged by this Success, she proceeded in her Plan. Observing that the new Settlers were very fond of a particular Kind of Cyder which they purchased of a Neighbour, who was in Friendship with their Father (the Apples proper for making this Cyder not growing on their own Farm) she published another Edict, obliging them to pay her a certain Stipend for every Barrel of Cyder used in their Families! To this likewise they submitted: Not yet seeing the Scope of her Designs against them.

After this Manner she proceeded, imposing Taxes upon them on various Pretences, and receiving the Fruits of their Industry with both Hands. Moreover she persuaded her Husband to send amongst them from Time to Time a Number of the most lazy and useless of his Servants, under the specious Pretext of defending them in their Settlements, and of assisting to destroy the wild Beasts; but in Fact to rid his own House of their Company, not having Employment for them; and at the same Time to be a Watch and a Check upon the People of the new Farm.

It was likewise ordered that these Protectors, as they were called, should be supplied with Bread and Butter cut in a particular Form: But the Head of one of the Families refused to comply with this Order. He engaged to give the Guests, thus forced upon him, Bread and Butter sufficient; but insisted that his Wife should have the Liberty of cutting it in what Shape she pleased.

This put the old Nobleman into a violent Passion, insomuch that he had his Son's Wife put into Gaol for presuming to cut her Loaf otherwise than as had been directed.

CHAPTER IV

As the old Gentleman advanced in Years he began to neglect the Affairs of his Family, leaving them chiefly to the Management of his Steward. Now the Steward had debauched his Wife, and by that Means gained an entire Ascendency over her. She no longer deliberated what would most benefit either the old Farm or the new; but said and did whatever the Steward pleased. Nay so much was she influenced by him that she could neither utter *Ay* or *No* but as he directed. For he had cunningly persuaded her that it was very fashionable for Women to wear Padlocks on their Lips, and that he was sure they would become her exceedingly. He therefore fastened a Padlock to each Corner of her Mouth; when the one was open, she could only say *Ay*; and when the other was loosed, could only cry *No*. He took Care to keep the Keys of these Locks himself; so that her Will became entirely subject to his Power.

Now the old Lady and the Steward had set themselves against the People of the new Farm; and began to devise Ways and Means to impoverish and distress them.

They prevailed on the Nobleman to sign an Edict against the new Settlers, in which it was declared that it was their Duty as Children to pay something towards the supplying their Father's Table with Provisions, and to the supporting the Dignity of his Family; for that Purpose it was ordained that all their Spoons, Knives and Forks, Plates and Porringers, should be marked with a certain Mark, by Officers appointed for that End; for which marking they were to pay a certain Stipend: And that they should not, under severe Penalties, presume to make use of any Spoon, Knife or Fork, Plate or Porringer, before it had been so marked, and the said Stipend paid to the Officer.

The Inhabitants of the new Farm began to see that their Father's Affections were alienated from them; and that their Mother was but a base Mother in Law debauched by their Enemy the Steward. They were thrown into great Confusion and Distress. They wrote the most supplicating Letters to the old Gentleman, in which they acknowledged him to be their Father in Terms of the greatest Respect and Affection—they recounted to him the Hardships and Difficulties they had suffered in settling his new Farm; and pointed out the great Addition of Wealth and Power his Family had acquired by the Improvement of that Wilderness; and showed him that all the Fruits of their Labours must in the natural Course of Things unite, in the long Run, in his Money

Box. They also, in humble Terms, reminded him of his Promises
and Engagements on their leaving Home, and of the Bonds he
had given them; of the Solemnity and Importance of the *Great
Paper* with the Curse annexed. They acknowledged that he ought
to be reimbursed the Expences he was at on their Account, and
that it was their Duty to assist in supporting the Dignity of his
Family. All this they declared they were ready and willing to do;
but requested that they might do it agreeable to the Purport of
the *Great Paper*, by applying to their several Wives for the Keys of
their Money Boxes and furnishing him from thence; and not be
subject to the Tyranny and Caprice of an avaricious Mother in
Law, whom they had never chosen, and of a Steward who was
their declared Enemy.

Some of these Letters were intercepted by the Steward; others
were delivered to the old Gentleman, who was at the same Time
persuaded to take no Notice of them; but, on the Contrary, to
insist the more strenuously upon the Right his Wife claimed of
marking their Spoons, Knives and Forks, Plates and Porringers.

The new Settlers observing how Matters were conducted in
their Father's Family became exceedingly distressed and mortified. They met together and agreed one and all that they would
no longer submit to the arbitrary Impositions of their Mother in
Law, and their Enemy the Steward. They determined to pay no
Manner of Regard to the new Decree, considering it as a Violation
of the *Great Paper*. But to go on and eat their Broth and Pudding
as usual. The Cooks also and Butlers served up their Spoons,
Knives and Forks, Plates and Porringers without having them
marked by the new Officers.

The Nobleman at length thought fit to reverse the Order which
had been made respecting the Spoons, Knives and Forks, Plates
and Porringers of the new Settlers. But he did this with a very ill
Grace: For he, at the same Time avowed and declared that he
and his Wife had a Right to mark all their Furniture, if they
pleased, from the Silver Tankard down to the very Chamber Pots:
That as he was their Father he had an absolute Controul over
them, and that their Liberties, Lives and Properties were at the
entire Disposal of him and his Wife: That it was not fit that he
who was allowed to be *Omnipresent, Immortal,* and *incapable of Error,*
should be confined by the Shackles of the *Great Paper*; or obliged

to fulfil the Bonds he had given them, which he averred he had a Right to cancel whenever he pleased.

His Wife also became intoxicated with Vanity. The Steward had told her that she was an *omnipotent* Goddess, and ought to be worshipped as such: That it was the Height of Impudence and Disobedience in the new Settlers to dispute her Authority, which, with Respect to them, was unlimited: That as they had removed from their Father's Family, they had forfeited all Pretensions to be considered as his Children, and lost the Privileges of the *Great Paper*: That, therefore, she might look on them only as Tenants at Will upon her Husband's Farm, and exact from them what Rent she pleased.

All this was perfectly agreeable to Madam, who admitted this new Doctrine in its full Sense.

The People of the new Farm however took little Notice of these pompous Declarations. They were glad the marking Decree was reversed, and were in Hopes that Things would gradually settle into their former Channel.

CHAPTER V

In the mean Time the new Settlers increased exceedingly, and as they increased, their Dealings at their Father's Shop were proportionatly enlarged.

It is true they suffered some Inconveniencies from the Protectors that had been sent amongst them, who became very troublesome in their Houses: They seduced their Daughters; introduced Riot and Intemperance into their Families, and derided and insulted the Orders and Regulations they had made for their own good Government. Moreover the old Nobleman had sent amongst them a great Number of Thieves, Ravishers and Murderers, who did a great deal of Mischief by practising those Crimes for which they had been banished the old Farm. But they bore these Grievances with as much Patience as could be expected; not choosing to trouble their aged Father with Complaints, unless in Cases of important Necessity.

Now the Steward continued to hate the new Settlers with exceeding great Hatred, and determined to renew his Attack upon their Peace and Happiness. He artfully insinuated to the old Gentleman and his foolish Wife, that it was very mean and unbecoming in them to receive the Contributions of the People of the new Farm, towards supporting the Dignity of his Family, through the Hands of their respective Wives: That upon this Footing it would be in their Power to refuse his Requisitions whenever they should be thought to be unreasonable, of which they would pretend to be Judges themselves; and that it was high Time they should be compelled to acknowledge his arbitrary Power, and his Wife's *Omnipotence.*

For this Purpose, another Decree was prepared and published, ordering that the new Settlers should pay a certain Stipend upon particular Goods, which they were not allowed to purchase any where but at their Father's Shop; and that this Stipend should not be deemed an Advance upon the original Price of the Goods, but be paid on their Arrival at the new Farm, for the express Purpose of supporting the Dignity of the old Gentleman's Family, and of defraying the Expences he affected to afford them.

This new Decree gave our Adventurers the utmost Uneasiness. They saw that the Steward and their Mother in Law were determined to oppress and enslave them. They again met together and wrote to their Father, as before, the most humble and persuasive Letters; but to little Purpose: A deaf Ear was turned to all their Remonstrances; and their dutiful Requests treated with Contempt.

Finding this moderate and decent Conduct brought them no Relief, they had Recourse to another Expedient. They bound themselves in a solemn Engagement not to deal any more at their Father's Shop until this unconstitutional Decree should be reversed; which they declared to be a Violation of the *Great Paper.*

This Agreement was so strictly adhered to, that in a few Months the Clerks and Apprentices in the old Gentleman's Shop began to make a sad Outcry. They declared that their Master's Trade was declining exceedingly, and that his Wife and Steward would, by their mischievous Machinations, ruin the whole Farm: They forthwith sharpened their Pens and attacked the Steward, and even the old Lady herself with great Severity. Insomuch that it was thought proper to withdraw this Attempt likewise upon the

Rights and Liberties of the new Settlers. One Part only of the new Decree remained unreversed—Viz. the Tax upon *Water Gruel.*

Now there were certain Men on the old Farm, who had obtained from the Nobleman an exclusive Right of selling *Water Gruel.* Vast Quantities of this *Gruel* were vended amongst the new Settlers; for it became very fashionable for them to use it in their Families in great Abundance. They did not however trouble themselves much about the Tax on *Water Gruel*: They were well pleased with the Reversal of the other Parts of the Decree, and considering *Gruel* as not absolutely necessary to the Comfort of Life, they were determined to endeavour to do without it, and by that Means avoid the remaining Effects of the new Decree.

The Steward found his Designs once more frustrated; but was not discouraged by this Disappointment. He formed another Scheme so artfully contrived that he thought himself sure of Success. He sent for the Persons who had the sole Right of vending *Water Gruel,* and after reminding them of the Obligations they were under to the Nobleman and his Wife for their exclusive Privilege, he desired that they would send sundry Waggon Loads of *Gruel* to the new Farm, promising that the accustomed Duty which they paid for their exclusive Right should be taken off from all the *Gruel* they should send amongst the new Settlers: And that in Case their Cargoes should come to any Damage, he would take Care that the Loss should be repaired out of the old Gentleman's Coffers.

The *Gruel* Merchants readily consented to this Proposal, knowing that if their Cargoes were sold, they would reap considerable Profits; and if they failed, the Steward was to make good the Damage. On the other Hand the Steward concluded that the new Settlers could not resist purchasing the *Gruel* to which they had been so long accustomed; and if they did purchase it when subject to the Tax aforesaid, this would be an avowed Acknowledgment on their Parts that their Father and his Wife had a Right to break through the Tenor of the *Great Paper,* and to lay on them what Impositions they pleased, without the Consent of their respective Wives.

But the new Settlers were well aware of this Decoy. They saw clearly that the *Gruel* was not sent to accommodate, but to enslave them; and that if they suffered any Part of it to be sold amongst them, it would be deemed a Submission to the assumed *Omnipotence* of the *Great Madam*.

CHAPTER VI

On the Arrival of the *Water Gruel*, the People of the new Farm were again thrown into great Alarms and Confusions. Some of them would not suffer the Waggons to be unloaded at all, but sent them immediately back to the *Gruel* Merchants: Others permitted the Waggons to unload, but would not touch the hateful Commodity; so that it lay neglected about their Roads and Highways until it grew sour and spoiled. But one of the new Settlers, whose Name was *Jack*, either from a keener Sense of the Injuries attempted against him, or from the Necessity of his Situation, which was such that he could not send back the *Gruel* because of a Number of Mercenaries whom his Father had stationed before his House to watch and be a Check upon his Conduct: He, I say, being almost driven to Despair, fell to Work, and with great Zeal stove to Pieces the Casks of *Gruel*, which had been sent him, and utterly demolished the whole Cargoe.

These Proceedings were soon known at the old Farm. Great and terrible was the Uproar there. The old Gentleman fell into great Wrath, declaring that his absent Children meant to throw off all Dependence upon him, and to become altogether disobedient. His Wife also tore the Padlocks from her Lips, and raved and stormed like a Billingsgate. The Steward lost all Patience and Moderation, swearing most prophanely that he would leave no Stone unturned 'till he had *humbled the Settlers of the new Farm at his Feet,* and caused their Father to trample on their Necks. Moreover the *Gruel* Merchants roared and bellowed for the Loss of their *Gruel*; and the Clerks and Apprentices were in the utmost Consternation lest the People of the new Farm should again agree to have no Dealings with their Father's Shop—Vengeance was immediately set on Foot, particularly against *Jack*. With him they determined to begin; hoping that by making an Example of him they should so terrify the other Families of the new Settlers, that they would all submit to the Designs of the Steward, and the *Omnipotence* of the old Lady.

A very large *Padlock* was, accordingly, prepared to be fastened upon *Jack's* great Gate; the Key of which was to be given to the old Gentleman; who was not to open it again until he had paid for the *Gruel* he had spilt, and resigned all Claim to the Privileges of the *Great Paper*: Nor then neither unless he thought fit. Secondly, a Decree was made to new model the Regulations and Œconomy of *Jack's* Family in such Manner that they might for the Future be more subject to the Will of the Steward: And, thirdly, a large Gallows was erected before the Mansion House in the old Farm, and an Order made that if any of Jack's Children or Servants should be suspected of Misbehaviour, they should not be convicted or acquitted by the Consent of their Brethren, agreeable to the Purport of the *Great Paper*, but be tied Neck and Heels and dragged to the Gallows at the Mansion House, and there be hanged without Mercy.

No sooner did Tidings of this undue Severity reach the new Farm, but the People were almost ready to despair. They were altogether at a Loss how to act, or by what Means they should avert the Vengeance to which they were doomed: But the old Lady and Steward soon determined the Matter; for the *Padlock* was sent over, and without Ceremony fastened upon *Jack's* great Gate. They did not wait to know whether he would pay for the *Gruel* or not, or make the required Acknowledgments; nor give him the least Opportunity to make his Defence—The great Gate was locked, and the Key given to the old Nobleman, as had been determined.

Poor *Jack* found himself in a most deplorable Condition. The great Inlet to his Farm was entirely blocked up, so that he could neither carry out the Produce of his Land for Sale, nor receive from abroad the Necessaries for his Family.

But this was not all—His Father, along with the *Padlock* aforesaid, had sent an Overseer to hector and domineer over him and his Family; and to endeavour to break his Spirit by exercising every possible Severity: For which Purpose he was attended by a great Number of Mercenaries, and armed with more than common Authorities.

On his first arrival in *Jack's* Family he was received with considerable Respect, because he was the Delegate of their aged Father: For, notwithstanding all that had past, the People of the new

Settlements loved and revered the old Gentleman with a truly filial Attachment; attributing his unkindness entirely to the Intrigues of their Enemy the Steward. But this fair Weather did not last long. The new Overseer took the first Opportunity of showing that he had no Intentions of living in Harmony and Friendship with the Family. Some of *Jack's* Domesticks had put on their Sunday Clothes, and attended the Overseer in the great Parlour, in Order to pay him their Compliments on his Arrival, and to request his Assistance in reconciling them to their Father: But he rudely stopped them short in the Midst of their Speech; called them a Parcel of disobedient Scoundrels, and bid them go about their Business. So saying, he turned upon his Heel, and with great Contempt left the Room.

CHAPTER VII

Now *Jack* and his Family finding themselves oppressed, insulted and tyrannised over in the most cruel and arbitrary Manner, advised with their Brethren what Measures should be adopted to relieve them from their intolerable Grievances. Their Brethren, one and all, united in sympathising with their Afflictions; they advised them to bear their Sufferings with Fortitude for a Time, assuring them that they looked on the Punishments and Insults laid upon them with the same Indignation as if they had been inflicted on themselves, and that they would stand by and support them to the last. But, above all, earnestly recommended it to them to be firm and steady in the Cause of Liberty and Justice, and never acknowledge the *Omnipotence* of their Mother in Law; nor yield to the Machinations of their Enemy the Steward.

In the mean Time, lest *Jack's* Family should suffer for Want of Necessaries, their great Gate being fast locked, liberal and very generous Contributions were raised among the several Families of the new Settlements, for their present Relief. This seasonable Bounty was handed to *Jack* over the Garden Wall—All Access to the Front of his House being shut up.

Now the Overseer observed that the Children and Domesticks of *Jack's* Family had frequent Meetings and Consultations together: Sometimes in the Garret, and sometimes in the Stable:

Understanding, likewise, that an Agreement not to deal in their Father's Shop, until their Grievances should be redressed, was much talked of amongst them, he wrote a thundering Prohibition, much like a Pope's Bull, which he caused to be pasted up in every Room in the House: In which he declared and protested that these Meetings were treasonable, traiterous and rebellious; contrary to the Dignity of their Father, and inconsistent with the *Omnipotence* of their Mother in Law: Denouncing also terrible Punishments against any two of the Family who should from thenceforth be seen whispering together, and strictly forbidding the Domesticks to hold any more Meetings in the Garret or Stable.

These harsh and unconstitutional Proceedings irritated *Jack* and the other Inhabitants of the new Farm to such a Degree that *************

Cætera desunt.

Benjamin Franklin
(1706–1790)

Scientist, inventor, printer, publisher, diplomat and politician, drafter and signer of the Declaration of Independence, founder of the University of Pennsylvania, attendee at the Constitutional Convention of 1787—it is hard to believe that Franklin had time left over to be an author as well. Yet his *Autobiography* is a classic of the genre, *Poor Richard's Almanack* is a little gem of gentle wit and down-to-earth philosophy, and his satirical writings are as sharp and skilled as any in the history of American literature. He was of course particularly adept at political satire, so here are several pieces in that genre. And we add a sardonic "model" letter of recommendation that is as lively and pertinent today as it was two hundred years ago.

On Sending Felons to America

FOR THE PENNSYLVANIA GAZETTE

Sir,

We may all remember the Time when our Mother Country, as a Mark of her parental Tenderness, emptied her Jails into our Habitations, *"for the* BETTER *Peopling,"* as she express'd it, *"of the Colonies."* It is certain that no due Returns have yet been made for these valuable Consignments. We are therefore much in her Debt on that Account; and, as she is of late clamorous for the

Payment of all we owe her, and some of our Debts are of a kind not so easily discharg'd, I am for doing however what is in our Power. It will show our good-will as to the rest. The Felons she planted among us have produc'd such an amazing Increase, that we are now enabled to make ample Remittance in the same Commodity. And since the Wheelbarrow Law is not found effectually to reform them, and many of our Vessels are idle through her Restraints on our Trade, why should we not employ those Vessels in transporting the Felons to Britain?

I was led into this Thought by perusing the Copy of a Petition to Parliament, which fell lately by Accident into my Hands. It has no Date, but I conjecture from some Circumstances, that it must have been about the year 1767 or 68. (It seems, if presented, it had no Effect, since the Act passed.) I imagine it may not be unacceptable to your Readers, and therefore transcribe it for your paper; viz.

To the Honourable the Knights, Citizens, and Burgesses of Great Britain, in Parliament assembled,

The PETITION of B. F., Agent for the Province of Pensilvania; Most humbly sheweth;

That the Transporting of Felons from England to the Plantations in America, is, and hath long been, a great Grievance to the said Plantations in general.

That the said Felons, being landed in America, not only continue their evil Practices to the Annoyance of his Majesty's good Subjects there, but contribute greatly to corrupt the Morals of the Servants and poorer People among whom they are mixed.

That many of the said Felons escape from the Servitude to which they were destined, into other Colonies, where their Condition is not known; and, wandering at large from one populous Town to another, commit many Burglaries, Robberies, and Murders, to the great Terror of the People; and occasioning heavy Charges for apprehending and securing such Felons, and bringing them to Justice.

That your Petitioner humbly conceives the Easing one Part of the British Dominions of their Felons, by burthening another Part with the same Felons, cannot increase the common Happiness of his Majesty's Subjects, and that therefore the Trouble and Expence of transporting them is upon the whole altogether useless.

That your petitioner, nevertheless, observes with extream Concern in the Votes of Friday last, that leave is given to bring in a Bill for extending to Scotland, the Act made in the 4th Year of the Reign of King George the First, whereby the aforesaid Grievances are, as he understands, to be greatly increased by allowing Scotland also to transport its Felons to America.

Your petitioner therefore humbly prays, in behalf of Pensilvania, and the other Plantations in America, that the House would take the Premises into Consideration, and in their great Wisdom and Goodness repeal all Acts, and Clauses of Acts, for transporting of Felons; or, if this may not at present be done, that they would at least reject the propos'd Bill for extending the said Acts to Scotland; or, if it be thought fit to allow of such Extension, that then the said Extension may be carried further, and the Plantations be also, by an equitable Clause in the same bill, permitted to transport their Felons to Scotland.

And your Petitioner, as in Duty bound, shall pray, &c.

This Petition, as I am informed, was not receiv'd by the House, and the Act passed.

On second Thoughts, I am of Opinion, that besides employing our own Vessels, as above propos'd, every English Ship arriving in our Ports with Goods for sale, should be obliged to give Bond, before she is permitted to Trade, engaging that she will carry back to Britain at least one Felon for every Fifty Tons of her Burthen. Thus we shall not only discharge sooner our Debts, but furnish our old Friends with the means of *"better Peopling,"* and with more Expedition, their promising new Colony of Botany Bay.

I am yours, &c.

A. Z.

The Sale of the Hessians

FROM THE COUNT DE SCHAUMBERGH TO THE BARON HOHENDORF, COMMANDING THE HESSIAN TROOPS IN AMERICA

Rome, February 18, 1777.

MONSIEUR LE BARON:—On my return from Naples, I received at Rome your letter of the 27th December of last year. I have learned with unspeakable pleasure the courage our troops exhibited at Trenton, and you cannot imagine my joy on being told that of the 1,950 Hessians engaged in the fight, but 345 escaped. There were just 1,605 men killed, and I cannot sufficiently commend your prudence in sending an exact list of the dead to my minister in London. This precaution was the more necessary, as the report sent to the English ministry does not give but 1,455 dead. This would make 483,450 florins instead of 643,500 which I am entitled to demand under our convention. You will comprehend the prejudice which such an error would work in my finances, and I do not doubt you will take the necessary pains to prove that Lord North's list is false and yours correct.

The court of London objects that there were a hundred wounded who ought not to be included in the list, nor paid for as dead; but I trust you will not overlook my instructions to you on quitting Cassel, and that you will not have tried by human succor to recall the life of the unfortunates whose days could not be lengthened but by the loss of a leg or an arm. That would be making them a pernicious present, and I am sure they would rather die than live in a condition no longer fit for my service. I do not mean by this that you should assassinate them; we should be humane, my dear Baron, but you may insinuate to the surgeons with entire propriety that a crippled man is a reproach to their profession, and that there is no wiser course than to let every one of them die when he ceases to be fit to fight.

I am about to send to you some new recruits. Don't economize them. Remember glory before all things. Glory is true wealth. There is nothing degrades the soldier like the love of money. He must care only for honour and reputation, but this reputation must be acquired in the midst of dangers. A battle gained without costing the conqueror any blood is an inglorious success, while the conquered cover themselves with glory by perishing with their arms in their hands. Do you remember that of the 300 Lacedæ-monians who defended the defile of Thermopylæ, not one re-turned? How happy should I be could I say the same of my brave Hessians!

It is true that their king, Leonidas, perished with them: but things have changed, and it is no longer the custom for princes of the empire to go and fight in America for a cause with which they have no concern. And besides, to whom should they pay the thirty guineas per man if I did not stay in Europe to receive them? Then, it is necessary also that I be ready to send recruits to replace the men you lose. For this purpose I must return to Hesse. It is true, grown men are becoming scarce there, but I will send you boys. Besides, the scarcer the commodity the higher the price. I am assured that the women and little girls have begun to till our lands, and they get on not badly. You did right to send back to Europe that Dr. Crumerus who was so successful in curing dys-entery. Don't bother with a man who is subject to looseness of the bowels. That disease makes bad soldiers. One coward will do more mischief in an engagement than ten brave men will do good. Better that they burst in their barracks than fly in a battle, and tarnish the glory of our arms. Besides, you know that they pay me as killed for all who die from disease, and I don't get a farthing for runaways. My trip to Italy, which has cost me enor-mously, makes it desirable that there should be a great mortality among them. You will therefore promise promotion to all who expose themselves; you will exhort them to seek glory in the midst of dangers; you will say to Major Maundorff that I am not at all content with his saving the 345 men who escaped the massacre of Trenton. Through the whole campaign he has not had ten men killed in consequence of his orders. Finally, let it be your principal object to prolong the war and avoid a decisive engagement on either side, for I have made arrangements for a grand Italian opera, and I do not wish to be obliged to give it up. Meantime I pray God, my dear Baron de Hohendorf, to have you in his holy and gracious keeping.

Model of a Letter of Recommendation

Paris April 2, 1777

Sir

The Bearer of this who is going to America, presses me to give him a Letter of Recommendation, tho' I know nothing of him, not even his Name. This may seem extraordinary, but I assure you it is not uncommon here. Sometimes indeed one unknown Person brings me another equally unknown, to recommend him; and sometimes they recommend one another! As to this Gentleman, I must refer you to himself for his Character and Merits, with which he is certainly better acquainted than I can possibly be; I recommend him however to those Civilities which every Stranger, of whom one knows no Harm, has a Right to, and I request you will do him all the good Offices and show him all the Favour that on further Acquaintance you shall find him to deserve. I have the honour to be, &c.

Rules by Which a Great Empire May Be Reduced to a Small One

[Presented privately to a *late Minister*, when he entered upon his Administration; and now first published.]

An ancient Sage valued himself upon this, that tho' he could not fiddle, he knew how to make a *great City* of a *little one*. The Science that I, a modern Simpleton, am about to communicate is the very reverse.

I address myself to all Ministers who have the Management of extensive Dominions, which from their very Greatness are become troublesome to govern, because the Multiplicity of their Affairs leaves no Time for *fiddling*.

I. In the first Place, Gentlemen, you are to consider, that a great Empire, like a great Cake, is most easily diminished at the Edges.

Turn your Attention therefore first to your remotest Provinces; that as you get rid of them, the next may follow in Order.

II. That the Possibility of this Separation may always exist, take special Care the Provinces are never incorporated with the Mother Country, that they do not enjoy the same common Rights, the same Privileges in Commerce, and that they are governed by *severer* Laws, all of *your enacting*, without allowing them any Share in the Choice of the Legislators. By carefully making and preserving such Distinctions, you will (to keep to my Simile of the Cake) act like a wise Gingerbread Baker, who, to facilitate a Division, cuts his Dough half through in those Places, where, when bak'd, he would have it *broken to Pieces*.

III. These remote Provinces have perhaps been acquired, purchas'd, or conquer'd, at the *sole Expence* of the Settlers or their Ancestors, without the Aid of the Mother Country. If this should happen to increase her *Strength* by their growing Numbers ready to join in her Wars, her *Commerce* by their growing Demand for her Manufactures, or her *Naval Power* by greater Employment for her Ships and Seamen, they may probably suppose some Merit in this, and that it entitles them to some Favour; you are therefore to *forget it all*, or resent it as if they had done you Injury. If they happen to be zealous Whigs, Friends of Liberty, nurtur'd in Revolution Principles, *remember all that* to their Prejudice, and contrive to punish it: For such Principles, after a Revolution is thoroughly established, are of *no more Use*, they are even *odious* and *abominable*.

IV. However peaceably your Colonies have submitted to your Government, shewn their Affection to your Interest, and patiently borne their Grievances, you are to *suppose* them always inclined to revolt, and treat them accordingly. Quarter Troops among them, who by their Insolence may *provoke* the rising of Mobs, and by their Bullets and Bayonets *suppress* them. By this Means, like the Husband who uses his Wife ill *from Suspicion*, you may in Time convert your *Suspicions* into *Realities*.

V. Remote Provinces must have *Governors*, and *Judges*, to represent the Royal Person, and execute every where the delegated Parts of his Office and Authority. You Ministers know, that much of the Strength of Government depends on the *Opinion* of the People; and much of that Opinion on the Choice of Rulers placed immediately over them. If you send them wise and good Men for

Governors, who study the Interest of the Colonists, and advance their Prosperity, they will think their King wise and good, and that he wishes the Welfare of his Subjects. If you send them learned and upright Men for Judges, they will think him a Lover of Justice. This may attach your Provinces more to his Government. You are therefore to be careful who you recommend for those Offices.—If you can find Prodigals who have ruined their Fortunes, broken Gamesters or Stock-Jobbers, these may do well as *Governors*; for they will probably be rapacious, and provoke the People by their Extortions. Wrangling Proctors and petty-fogging Lawyers too are not amiss, for they will be for ever disputing and quarrelling with their little Parliaments. If withal they should be ignorant, wrong-headed and insolent, so much the better. Attorneys Clerks and Newgate Solicitors will do for *Chief-Justices*, especially if they hold their Places *during your Pleasure.*—And all will contribute to impress those ideas of your Government that are proper for a People *you would wish to renounce it.*

VI. To confirm these Impressions, and strike them deeper, whenever the Injured come to the Capital with Complaints of Maladministration, Oppression, or Injustice, punish such Suitors with long Delay, enormous Expence, and a final Judgment in Favour of the Oppressor. This will have an admirable Effect every Way. The Trouble of future Complaints will be prevented, and Governors and Judges will be encouraged to farther Acts of Oppression and Injustice; and thence the People may become more disaffected, *and at length desperate.*

VII. When such Governors have crammed their Coffers, and made themselves so odious to the People that they can no longer remain among them with Safety to their Persons, recall and *reward* them with Pensions. You may make them *Baronets* too, if that respectable Order should not think fit to resent it. All will contribute to encourage new Governors in the same Practices, and make the supreme Government *detestable.*

VIII. If when you are engaged in War, your Colonies should vie in liberal Aids of Men and Money against the common Enemy, upon your simple Requisition, and give far beyond their Abilities, reflect, that a Penny taken from them by your Power is more honourable to you than a Pound presented by their Benevolence. Despise therefore their voluntary Grants, and resolve to harrass them with novel Taxes. They will probably complain to your Parliaments that they are taxed by a Body in which they have no Representative, and that this is contrary to common Right. They will petition for Redress. Let the Parliaments flout their Claims, reject their Petitions, refuse even to suffer the reading of them, and treat the Petitioners with the utmost Contempt. Nothing can have a better Effect, in producing the Alienation proposed; for though many can forgive Injuries, *none ever forgave Contempt.*

IX. In laying these Taxes, never regard the heavy Burthens those remote People already undergo, in defending their own Frontiers, supporting their own provincial Governments, making new Roads, building Bridges, Churches and other public Edifices, which in old Countries have been done to your Hands by your Ancestors, but which occasion constant Calls and Demands on the Purses of a new People. Forget the *Restraints* you lay on their Trade for *your own* Benefit, and the Advantage a *Monopoly* of this Trade gives your exacting Merchants. Think nothing of the Wealth those Merchants and your Manufacturers acquire by the Colony Commerce; their encreased Ability thereby to pay Taxes at home; their accumulating, in the Price of their Commodities, most of those Taxes, and so levying them from their consuming Customers: All this, and the Employment and Support of Thousands of your Poor by the Colonists, you are *intirely to forget.* But remember to make your arbitrary Tax more grievous to your Provinces, by public Declarations importing that your Power of taxing them has *no Limits*, so that when you take from them without their Consent a Shilling in the Pound, you have a clear Right to the other nineteen. This will probably weaken every Idea of *Security in their Property*, and convince them that under such a Government *they have nothing they can call their own*; which can scarce fail of producing *the happiest Consequences*!

X. Possibly indeed some of them might still comfort themselves, and say, 'Though we have no Property, we have yet *something* left that is valuable; we have constitutional *Liberty* both of Person and of Conscience. This King, these Lords, and these Commons, who it seems are too remote from us to know us and feel for us, cannot take from us our *Habeas Corpus* Right, or our Right of Trial *by a Jury of our Neighbours*: They cannot deprive us of the Exercise of our Religion, alter our ecclesiastical Constitutions, and compel us

to be Papists if they please, or Mahometans.' To annihilate this
Comfort, begin by Laws to perplex their Commerce with infinite
Regulations impossible to be remembered and observed; ordain
Seizures of their Property for every Failure; take away the Trial of
such Property by Jury, and give it to arbitrary Judges of your own
appointing, and of the lowest Characters in the Country, whose
Salaries and Emoluments are to arise out of the Duties or Con-
demnations, and whose Appointments are *during Pleasure*. Then
let there be a formal Declaration of both Houses, that Opposition
to your Edicts is *Treason*, and that Persons suspected of Treason
in the Provinces may, according to some obsolete Law, be seized
and sent to the Metropolis of the Empire for Trial; and pass an
Act that those there charged with certain other Offences shall be
sent away in Chains from their Friends and Country to be tried
in the same Manner for Felony. Then erect a new Court of Inquisition among them, accompanied by an armed Force, with Instructions to transport all such suspected Persons, to be ruined
by the Expence if they bring over Evidences to prove their Innocence, or be found guilty and hanged if they can't afford it.
And lest the People should think you cannot possibly go any farther, pass another solemn declaratory Act, that 'King, Lords, and
Commons had, hath, and of Right ought to have, full Power and
Authority to make Statutes of sufficient Force and Validity to bind
the unrepresented Provinces IN ALL CASES WHATSOEVER.' This will
include *spiritual* with temporal; and taken together, must operate
wonderfully to your Purpose, by convincing them, that they are
at present under a Power something like that spoken of in the
Scriptures, which can not only *kill their Bodies*, but *damn their Souls*
to all Eternity, by compelling them, if it pleases, *to worship the
Devil*.

XI. To make your Taxes more odious, and more likely to procure Resistance, send from the Capital a Board of Officers to su-
perintend the Collection, composed of the most *indiscreet, ill-bred*
and *insolent* you can find. Let these have large Salaries out of the
extorted Revenue, and live in open grating Luxury upon the
Sweat and Blood of the Industrious, whom they are to worry continually with groundless and expensive Prosecutions before the
above-mentioned arbitrary Revenue-Judges, all *at the Cost of the
Party prosecuted* tho' acquitted, because *the King is to pay no Costs*.

—Let these Men *by your Order* be exempted from all the common Taxes and Burthens of the Province, though they and their Property are protected by its Laws. If any Revenue Officers are *suspected* of the least Tenderness for the People, discard them. If others are justly complained of, protect and reward them. If any of the Underofficers behave so as to provoke the People to drub them, promote those to better Offices: This will encourage others to procure for themselves such profitable Drubbings, by multiplying and enlarging such Provocations, and *all with work towards the End you aim at.*

XII. Another Way to make your Tax odious, is to misapply the Produce of it. If it was originally appropriated for the *Defence* of the Provinces and the better Support of Government, and the Administration of Justice where it may be *necessary*, then apply none of it to that *Defence*, but bestow it where it is *not necessary*, in augmented Salaries or Pensions to every Governor who has distinguished himself by his Enmity to the People, and by calumniating them to their Sovereign. This will make them pay it more unwillingly, and be more apt to quarrel with those that collect it, and those that imposed it, who will quarrel again with them, and all shall contribute to your *main Purpose* of making them *weary of your Government.*

XIII. If the People of any Province have been accustomed to support their own Governors and Judges to Satisfaction, you are to apprehend that such Governors and Judges may be thereby influenced to treat the People kindly, and to do them Justice. This is another Reason for applying Part of that Revenue in larger Salaries to such Governors and Judges, given, as their Commissions are, *during your Pleasure* only, forbidding them to take any Salaries from their Provinces; that thus the People may no longer hope any Kindness from their Governors, or (in Crown Cases) any Justice from their Judges. And as the Money thus mis-applied in one Province is extorted from all, probably *all will resent the Misapplication.*

XIV. If the Parliaments of your Provinces should dare to claim Rights or complain of your Administration, order them to be harass'd with repeated *Dissolutions*. If the same Men are continually return'd by new Elections, adjourn their Meetings to some Country Village where they cannot be accommodated, and there keep them *during Pleasure*; for this, you know, is your PREROGATIVE; and an excellent one it is, as you may manage it, to promote Discontents among the People, diminish their Respect, and *increase their Disaffection.*

XV. Convert the brave honest Officers of your Navy into pimping Tide-waiters and Colony Officers of the Customs. Let those who in Time of War fought gallantly in Defence of the Commerce of their Countrymen, in Peace be taught to prey upon it. Let them learn to be corrupted by great and real Smugglers, but (to shew their Diligence) scour with armed Boats every Bay, Harbour, River, Creek, Cove or Nook throughout the Coast of your Colonies, stop and detain every Coaster, every Wood-boat, every Fisherman, tumble their Cargoes, and even their Ballast, inside out and upside down; and if a Penn'orth of Pins is found un-entered, let the Whole be seized and confiscated. Thus shall the Trade of your Colonists suffer more from their Friends in Time of Peace, than it did from their Enemies in War. Then let these Boats Crews land upon every Farm in their Way, rob the Orchards, steal the Pigs and Poultry, and insult the Inhabitants. If the injured and exasperated Farmers, unable to procure other Justice, should attack the Agressors, drub them and burn their Boats, you are to call this *High Treason* and *Rebellion,* order Fleets and Armies into their Country, and threaten to carry all the Offenders three thousand Miles to be hang'd, drawn and quartered. *O! this will work admirably!*

XVI. If you are told of Discontents in your Colonies, never believe that they are general, or that you have given Occasion for them; therefore do not think of applying any Remedy, or of changing any offensive Measure. Redress no Grievance, lest they should be encouraged to demand the Redress of some other Grievance. Grant no Request that is just and reasonable, lest they should make another that is unreasonable. Take all your Informations of the State of the Colonies from your Governors and Officers in Enmity with them. Encourage and reward these *Leasing-makers*; secrete their lying Accusations lest they should be confuted; but act upon them as the clearest Evidence, and believe nothing you hear from the Friends of the People. Suppose all *their* Complaints to be invented and promoted by a few factious Demagogues, whom if you could catch and hang, all would be quiet. Catch and hang a few of them accordingly; and the *Blood of the Martyrs* shall *work Miracles* in favour of your Purpose.

XVII. If you see *rival Nations* rejoicing at the Prospect of your Disunion with your Provinces, and endeavouring to promote it: If they translate, publish and applaud all the Complaints of your discontented Colonists, at the same Time privately stimulating you to severer Measures; let not that *alarm* or offend you. Why should it? since you all mean *the same Thing*.

XVIII. If any Colony should at their own Charge erect a Fortress to secure their Port against the Fleets of a foreign Enemy, get your Governor to betray that Fortress into your Hands. Never think of paying what it cost the Country, for that would *look*, at least, like some Regard for Justice; but turn it into a Citadel to awe the Inhabitants and curb their Commerce. If they should have lodged in such Fortress the very Arms they bought and used to aid you in your Conquests, seize them all, 'twill provoke like *Ingratitude* added to *Robbery*. One admirable Effect of these Operations will be, to discourage every other Colony from erecting such Defences, and so their and your Enemies may more easily invade them, to the great Disgrace of your Government, and of course *the Furtherance of your Project*.

XIX. Send Armies into their Country under Pretence of protecting the Inhabitants; but instead of garrisoning the Forts on their Frontiers with those Troops, to prevent Incursions, demolish those Forts, and order the Troops into the Heart of the Country, that the Savages may be encouraged to attack the Frontiers, and that the Troops may be protected by the Inhabitants: This will seem to proceed from your Ill will or your Ignorance, and contribute farther to produce and strengthen an Opinion among them, *that you are no longer fit to govern them*.

XX. Lastly, Invest the General of your Army in the Provinces with great and unconstitutional Powers, and free him from the Controul of even your own Civil Governors. Let him have Troops enow under his Command, with all the Fortresses in his Possession; and who knows but (like some provincial Generals in the Roman Empire, and encouraged by the universal Discontent you have produced) he may take it into his Head to set up for himself. If he should, and you have carefully practised these few *excellent Rules* of mine, take my Word for it, all the Provinces will immediately join him, and you will that Day (if you have not done it sooner) get rid of the Trouble of governing them, and all the *Plagues* attending their *Commerce* and Connection from thenceforth and for ever.

Q. E. D.

The Public Advertiser, September 11, 1773

Humourous Reasons for Restoring Canada

Mr. Chronicle,

We Britons are a nation of statesmen and politicians; we are privy councellors by birthright; and therefore take it much amiss when we are told by some of your correspondents, 'that it is not proper to expose to public view the many good reasons there are for restoring Canada,' (*if we reduce it.*)

I have, with great industry, been able to procure a full account of those reasons, and shall make no secret of them among ourselves. Here they are.—Give them to all your readers; that is, to all that can read, in the King's dominions.

1. We should restore Canada; because an uninterrupted trade with the Indians throughout a vast country, where the communication by water is so easy, would encrease our commerce, *already too great*, and occasion a large additional demand for our manufactures,* *already too dear.*

2. We should restore it, lest, thro' a greater plenty of beaver, broad-brimmed hats become cheaper to that unmannerly sect, the Quakers.

3. We should restore Canada, that we may *soon* have a new war, and another opportunity of spending two or three millions a year in America; there being great danger of our growing too rich, our

---

* Every Indian now wears a woollen blanket, a linnen shirt, and cloth stockings; besides a knife, a hatchet and a gun; and they use a variety of other European and Indian goods, which they pay for in skins and furs.

European expences not being sufficient to drain our immense treasures.

4. We should restore it, that we may have occasion constantly to employ, in time of war, a fleet and army in those parts; for otherwise we might be too strong at home.

5. We should restore it, that the French may, by means of their Indians, carry on, (as they have done for these 100 years past even in times of peace between the two crowns) a constant scalping war against our colonies, and thereby stint their growth; for, otherwise, the children might in time be as tall as their mother*.

6. What tho' the blood of thousands of unarmed English farmers, surprized and assassinated in their fields; of harmless women and children murdered in their beds; doth at length call for vengeance;—what tho' the Canadian measure of iniquity be full, and if ever any country did, that country now certainly does, deserve the judgment of *extirpation*;—yet let not us be the executioners of Divine justice;—it will look as if Englishmen were revengeful.

7. Our colonies, 'tis true, have exerted themselves beyond their strength, on the expectations we gave them of driving the French from Canada; but tho' we ought to keep faith with our Allies, it is not necessary with our children. That might teach them (against Scripture) to *put their trust in Princes*: Let 'em learn to trust in God.

8. Should we not restore Canada, it would look as if our statesmen had *courage* as well as our soldiers; but what have statesmen to do with *courage*? Their proper character is *wisdom*.

9. What can be *braver*, than to show all Europe we can afford to lavish our best blood as well as our treasure, in conquests we do not intend to keep? Have we not plenty of *Howe's*, and *Wolfe's*, &c. &c. &c. in every regiment?

10. The French† have long since openly declar'd, *'que les Anglois & les François sont incompatible dans cette partie de l'Amerique;'* 'that our people and theirs were incompatible in that part of the continent of America:' *'que rien n'etoit plus important à l'etat, que de*

---

* This reason is seriously given by some who do not wish well to the Colonies: But, is it not too like the Egyptian Politics practised by Pharoah, destroying the young males to prevent the increase of the children of Israel?

† Histoire Generale de la Nouvelle France, par Charlevoix. Liv. XII.

delivrer leur colonie du facheux voisinage des Anglois;' 'that nothing
was of more importance to France, than delivering its colony from
the troublesome neighbourhood of the English;' to which end,
there was an avowed project on foot *'pour chasser premierement les
Anglois de la Nouvelle York;'* 'to drive the English in the first place
out of the province of New York;' *'& apres la prise de la capitale,
il falloit* (says the scheme) *la* BRULER *&* RUINER *le pays jusqu' à
Orange;'* 'and after taking the capital, to *burn it,* and *ruin* (that is,
make a desart of) the whole country, quite up to Albany.' Now, if
we do not fairly leave the French in Canada, till they have a favourable opportunity of putting their *burning* and *ruining* schemes
in execution, will it not look as if we were afraid of them?

11. Their historian, Charlevoix, in his IVth book, also tells us,
that when Canada was formerly taken by the English, it was a
question at the court of France, whether they should endeavour
to recover it; for, says he, *'bien de gens douterent si l'on avoit fait une
veritable perte;'* 'many thought it was not really a loss.' But tho'
various reasons were given why it was scarce worth recovering, *'le
seul motive* (says he) *d'empecher les Anglois de se rendre trop puissans
—étoit plus que suffissant pour nous engager a recouvrer Quebec, a quel-
que prix que ce fût;'* 'the single motive of preventing the increase
of *English* power, was more than sufficient to engage us in recovering Quebec, *what price soever it might cost us.'* Here we see the
high value they put on that country, and the reason of their valu-
ing it so highly. Let us then, *oblige them* in this (to them) so important an article, and be assured they will *never prove ungrateful.*

I will not dissemble, Mr. *Chronicle*; that in answer to all these
reasons and motives for restoring Canada, I have heard one that
appears to have some weight on the other side of the question.
It is said, that nations, as well as private persons, should, for their
honour's sake, take care to preserve a *consistence of character*: that
it has always been the character of the English to fight strongly,
and negotiate weakly; generally agreeing to restore, at a peace,
what they ought to have kept, and to keep what they had better
have restored: then, if it would really, according to the preceding
reasons, be prudent and right to restore Canada, we ought, say
these objectors, to keep it; otherwise *we shall be inconsistent with
ourselves.* I shall not take upon myself to weigh these different
reasons, but offer the whole to the consideration of the public.

Only permit me to suggest, that there is one method of avoiding fairly all future dispute about the propriety of *keeping* or *restoring* Canada; and that is, *let us never take it.* The French still hold out at Montreal and Trois Rivieres, in hopes of succour from France. Let us be but *a little too late* with our ships in the river St. Laurence, so that the enemy may get their supplies up next spring, as they did the last, with reinforcements sufficient to enable them to recover Quebec, and there is an end of the question. I am, Sir, Yours, &c.

A. Z.

Alexander Hamilton

(1712–1756)

Alexander Hamilton (not to be confused with the secretary of the treasury who died in a duel with Aaron Burr) was a Scottish physician who emigrated to Maryland in 1738 shortly after graduating from the University of Edinburgh. Hamilton worked as a doctor and druggist, a common combination at the time, and ran successfully for the common council of the city of Annapolis. By 1745 he had founded the Tuesday Club, a social and literary organization whose members and visitors included most of the eminent names of Maryland. Hamilton undertook to write a history of the club, but died before he was finished. But the book, *The History of the Ancient and Honorable Tuesday Club*, survives, a collection of pseudo-scholarly articles, amusing speeches, riddles and jokes, farce, political satire, and sometimes scatological humor that is unique in eighteenth-century literature. The book in its full version is more than 1400 pages long, but Hamilton suggested that the reader "begin in the middle of the Book & read backwards, then forwards & skip about; I think now & then you will find something that will set you a roaring."

The Tuesday Club

CHAPTER 6

Some of the Members seized with a furor poeticus, *and some account of the Baltimore Bards.*

Much about this time, appeared an epidemical distemper in the Club, which broke out, no body can tell how, it was what Physicians might properly call a κακο-ηθεια or μαγια§ ποιητικη§, *malignitas poetica,* or *Furor poeticus,* several of the members having been taken in an unaccountable manner, with fits of Rhiming, and writing of Rhimes, those that seemed to be most affected with it were Messiurs Sly, Motely, Blunt, Quaint and Scribble, tho' none were writers but the two last, however, the whole Club was in some measure touched with this malignity, so that they could scarce speak to one another, but in Rhime and Jingle, and even Mr Solo Neverout, sometime after, admitted a Member of the Club, who had never before shown the least genius or turn to Rhiming or versification, nay even made a Jest of it in his laughing way, and ridiculed all poets and poetasters, was so Infected as to break all at once into blank verse, and with great violence and vociferation, exclaimed to the Surprize of all present,

With dowble Lustre, Beckie's beauties shine.

And when he was desired to proceed farther, and make a Couplet of it, he bawld out in a furious manner,

Rise Jupiter, and snuff the moon!—

Upon which the company thinking he was crazed left him to himself, and urged no more questions. . . .

We have reason to believe, that this poetical Contagion took its rise first in the north, and therefore was of the frigid Sort, for, in the county of Baltimore, there appeared two Celebrated Bards, vizt: Bard Bavius, and Bard Mevius, who, having broke out into most violent fits of Rhiming and versifying, Infected many people around them with the same distemper. . . .

The first bold Stroke that appeared of this kind was from the celebrated Bard Mevius, who, one day being In church, hearing the Reverend and pious Mr George Whitefield hold forth, was diverted in his attention to the Sweet words of that Inspired Saint, by some Ladies, who sat in a pew Just before him, with the whiteness and beautiful Length of whose Necks . . . he was so miraculously Charmed, that, Intirely forgetting where he was, he fell directly to Composing of verses on this delightful Subject, and hammered out a very pritty epigram of eight lines, the Stile and turn of which was so peculiar, that it is yet unequalled by any bard that has since appeared, and is really an original, having never been paralelled in former ages, by any of the Bards of Antiquity.

Immediatly, upon the appearance of this amorous epigram, . . . the critics were in an uproar against it, they took this poor Bards performance all to pieces, as is the custom with Critics in these our degenerate days, and discried more blunders and Inaccuracies in it than there were words, Some of the Longstanding members of the Ancient and honorable Tuesday Club were among these Critics, particularly Messieurs Blunt, Sly, Quaint and Scribble, who exercised the acuteness of wit and Genius pritty Smartly upon this unfortunate Bard, and were Joined by others, . . . from Criticising in prose, they went to Satyrizing and Lampooning in Rhime, So the Baltimore Bards & the Critics of the Tuesday Club strenuously contended who should outrhime, and who should outcriticise each other, . . . and some who thought them wiser than themselves admired much their wit, while others who had no opinion of their wisdom laughed at their folly and assurance, and condemned them much, as Idle and mischievous, in trowbling people that thought no harm with such poetical Jargon. . . .

It came at last to that pitch, that even the weekly Journal of Mr Jonathan Grog, entituled the *Maryland Gazette*, was stuffed with comments, Reflections and Satyrs on this unfortunate Bard and his performances, so, that it is thought he must Infallibly have sunk under the pressure, of this formidable hostile power of Critics, had not an Invulnerable Champion, stood up in his defence, vizt: the tremendous Bard Bavius, who was reckoned by many the compleatest bard of the two, and Indeed, the most extraordinary bard, that was to be found, far or near, and not to be daunted, or put out of countenance, by the conjoint forces of all the Critics put together.

This Illustrious Bard, was of a stern, Severe countenance, whose Severity and Sterness, was of great use to the other, naturally mild,

modest and timorous, since he was much asisted thereby, in bearing the violence and fury of the Attacks made upon him, by his
professd foes, the Critics and Bards of the Tuesday Club.

This Gygantic auxiliary Bard, mustering up all his force and
straining the Sublime of his genius to the utmost, advised the
other, to show the dignity of his muse, by outsoaring all those pitiful bards and Critics, that set up against him, and, that he should
have his assistance, in whatever Subject he undertook, it was then
resolved, by these two eminent Baltimore Bards, over a bowl of
punch and a pipe of tobacco, to pen a Sublime panegyric on the
celebrated toasts and beauties of their county, under the title of *The
Baltimore Belles.* This piece was then Immediatly set about, and
the Muses Invoked, and being finished by these rapid Geniuses in a
few hours, was carefully revised, corrected, and wrote out fair. It was
read by Bard Bavius, in a Sonorous and theatrical tone of voice,
much approved of by both bards, and after a Second third and
fourth reading, was left lying on the table for further perusal and
consideration, or, rather to be exposed to the eye of the public,
that it might meet with the applause it so Justly deserved; being
such a specimen of the Sublime, as exceeded the execution of all
Bards whatsoever, either ancient or modern, since the days of Pindar.

The news of this soon reached the Clubical Bards and Critics
at Annapolis, together with a copy of the composition it Self, who
set about it, tooth and nail, and gave it no quarter. One, under
the name of Doctor Philalethes, published in the *Gazette* No 34
an Infallible receipt to cure the Epidemical and afflicting distem-
pers of Love and the poetical Itch. Soon after, another Learned
Physician, who stiles himself Doctor Polypharmacus, in *Gazette* No
41 publishes another recipe, and seems to be diffident of the
efficacy of the former, according to the humor of great Physicians,
who commonly prefer their own Nostrums, to those of all the
faculty besides, this Learned Gentleman, describes Bard Bavius,
under a violent delirium or *furor poeticus,* excited by a *febris Ama-
toria,* . . . on the Doctor's first feeling his pulse, he exclaims thus.

A well turn'd praise requires the nicest Skill,
And he who writes ill natur'd must write ill.

And again, upon being asked how he did, he bawls out

Then let the Muse her tuneful numbers raise
And praise the beauties for the Sake of praise.

Upon this the Doctor applies cupping Glasses, as he says, to his
head, and gives him a large dose of hellebore, which procures a
copious and fætid Stool, after which the Bard exclaims

Maria sings, now bid the Muses hear
Or Call Apollo from the Crystal Sphere.

Polypharmacus on this, suspects a calenture, plies him with cooling Glysters to Relieve the encephalon, and Claps Sinapisms to
his feet, and soon after, he breaks out thus.

See, Lovely Risteau! happy, hapless Maid!—
Happy the man whom this fair Maiden loves,
O happiest he, whom this fair maid approves,
Great is her worth, yet useless and unknown,
Or useful to her charming Self alone.

This last, the Physician observes, is a most remarkable Instance of
the Bathos, and by this, he percieved that the Violence of the
Distemper abated, and gives him his famous remedy, which he
calls his *Neutrum quid.* . . .

Soon after this Bard Bavius wrote his celebrated Letter to the
City of Annapolis, which he Intends as a kind of prose Dunciad,
Introducing all his critics and opponent Bards in some Ridiculous
Character or other, here he learnedly criticises on the term *Neutrum Quid*, and, assuming the Character of a Physician himself, he
proposes a Remedy, or *Methodus Medendi*, so very much out of the
common road, that never any thing like it was seen either before
or since, nor, I believe, ever will be, in this transient world, the
piece it self being Inimitable, and extraneously extravagant, in
short, to cure those frantic poets, as he calls them, Mr Jonathan
Grog . . . was to put them into his press or typographical machine,
and, an operator with a Spatula was to extract excrementitious
matter from their fundament, while Parson Sly was to sing a
Psalm, to Comfort them under the operation; in this prophylactic
dissertation our Bard displays his profound skill and knowledge
in Chemistry, by absolutely pronouncing Doctor Polypharmacus

a dunce, for using the term *Neutrum quid*, which he says is in it
Self Stark nonsense, as Intending something that is only chip in
porridge, or neither Chalk nor Cheese, then he slides into a
Learned Enquiry into the nature of Ordure and excrement, to
which he elegantly compars the works and compositions of his
Antagonist Bards.

This Learned Epistle made some noise for a time among the
wits and critics, particularly of Annapolis, and produced several
learned criticisms, dissertations and essays; and certain critical and
Explanatory Notes were wrote upon it in the names of Martinus
Scriblerus & Hurlothrumbo, the first in a grave, the other in a
Burlesque Stile. . . .

Bard Bavius, the only person now aimed at (since his associate
Mevius, had altogether retired and absconded,) was also attacked
by another wit, who appeared in the *Maryland Gazette* No 47, under the Character of an advertiser; This wit assumes to himself,
the name of Jehoiakim Jerkum, and is thought to have been per-
sonated, by one or more of the Longstanding members, of the
ancient and honorable Tuesday Club, takeing upon them the
Character of a Master advertising his run away Servant; Bard Bavius is mentioned in this advertisement, under the names of Bard
& Bavius, he is described as a fellow disordered in his Senses,
wearing a String of Bells about his neck, carrying with him several
Stollen materials from the works of Pope & Prior, together with
abundance of Trash of his own. A nasty Fellow, whose discourse
turns chiefly on excrementitious Subjects, of uncertain parentage,
and therefore, in himself an original, praising for the Sake of
praise, and Censuring for the Sake of censure, apt to bewray himself in company, thro' a relaxation of the *Sphincter ani*, and then
lay the blame on others, an Enimy to the Presbyterians, tho' himself a Muggletonian, the profit of his poems for one hundred
years to come, is offered to those who go on the *Chace* after him,
and apprehend him, as it appears to be a difficult thing so to do,
besides what the Law allows in such cases.

This Burlesque advertisement, utterly silenced Bard Bavius, and
consequently, the other Baltimore Bard, whose Champion he was,
and effectually cured that pestiferous *furor poeticus*, which had for
some time raged in Baltimore, and set many people a quarrelling,
and as many a Laughing, and, the members of the ancient and

honorable Tuesday Club, that were concerned in this conflict and victory, valued themselves much upon it, as having largely Contributed to the peace and quiet of the public, nothing being more destructive to the good order of Society and private families, than the Scribble of the *Poætæ Minorum Gentium*, whether Panegyrical or Satyrical, handed about either in Manuscript, or from the press.

BOOK V

From the first grand Anniversary procession,
to the foundation of the Eastren Shore Triumvirate.

CHAPTER 1

A Chapter of Triffles, and concerning Clubbical Critics
and Anticlubarians.

Were it not for triffles, says a certain philosopher, (which I know only by hearsay) the world would be but very scurvily entertained, and life would hang on us like a heavy Clog, . . . whoever doubts of this doctrine, let him read the works of Solomon, that Royal preacher, whom I look upon to be a philosopher of no mean degree, that knew well the nature of triffles and vanities, among which he Classes all Sublunary enjoyments, after having himself had a taste of all.

Triffles and vanities are but Synonomous terms, and therefore, all that passes in this transitory life, this petty scantling of time, which we have allotted us to peregrinate thro' this absurd worldly wilderness, and to rant our Comical, or (as some are pleased to call it) tragical parts out upon this terrestrial Stage, is but of a triffling nature, why should any saucy, pert, demure, pricise, finical coxcomb of a Clubical Critic, to say no worse of him, nay, any Chuckleheaded, unexperienced, raw, Saucy Jackanapes pretend to say, that this our famous History, is more triffling than any other history, or this our ancient and honorable Club more triffling in its constitution, government, model, form and Conversation, than any other Society whatsoever, great or small, be it Empire kingdom, Commonwealth corporation or Club.

But, to particularize alittle, what did Cæsar Conquer for? a Triffle; . . . what was the Grandure of the Roman Empire? a triffle a vapor, an evanescent Smoke; . . . what is the learning and wisdom of philosophers? a triffle; what is the Splendor, equipage and pomp of great princes? a triffle; what are Crowns, triple Crowns, Coronets, mitres, . . . truncheons, Stars and Garters? all transitory, vain, perishing triffles, bawbles, toys, in which the great babies of this world delight; What is a great man, attended by his Levee of pimps, liars, flatterers, Sycophants, parasites and hungry dependants? a damnd Superlative, unequalled unparalelled triffle, a paragon of triffles, the Sum Substance, essence and cause efficient of all the other evanescent triffles about him, since he contains them all, and they him, since they think by him, act by him, live by him, move by him, breath by him, and by him they have their being, not as rational men, which god made them, before they mangled god's work—but as fools, prigs and Coxcombs, which their foolish patron molded them into. . . . What are all human Enquiries, learned discourses, Dissertations, explications, comments, paraphrases and Annotations? Triffles! Triffles! the mockery of Learning, and the very Image of Ignorance. What are all the Charms of the fair Sex, all their allurements, all their Smiles, all their blandishments, all the pleasures in the lump, which they are able to afford? perfect, paultry perishing, good for nothing triffles. To sum up all, what is this Globe and all its Contents, compared to the General System of nature? an atom, a triffle, a thing of nothing; what the General System of Nature compared to endless space? a Spec, a triffle, a grain of dust; and what are all these to the Supreme Essence? more than a triffle, and less than nothing if possible.

Say then, ye wise men of Gotham, ye round heads of this world, with what face of Impudence can you assert, that this here History of ours, is a triffling History and this here Club a triffling Club, comparatively speaking, since there is not an ace difference between what you call Serious, Solid and rational, and all the triffles that you can ransac and cull out, in this our history, . . . which In fact are not more arrant triffles, than these other triffles that are to be met with in the histories of great Empires kingdoms, commonwealths, and in the Memoirs of the Characters and lives of mighty Emperors, kings, Generals and Commanders of armies.

Will you have the Impudence to say, that Julius Cæsar was a greater man than Nasifer Jole Esqr, because the first was Emperor over great territories, and the latter only President of a little paltry Club; Surely no, consider the Inscription, which Cyrus the great ordered to be put upon his tomb, and you'll find no difference between great Emperors and presidents of Clubs, The Inscription runs thus, *"O Man, whosoever thou art, and from whence soever thou comest, for I know thou wilt come, I am Cyrus, the founder of the great persian Empire, do not envy me this little portion of earth that covers my body,"* and pray does not an emperor take as small a portion of the Earth to lye in, as a president of a Club. . . . Again, will you pretend to assert with a grave composed countenance, . . . that the Roman, or the Russian, or the Turkish or the Persian or the Chinese Empires, are greater than this here Club, because they are Empires, & this here Club only a Club? Surely no,—and why pray? Why thus,—Is there any difference but in Size or Magnitude? are not the parts of a mite, as perfect as those of an Elephant, tho smaller? has not a mite its Sinews, nerves, arteries, veins, . . . Stomach, Intestines, genitals, legs, feet, toes, hair, Skin &ct: as well as an Elephant, and wherein do they differ but in magnitude of body? Has not the Tuesday club, it's president, State officers, officers of the Commons, Longstanding members, honorary members, and an Empire or kingdom, it's Emperor or king, prime ministers, rulers, nobles, commons &ct: and wherein I pray do they differ but in bulk.

But take me along with you, ye conceited Sophisters, ye paultry reasoners of this world, Pray does not an Emperor eat, drink and sleep as much as a president; does he not stink at times as hideously as a president? does he not prevaricate, swear, cheat and lie as grossly as a president? does he not tyrannize, oppress, fornicate, whore, kill and massacre as much, nay more than any president? . . . may he not be poxed as well as a president? may he not have the plague, the hyppo, the palsey, . . . the Ripples, the whiffles, nay the Itch as well as a president? Nay, may he not play the fool as much as a president? what then is the difference between an Emperor and a president, and in what does it consist, a triffle, believe me, a very triffle, and not worth Contending for.

I question not, but I shall be asked, why I should fall into this odd Rhapsody, this rant, which they'll say looks as if it had been hatched in Bedlam? but let me tell you my grave, Serious friends, (whom I shall take the liberty to call by no worse name than Anticlubarians,) that your ridiculous, Silly, and Idle remarks, uttered with a grave tho unmeaning face, and an Empty head, against the Lawful recreations of Innocent mirth, and Inoffensive drollery, has been the occasion of all this rant, so, if I have Committed any mortal Sin, at your doors I lay it, ye Impertinent, precise, Stiff, Starch'd up, Cynical Logerheads.

I know you'll say, ye good for nothing wiseacres, ye mock critics, and bungling molders of modes and manners, that such Clubical pastime is beneath the dignity of rational creatures, and wise men; but tell me, ye pragmatical dunces, . . . are you never Employed about amusements less becoming a rational nature, than these droll, facetious, gelastic and harmless Clubical recreations? do you never whore? do you never game? do you never swear? do you never lie? do you never flatter? do you never Idle your time away in insipid flat, childish and unprofitable Conversation? among fops like yourselves? . . . Wise men indeed! pray who made you wise men? on what ground do you claim that title to yourselves? is it on account of your knowledge? is it on account of your Learning? your knowledge is nothing, when compared to your vanity and Self conceit, and your Learning is Collected from broken Scraps of plays, Romances, Lewd authors, title pages and hearsay, do you pretend to know more than Socrates, who, tho' the wisest of the Athenians,—of the greeks, and consequently of the whole world in his time, yet declared that *he knew nothing.* . . . But if you persist still, and say these Low clubical humors are Inconsistent with philosophy, pray what do you take Philosophy to be? . . . I tell you ye dunces, that there is nothing more gay, more frolicksome and (if I may so speak) more Jocose than Philosophy.

But I shall leave you here, ye Incorrigible Anticlubarians, . . . ye Eternal trifflers, I shall bid you an eternal Adieu in this very place, and henceforth take no more notice of you than if you were not in being, or never had been hatched, which, had things really turned out so, would not have been a farthing's matter, either of profit or Loss to the world. . . .

Let me only conclude with this condolatory exclamation; Oh how I pity you, for your want of the true taste of life; for the want of that blessed humor, which set Democritus a Laughing, and Heraclitus a crying, . . . for, ye dry withered Stocks of human Society, Ye Statues and poppets in human form, you can neither laugh nor Cry in earnest, nature has absolutely denyed you the power of both, and like a parcel of upstart mushrooms, ye come into the world, and like a flitch of Smoked bacon, whose Salt is soaked out, you go out of it, dry, dead, musty, Insipid and Sapless, having never in your lives enjoyed the Sweets and delights of club-ical humors and recreations, without which life is not worth en-joying, but is a *tabula rasa*, or a *Cart Blanch*, or rather a blotted Scroll or Scutcheon, in which nothing of Sense or Significancy can be read or discerned. . . .

Philip Freneau

(1752–1832)

Freneau was a Princeton graduate who studied for the ministry, but when the Revolutionary War began he turned to writing satire directed against the Crown. He fought in the war as well, beginning in 1778 as a member of the New Jersey militia, sailing through the British blockade of the West Indies, and finally being captured by the British in 1780—a captivity that produced on his release a bitter poem, "The British Prison Ship." Freneau was also a newspaper writer who edited the *National Gazette* in Philadelphia from 1791 to 1793, after which he worked alternately as a ship's captain and newspaper columnist until his retirement. He was an enthusiastic propagandist for the American Revolution, and some call him the first American journalist. "The British Prison Ship" is a biting satire, as well as an effective piece of political advocacy.

The British Prison Ship

Written 1780

CANTO I.—THE CAPTURE

Amid these ills no tyrant dared refuse
My right to pen the dictates of the muse,
To paint the terrors of the infernal place,
And fiends from Europe, insolent as base.

Assist me, Clio! while in verse I tell
The dire misfortunes that a ship befell,
Which outward bound, to St. Eustatia's shore,
Death and disaster through the billows bore.
  From Philadelphia's crowded port she came;
For there the builder plann'd her lofty frame,
With wond'rous skill, and excellence of art
He form'd, dispos'd, and order'd every part,
With joy beheld the stately fabric rise
To a stout bulwark of stupendous size,
'Till launch'd at last, capacious of the freight,
He left her to the Pilots, and her fate.
  First from her depths the tapering masts ascend,
On whose firm bulk the transverse yards depend,
By shrouds and stays secur'd from side to side
Trees grew on trees, suspended o'er the tide,
Firm to the yards extended, broad and vast
They hung the sails susceptive of the blast,
Far o'er the prow the lengthy bowsprit lay,
Supporting on the extreme the taught Gib-stay,
Twice ten six pounders at their port holes plac'd
And rang'd in rows, stood hostile in the waist:
Thus all prepar'd, impatient for the seas,
She left her station with an adverse breeze,
This her first outset from her native shore,
To seas a stranger, and untry'd before.
  From the bright radiance that his glories spread
Ere from the east gay Phœbus lifts his head,
From the sweet morn, a kindred name she won,
Aurora call'd, the offspring of the sun,
Whose form projecting, the broad prow displays,
Far glittering o'er the wave, a mimic blaze.
  The gay ship now, in all her pomp and pride,
With sails expanded, flew along the tide;
'Twas thy deep stream, O Delaware, that bore
This pile intended for a southern shore,
Bound to those isles where endless summer reigns,
Fair fruits, gay blossoms, and enamell'd plains;
Where sloping lawns the roving swain invite,

And the cool morn succeeds the breezy night,
Where each glad day a heaven unclouded brings
And sky-topt mountains teem with golden springs.
   From Cape Henlopen, urg'd by favouring gales,
When morn emerg'd, we sea-ward spread our sails,
Then east-south-east explor'd the briny way,
Close to the wind, departing from the bay;
No longer seen the hoarse resounding strand,
With hearts elate we hurried from the land,
Escap'd the dangers of that shelvy ground,
To sailors fatal, and for wrecks renown'd.—
   The gale increases as we stem the main,
Now scarce the hills their sky-blue mist retain,
At last they sink beneath the rolling wave
That seems their summits, as they sink, to lave;
Abaft the beam the freshening breezes play,
No mists advancing to deform the day,
No tempests rising o'er the splendid scene,
A sea unruffled, and a heaven serene.
   Now Sol's bright lamp, the heav'n born source of light,
Had pass'd the line of his meridian height,
And westward hung—retreating from the view
Shores disappear'd, and every hill withdrew,
When, still suspicious of some neighbouring foe,
Aloft the Master bade a Seaman go,
To mark if, from the mast's aspiring height
Through all the round a vessel came in sight.
   Too soon the Seaman's glance, extending wide,
Far distant in the east a ship espy'd,
Her lofty masts stood bending to the gale,
Close to the wind was brac'd each shivering sail;
Next from the deck we saw the approaching foe,
Her spangled bottom seem'd in flames to glow
When to the winds she bow'd in dreadful haste
And her lee-guns lay delug'd in the waste:
From her top-gallant flow'd an English Jack;
With all her might she strove to gain our track,
Nor strove in vain—with pride and power elate,
Wing'd on by hell, she drove us to our fate;

No stop no stay her bloody crew intends,
(So flies a comet with its host of fiends)
Nor oaths, nor prayers arrest her swift career,
Death in her front, and ruin in her rear.
  Struck at the sight, the Master gave command
To change our course, and steer toward the land—
Swift to the task the ready sailors run,
And while the word was utter'd, half was done:
As from the south the fiercer breezes rise
Swift from her foe alarm'd *Aurora* flies,
With every sail extended to the wind
She fled the unequal foe that chac'd behind;
Along her decks dispos'd in close array
Each at its port, the grim artillery lay,
Soon on the foe with brazen throat to roar;
But, small their size, and narrow was their bore;
Yet faithful they their destin'd station keep
To guard the barque that wafts them o'er the deep,
Who now must bend to steer a homeward course
And trust her swiftness rather than her force,
Unfit to combat with a powerful foe;
Her decks too open, and her waist too low.
  While o'er the wave with foaming prow she flies,
Once more emerging, distant landscapes rise;
High in the air the starry streamer plays,
And every sail its various tribute pays:
To gain the land we bore the weighty blast;
And now the wish'd for cape appear'd at last;
But the vext foe, impatient of delay,
Prepar'd for ruin, press'd upon her prey;
Near, and more near, in awful grandeur came
The frigate *Iris*, not unknown to fame;
Iris her name, but *Hancock* once she bore,
Fram'd and completed on New Albion's shore,
By Manly lost, the swiftest of the train
That fly with wings of canvas o'er the main.
  Now, while for combat some with zeal prepare,
Thus to the heavens the Boatswain sent his prayer:
"List, all ye powers that rule the skies and seas!

"Shower down perdition on such thieves as these,
"Fate, strike their hearts with terror and dismay,
"And sprinkle on their powder salt-sea spray!
"May bursting cannon, while his aim he tries,
"Destroy the Gunner, and be-damn his eyes—
"The chief who awes the quarter-deck, may he,
"Tripp'd from his stand, be tumbled in the sea.
"May they who rule the round-top's giddy height
"Be canted headlong to perpetual night;
"May fiends torment them on a leeward coast,
"And help forsake them when they want it most—
"From their wheel'd engines torn be every gun—
"And now, to sum up every curse in one,
"May latent flames, to save us, intervene,
"And hell-ward drive them from their magazine!"—
   The Frigate now had every sail unfurl'd,
And rush'd tremendous o'er the wat'ry world;
Thus fierce Pelides, eager to destroy,
Chac'd the proud Trojan to the gates of Troy—
Swift o'er the waves while hostile they pursue
As swiftly from their fangs *Aurora* flew,
At length Henlopen's cape we gain'd once more,
And vainly strove to force the ship ashore;
Stern fate forbade the barren shore to gain,
Denial sad, and source of future pain!
For then the inspiring breezes ceas'd to blow,
Lost were they all, and smooth the seas below;
By the broad cape becalm'd, our lifeless sails
No longer swell'd their bosoms to the gales;
The ship, unable to pursue her way,
Tumbling about, at her own guidance lay,
No more the helm its wonted influence lends,
No oars assist us, and no breeze befriends;
Meantime the foe, advancing from the sea,
Rang'd her black cannon, pointed on our lee,
Then up she luff'd, and blaz'd her entrails dire,
Bearing destruction, terror, death and fire.
   Vext at our fate, we prim'd a piece, and then
Return'd the shot, to shew them we were men.

Dull night at length her dusky pinions spread,
And every hope to 'scape the foe was fled;
Close to they cape, Henlopen, though we press'd,
We could not gain they desert, dreary breast;
Though ruin'd trees beshroud they barren shore
With mounds of sand half hid, or cover'd o'er,
Though ruffian winds disturb they summit bare,
Yet every hope and every wish was there;
In vain we sought to reach the joyless strand,
Fate stood between, and barr'd us from the land.
   All dead becalm'd, and helpless as we lay,
The ebbing current forc'd us back to sea,
While vengeful *Iris*, thirsting for our blood,
Flash'd her red lightnings o'er the trembling flood,
At every flash a storm of ruin came
'Till our shock'd vessel shook through all her frame—
Mad for revenge, our breasts with fury glow
To wreak returns of vengeance on the foe;
Full at his hull our pointed guns we rais'd,
His hull resounded as the cannon blaz'd;
Through his main top-sail one a passage tore,
His sides re-echo'd to the dreadful roar,
Alternate fires dispell'd the shades of night—
But how unequal was this daring fight!
Our stoutest guns threw but a six-pound ball,
Twelve pounders from the foe our sides did maul,
And, while no power to save him intervenes,
A bullet struck our captain of Marines;
Fierce, though he bid defiance to the foe
He felt his death and ruin in the blow,
Headlong he fell, distracted with the wound,
The deck distain'd, and heart blood streaming round.
Another blast, as fatal in its aim,
Wing'd by destruction, through our rigging came,
And, whistling tunes from hell upon its way,
Shrouds, stays, and braces tore at once away,
Sails, blocks, and oars in scatter'd fragments fly—
Their softest language was—*submit, or die!*
   Repeated cries throughout the ship resound;

Now every bullet brought a different wound;
'Twixt wind and water, one assail'd the side,
Through this aperture rush'd the briny tide—
'Twas then the Master trembled for his crew,
And bade thy shores, O Delaware, adieu!—
And must we yield to yon' destructive ball,
And must our colours to these ruffians fall!—
They fall!—his thunders forc'd our pride to bend,
The lofty topsails with their yards descend,
And the proud foe, such leagues of ocean pass'd,
His wish completed in our woe at last.
    Convey'd to York, we found, at length, too late,
That Death was better than the prisoner's fate;
There doom'd to famine, shackles and despair,
Condemn'd to breathe a foul, infected air
In sickly hulks, devoted while we lay,
Successive funerals gloom'd each dismal day—
But what on captives British rage can do,
Another Canto, friend, shall let you know.

Canto II.—The Prison Ship

The various horrors of these hulks to tell,
These Prison Ships where pain and horror dwell,
Where death in tenfold vengeance holds his reign,
And injur'd ghosts, yet unaveng'd, complain;
This be my task—ungenerous Britons, you
Conspire to murder those you can't subdue.—
    Weak as I am, I'll try my strength to-day
And my best arrows at these hell-hounds play,
To future years one scene of death prolong,
And hang them up to infamy, in song.
    That Britain's rage should dye our plains with gore,
And desolation spread through every shore,
None e'er could doubt, that her ambition knew,
This was to rage and disappointment due;
But that those monsters whom our soil maintain'd,
Who first drew breath in this devoted land,

Like famish'd wolves, should on their country prey,
Assist its foes, and wrest our lives away,
This shocks belief—and bids our soil disown
Such friends, subservient to a bankrupt crown,
By them the widow mourns her partner dead,
Her mangled sons to darksome prisons led,
By them—and hence my keenest sorrows rise,
My friend, my guardian, my Orestes dies;
Still for that loss must wretched I complain,
And sad Ophelia mourn her favourite swain.

   Ah! come the day when from this bloody shore
Fate shall remove them to return no more—
To scorch'd Bahama shall the traitors go
With grief and rage, and unremitting woe,
On burning sands to walk their painful round,
And sigh through all the solitary ground,
Where no gay flower their haggard eyes shall see,
And find no shade but from the cypress tree.

   So much we suffer'd from the tribe I hate,
So near they shov'd me to the brink of fate,
When two long months in these dark hulks we lay,
Barr'd down by night, and fainting all the day
In the fierce fervours of the solar beam,
Cool'd by no breeze on Hudson's mountain-stream;
That not unsung these threescore days shall fall
To black oblivion that would cover all!—

   No masts or sails these crowded ships adorn,
Dismal to view, neglected and forlorn!
Here, mighty ills oppress the imprison'd throng,
Dull were our slumbers, and our nights too long—
From morn to eve along the decks we lay
Scorch'd into fevers by the solar ray;
No friendly awning cast a welcome shade,
Once was it promis'd, and was never made;
No favours could these sons of death bestow,
'Twas endless cursing, and continual woe:
Immortal hatred doth their breasts engage,
And this lost empire swells their souls with rage.

   Two hulks on Hudson's stormy bosom lie,

Two, farther south, affront the pitying eye—
There, the black *Scorpion* at her mooring rides,
There, *Strombolo* swings, yielding to the tides;
Here, bulky *Jersey* fills a larger space,
And *Hunter*, to all hospitals disgrace—
Thou, *Scorpion*, fatal to thy crowded throng,
Dire theme of horror and Plutonian song,
Requir'st my lay—thy sultry decks I know,
And all the torments that exist below!
The briny wave that Hudson's bosom fills
Drain'd through her bottom in a thousand rills,
Rotten and old, replete with sighs and groans,
Scarce on the waters she sustain'd her bones;
Here, doom'd to toil, or founder in the tide,
At the moist pumps incessantly we ply'd,
Here, doom'd to starve, like famish'd dogs we tore
The scant allowance, that our tyrants bore.
   Remembrance shudders at this scene of fears—
Still in my view some English brute appears,
Some base-born Hessian slave walks threat'ning by,
Some servile Scot with murder in his eye
Still haunts my sight, as vainly they bemoan
Rebellions manag'd so unlike their own!
O may I never feel the poignant pain
To live subjected to such fiends again,
Stewards and Mates that hostile Britain bore,
Cut from the gallows on their native shore;
Their ghastly looks and vengeance-beaming eyes
Still to my view in dismal colours rise—
O may I ne'er review these dire abodes,
These piles for slaughter, floating on the floods,—
And you, that o'er the troubled ocean go,
Strike not your standards to this miscreant foe,
Better the greedy wave should swallow all,
Better to meet the death-conducted ball,
Better to sleep on ocean's deepest bed,
At once destroy'd and number'd with the dead,
Than thus to perish in the face of day
Where twice ten thousand deaths one death delay.

When to the ocean dives the western sun,
And the scorch'd Tories fire their evening gun,
"Down, rebels, down!" the angry Scotchmen cry,
"Damn'd dogs, descend, or by our broad swords die!"
  Hail, dark abode! what can with thee compare—
Heat, sickness, famine, death, and stagnant air—
Pandora's box, from whence all mischief flew,
Here real found, torments mankind anew!—
Swift from the guarded decks we rush'd along,
And vainly sought repose, so vast our throng:
Three hundred wretches here, denied all light,
In crowded mansions pass the infernal night,
Some for a bed their tatter'd vestments join,
And some on chests, and some on floors recline;
Shut from the blessings of the evening air,
Pensive we lay with mingled corpses there,
Meagre and wan, and scorch'd with heat below,
We loom'd like ghosts, ere death had made us so—
How could we else, where heat and hunger join'd
Thus to debase the body and the mind,
Where cruel thirst the parching throat invades,
Dries up the man, and fits him for the shades.
  No waters laded from the bubbling spring
To these dire ships the British monsters bring—
By planks and ponderous beams completely wall'd
In vain for water, and in vain, I call'd—
No drop was granted to the midnight prayer,
To Dives in these regions of despair!—
The loathsome cask a deadly dose contains,
Its poison circling through the languid veins;
"Here, generous Britain, generous, as you say,
"To my parch'd tongue one cooling drop convey,
"Hell has no mischief like a thirsty throat,
"Nor one tormentor like your David Sproat."
  Dull flew the hours, till, from the East display'd,
Sweet morn dispells the horrors of the shade;
On every side dire objects meet the sight,
And pallid forms, and murders of the night,
The dead were past their pain, the living groan,

Nor dare to hope another morn their own;
But what to them is morn's delightful ray,
Sad and distressful as the close of day,
O'er distant streams appears the dewy green,
And leafy trees on mountain tops are seen,
But they no groves nor grassy mountains tread,
Mark'd for a longer journey to the dead.
  Black as the clouds that shade St. Kilda's shore,
Wild as the winds that round her mountains roar,
At every post some surly vagrant stands,
Pick'd from the British or the Irish bands,
Some slave from Hesse, some hangman's son at least
Sold and transported, like his brother beast—
Some miscreant Tory, puff'd with upstart pride,
Led on by hell to take the royal side;
Dispensing death triumphantly they stand,
Their musquets ready to obey command;
Wounds are their sport, as ruin is their aim;
On their dark souls compassion has no claim,
And discord only can their spirits please:
Such were our tyrants here, and such were these.
  Ingratitude! no curse like thee is found
Throughout this jarring world's extended round,
Their hearts with malice to our country swell
Because in former days we us'd them well!—
This pierces deep, too deeply wounds the breast;
We help'd them naked, friendless, and distrest,
Receiv'd their vagrants with an open hand,
Bestow'd them buildings, privilege, and land—
Behold the change!—when angry Britain rose,
These thankless tribes became our fiercest foes,
By them devoted, plunder'd, and accurst,
Stung by the serpents whom ourselves had nurs'd.
  But such a train of endless woes abound,
So many mischiefs in these hulks are found,
That on them all a poem to prolong
Would swell too high the horrors of my song—
Hunger and thirst to work our woe combine,
And mouldy bread, and flesh of rotten swine,

The mangled carcase, and the batter'd brain,
The doctor's poison, and the captain's cane,
The soldier's musquet, and the steward's debt,
The evening shackle, and the noon-day threat.
    That juice destructive to the pangs of care
Which Rome of old, nor Athens could prepare,
Which gains the day for many a modern chief
When cool reflection yields a faint relief,
That charm, whose virtue warms the world beside,
Was by these tyrants to our use denied,
While yet they deign'd that healthy juice to lade
The putrid water felt its powerful aid;
But when refus'd—to aggravate our pains—
Then fevers rag'd and revel'd through our veins;
Throughout my frame I felt its deadly heat,
I felt my pulse with quicker motions beat:
A pallid hue o'er every face was spread,
Unusual pains attack'd the fainting head,
No physic here, no doctor to assist,
My name was enter'd on the sick man's list;
Twelve wretches more the same dark symptoms took,
And these were enter'd on the doctor's book;
The loathsome *Hunter* was our destin'd place,
The *Hunter*, to all hospitals disgrace;
With soldiers sent to guard us on our road,
Joyful we left the *Scorpion's* dire abode;
Some tears we shed for the remaining crew,
Then curs'd the hulk, and from her sides withdrew.

CANTO III.—THE HOSPITAL PRISON SHIP

    Now tow'rd the *Hunter's* gloomy sides we came,
A slaughter-house, yet hospital in name;
For none came there (to pass through all degrees)
'Till half consum'd, and dying with disease;—
But when too near with labouring oars we ply'd,
The Mate with curses drove us from the side;
That wretch who, banish'd from the navy crew,

Grown old in blood, did here his trade renew;
His serpent's tongue, when on his charge let loose,
Utter'd reproaches, scandal, and abuse,
Gave all to hell who dar'd his king disown,
And swore mankind were made for George alone:
Ten thousand times, to irritate our woe,
He wish'd us founder'd in the gulph below;
Ten thousand times he brandish'd high his stick,
And swore as often that we were not sick—
And yet so pale!—that we were thought by some
A freight of ghosts from Death's dominions come—
But calm'd at length—for who can always rage,
Or the fierce war of endless passion wage,
He pointed to the stairs that led below
To damps, disease, and varied shapes of woe—
Down to the gloom I took my pensive way,
Along the decks the dying captives lay;
Some struck with madness, some with scurvy pain'd,
But still of putrid fevers most complain'd!
On the hard floors these wasted objects laid,
There toss'd and tumbled in the dismal shade,
There no soft voice their bitter fate bemoan'd,
And Death strode stately, while the victims groan'd;
Of leaky decks I heard them long complain,
Drown'd as they were in deluges of rain,
Deny'd the comforts of a dying bed,
And not a pillow to support the head—
How could they else but pine, and grieve, and sigh,
Detest a wretched life—and wish to die?
  Scarce had I mingled with this dismal band
When a thin spectre seiz'd me by the hand—
"And art thou come, (death heavy on his eyes)
"And art thou come to these abodes," he cries;
"Why didst thou leave the *Scorpion*'s dark retreat,
"And hither haste a surer death to meet?
"Why didst thou leave thy damp infected cell?
"If that was purgatory, this is hell—
"We, too, grown weary of that horrid shade,
"Petitioned early for the doctor's aid;

"His aid denied, more deadly symptoms came,
"Weak, and yet weaker, glow'd the vital flame;
"And when disease had worn us down so low
"That few could tell if we were ghosts or no,
"And all asserted, death would be our fate—
"Then to the doctor we were sent—too late.
"Here wastes away Autolycus the brave,
"Here young Orestes finds a wat'ry grave,
"Here gay Alcander, gay, alas! no more,
"Dies far sequester'd from his native shore;
"He late, perhaps, too eager for the fray,
"Chac'd the vile Briton o'er the wat'ry way
" 'Till fortune jealous, bade her clouds appear,
"Turn'd hostile to his fame, and brought him here.
    "Thus do our warriors, thus our heroes fall,
"Imprison'd here, base ruin meets them all,
"Or, sent afar to Britain's barbarous shore,
"There die neglected, and return no more:
"Ah! rest in peace, poor, injur'd, parted shade,
"By cruel hands in death's dark weeds array'd,
"But happier climes, where suns unclouded shine,
"Light undisturb'd, and endless peace are thine."—
    From Brookland groves a Hessian doctor came,
Not great his skill, nor greater much his fame;
Fair Science never call'd the wretch her son,
And Art disdain'd the stupid man to own;—
Can you admire that Science was so coy,
Or Art refus'd his genius to employ!—
Do men with brutes an equal dullness share,
Or cuts yon' grovelling mole the midway air?
In polar worlds can Eden's blossoms blow?
Do trees of God in barren desarts grow?
Are loaded vines to Etna's summit known,
Or swells the peach beneath the torrid zone?—
Yet still he doom'd his genius to the rack,
And, as you may suppose, was own'd a quack.
    He on his charge the healing work begun
With antimonial mixtures, by the tun,
Ten minutes was the time he deign'd to stay,

The time of grace allotted once a day—
He drencht us well with bitter draughts, 'tis true,
Nostrums from hell, and cortex from Peru—
Some with his pills he sent to Pluto's reign,
And some he blister'd with his flies of Spain;
His cream of Tartar walk'd its deadly round,
Till the lean patient at the potion frown'd,
And swore that hemlock, death, or what you will,
Were nonsense to the drugs that stuff'd his bill.—
On those refusing he bestow'd a kick,
Or menac'd vengeance with his walking stick;
Here uncontroul'd he exercis'd his trade,
And grew experienced by the deaths he made;
By frequent blows we from his cane endur'd
He kill'd at least as many as he cur'd;
On our lost comrades built his future fame,
And scatter'd fate, where'er his footsteps came.

   Some did not seem obedient to his will,
And swore he mingled poison with his pill,
But I acquit him by a fair confession,
He was no Englishman—he was a Hessian—
Although a dunce, he had some sense of sin,
Or else the Lord knows where we now had been;
Perhaps in that far country sent to range
Where never prisoner meets with an exchange—
Then had we all been banish'd out of time
Nor I return'd to plague the world with rhyme.

   Fool though he was, yet candour must confess
Not chief Physician was this dog of Hesse—
One master o'er the murdering tribe was plac'd,
By him the rest were honour'd or disgrac'd;—
Once, and but once, by some strange fortune led
He came to see the dying and the dead—
He came—but anger so deform'd his eye,
And such a faulchion glitter'd on his thigh,
And such a gloom his visage darken'd o'er,
And two such pistols in his hands he bore!
That, by the gods!—with such a load of steel
He came, we thought, to murder, not to heal—

Hell in his heart, and mischief in his head,
He gloom'd destruction, and had smote us dead,
Had he so dar'd—but fate with-held his hand—
He came—blasphem'd—and turn'd again to land.
    From this poor vessel, and her sickly crew
An English ruffian all his titles drew,
Captain, esquire, commander, too, in chief,
And hence he gain'd his bread, and hence his beef,
But, sir, you might have search'd creation round
Ere such another miscreant could be found—
Though unprovok'd, an angry face he bore,
We stood astonish'd at the oaths he swore;
He swore, till every prisoner stood aghast,
And thought him Satan in a brimstone blast;
He wish'd us banish'd from the public light,
He wish'd us shrouded in perpetual night!
That were he king, no mercy would he show,
But drive all rebels to the world below;
That if we scoundrels did not scrub the decks
His staff should break our damn'd rebellious necks;
He swore, besides, that if the ship took fire
We too should in the pitchy flame expire;
And meant it so—this tyrant, I engage,
Had lost his breath to gratify his rage.—
    If where he walk'd a captive carcase lay,
Still dreadful was the language of the day—
He call'd us dogs, and would have us'd us so,
But vengeance check'd the meditated blow,
The vengeance from our injur'd nation due
To him, and all the base, unmanly crew.
    Such food they sent, to make complete our woes,
It look'd like carrion torn from hungry crows,
Such vermin vile on every joint were seen,
So black, corrupted, mortified, and lean
That once we try'd to move our flinty chief,
And thus address'd him, holding up the beef:
    "See, captain, see! what rotten bones we pick,
"What kills the healthy cannot cure the sick:
"Not dogs on such by Christian men are fed,

"And see, good master, see, what lousy bread!"
  "Your meat or bread (this man of flint replied)
"Is not my care to manage or provide—
"But this, damn'd rebel dogs, I'd have you know,
"That better than you merit we bestow;
"Out of my sight!"——nor more he deign'd to say,
But whisk'd about, and frowning, strode away.
  Each day, at least three carcases we bore,
And scratch'd them graves along the sandy shore;
By feeble hands the shallow graves were made,
No stone memorial o'er the corpses laid;
In barren sands, and far from home, they lie,
No friend to shed a tear, when passing by;
O'er the mean tombs insulting Britons tread,
Spurn at the sand, and curse the rebel dead.
  When to your arms these fatal islands fall,
(For first or last they must be conquer'd all)
Americans! to rites sepulchral just,
With gentlest footstep press this kindred dust,
And o'er the tombs, if tombs can then be found,
Place the green turf, and plant the myrtle round.
  Americans! a just resentment shew,
And glut revenge on this detested foe;
While the warm blood exults the glowing vein
Still shall resentment in your bosoms reign,
Can you forget the greedy Briton's ire,
Your fields in ruin, and your domes on fire,
No age, no sex from lust and murder free,
And, black as night, the hell born refugee!
Must York forever your best blood entomb,
And these gorg'd monsters triumph in their doom,
Who leave no art of cruelty untry'd;
Such heavy vengeance, and such hellish pride!
Death has no charms—his realms dejected lie
In the dull climate of a clouded sky:
Death has no charms, except in British eyes,
See, arm'd for death, the infernal miscreants rise;
See how they pant to stain the world with gore,
And millions murder'd, still would murder more;

This selfish race, from all the world disjoin'd,
Perpetual discord spread throughout mankind,
Aim to extend their empire o'er the ball,
Subject, destroy, absorb, and conquer all,
As if the power that form'd us did condemn
All other nations to be slaves to them—
Rouse from your sleep, and crush the thievish band,
Defeat, destroy, and sweep them from the land,
Ally'd like you, what madness to despair,
Attack the ruffians while they linger there;
There Tryon sits, a monster all complete,
See Clinton there with vile Knyphausen meet,
And every wretch whom honour should detest
There finds a home—and Arnold with the rest.
Ah! traitors, lost to every sense of shame,
Unjust supporters of a tyrant's claim;
Foes to the rights of freedom and of men,
Flush'd with the blood of thousands you have slain,
To the just doom the righteous skies decree
We leave you, toiling still in cruelty,
Or on dark plains in future herds to meet,
Plans form'd in hell, and projects half complete:
The years approach that shall to ruin bring
Your lords, your chiefs, your miscreant of a king,
Whose murderous acts shall stamp his name accurs'd,
And his last triumphs more than damn the first.

Hugh Brackenridge

(1748–1816)

Brackenridge grew up a poor farmer's son in Pennsylvania, but a local minister taught him Latin and Greek, and he studied theology at Princeton University (then called the College of New Jersey), receiving a B.A. in 1771 and a master's degree in 1774. He immediately saw service in the Revolutionary War as a chaplain, and began a career in writing with two patriotic plays that were produced on an amateur level. He also contributed sermons to the American cause, and edited a patriotic periodical called *United States Magazine*. By 1781 he had given up theology, and set up practice as a lawyer in Pittsburgh, where he also helped found the *Pittsburgh Gazette* and pursued a career in politics. In 1799 he was appointed to the Supreme Court of Pennsylvania, where he served until he died.

Modern Chivalry, his satirical novel, was published between 1792 and 1815. It is immense—probably five times the length of an ordinary novel—and immensely satirical on the subject of bad government. Mirroring *Don Quixote* in form, *Modern Chivalry* is a picaresque adventure of a trip through Pennsylvania by Captain Farrago, a "peripatetic philosopher," and his man Teague Oregan, a dishonest, blundering oaf, always getting himself into some sort of trouble from which his master is forced to extricate him. Although Brackenridge satirizes democracy in this book—especially the crude form that flourished in the early republic—his real targets are dishonesty and corruption, especially corruption in high places, and not democracy itself as a political ideology.

Modern Chivalry

INTRODUCTION

It has been a question for some time past, what would be the best means to fix the English language. Some have thought of Dictionaries, others of Institutes, for that purpose. Swift, I think it was, who proposed, in his letters to the Earl of Oxford, the forming an academy of learned men, in order by their observations and rules, to settle the true spelling, accentuation, and pronunciation, as well as the proper words, and the purest, most simple, and perfect phraseology of language. It has always appeared to me, that if some great master of stile should arise, and without regarding sentiment, or subject, give an example of good language in his composition, which might serve as a model to future speakers and writers, it would do more to fix the orthography, choice of words, idiom of phrase, and structure of sentence, than all the Dictionaries and Institutes that have been ever made. For certainly, it is much more conducive to this end, to place before the eyes what is good writing, than to suggest it to the ear, which may forget in a short time all that has been said.

It is for this reason, that I have undertaken this work; and that it may attain the end the more perfectly, I shall consider language only, not in the least regarding the matter of the work; but as musicians, when they are about to give the most excellent melody, pay no attention to the words that are set to music; but take the most unmeaning phrases, such as sol, fa, la; so here, culing out the choicest flowers of diction, I shall pay no regard to the idea; for it is not in the power of human ingenuity to attain two things perfectly at once. Thus we see that they mistake greatly, who think to have a clock that can at once tell the hour of the day, the age of the moon, and the day of the week, month, or year; because the complexness of the machine hinders that perfection which the simplicity of the works and movements can alone give. For it is not in nature to have all things in one. If you are about to chuse a wife, and expect beauty, you must give up family and fortune; or if you attain these, you must at least want good temper, health, or some other advantage: so to expect good language and good sense, at the same time, is absurd, and not in the compass of common nature to produce. Attempting only one thing, therefore, we may entertain the idea of hitting the point of perfection. It has been owing to an inattention to this principle, that so many fail in their attempts at good writing. A Jack of all Trades, is proverbial of a bungler; and we scarcely ever find any one who excels in two parts of the same art; much less in two arts at the same time. The smooth poet wants strength; and the orator of a good voice, is destitute of logical reason and argument. How many have I heard speak, who, were they to attempt voice only, might be respectable; but undertaking, at the same time, to carry sense along with them, they utterly fail, and become contemptible. One thing at once, is the best maxim that ever came into the mind of man. This might be illustrated by a thousand examples; but I shall not trouble myself with any; as it is not so much my object to convince others as to shew the motives by which I myself am governed. Indeed, I could give authority which is superior to all examples; *viz.* that of the poet Horace; who, speaking on this very subject of excellence in writing, says, *Quidvis*, that is, whatever you compose, let it be, *simplex duntaxit & unum*: that is, simple, and one thing only.

It will be needless for me to say any thing about the critics; for as this work is intended as a model or rule of good writing, it cannot be the subject of criticism. It is true, Homer has been criticised by a Zoilus and an Aristotle; but the one contented himself with pointing out defects; the other, beauties. But Zoilus has been censured, Aristotle praised; because in a model there can be no defect; error consisting in a deviation from the truth, and faults, in an aberration from the original of beauty; so that where there are no faults there can be no food for criticism, taken in the unfavourable sense of finding fault with the productions of an author. I have no objections, therefore, to any praise that may be given to this work; but to censure or blame must appear absurd; because it cannot be doubted but that it will perfectly answer the end proposed.

Being a book without thought, or the smallest degree of sense, it will be useful to young minds, not fatiguing their understandings, and easily introducing a love of reading and study. Acquiring language at first by this means, they will afterwards gain knowledge. It will be useful especially to young men of light minds intended for the bar or pulpit. By heaping too much upon them, stile and matter at once, you surfeit the stomach, and turn away the appetite from literary entertainment, to horse-racing and cock-fighting. I shall consider myself, therefore, as having performed an acceptable service, to all weak and visionary people, if I can give them something to read without the trouble of thinking. But these are collateral advantages of my work, the great object of which is, as I have said before, to give a model of perfect stile in writing. If hereafter any author of supereminent abilities, should chuse to give this stile a body, and make it the covering to some work of sense, as you would wrap fine silk round a beautiful form, so that there may be, not only vestment, but life in the object, I have no objections; but shall be rather satisfied with having it put to so good a use.

CHAPTER I

JOHN FARRAGO, was a man of about fifty-three years of age, of good natural sense, and considerable reading; but in some things whimsical, owing perhaps to his greater knowledge of books than of the world; but, in some degree, also, to his having never married, being what they call an old batchelor, a characteristic of which is, usually, singularity and whim. He had the advantage of having had in early life, an academic education; but having never applied himself to any of the learned professions, he had lived the greater part of his life on a small farm, which he cultivated with servants or hired hands, as he could conveniently supply himself with either. The servant that he had at this time, was an Irishman, whose name was Teague Oregan. I shall say nothing of the character of this man, because the very name imports what he was.

A strange idea came in to the head of Captain Farrago about this time; for, by the bye, I had forgot to mention that having been chosen captain of a company of militia in the neighbourhood, he had gone by the name of Captain ever since; for the rule is, once a captain, and always a captain; but, as I was observing, the idea had come in to his head, to saddle an old horse that he had, and ride about the world a little, with his man Teague at his heels, to see how things were going on here and there, and to observe human nature. For it is a mistake to suppose, that a man cannot learn man by reading him in a corner, as well as on the widest space of transaction. At any rate, it may yield amusement.

It was about a score of miles from his own house, that he fell in with what we call Races. The jockeys seeing him advance, with Teague by his side, whom they took for his groom, conceived him to be some person who had brought his horse to enter for the purse. Coming up and accosting him, said they, You seem to be for the races, Sir; and have a horse to enter. Not at all, said the Captain; this is but a common palfrey, and by no means remarkable for speed or bottom; he is a common plough horse which I have used on my farm for several years, and can scarce go beyond a trot; much less match himself with your blooded horses that are going to take the field on this occasion.

The jockeys were of opinion, from the speech, that the horse was what they call a bite, and that under the appearance of leanness and stiffness, there was concealed some hidden quality of swiftness uncommon. For they had heard of instances, where the most knowing had been taken in by mean looking horses; so that having laid two, or more, to one, they were nevertheless bit by the bet; and the mean looking nags, proved to be horses of a more than common speed and bottom. So that there is no trusting appearances. Such was the reasoning of the jockeys. For they could have no idea, that a man could come there in so singular a manner, with a groom at his foot, unless he had some great object of making money by the adventure. Under this idea, they began to interrogate him with respect to the blood and pedigree of his horse: whether he was of the Dove, or the bay mare that took the purse; and was imported by such a one at such a time? whether his sire was Tamerlane or Bajazet?

The Captain was irritated at the questions, and could not avoid answering.—Gentlemen, said he, it is a strange thing that you should suppose that it is of any consequence what may be the pedigree of a horse. For even in men it is of no avail. Do we not find that sages have had blockheads for their sons; and that blockheads have had sages? It is remarkable, that as estates have seldom

lasted three generations, so understanding and ability have seldom been transmitted to the second. There never was a greater
man, take him as an orator and philosopher, than Cicero: and
never was there a person who had greater opportunities than his
son Marcus; and yet he proved of no account or reputation. This
is an old instance, but there are a thousand others. Chesterfield
and his son are mentioned. It is true, Philip and Alexander may
be said to be exceptions: Philip of the strongest possible mind;
capable of almost every thing we can conceive; the deepest policy
and the most determined valour; his son Alexander not deficient
in the first, and before him in the last; if it is possible to be before
a man than whom you can suppose nothing greater. It is possible,
in modern times, that Tippo Saib may be equal to his father Hy-
der Ali. Some talk of the two Pitts. I have no idea that the son is,
in any respect, equal to old Sir William. The one is a laboured
artificial minister; the other spoke with the thunder, and acted
with the lightning of the gods. I will venture to say, that when the
present John Adamses, and Lees, and Jeffersons, and Jays, and
Henrys, and other great men, who figure upon the stage at this
time, have gone to sleep with their fathers, it is an hundred to
one if there is any of their descendents who can fill their places.
Was I to lay a bet for a great man, I would sooner pick up the
brat of a tinker, than go into the great houses to chuse a piece
of stuff for a man of genius. Even with respect to personal appearance, which is more in the power of natural production, we
do not see that beauty always produces beauty; but on the contrary, the homeliest persons have oftentimes the best favoured
offspring; so that there is no rule or reason in these things. With
respect to this horse, therefore, it can be of no moment whether
he is blooded or studed, or what he is. He is a good old horse,
used to the plough, and carries my weight very well; and I have
never yet made enquiry with respect to his ancestors, or affronted
him so much as to cast up to him the defect of parentage. I
bought him some years ago from Neil Thomas, who had him from
a colt. As far as I can understand, he was of a brown mare that
John M'Neis had; but of what horse I know no more than the
horse himself. His gaits are good enough, as to riding a short
journey of seven or eight miles, or the like; but he is rather a
pacer than a troter; and though his bottom may be good enough

in carrying a bag to the mill, or going in the plough, or the sled, or the harrow, &c. yet his wind is not so good, nor his speed, as to be fit for the heats.

The jockeys thought the man a fool, and gave themselves no more trouble about him.

The horses were now entered, and about to start for the purse. There was Black and all Black, and Snip, John Duncan's Barbary Slim, and several others. The riders had been weighed, and when mounted, the word was given. It is needless to describe a race; every body knows the circumstances of it. It is sufficient to say, that from the bets that were laid, there was much anxiety, and some passion in the minds of those concerned: So, that as two of the horses, Black and all-Black, and Slim, came out near together; there was dispute and confusion. It came to kicking and cuffing in some places. The Captain was a good deal hurt with such indecency amongst gentlemen, and advancing, addressed them in the following manner: Gentlemen, this is an unequal and unfair proceeding. It is unbecoming modern manners, or even the ancient. For at the Olympic games of Greece, where were celebrated horse and chariot races, there was no such hurry scurry as this; and in times of chivalry itself, where men ate, drank, and slept on horseback, though there was a great deal of pell-meling, yet no such disorderly work as this. If men had a difference, they couched their lances, and ran full tilt at one another; but no such indecent expressions, as villain, scoundrel, liar, ever came out of their mouths. There was the most perfect courtesy in those days of heroism and honour; and this your horse-racing, which is a germ of the amusement of those times, ought to be conducted on the same principles of decorum, and good breeding.

As he was speaking, he was jostled by some one in the croud, and thrown from his horse; and had it not been for Teague, who was at hand, and helped him on again, he would have suffered damage. As it was, he received a contusion in his head, of which he complained much; and having left the race-ground, and coming to a small cottage, he stopped a little, to alight and dress the wound. An old woman who was there, thought they ought to take a little of his water, and see how it was with him; but the Captain having no faith in telling disorders by the urine, thought proper to send for a surgeon who was hard by, to examine the bruise, and apply bandages. The surgeon attended, and examining the part, pronounced it a contusion of the cerebrum. But as there appeared but little laceration, and no fracture, simple or compound, the pia mater could not be injured; nor even could there be more than a slight impression on the dura mater. So that trepaning did not at all appear necessary. A most fortunate circumstance; for a wound in the head, is of all places the most dangerous; because there can be no amputation to save life. There being but one head to a man, and that being the residence of the five senses, it is impossible to live without it. Nevertheless, as the present case was highly dangerous, as it might lead to a subsultus tendinum, or lock-jaw, it was necessary to apply cataplasms in order to reduce inflammation, and bring about a sanative disposition of the parts. Perhaps it might not be amiss, to take an anodyne as a refrigerant. Many patients had been lost by the ignorance of empirics prescribing bracers; whereas, in the first stage of a contusion, relaxing and antifebrile medicines are proper. A little phlebotomy was no doubt necessary, to prevent the bursting of the blood vessels.

The Captain hearing so many hard words, and bad accounts of this case, was much alarmed. Nevertheless he did not think it could be absolutely so dangerous. For it seemed to him that he was not sick at heart, or under any mortal pain. The surgeon observed, that in this case he could not himself be a judge. For the very part was affected by which he was to judge, *viz.* the head; that it was no uncommon thing for men in the extremest cases to imagine themselves out of danger; whereas in reality, they were in the greatest possible: that notwithstanding the symptoms were mild, yet from the contusion, a mortification might ensue. Hypocrates, who might be stiled an elementary physician, and has a treatise on this very subject, is of opinion, that the most dangerous symptom is a topical insensibility; but among the moderns, Sydenham considers it in another point of view, and thinks that where there is no pain, there is as great reason to suppose that there is no hurt, as that there is a mortal one. Be this as it may, antiseptic medicines might be very proper.

The Captain hearing so much jargon, and conscious to himself that he was by no means in so bad a state as this son of Escalapius would represent, broke out into some passion. It is, said he, the craft of your profession to make the case worse than it is, in order to increase the perquisites. But if there is any faith in you, make the same demand, and let me know your real judgment. The surgeon was irritated with his distrust, and took it into his head to fix some apprehension in the mind of his patient, if possible, that his case was not without danger. Looking stedfastly at him for some time, and feeling his pulse, there is, said he, an evident delirium approaching. This argues an affection of the brain, but it will be necessary, after some soporiferous draughts, to put the patient to sleep. Said the Captain, If you will give me about a pint of whiskey and water, I will try to go to sleep myself. A deleterious mixture, in this case, said the surgeon, cannot be proper; especially a distillation of that quality. The Captain would hear no more; but requesting the man of the cabin, to let him have the spirits proposed, drank a pint or two of grog, and having bound up his head with a handkerchief, went to bed.

CHAPTER II

Containing Some General Reflections

THE first reflection that arises, is, the good sense of the Captain; who was unwilling to impose his horse for a racer; not being qualified for the course. Because, as an old lean beast, attempting a trot, he was respectable enough; but going out of his nature and affecting speed, he would have been contemptible. The great secret of preserving respect, is the cultivating and shewing to the best advantage the powers that we possess, and the not going beyond them. Every thing in its element is good, and in their proper sphere all natures and capacities are excellent. This thought might be turned into a thousand different shapes, and cloathed with various expressions; but after all, it comes to the old proverb at last, *Ne sutor ultra crepidam,* Let the cobler stick to his last; a sentiment we are about more to illustrate in the sequel of this work.

The second reflection that arises, is, the simplicity of the Captain; who was so unacquainted with the world, as to imagine that jockeys and men of the turf could be composed by reason and good sense; whereas there are no people who are by education of a less philosophic turn of mind. The company of horses is by no means favourable to good taste and genius. The rubbing and currying them, but little enlarges the faculties, or improves the mind; and even riding, by which a man is carried swiftly through the air, though it contributes to health, yet stores the mind with few or no ideas; and as men naturally consimilate with their company, so it is observable that your jockeys are a class of people not far removed from the sagacity of a good horse. Hence most probably the fable of the centaur, among the ancients; by which they held out the moral of the jockey and the horse being one beast.

A third reflection is, that which he exprest; *viz.* the professional art of the surgeon to make the most of the case, and the technical terms used by him. I have to declare, that it is with no attempt at wit, that the terms are set down, or the art of the surgeon hinted at; because it is so common place a thing to ridicule the peculiarities of a profession, that it savours of mean parts to indulge it. For a man of real genius will never walk in the beaten track, because his object is what is new and uncommon. This surgeon does not appear to have been a man of very great ability; but the Captain was certainly wrong in declining his prescriptions; for the maxim is, *Unicuique in arte, sua perito, credendum est*; every one is to be trusted in his profession.

CHAPTER III

The Captain rising early next morning, and setting out on his way, had now arrived at a place where a number of people were convened, for the purpose of electing persons to represent them in the legislature of the state. There was a weaver who was a candidate for this appointment, and seemed to have a good deal of interest among the people. But another, who was a man of education was his competitor. Relying on some talent of speaking which he thought he possessed, he addressed the multitude.

Fellow citizens, said he, I pretend not to any great abilities; but am conscious to myself that I have the best good will to serve you. But it is very astonishing to me, that this weaver should conceive himself qualified for the trust. For though my requirements are not great, yet his are still less. The mechanical business which he pursues, must necessarily take up so much of his time, that he cannot apply himself to political studies. I should therefore think it would be more answerable to your dignity, and conducive to your interest, to be represented by a man at least of some letters, than by an illiterate handicraftsman like this. It will be more honourable for himself, to remain at his loom and knot threads, than to come forward in a legislative capacity; because in the one case, he is in the sphere suited to his education; in the other, he is like a fish out of water, and must struggle for breath in a new element.

Is it possible he can understand the affairs of government whose mind has been concentered to the small object of weaving webs; to the price by the yard, the grist of the thread, and such like matters as concern the manufacturer of cloths? The feet of him who weaves, are more occupied than the head, or at least as much; and therefore he must be, at least, but in half, accustomed to exercise his mental powers. For these reasons, all other things set aside, the chance is in my favour, with respect to information. However, you will decide, and give your suffrages to him or to me, as you shall judge expedient.

The Captain hearing these observations, and looking at the weaver, could not help advancing, and undertaking to subjoin something in support of what had been just said. Said he, I have no prejudice against a weaver more than another man. Nor do I know any harm in the trade; save that from the sedentary life in a damp place, there is usually a paleness of the countenance: but this is a physical, not a moral evil. Such usually occupy subterranean apartments; not for the purpose, like Demosthenes, of shaving their heads and writing over eight times the history of Thucydides, and perfecting a style of oratory; but rather to keep the thread moist; or because this is considered but as an inglorious sort of trade, and is frequently thrust away into cellars, and damp out-houses, which are not occupied for a better use.

But to rise from the cellar to the senate house, would be an unnatural hoist. To come from counting threads, and adjusting them to the splits of a reed, to regulate the finances of a government, would be preposterous; there being no congruity in the case. There is no analogy between knotting threads and framing laws. It would be a reversion of the order of things. Not that a manufacturer of linen or woolen, or other stuffs, is an inferior character, but a different one, from that which ought to be employed in affairs of state. It is unnecessary to enlarge on this subject; for you must all be convinced of the truth and propriety of what I say. But if you will give me leave to take the manufacturer aside a little, I think I can explain to him my ideas on the subject; and very probably prevail with him to withdraw his pretensions. The people seeming to acquiesce, and beckoning to the weaver, they withdrew aside, and the Captain addressed him in the following words:

Mr. Traddle, said he, for that was the name of the manufacturer, I have not the smallest idea of wounding your sensibility; but it would seem to me, it would be more your interest to pursue your occupation, than to launch out into that of which you have no knowledge. When you go to the senate house, the application to you will not be to warp a web; but to make laws for the commonwealth. Now, suppose that the making these laws, requires a knowledge of commerce, or of the interests of agriculture, or those principles upon which the different manufactures depend, what service could you render? It is possible you might think justly enough; but could you speak? You are not in the habit of public speaking. You are not furnished with those common place ideas, with which even very ignorant men can pass for knowing something. There is nothing makes a man so ridiculous, as to attempt what is above his sphere. You are no tumbler for instance; yet should you give out that you could vault upon a man's back; or turn heels over head like the wheels of a cart; the stiffness of your joints would encumber you; and you would fall upon your posteriors to the ground. Such a squash as that, would do you damage. The getting up to ride on the state is an unsafe thing to those who are not accustomed to such horsemanship. It is a disagreeable thing for a man to be laughed at, and there is no way of keeping one's self from it but by avoiding all affectation.

While they were thus discoursing, a bustle had taken place among the crowd. Teague hearing so much about elections, and serving the government, took it into his head, that he could be a legislator himself. The thing was not displeasing to the people, who seemed to favour his pretensions; owing, in some degree, to there being several of his countrymen among the crowd; but more epecially to the fluctuation of the popular mind, and a disposition to what is new and ignoble. For though the weaver was not the most elevated object of choice, yet he was still preferable to this tatter-demalion, who was but a menial servant, and had so much of what is called the brogue on his tongue, as to fall far short of an elegant speaker.

The Captain coming up, and finding what was on the carpet, was greatly chagrined at not having been able to give the multitude a better idea of the importance of a legislative trust; alarmed also, from an apprehension of the loss of his servant. Under these impressions he resumed his address to the multitude. Said he, this is making the matter still worse, gentlemen: this servant of mine is but a bog-trotter, who can scarcely speak the dialect in which your laws ought to be written; but certainly has never read a single treatise on any political subject; for the truth is, he cannot read at all. The young people of the lower class, in Ireland, have seldom the advantage of a good education; especially the descendants of the ancient Irish, who have most of them a great assurance of countenance, but little information or literature. This young man, whose family name is O'Regan, has been my servant for several years; and, except a too great fondness for women, which now and then brings him into scrapes, he has demeaned himself in a manner tolerable enough. But he is totally ignorant of the great principles of legislation; and more especially the particular interests of the government. A free government is a noble acquisition to a people: and this freedom consists in an equal right to make laws, and to have the benefit of the laws when made. Though doubtless, in such a government, the lowest citizen may become chief magistrate; yet it is sufficient to possess the right, not absolutely necessary to exercise it. Or even if you should think proper, now and then, to show your privilege, and exert, in a signal manner, the democratic prerogative, yet is it not descending too low to filch away from me a hireling, which I cannot well spare? You are surely carrying the matter too far, in thinking to make a senator of this ostler; to take him away from an employment to which he has been bred, and put him to another, to which he has served no apprenticeship: to set those hands which have been lately employed in currying my horse, to the draughting bills, and preparing business for the house.

The people were tenacious of their choice, and insisted on giving Teague their suffrages; and by the frown upon their brows, seemed to indicate resentment at what had been said; as indirectly charging them with want of judgment; or calling in question their privilege to do what they thought proper. It is a very strange thing, said one of them, who was a speaker for the rest, that after having conquered Burgoyne and Cornwallis, and got a government of our own, we cannot put in it whom we please. This young man may be your servant, or another man's servant; but if we chuse to make him a delegate, what is that to you? He may not be yet skilled in the matter, but there is a good day coming. We will empower him; and it is better to trust a plain man like him, than one of your high-flyers, that will make laws to suit their own purposes.

I had much rather, said the Captain, you would send the weaver, though I thought that improper, than to invade my household, and thus detract from me the very person that I have about me to brush my boots, and clean my spurs.

The prolocutor of the people gave him to understand that his objections were useless, for the people had determined on the choice, and Teague they would have, for a representative.

Finding it answered no end to expostulate with the multitude, he requested to speak a word with Teague by himself. Stepping aside, he said to him, composing his voice, and addressing him in a soft manner: Teague you are quite wrong in this matter they have put into your head. Do you know what it is to be a member of a deliberative body? What qualifications are necessary? Do you understand any thing of geography? If a question should be put to make a law to dig a canal in some part of the state, can you describe the bearing of the mountains, and the course of the rivers? Or if commerce is to be pushed to some new quarter, by the force of regulations, are you competent to decide in such a case? There will be questions of law, and astronomy on the carpet. How you must gape and stare like a fool, when you come to be asked your opinion on these subjects! Are you acquainted with the abstract principles of finance; with the funding public securities; the ways and means of raising the revenue; providing for the discharge of the public debts, and all other things which respect the economy of the government? Even if you had knowledge, have you a facility of speaking? I would suppose you would have too much pride to go to the house just to say, ay, or no. This is not the fault of your nature, but of your education; having been accustomed to dig turf in your early years, rather than instructing yourself in the classics, or common school books.

When a man becomes a member of a public body, he is like a racoon, or other beast that climbs up the fork of a tree; the boys pushing at him with pitchforks, or throwing stones or shooting at him with an arrow, the dogs barking in the mean time. One will find fault with your not speaking; another with your speaking, if you speak at all. They will put you in the newspapers, and ridicule you as a perfect beast. There is what they call the caricatura; that is, representing you with a dog's head, or a cat's claw. As you have a red head, they will very probably make a fox of you, or a sorrel horse, or a brindled cow. It is the devil in hell to be exposed to the squibs and crackers of the gazette wits and publications. You know no more about these matters than a goose; and yet you would undertake rashly, without advice, to enter on the office; nay, contrary to advice. For I would not for a thousand guineas, though I have not the half to spare, that the breed of the O'Regans should come to this; bringing on them a worse stain than stealing sheep; to which they are addicted. You have nothing but your character, Teague, in a new country to depend upon. Let it never be said, that you quitted an honest livelihood, the taking care of my horse, to follow the new fangled whims of the times, and be a statesman.

Teague was moved chiefly with the last part of the address, and consented to relinquish his pretensions.

The Captain, glad of this, took him back to the people, and announced his disposition to decline the honour which they had intended him.

Teague acknowledged that he had changed his mind, and was willing to remain in a private station.

The people did not seem well pleased with the Captain; but as nothing more could be said about the matter, they turned their attention to the weaver, and gave him their suffrages.

CHAPTER IV

CAPTAIN FARRAGO leaving this place, proceeded on his way; and at the distance of a mile or two, met a man with a bridle in his hand; who had lost a horse, and had been at a conjurer's to make enquiry, and recover his property.

It struck the mind of the Captain to go to this conjuring person, and make a demand of him, what was the cause that the multitude were so disposed to elevate the low to the highest station. He had rode but about a mile, when the habitation of the conjurer, by the direction and description of the man who had lost the horse had given, began to be in view. Coming up to the door, and enquiring if that was not where conjurer Kolt lived, they were answered Yes. Accordingly alighting, and entering the domicile, all those things took place which usually happen, or are described in cases of this nature, *viz.* there was the conjurer's assistant, who gave the Captain to understand that master had withdrawn a little, but would be in shortly.

In the mean time, the assistant endeavoured to draw from him some account of the occasion of his journey; which the other readily communicated; and the conjurer, who was listening through a crack in the partition, overheard. Finding it was not a horse or a cow, or a piece of linen that was lost, but an abstract question of political philosophy which was to be put, he came from his lurking place, and entered, as if not knowing that any person had been waiting for him.

After mutual salutations, the Captain gave him to understand the object which he had in view by calling on him.

Said the conjurer, This lies not at all in my way. If it had been a dozen of spoons, or a stolen watch, that you had to look for, I could very readily, by the assistance of my art, have assisted you in the recovery; but as to this matter of man's imaginations and attachments in political affairs, I have no more understanding than another man.

It is very strange, said the Captain, that you who can tell by what means a thing is stolen, and the place where it is deposited, though at a thousand miles distance, should know so little of what is going on in the breast of man, as not to be able to develope his secret thoughts, and the motives of his actions.

It is not of our business, said the other; but should we undertake it, I do not see that it would be very difficult to explain all
that puzzles you at present. There is no need of a conjurer to tell
why it is that the common people are more disposed to trust one
of their own class, than those who may affect to be superior. Besides, there is a certain pride in man, which leads him to elevate
the low, and pull down the high. There is a kind of creating power
exerted in making a senator of an unqualified person; which
when the author has done, he exults over the work, and like the
Creator himself when he made the world, sees that "it is very
good." Moreover, there is in every government a patrician class,
against whom the spirit of the multitude naturally militates: And
hence a perpetual war; the aristocrats endeavouring to detrude
the people, and the people contending to obtrude themselves.
And it is right it should be so; for by this fermentation, the spirit
of democracy is kept alive.

The Captain, thanking him for his information, asked him what
was to pay; at the same time pulling out half a crown from a green
silk purse which he had in his breeches pocket. The conjurer gave
him to understand, that as the solution of these difficulties was
not within his province, he took nothing for it. The Captain expressing his sense of his disinterested service, bade him adieu.

CHAPTER V

Containing Reflections

A DEMOCRACY is beyond all question the freest government:
because under this, every man is equally protected by the laws,
and has equally a voice in making them. But I do not say an equal
voice; because some men have stronger lungs than others, and
can express more forcibly their opinions of public affairs. Others,
though they may not speak very loud, yet have a faculty of saying
more in a short time; and even in the case of others, who speak
little or none at all, yet what they do say containing good sense,
comes with greater weight; so that all things considered, every
citizen, has not, in this sense of the word, an equal voice. But the
right being equal, what great harm if it is unequally exercised? is

it necessary that every man should become a statesman? No more than that every man should become a poet or a painter. The sciences, are open to all; but let him only who has taste and genius pursue them. If any man covets the office of a bishop, says St. Paul, he covets a good work. But again, he adds this caution, Ordain not a novice, lest being lifted up with pride, he falls into the condemnation of the devil. It is indeed making a devil of a man to lift him up to a state to which he is not suited. A ditcher is a respectable character, with his over-alls on, and a spade in his hand; but put the same man to those offices which require the head whereas he has been accustomed to impress with his foot, and there appears a contrast between the individual and the occupation.

There are individuals in society, who prefer honour to wealth; or cultivate political studies as a branch of literary pursuits; and offer themselves to serve public bodies, in order to have an opportunity of discovering their knowledge, and exercising their judgment. It must be chagrining to these, and hurtful to the public, to see those who have no talent this way, and ought to have no taste, preposterously obtrude themselves upon the government. It is the same as if a brick-layer should usurp the office of a taylor, and come with his square and perpendicular, to take the measure of a pair of breeches.

It is proper that those who cultivate oratory, should go to the house of orators. But for an Ay and No man to be ambitious of that place, is to sacrifice his credit to his vanity.

I would not mean to insinuate that legislators are to be selected from the more wealthy of the citizens, yet a man's circumstances ought to be such as afford him leisure for study and reflection. There is often wealth without taste or talent. I have no idea, that because a man lives in a great house and has a cluster of bricks or stones about his backside, that he is therefore fit for a legislator. There is so much pride and arrogance with those who consider themselves the first in a government, that it deserves to be checked by the populace, and the evil most usually commences on this side. Men associate with their own persons, the adventitious circumstances of birth and fortune: So that a fellow blowing with fat and repletion, conceives himself superior to the poor lean man, that lodges in an inferior mansion. But as in all cases, so in this, there is a medium. Genius and virtue are independent of rank and fortune; and it is neither the opulent, nor the indigent, but the man of ability and integrity that ought to be called forth to serve his country: and while, on the one hand, the aristocratic part of the government, arrogates a right to represent; on the other hand, the democratic contends the point; and from this conjunction and opposition of forces, there is produced a compound resolution, which carries the object in an intermediate direction. When we see therefore, a Teague Oregan lifted up, the philosopher will reflect, that it is to balence some purse-proud fellow, equally as ignorant, that comes down from the sphere of aristocratic interest.

But every man ought to consider for himself, whether it is his use to be this draw-back, on either side. For as when good liquor is to be distilled, you throw in some material useless in itself to correct the effervescence of the spirit; so it may be his part to act as a sedative. For though we commend the effect, yet still the material retains but its original value.

But as the nature of things is such, let no man who means well to the commonwealth, and offers to serve it, be hurt in his mind when some one of meaner talents is preferred. The people are a sovereign, and greatly despotic; but, in the main, just.

I have a great mind, in order to elevate the composition, to make quotations from the Greek and Roman history. And I am conscious to myself, that I have read the writers on the government of Italy and Greece, in ancient, as well as in modern times. But I have drawn a great deal more from reflection on the nature of things, than from all the writings I have ever read. Nay, the history of the election, which I have just given, will afford a better lesson to the American mind, than all that is to be found in other examples. We have seen here, a weaver a favoured candidate, and in the next instance, a bog-trotter superseding him. Now it may be said, that this is fiction; but fiction, or no fiction, the nature of the thing will make it a reality. But I return to the adventures of the Captain, whom I have upon my hands; and who, as far as I can yet discover, is a good honest man; and means what is benevolent and useful; though his ideas may not comport with the ordinary manner of thinking, in every particular.

Washington Irving

(1783–1859)

Washington Irving was born in New York City, and much of his writing is set in New York and the Hudson River Valley. He was adept at the humorous essay, and his burlesque *A History of New York* (1809), written under the pseudonym Diedrich Knicker-bocker, is considered by some to be the first American master-piece of comic literature. Later, his short stories would gain him an international audience: "Rip Van Winkle" and "The Legend of Sleepy Hollow," first published in a collection called *The Sketch Book of Geoffrey Crayon, Gent.* (1820), remain among his most-read works. Irving was trained in the law, and spent more than two decades in Europe traveling and working. *The Sketch Book* was writ-ten during his stay in England, and he became a literary celebrity in both London and Paris. He served as a diplomat in Spain, where he wrote nonfiction on Spanish subjects. He also wrote on the American West, and published biographies of Christopher Co-lumbus and Oliver Goldsmith, among others, as well as a monu-mental five-volume life of George Washington.

Irving was a gentle and refined satirist, as these "anecdotes of literary life" demonstrate. These essays appeared in a collection called *Tales of a Traveler*, published in 1824.

Tales of a Traveler

LITERARY LIFE

Among other subjects of a traveller's curiosity, I had at one time a great craving after anecdotes of literary life; and being at London, one of the most noted places for the production of books, I was excessively anxious to know something of the animals which produced them. Chance fortunately threw me in the way of a literary man by the name of Buckthorne, an eccentric personage, who had lived much in the metropolis, and could give me the natural history of every odd animal to be met with in that wilderness of men. He readily imparted to me some useful hints upon the subject of my inquiry.

"The literary world," said he, "is made up of little confederacies, each looking upon its own members as the lights of the universe; and considering all others as mere transient meteors, doomed soon to fall and be forgotten, while its own luminaries are to shine steadily on to immortality."

"And pray," said I, "how is a man to get a peep into those confederacies you speak of? I presume an intercourse with authors is a kind of intellectual exchange, where one must bring his commodities to barter, and always give a quid pro quo."

"Pooh, pooh—how you mistake," said Buckthorne, smiling: "you must never think to become popular among wits by shining. They go into society to shine themselves, not to admire the brilliancy of others. I once thought as you do, and never went into literary society without studying my part before hand. The consequence was, I soon got the name of an intolerable proser, and should in a little while have been completely excommunicated had I not changed my plan of operations. No, sir, no character succeeds so well among wits as that of a good listener, or if ever you are eloquent, let it be when tête-à-tête with an author, and then in praise of his own works, or what is nearly as acceptable, in disparagement of the works of his contemporaries. If ever he speaks favourably of the productions of a particular friend, dissent boldly from him; pronounce his friend to be a blockhead; never fear his being vexed; much as people speak of the irritability of authors, I never found one to take offense at such contradictions. No-no sir, authors are particularly candid in admitting the faults of their friends.

"Indeed I would advise you to be extremely sparing of remarks on all modern works, excepting to make sarcastic observations on the most distinguished writers of the day."

"Faith," said I, "I'll praise none that have not been dead for at least half a century."

"Even then," observed Mr. Buckthorne, "I would advise you to be rather cautious; for you must know that many old writers have been enlisted under the banners of different sects, and their merits have become as complete topics of party discussion as the merits of living statesmen and politicians. Nay, there have been whole periods of literature absolutely *taboo'd*, to use a South Sea phraze. It is, for example, as much as a man's critical reputation is worth, in some circles, to say a word in praise of any writers of the reign of Charles the Second, or even of Queen Anne; they being all declared Frenchmen in disguise."

"And pray then," said I, "when am I to know that I am on safe grounds; being totally unacquainted with the literary landmarks and the boundary lines of fashionable taste?"

"Oh," replied he, "there is fortunately one tract of literature which forms a kind of neutral ground, on which all the literary meet amicably, and run riot in the excess of their good humour. And this is, the reigns of Elizabeth and James. Here you may praise away at random; here it is 'cut and come again,' and the more obscure the author, and the more quaint and crabbed his style, the more your admiration will smack of the real relish of the Connoisseur; whose taste, like that of an Epicure, is always for game that has an antiquated flavour.

"But," continued he, "as you seem anxious to know something of literary society I will take an opportunity to introduce you to some coterie, where the talents of the day are assembled. I cannot promise you, however, that they will all be of the first order. Some how or other, our great geniuses are not gregarious, they do not go in flocks; but fly singly in general society. They prefer mingling, like common men, with the multitude; and are apt to carry nothing of the author about them but the reputation. It is only the inferior orders that herd together, acquire strength and importance by their confederacies, and bear all the distinctive characteristics of their species.''

A Literary Dinner

A few days after this conversation with Mr. Buckthorne, he called upon me, and took me with him to a regular literary dinner. It was given by a great Bookseller, or rather a company of Booksellers, whose firm surpassed in length even that of Shadrach, Meshach and Abed-nego.

I was surprised to find between twenty and thirty guests assembled, most of whom I had never seen before. Buckthorne explained this to me, by informing me that this was a "business dinner," or kind of field day which the house gave about twice a year to its authors. It is true they did occasionally give snug dinners to three or four literary men at a time; but then these were generally select authors; favourites of the public; such as had arrived at their sixth or seventh editions. "There are," said he, "certain geographical boundaries in the land of literature, and you may judge tolerably well of an author's popularity, by the wine his bookseller gives him. An author crosses the port line about the third edition and gets into claret, but when he has reached the sixth and seventh, he may revel in champagne and burgundy.''

"And pray," said I, "how far may these gentlemen have reached that I see around me; are any of these claret drinkers?''

"Not exactly, not exactly. You find at these great dinners the common steady run of authors, one, two-edition men; or if any others are invited they are aware that it is a kind of republican meeting.—You understand me—a meeting of the republic of letters, and that they must expect nothing but plain substantial fare.''

These hints enabled me to comprehend more fully the arrangement of the table. The two ends were occupied by two partners of the House—and the host seemed to have adopted Addison's idea as to the literary precedence of his guests. A popular poet had the post of honour, opposite to whom was a hotpressed traveller in Quarto with plates. A grave looking antiquarian, who had produced several solid works, which were much quoted and little read, was treated with great respect, and seated next to a neat dressy gentleman in black, who had written a thin, genteel, hot-pressed octavo on political economy that was getting into fashion. Several three volume duodecimo men of fair currency were placed about the centre of the table; while the lower end was taken up with small poets, translators and authors who had not as yet risen into much notoriety.

The conversation during dinner was by fits and starts; breaking out here and there in various parts of the table in small flashes, and ending in smoke. The poet who had the confidence of a man on good terms with the world and independent of his bookseller, was very gay and brilliant, and said many clever things, which set the partner next him in a roar, and delighted all the company. The other partner, however, maintained his sedateness and kept carving on, with the air of a thorough man of business, intent upon the occupation of the moment. His gravity was explained to me by my friend Buckthorne. He informed me that the concerns of the house were admirably distributed among the partners. "Thus, for instance," said he, "the grave gentleman is the carving partner who attends to the joints, and the other is the laughing partner who attends to the jokes."

The general conversation was chiefly carried on at the upper end of the table; as the authors there seemed to possess the greatest courage of the tongue. As to the crew at the lower end, if they did not make much figure in talking they did in eating. Never was there a more determined, inveterate, thoroughly sustained attack on the trencher, than by this phalanx of masticators. When the cloth was removed, and the wine began to circulate, they grew very merry and jocose among themselves. Their jokes, however, if by chance any of them reached the upper end of the table, seldom produced much effect. Even the laughing partner did not think it necessary to honour them with a smile; which my neighbour Buckthorne accounted for, by informing me that there was a certain degree of popularity to be obtained, before a bookseller could afford to laugh at an author's jokes.

Among this crew of questionable gentlemen thus seated below the salt, my eye singled out one in particular. He was rather shabbily dressed; though he had evidently made the most of a rusty black coat, and wore his shirt frill plaited and puffed out voluminously at the bosom. His face was dusky, but florid, perhaps a little too florid, particularly about the nose; though the rosy hue gave the greater lustre to a twinkling black eye. He had a little the look of a boon companion, with that dash of the poor devil in it which gives an inexpressibly mellow tone to a man's humour. I had seldom seen a face of richer promise; but never was promise so ill kept. He said nothing; ate and drank with the keen appetite of a Garretteer, and scarcely stopped to laugh even at the good jokes from the upper end of the table. I inquired who he was. Buckthorne looked at him attentively; "Gad," said he, "I have seen that face before but where I cannot recollect. He cannot be an author of any note. I suppose some writer of sermons or grinder of foreign travels."

After dinner we retired to another room to take tea and coffee, where we were reinforced by a cloud of inferior guests. Authors of small volumes in boards, and pamphlets stitched in blue paper. These had not as yet arrived to the importance of a dinner invitation, but were invited occasionally to pass the evening "in a friendly way." They were very respectful to the partners, and indeed seemed to stand a little in awe of them; but they paid devoted court to the lady of the house, and were extravagantly fond of the children. Some few, who did not feel confidence enough to make such advances, stood shyly off in corners, talking to one another; or turned over the portfolios of prints, which they had not seen above five thousand times, or moused over the music on the forte-piano.

The poet and the thin octavo gentleman were the persons most current and at their ease in the drawing room; being men evidently of circulation in the west end. They got on each side of the lady of the house, and paid her a thousand compliments and civilities, at some of which I thought she would have expired with delight. Every thing they said and did had the odour of fashionable life. I looked round in vain for the poor devil author in the rusty black coat; he had disappeared immediately after leaving the table; having a dread, no doubt, of the glaring light of a drawing room. Finding nothing further to interest my attention, I took my departure soon after coffee had been served, leaving the poet and the thin, genteel, hotpressed, octavo gentleman, masters of the field.

THE CLUB OF QUEER FELLOWS

I think it was but the very next evening that in coming out of Covent Garden theatre with my excentric friend Buckthorne, he proposed to give me another peep at life and character. Finding me willing for any research of the kind, he took me through a variety of the narrow courts and lanes about Covent Garden until we stopped before a tavern from which we heard the bursts of merriment of a jovial party. There would be a loud peal of laughter, then an interval, then another peal, as if a prime wag were telling a story. After a little while there was a song, and at the close of each stanza a hearty roar and a vehement thumping on the table.

"This is the place," whispered Buckthorne. "It is the 'club of queer fellows,' a great resort of the small wits, third rate actors, and newspaper critics of the theatres. Any one can go in, on paying a sixpence at the bar for the use of the club."

We entered, therefore, without ceremony and took our seats at a lone table in a dusky corner of the room. The club was assembled round a table, on which stood beverages of various kinds, according to the taste of the individual. The members were a set of queer fellows indeed; but what was my surprize on recognizing in the prime wit of the meeting the poor devil author, whom I had remarked at the Booksellers' dinner for his promising face and his complete taciturnity. Matters, however, were entirely changed with him. There he was a mere cypher: here he was lord of the ascendant; the choice spirit, the dominant genius. He sat at the head of the table with his hat on, and an eye beaming even more luminously than his nose. He had a quip and a fillip for every one, and a good thing on every occasion. Nothing could be said or done without eliciting a spark from him; and I solemnly declare I have heard much worse wit even from noblemen. His jokes it must be confessed, were rather wet, but they suited the circle in which he presided. The company were in that maudlin mood when a little wit goes a great way. Every time he opened his lips there was sure to be a roar, and even sometimes before he had time to speak.

We were fortunate enough to enter in time for a glee composed by him expressly for the club, and which he sang with two boon companions who would have been worthy subjects for Hogarth's pencil. As they were each provided with a written copy; I was enabled to procure the reading of it.

> Merrily, merrily push round the glass,
> And merrily troll the glee,
> For he who won't drink till he wink is an ass,
> So neighbour I drink to thee.
>
> Merrily, merrily fuddle thy nose,
> Until it right rosy shall be;
> For a jolly red nose, I speak under the rose,
> Is a sign of good company.

We waited until the party broke up, and no one but the wit remained. He sat at the table with his legs stretched under it, and wide apart; his hands in his breeches pockets; his head drooped upon his breast; and gazing with lack lustre countenance on an empty tankard. His gaiety was gone, his fire completely quenched.

My companion approached and startled him from his fit of brown study, introducing himself on the strength of their having dined together at the Booksellers'.

"By the way," said he, "it seems to me I have seen you before; your face is surely that of an old acquaintance, though for the life of me I cannot tell where I have known you."

"Very likely," replied he with a smile; "many of my old friends have forgotten me. Though, to tell the truth my memory in this instance is as bad as your own. If however it will assist your recollection in any way, my name is Thomas Dribble, at your service."

"What. Tom Dribble, who was at old Birchell's school in Warwickshire—"

"The same," said the other, coolly.

"Why then we are old schoolmates, though it's no wonder you don't recollect me. I was your junior by several years; don't you recollect little Jack Buckthorne?"

Here then ensued a scene of school fellow recognition—and a world of talk about old school times and school pranks. Mr. Dribble ended by observing with a heavy sigh "that times were sadly changed since those days."

"Faith, Mr. Dribble," said I, "you seem quite a different man here from what you were at dinner. I had no idea that you had so much stuff in you. There you were all silence; but here you absolutely keep the table in a roar."

"Ah my dear sir," replied he, with a shake of the head and a shrug of the shoulder, "I'm a mere glow worm. I never shine by daylight. Besides, it's a hard thing for a poor devil of an author to shine at the table of a rich bookseller. Who, do you think, would laugh at any thing I could say, when I had some of the current wits of the day about me? But, here, though a poor devil, I am among still poorer devils than myself: men who look up to me as a man of letters and a bel esprit, and all my jokes pass as sterling gold from the mint."

"You surely do yourself injustice, sir," said I. "I have certainly heard more good things from you this evening, than from any of those beaux esprits by whom you appear to have been so daunted."

"Ah, sir! but they have luck on their side; they are in the fashion—there's nothing like being in fashion. A man that has once got his character up for a wit, is always sure of a laugh, say what he may. He may utter as much nonsense as he pleases, and all will pass current. No one stops to question the coin of a rich man; but a poor devil cannot pass off either a joke or a guinea, without its being examined on both sides. Wit and coin are always doubted with a threadbare coat.

"For my part," continued he, giving his hat a twitch a little more on one side, "for my part, I hate your fine dinners; there's nothing, sir, like the freedom of a chop house. I'd rather, any time, have my steak and tankard among my own set, than drink claret and eat venison with your cursed civil, elegant company who never laugh at a good joke from a poor devil for fear of its being vulgar. A good joke grows in a wet soil; it flourishes in low places, but withers on your d——d high, dry grounds. I once kept high company, sir, until I nearly ruined myself, I grew so dull, and vapid and genteel. Nothing saved me but being arrested by my Landlady and thrown into prison; where a course of catch clubs, eightpenny ale and poor devil company, manured my mind and brought it back to itself again."

As it was now growing late we parted for the evening; though

I felt anxious to know more of this practical philosopher. I was glad therefore when Buckthorne proposed to have another meeting to talk over old school times, and inquired his schoolmate's address. The latter seemed at first a little shy of naming his lodgings; but suddenly assuming an air of hardihood—"Green Arbour Court Sir," exclaimed he—"number——in Green Arbour Court. You must know the place. Classic ground, sir! classic ground! It was there Goldsmith wrote his Vicar of Wakefield—I always like to live in literary haunts—"

I was amused with this whimsical apology for shabby quarters. On our way homewards Buckthorne assured me that this Dribble had been the prime wit and great wag of the school in their boyish days and one of those unlucky urchins denominated bright geniuses. As he perceived me curious respecting his old schoolmate he promised to take me with him in his proposed visit to Green Arbour Court.

A few mornings afterwards he called upon me and we set forth on our Expedition. He led me through a variety of singular alleys, and courts, and blind passages; for he appeared to be profoundly versed in all the intricate geography of the metropolis. At length we came out upon Fleet Market and traversing it turned up a narrow street to the bottom of a long steep flight of stone steps called Break neck Stairs. These he told me led up to Green Arbour Court, and that, down them poor Goldsmith might many a time have risked his neck. When we entered the court, I could not but smile to think in what out of the way corners genius produces her bantlings! And the muses, those capricious dames, who forsooth, so often refuse to visit palaces, and deny a single smile to votaries in splendid studies and gilded drawing rooms,—what holes and burrows will they frequent to lavish their favours on some ragged disciple!

This Green Arbour Court I found to be a small square surrounded by tall miserable houses, the very intestines of which seemed turned inside out, to judge from the old garments and frippery fluttering from every window. It appeared to be a region of washerwomen, and lines were stretched about the little square, on which clothes were dangling to dry. Just as we entered the square, a scuffle took place between two viragos about a disputed right to a washtub, and immediately the whole community was in a hubbub. Heads in mob caps popped out of every window, and such a clamour of tongues ensued that I was fain to stop my ears. Every Amazon took part with one or other of the disputants, and brandished her arms dripping with soapsuds, and fired away from her window as from the embrazure of a fortress; while the swarms of children nestled and cradled in every procreant chamber of this hive, waking with the noise, set up their shrill pipes to swell the general concert.

Poor Goldsmith! what a time must he have had of it, with his quiet disposition and nervous habits, penned up in this den of noise and vulgarity. How strange that while every sight and sound was sufficient to embitter the heart and fill it with misanthropy, his pen should be dropping the honey of Hybla. Yet it is more than probable that he drew many of his inimitable pictures of low life from the scenes which surrounded him in this abode. The circumstance of Mrs. Tibbs being obliged to wash her husband's two shirts in a neighbour's house, who refused to lend her wash-tub, may have been no sport of fancy, but a fact passing under his own eye. His landlady may have sat for the picture, and Beau Tibbs' scanty wardrobe have been a fac simile of his own.

It was with some difficulty that we found our way to Dribble's lodgings. They were up two pair of stairs, in a room that looked upon the Court, and when we entered he was seated on the edge of his bed, writing at a broken table. He received us, however, with a free, open, poor devil air, that was irresistible. It is true he did at first appear slightly confused; but toned up his waistcoat a little higher and tucked in a stray frill of linen. But he recollected himself in an instant; gave a half swagger, half leer as he stepped forth to receive us; drew a three legged stool for Mr. Buckthorne; pointed me to a lumbering old Damask chair that looked like a dethroned monarch in exile, and bade us welcome to his garret.

We soon got engaged in conversation. Buckthorne and he had much to say about early school scenes, and as nothing opens a man's heart more than recollections of the kind we soon drew from him a brief outline of his literary career.

THE POOR DEVIL AUTHOR

I began life unluckily by being the wag and bright fellow at school; and I had the further misfortune of becoming the great genius of my native village. My father was a country attorney, and intended I should succeed him in business; but I had too much genius to study, and he was too fond of my genius to force it into the traces. So I fell into bad company and took to bad habits. Do not mistake me. I mean that I fell into the company of village literati and village blues, and took to writing village poetry.

It was quite the fashion in the village to be literary. There was a little knot of choice spirits of us who assembled frequently together, formed ourselves into a Literary, Scientific and Philosophical Society, and fancied ourselves the most learned philos in existence. Every one had a great character assigned him, suggested by some casual habit or affectation. One heavy fellow drank an enormous quantity of tea; rolled in his arm chair, talked sententiously, pronounced dogmatically, and was considered a second Dr. Johnson; another who happened to be a curate uttered coarse jokes, wrote doggerel rhymes, and was the Swift of our association. Thus we had also our Popes, and Goldsmiths and Addisons, and a blue stocking lady whose drawing room we frequented, who corresponded about nothing, with all the world, and wrote letters with the stiffness and formality of a printed book, was cried up as another Mrs. Montagu. I was, by common consent, the juvenile prodigy, the poetical youth, the great genius, the pride and hope of the village, through whom it was to become one day as celebrated as Stratford on Avon.

My father died and left me his blessing and his business. His blessing brought no money into my pocket; and as to his business it soon deserted me: for I was busy writing poetry, and could not attend to law; and my clients, though they had great respect for my talents, had no faith in a poetical attorney.

I lost my business, therefore, spent my money and finished my poem. It was the Pleasures of Melancholy, and was cried up to the skies by the whole circle. The Pleasures of Imagination, the Pleasures of Hope and the Pleasures of Memory though each had placed its author in the first rank of poets, were blank prose in comparison. Our Mrs. Montagu would cry over it from beginning to end. It was pronounced by all the members of the Literary, Scientific and Philosophical Society, the greatest poem of the age, and all anticipated the noise it would make in the great world. There was not a doubt but the London booksellers would be mad after it, and the only fear of my friends was, that I would make a sacrifice by selling it too cheap. Every time they talked the matter over they encreased the price. They reckoned up the great sums given for the poems of certain popular writers, and determined that mine was worth more than all put together, and ought to be paid for accordingly. For my part, I was modest in my expectations, and determined that I would be satisfied with a thousand guineas. So I put my poem in my pocket and set off for London.

My journey was joyous. My heart was light as my purse, and my head full of anticipations of fame and fortune. With what swelling pride did I cast my eyes upon old London from the heights of Highgate. I was like a general looking down upon a place he expects to conquer. The great metropolis lay stretched before me, buried under a home made cloud of murky smoke, that wrapped it from the brightness of a sunny day, and formed for it a kind of artificial bad weather. At the outskirts of the city, away to the west, the smoke gradually decreased until all was clear and sunny, and the view stretched uninterrupted to the blue line of the Kentish Hills.

My eye turned fondly to where the mighty cupola of St. Paul's swelled dimly through this misty chaos, and I pictured to myself the solemn realm of learning that lies about its base. How soon should the Pleasures of Melancholy throw this world of Booksellers and printers into a bustle of business and delight! How soon should I hear my name repeated by printers' devils throughout Paternoster Row, and Angel Court, and Ave Maria Lane, until Amen Corner should echo back the sound!

Arrived in town, I repaired at once to the most fashionable publisher. Every new author patronizes him of course. In fact, it had been determined in the village circle that he should be the fortunate man. I cannot tell you how vaingloriously I walked the streets; my head was in the clouds. I felt the airs of heaven playing about it, and fancied it already encircled by a halo of literary glory. As I passed by the windows of bookshops, I anticipated the time when my work would be shining among the hotpressed wonders of the day; and my face, scratched on copper, or cut in wood, figuring in fellowship with those of Scott and Byron and Moore.

When I applied at the publisher's house there was something in the loftiness of my air, and the dinginess of my dress, that struck the clerks with reverence. They doubtless took me for some person of consequence, probably a digger of Greek roots or a penetrater of pyramids. A proud man in a dirty shirt is always an imposing character in the world of letters; one must feel intellectually secure before he can venture to dress shabbily; none but a great scholar or a great genius dares to be dirty; so I was ushered at once, to the sanctum sanctorum of this high priest of Minerva.

The publishing of books is a very different affair now adays, from what it was in the time of Bernard Lintot. I found the publisher a fashionably dressed man, in an elegant drawing room, furnished with sophas; and portraits of celebrated authors, and cases of splendidly bound books. He was writing letters at an elegant table. This was transacting business in style. The place seemed suited to the magnificent publications that issued from it. I rejoiced at the choice I had made of a publisher, for I always liked to encourage men of taste and spirit.

I stepped up to the table with the lofty poetical port I had been accustomed to maintain in our village circle; though I threw in it something of a patronizing air, such as one feels when about to make a man's fortune. The publisher paused with his pen in hand, and seemed waiting in mute suspense to know what was to be announced by so singular an apparition.

I put him at his ease in a moment, for I felt that I had but to come, see and conquer. I made known my name, and the name of my poem; produced my precious roll of blotted manuscript, laid it on the table with an emphasis, and told him at once, to save time and come directly to the point, the price was one thousand guineas.

I had given him no time to speak, nor did he seem so inclined. He continued looking at me for a moment with an air of whimsical perplexity; scanned me from head to foot; looked down at the manuscript; then up again at me, then pointed to a chair; and whistling softly to himself, went on writing his letter.

I sat for some time waiting his reply; supposing he was making up his mind; but he only paused occasionally to take a fresh dip of ink; to stroke his chin or the tip of his nose and then resumed his writing. It was evident his mind was intently occupied upon some other subject; but I had no idea that any other subject should be attended to and my poem lie unnoticed on the table. I had supposed that every thing would make way for the Pleasures of Melancholy.

My gorge at length rose within me. I took up my manuscript; thrust it into my pocket, and walked out of the room; making some noise as I went, to let my departure be heard. The publisher, however, was too much buried in minor concerns to notice it. I was suffered to walk down stairs without being called back. I sallied forth into the street, but no clerk was sent after me; nor did the publisher call after me from the drawing room window. I have been told since, that he considered me either a madman or a fool. I leave you to judge how much he was in the wrong in his opinion.

When I turned the corner my crest fell. I cooled down in my pride and my expectations, and reduced my terms with the next bookseller to whom I applied. I had no better success: nor with a third; nor with a fourth. I then desired the booksellers to make an offer themselves; but the deuce an offer would they make. They told me poetry was a mere drug; every body wrote poetry; the market was overstocked with it. And then, they said, the title of my poem was not taking: that pleasures of all kinds were worn threadbare, nothing but horrors did now adays, and even those were almost worn out. Tales of Pirates, Robbers and bloody Turks might answer tolerably well; but then they must come from some established well known name, or the public would not look at them.

At last I offered to leave my poem with a bookseller to read it and judge for himself. "Why really, my dear Mr.——a—a—I forget your name," said he, cutting an eye at my rusty coat and shabby gaiters, "really, sir, we are so pressed with business just now, and have so many manuscripts on hand to read, that we have not time to look at any new production, but if you can call again in a week or two, or say the middle of next month, we may be able to look over your writings and give you an answer. Don't forget, the month after next——good morning, sir—happy to see you any time you are passing this way—"; so saying he bowed me out in the civilest way imaginable.—In short, sir, instead of an eager competition to secure my poem, I could not even get it read! In the meantime I was harrassed by letters from my friends, wanting to know when the work was to appear; who was to be my publisher; but above all things warning me not to let it go too cheap.

There was but one alternative left. I determined to publish the poem myself; and to have my triumph over the booksellers, when it should become the fashion of the day. I accordingly published the Pleasures of Melancholy and ruined myself. Excepting the copies sent to the reviews, and to my friends in the country, not one I believe ever left the bookseller's ware house. The printer's bill drained my purse, and the only notice that was taken of my work was contained in the advertisements paid for by myself.

I could have borne all this, and have attributed it as usual to the mismanagement of the publisher; or the want of taste in the public; and could have made the usual appeal to posterity; but my village friends would not let me rest in quiet. They were picturing me to themselves feasting with the great, communing with the literary, and in the high career of fortune and renown. Every little while, some one would call on me with a letter of introduction from the village circle, recommending him to my attentions, and requesting that I would make him known in society: with a hint that an introduction to a celebrated literary nobleman would be extremely agreeable.

I determined, therefore, to change my lodgings, drop my correspondence, and disappear altogether from the view of my village admirers. Besides, I was anxious to make one more poetic attempt. I was by no means disheartened by the failure of my first. My poem was evidently too didactic. The public was wise enough. It no longer read for instruction. "They want horrors, do they?" said I, "I'faith then they shall have enough of them." So I looked out for some quiet retired place, where I might be out of reach of my friends, and have leisure to cook up some delectable dish of poetical "hell-broth."

I had some difficulty in finding a place to my mind, when chance threw me in the way of Canonbury Castle. It is an ancient brick tower, hard by "merry Islington;" the remains of a hunting seat of Queen Elizabeth, where she took the pleasures of the country, when the neighbourhood was all woodland. What gave it particular interest in my eyes was the circumstance that it had been the residence of a Poet. It was here Goldsmith resided when he wrote his Deserted Village. I was shown the very apartment. It was a relique of the original style of the castle, with pannelled wainscots and Gothic windows. I was pleased with its air of antiquity, and with its having been the residence of poor Goldy. "Goldsmith was a pretty poet," said I to myself, "a very pretty poet; though rather of the old school. He did not think and feel so strongly as is the fashion now adays; but had he lived in these times of hot hearts and hot heads, he would no doubt have written quite differently."

In a few days I was quietly established in my new quarters; my books all arranged, my writing desk placed by a window looking out into the fields; and I felt as snug as Robinson Crusoe, when he had finished his bower. For several days I enjoyed all the novelty of change and the charms which grace new lodgings before one has found out their defects. I rambled about the fields where I fancied Goldsmith had rambled. I explored merry Islington; ate my solitary dinner at the Black Bull, which according to tradition was a country seat of Sir Walter Raleigh, and would sit and sip my wine and muse on old times in a quaint old room, where many a council had been held.

All this did very well for a few days; I was stimulated by novelty; inspired by the associations awakened in my mind by these curious haunts; and began to think I felt the spirit of composition stirring within me; but Sunday came, and with it the whole city world, swarming about Canonbury Castle. I could not open my window but I was stunned with shouts and noises from the cricket ground. The late quiet road beneath my window, was alive with the tread of feet and clack of tongues, and to complete my misery, I found that my quiet retreat was absolutely a "show house!" the tower and its contents being shewn to strangers at sixpence a head.

There was a perpetual tramping up stairs of citizens and their families, to look about the country from the top of the tower, and to take a peep at the city through the telescope, to try if they could discern their own chimnies. And then, in the midst of a vein of thought, or a moment of inspiration, I was interrupted and all my ideas put to flight, by my intolerable landlady's tapping at the door, and asking me, if I would "jist please to let a lady and gentleman come in to take a look at Mr. Goldsmith's room."

If you know any thing what an author's study is, and what an author is himself, you must know that there was no standing this. I put a positive interdict on my room's being exhibited; but then it was shewn when I was absent and my papers put in confusion; and on returning home one day, I absolutely found a cursed tradesman and his daughters gaping over my manuscripts; and my landlady in a panic at my appearance. I tried to make out a little longer by taking the key in my pocket, but it would not do. I overheard mine hostess one day telling some of her customers on the stairs that the room was occupied by an author, who was always in a tantrum if interrupted; and I immediately perceived, by a slight noise at the door, that they were peeping at me through the keyhole. By the head of Apollo, but this was quite too much! With all my eagerness for fame, and my ambition of the stare of the million, I had no idea of being exhibited by retail at sixpence a head, and that through a Key hole. So I bade adieu to Canonbury Castle, Merry Islington, and the haunts of poor Goldsmith, without having advanced a single line in my labours.

My next quarters were at a small white washed cottage, which stands not far from Hampstead, just on the brow of a hill; looking over Chalk Farm, and Camden Town, remarkable for the rival houses of Mother Red Cap and Mother Black Cap; and so across Crackscull Common to the distant city.

The cottage was in no wise remarkable in itself; but I regarded it with reverence, for it had been the asylum of a persecuted author. Hither poor Steele had retreated and lain perdu, when persecuted by creditors and bailiffs; those immemorial plagues of authors and free spirited gentlemen; and here he had written many numbers of the Spectator. It was hence, too, that he had dispatched those little notes to his lady, so full of affection and whimsicality; in which the fond husband, the careless gentleman, and the shifting spendthrift, were so oddly blended. I thought, as I first eyed the window of his apartment, that I could sit within it, and write volumes.

No such thing! It was Haymaking season, and, as ill luck would have it, immediately opposite the cottage was a little ale house with the sign of the Load of Hay. Whether it was there in Steele's time I cannot say; but it set all attempts at conception or inspiration at defiance. It was the resort of all the Irish Haymakers who mow the broad fields in the neighbourhood; and of drovers and teamsters who travel that road. Here would they gather in the endless summer twilight, or by the light of the harvest moon, and sit round a table at the door; and tipple, and laugh, and quarrel, and fight, and sing drowsy songs, and dawdle away the hours until the deep solemn notes of St. Paul's clock would warn the varlets home.

In the day time I was still less able to write. It was broad summer. The haymakers were at work in the fields, and the perfume of the new mown hay brought with it the recollection of my native fields. So instead of remaining in my room to write, I went wandering about Primrose Hill and Hampstead Heights and Shepherd's Fields; and all those Arcadian scenes so celebrated by London Bards. I cannot tell you how many delicious hours I have passed lying on the cocks of new mown hay, on the pleasant slopes of some of those hills, inhaling the fragrance of the fields; while the summer fly buzzed about me, or the grasshopper leaped into my bosom; and how I have gazed with half shut eye upon the smoky mass of London, and listened to the distant sound of its population; and pitied the poor sons of earth, toiling in its bowels, like Gnomes in the "dark gold mine."

People may say what they please about Cockney pastorals; but after all, there is a vast deal of rural beauty about the western vicinity of London; and any one that has looked down upon the valley of West End, with its soft bosom of green pasturage, lying open to the south and dotted with cattle; the steeple of Hampstead rising among rich groves on the brow of the hill; and the learned height of Harrow in the distance; will confess that never has he seen a more absolutely rural landscape in the vicinity of a great metropolis.

Still, however, I found myself not a whit the better off for my frequent change of lodgings; and I began to discover that in literature, as in trade, the old proverb holds good, "a rolling stone gathers no moss."

The tranquil beauty of the country played the very vengeance with me. I could not mount my fancy into the termagant vein. I could not conceive, amidst the smiling landscape, a scene of blood and murder; and the smug citizens in breeches and gaiters, put all ideas of heroes and Bandits out of my brain. I could think of nothing but dulcet subjects—"the pleasures of spring"— "the pleasures of solitude"—"the pleasures of tranquility"—"the pleasures of sentiment"—nothing but pleasures; and I had the painful experience of "the pleasures of melancholy" too strongly in my recollection to be beguiled by them.

Chance at length befriended me. I had frequently in my ramblings loitered about Hampstead Hill; which is a kind of Parnassus of the metropolis. At such times I occasionally took my dinner at Jack Straw's Castle. It is a country Inn so named. The very spot where that notorious rebel and his followers held their council of war. It is a favourite resort of citizens when rurally inclined, as it commands fine fresh air and a good view of the city.

I sat one day in the public room of this Inn, ruminating over a beefsteak and a pint of port, when my imagination kindled up with ancient and heroic images. I had long wanted a theme and a hero; both suddenly broke upon my mind; I determined to write a poem on the history of Jack Straw. I was so full of my subject that I was fearful of being anticipated; I wondered that none of the poets of the day, in their search after ruffian heroes, had ever thought of Jack Straw. I went to work pell mell, blotted several sheets of paper with choice floating thoughts, and battles and descriptions, to be ready at a moment's warning. In a few days' time I sketched out the skeleton of my poem, and nothing was wanting but to give it flesh and blood. I used to take my manuscript and stroll about Caen Wood, and read aloud; and would dine at the castle, by way of keeping up the vein of thought.

I was there one day, at rather a late hour, in the public room. There was no other company but one man, who sat enjoying his pint of port at a window, and noticing the passers by. He was dressed in a green shooting coat. His countenance was strongly marked. He had a hooked nose, a romantic eye, excepting that it had something of a squint, and altogether, as I thought, a poetical style of head. I was quite taken with the man, for you must know I am a little of a physiognomist; I set him down at once for either a poet or a philosopher.

As I like to make new acquaintances, considering every man a volume of human nature, I soon fell into conversation with the stranger, who, I was pleased to find, was by no means difficult of access. After I had dined, I joined him at the window, and we became so sociable that I proposed a bottle of wine together, to which he most cheerfully assented.

I was too full of my poem to keep long quiet on the subject, and began to talk about the origin of the tavern and the history of Jack Straw. I found my new acquaintance to be perfectly at home on the topic, and to jump exactly with my humour in every respect. I became elevated by the wine and the conversation. In the fullness of an author's feelings, I told him of my projected poem, and repeated some passages, and he was in raptures. He was evidently of a strong poetical turn.

"Sir," said he, filling my glass at the same time, "our poets don't look at home. I don't see why we need go out of old England for robbers and rebels to write about. I like your Jack Straw, sir. He's a home made hero. I like him, sir. I like him exceedingly. He's English to the back bone—damme—Give me honest old England after all; them's my sentiments, sir!"

"I honour your sentiment," cried I zealously, "it is exactly my own. An English ruffian is as good a ruffian for poetry as any in Italy, or Germany, or the Archipelago; but it is hard to make our poets think so."

"More shame for them!" replied the man in green. "What a plague would they have? What have we to do with their Archipelagos of Italy and Germany? Haven't we heaths and commons and high ways on our own little island?—Aye and stout fellows to pad the hoof over them too? Stick to home, I say—them's my sentiments.—Come sir, my service to you—I agree with you perfectly."

"Poets in old times had right notions on this subject," continued I; "witness the fine old ballads about Robin Hood, Allan a'Dale and other staunch blades of yore." "Right, sir, right," interrupted he. "Robin Hood! He was the lad to cry stand! to a man, and never flinch."

"Ah sir!" said I, "they had famous bands of robbers in the good old times. Those were glorious poetical days. The merry crew of Sherwood Forest, who led such a roving picturesque life, 'under the greenwood tree.' I have often wished to visit their haunts, and tread the scenes of the exploits of Friar Tuck, and Clym of the Clough, and Sir William of Cloudeslie."

"Nay sir," said the gentleman in green, "we have had several very pretty gangs since their day. Those gallant dogs that kept about the great heaths in the neighbourhood of London; about Bagshot, and Hounslow, and Blackheath, for instance. Come sir, my service to you. You don't drink."

"I suppose," said I, emptying my glass, "I suppose you have heard of the famous Turpin who was born in this very village of Hampstead, and who used to lurk with his gang in Epping Forest, about a hundred years since."

"Have I?" cried he. "To be sure I have! A hearty old blade that, sound as pitch. Old Turpentine!—as we used to call him. A famous fine fellow, sir."

"Well sir," continued I, "I have visited Waltham Abbey, and Chingford Church merely from the stories I heard when a boy of his exploits there, and I have searched Epping Forest for the cavern where he used to conceal himself. You must know," added I, "that I am a sort of amateur of Highwaymen. They were dashing, daring fellows; the last apologies that we had for the Knights errants of yore. Ah sir! the country has been sinking gradually into tameness and common place. We are losing the old English spirit. The bold Knights of the Post have all dwindled down into lurking footpads and sneaking pickpockets. There's no such thing as a dashing gentlemanlike robbery committed now adays on the King's high way. A man may roll from one end of England to the other, in a drowsy coach or jingling postchaise without any other adventure than that of being occasionally overturned, sleeping in damp sheets, or having an ill cooked dinner.

"We hear no more of public coaches being stopped and robbed by a well mounted gang of resolute fellows with pistols in their hands and crapes over their faces. What a pretty poetical incident was it for example, in domestic life, for a family carriage, on its way to a country seat, to be attacked about dusk, the old gentleman eased of his purse and watch, the ladies of their necklaces and ear rings, by a politely spoken Highwayman on a blood mare, who afterwards leaped the hedge and galloped across the country, to the admiration of Miss Carolina the daughter, who would write a long and romantic account of the adventure to her friend

Miss Juliana in town. Ah sir! we meet with nothing of such inci-
dents now adays!"

"That, sir,—" said my companion, taking advantage of a pause,
when I stopped to recover breath and to take a glass of wine,
which he had just poured out—"that, sir, craving your pardon, is
not owing to any want of old English pluck. It is the effect of this
cursed system of banking. People do not travel with bags of gold,
as they did formerly. They have post notes and drafts on Bankers.
To rob a coach is like catching a crow; where you have nothing
but carrion flesh and feathers for your pains. But a coach in old
times, sir, was as rich as a Spanish Galloon. It turned out the
yellow boys bravely. And a private carriage was a cool hundred or
two at least."

I cannot express how much I was delighted with the sallies of
my new acquaintance. He told me that he often frequented the
castle, and would be glad to know more of me; and I promised
myself many a pleasant afternoon with him, when I should read
him my poem, as it proceeded, and benefit by his remarks; for it
was evident he had the true poetical feeling.

"Come, sir!" said he, pushing the bottle, "Damme I like you!
—You're a man after my own heart; I'm cursed slow in making
new acquaintances. One must be on the reserve, you know. But
when I meet with a man of your kidney, damme my heart jumps
at once to him—Them's my sentiments, sir—Come, sir, here's
Jack Straw's health! I presume one can drink it now adays without
treason!"

"With all my heart," said I gaily, "and Dick Turpin's into the
bargain!"

"Ah, sir!" said the man in green, "those are the kind of men
for poetry. The Newgate Kalender, sir! the Newgate Kalender is
your only reading! There's the place to look for bold deeds and
dashing fellows."

We were so much pleased with each other that we sat until a
late hour. I insisted on paying the bill, for both my purse and my
heart were full, and I agreed that he should pay the score at our
next meeting. As the coaches had all gone that run between
Hampstead and London he had to return on foot. He was so
delighted with the idea of my poem that he could talk of nothing
else. He made me repeat such passages as I could remember, and

though I did it in a very mangled manner, having a wretched memory, yet he was in raptures.

Every now and then he would break out with some scrap which he would misquote most terribly, but would rub his hands and exclaim, "By Jupiter that's fine! that's noble! Damme, sir, if I can conceive how you hit upon such ideas!"

I must confess I did not always relish his misquotations, which sometimes made absolute nonsense of the passages; but what author stands upon trifles when he is praised?

Never had I spent a more delightful evening. I did not perceive how the time flew. I could not bear to separate but continued walking on, arm in arm, with him, past my lodgings, through Camden Town, and across Crackscull Common talking the whole way about my poem.

When we were half way across the common he interrupted me in the midst of a quotation by telling me that this had been a famous place for footpads, and was still occasionally infested by them; and that a man had recently been shot there in attempting to defend himself.

"The more fool he!" cried I. "A man is an ideot to risk life, or even limb, to save a paltry purse of money. It's quite a different case from that of a duel, where one's honour is concerned. For my part," added I, "I should never think of making resistance against one of those desperadoes."

"Say you so?" cried my friend in green, turning suddenly upon me, and putting a pistol to my breast, "Why then have at you my lad!—come—disburse! empty! unsack!"

In a word, I found that the muse had played me another of her tricks, and had betrayed me into the hands of a footpad. There was no time to parley; he made me turn my pockets inside out; and hearing the sound of distant footsteps, he made one fell swoop upon purse, watch and all, gave me a thwack over my unlucky pate that laid me sprawling on the ground; and scampered away with his booty.

I saw no more of my friend in green until a year or two afterwards; when I caught a sight of his poetical countenance among a crew of scapegraces, heavily ironed, who were on the way for transportation. He recognized me at once, tipped me an impudent wink, and asked me how I came on with the history of Jack Straw's Castle.

The catastrophe at Crackscull Common put an end to my summer's campaign. I was cured of my poetical enthusiasm for rebels, robbers and highwaymen. I was put out of conceit of my subject, and what was worse I was lightened of my purse, in which was almost every farthing I had in the world. So I abandoned Sir Richard Steele's cottage in despair, and crept into less celebrated, though no less poetical and airy lodgings in a garret in town.

I now determined to cultivate the society of the literary, and to enrol myself in the fraternity of authorship. It is by the constant collision of mind, thought I, that authors strike out the sparks of genius, and kindle up with glorious conceptions. Poetry is evidently a contagious complaint: I will keep company with poets; who knows but I may catch it as others have done?

I found no difficulty in making a circle of literary acquaintances, not having the sin of success lying at my door; indeed, the failure of my poem was a kind of recommendation to their favour. It is true my new friends were not of the most brilliant names in literature; but then, if you would take their words for it, they were like the prophets of old, men of whom the world was not worthy; and who were to live in future ages, when the ephemeral favourites of the day should be forgotten.

I soon discovered, however, that the more I mingled in literary society, the less I felt capacitated to write; that poetry was not so catching as I imagined; and that in familiar life there was often nothing less poetical than a poet. Besides, I wanted the *esprit du corps* to turn these literary fellowships to any account. I could not bring myself to enlist in any particular sect: I saw something to like in them all, but found that would never do, for that the tacit condition on which a man enters into one of these sects is, that he abuses all the rest.

I perceived that there were little knots of authors who lived with, and for, and by one another. They considered themselves the salt of the earth. They fostered and kept up a conventional vein of thinking and talking, and joking on all subjects; and they cried each other up to the skies. Each sect had its particular creed; and set up certain authors as divinities, and fell down and worshipped them; and considered every one who did not worship them, or who worshipped any other, as a heretic and an infidel.

In quoting the writers of the day, I generally found them extolling names of which I had scarcely heard, and talking slight-

ingly of others who were the favourites of the public. If I
mentioned any recent work from the pen of a first rate author,
they had not read it; they had not time to read all that was
spawned from the press; he wrote too much to write well;—and
then they would break out into raptures about some Mr. Timson,
or Tomson, or Jackson, whose works were neglected at the present
day, but who was to be the wonder and delight of posterity. Alas!
what heavy debts is this neglectful world daily accumulating on
the shoulders of poor posterity!

But above all, it was edifying to hear with what contempt they
would talk of the great. Ye gods! how immeasurably the great are
despised by the small fry of literature! It is true, an exception was
now and then made of some nobleman, with whom, perhaps, they
had casually shaken hands at an election, or hob or nobbed at a
public dinner, and who was pronounced a "devilish good fellow,"
and "no humbug;" but, in general, it was enough for a man to
have a title to be the object of their sovereign disdain: you have
no idea how poetically and philosophically they would talk of
nobility.

For my part, this affected me but little; for though I had no
bitterness against the great, and did not think the worse of a man
for having innocently been born to a title, yet I did not feel myself
at present called upon to resent the indignities poured upon
them by the little. But the hostility to the great writers of the day
went sorely against the grain with me. I could not enter into such
feuds, nor participate in such animosities. I had not become author sufficiently to hate other authors. I could still find pleasure
in the novelties of the press, and could find it in my heart to
praise a contemporary, even though he were successful. Indeed,
I was miscellaneous in my taste, and could not confine it to any
age or growth of writers. I could turn with delight from the glowing pages of Byron to the cool and polished raillery of Pope; and,
after wandering among the sacred groves of Paradise Lost, I could
give myself up to voluptuous abandonment in the enchanted bow-
ers of Lalla Rookh.

"I would have my authors," said I, "as various as my wines, and,
in relishing the strong and the racy, would never decry the sparkling and exhilarating. Port and sherry are excellent stand-by's,
and so is Madeira; but claret and Burgundy may be drunk now

and then without disparagement to one's palate; and Champagne
is a beverage by no means to be despised."

Such was the tirade I uttered one day, when a little flushed with
ale, at a literary club. I uttered it, too, with something of a flour-
ish, for I thought my simile a clever one. Unluckily, my auditors
were men who drank beer and hated Pope; so my figure about
wines went for nothing, and my critical toleration was looked
upon as downright heterodoxy. In a word, I soon became like a
freethinker in religion, an outlaw from every sect, and fair game
for all. Such are the melancholy consequences of not hating in
literature.

I see you are growing weary, so I will be brief with the residue
of my literary career. I will not detain you with a detail of my
various attempts to get astride of Pegasus; of the poems I have
written which were never printed, the plays I have presented
which were never performed, and the tracts I have published
which were never purchased.—It seemed as if booksellers, man-
agers, and the very public, had entered into a conspiracy to starve
me. Still I could not prevail upon myself to give up the trial nor
abandon those dreams of renown in which I had indulged. How
should I ever be able to look the literary circle of my native village
in the face, if I were so completely to falsify their predictions. For
some time longer therefore I continued to write for fame, and of
course was the most miserable dog in existence, besides being in
continual risk of starvation. I accumulated loads of literary treasure on my shelves—loads which were to be treasures to posterity;
but, alas! they put not a penny into my purse. What was all this
wealth to my present necessities? I could not patch my elbows with
an ode; nor satisfy my hunger with blank verse. "Shall a man fill
his belly with the east wind?" says the proverb. He may as well do
so as with poetry.

I have many a time strolled sorrowfully along, with a sad heart
and an empty stomach, about five o'clock, and looked wistfully
down the areas in the west end of the town; and seen through
the kitchen windows the fires gleaming, and the joints of meat
turning on the spits and dripping with gravy; and the cook maids
beating up puddings, or trussing turkeys, and felt for the moment
that if I could but have the run of one of those kitchens, Apollo
and the muses might have the hungry heights of Parnassus for

me. Oh sir! talk of meditations among the tombs—they are nothing so melancholy as the meditations of a poor devil without
penny in pouch, along a line of kitchen windows towards dinner
time.

At length, when almost reduced to famine and despair, the idea
all at once entered my head, that perhaps I was not so clever a
fellow as the village and myself had supposed. It was the salvation
of me. The moment the idea popped into my brain it brought
conviction and comfort with it. I awoke as from a dream. I gave
up immortal fame to those who could live on air; took to writing
for mere bread; and have ever since led a very tolerable life of it.
There is no man of letters so much at his ease, sir, as he who has
no character to gain or lose. I had to train myself to it a little,
and to clip my wings short at first, or they would have carried me
up into poetry in spite of myself. So I determined to begin by the
opposite extreme, and abandoning the higher regions of the craft
I came plump down to the lowest, and turned Creeper.

"Creeper! and pray what is that?" said I. "Oh sir! I see you are
ignorant of the language of the craft; a creeper is one who fur-
nishes the newspapers with paragraphs at so much a line: one
who goes about in quest of misfortunes; attends the Bow Street
Office; the courts of justice and every other den of mischief and
iniquity. We are paid at the rate of a penny a line, and as we can
sell the same paragraph to almost every paper, we sometimes pick
up a very decent day's work. Now and then the muse is unkind,
or the day uncommonly quiet, and then we rather starve; and
sometimes the unconscionable editors will clip our paragraphs
when they are a little too rhetorical, and snip off twopence or
threepence at a go. I have many a time had my pot of porter
snipped off of my dinner in this way; and have had to dine with
dry lips. However I cannot complain. I rose gradually in the lower
ranks of the craft, and am now I think in the most comfortable
region of literature."

"And pray," said I, "what may you be at present?"

"At present," said he, "I am a regular job writer and turn my
hand to any thing. I work up the writings of others at so much a
sheet; turn off translations; write second rate articles to fill up
reviews and magazines; compile travels and voyages, and furnish
theatrical criticisms for the newspapers. All this authorship, you

perceive, is anonymous; it gives no reputation, except among the trade, whe e I am considered an author of all work, and am always sure of employ. That's the only reputation I want. I sleep soundly, without dread of duns or critics, and leave immortal fame to those that choose to fret and fight about it. Take my word for it, the only happy author in this world is he who is below the care of reputation."

NOTORIETY

When we had emerged from the literary nest of honest Dribble, and had passed safely through the dangers of Break neck Stairs, and the labyrinths of Fleet Market, Buckthorne indulged in many comments upon the peep into literary life which he had furnished me.

I expressed my surprise at finding it so different a world from what I had imagined. "It is always so," said he, "with strangers. The land of literature is a fairy land to those who view it from a distance, but like all other landscapes, the charm fades on a nearer approach, and the thorns and briars become visible. The republic of letters is the most factious and discordant of all republics, ancient or modern."

"Yet," said I, smiling, "you would not have me take honest Dribble's experience as a view of the land. He is but a mousing owl; a mere groundling. We should have quite a different strain from one of those fortunate authors whom we see sporting about the empyreal heights of fashion, like swallows in the blue sky of a summer's day."

"Perhaps we might," replied he, "but I doubt it. I doubt whether if any one, even of the most successful, were to tell his actual feelings, you would not find the truth of friend Dribble's philosophy with respect to reputation. One you would find carrying a gay face to the world, while some vulture critic was preying upon his very liver. Another, who was simple enough to mistake fashion for fame, you would find watching countenances, and cultivating invitations, more ambitious to figure in the *beau monde* than the world of letters, and apt to be rendered wretched by the neglect of an illiterate peer, or a dissipated duchess. Those who were rising to fame, you would find tormented with anxiety to get higher; and those who had gained the summit, in constant apprehension of a decline.

"Even those who are indifferent to the buzz of notoriety, and the farce of fashion, are not much better off, being incessantly harassed by intrusions on their leisure, and interruptions of their pursuits; for, whatever may be his feelings, when once an author is launched into notoriety, he must go the rounds until the idle curiosity of the day is satisfied, and he is thrown aside to make way for some new caprice. Upon the whole, I do not know but he is most fortunate who engages in the whirl through ambition, however tormenting; as it is doubly irksome to be obliged to join in the game without being interested in the stake.

"There is a constant demand in the fashionable world for novelty; every nine days must have its wonder, no matter of what kind. At one time it is an author; at another a fire eater; at another a composer, an Indian juggler, or an Indian chief; a man from the North Pole or the Pyramids: each figures through his brief term of notoriety, and then makes way for the succeeding wonder. You must know that we have oddity fanciers among our ladies of rank, who collect about them all kinds of remarkable beings: fiddlers, statesmen, singers, warriors, artists, philosophers, actors, and poets; every kind of personage, in short, who is noted for something peculiar: so that their routs are like fancy balls, where every one comes 'in character.'

"I have had infinite amusement at these parties in noticing how industriously every one was playing a part, and acting out of his natural line. There is not a more complete game at cross purposes than the intercourse of the literary and the great. The fine gentleman is always anxious to be thought a wit, and the wit a fine gentleman.

"I have noticed a lord endeavouring to look wise and to talk learnedly with a man of letters, who was aiming at a fashionable air, and the tone of a man who had lived about town. The peer quoted a score or two of learned authors, with whom he would fain be thought intimate, while the author talked of Sir John this, and Sir Harry that, and extolled the Burgundy he had drank at Lord Such-a-one's.—Each seemed to forget that he could only be interesting to the other in his proper character. Had the peer been merely a man of erudition, the author would never have listened to his prosing; and had the author known all the nobility in the Court Calendar, it would have given him no interest in the eyes of the peer.

"In the same way I have seen a fine lady, remarkable for beauty, weary a philosopher with flimsy metaphysics, while the philosopher put on an awkward air of gallantry, played with her fan, and prattled about the Opera. I have heard a sentimental poet talk very stupidly with a statesman about the national debt; and on joining a knot of scientific old gentlemen conversing in a corner, expecting to hear the discussion of some valuable discovery, I found they were only amusing themselves with a fat story."

Nathaniel Hawthorne
(1804–1864)

Nathaniel Hawthorne's writings and the intellectual life of New England in the nineteenth century are so closely tied together that it is almost impossible to consider one without weighing the other. *The Scarlet Letter*, produced in four intensive months of concentrated writing in 1849, stands as one of the greatest of American novels, its exegesis of the somber spirit of Puritanism now familiar not only to scholars of American literature, but to almost every high school English student. Hawthorne is also the author of *Twice-Told Tales* (a two-volume collection of short stories published in 1837 for the first volume and 1842 for the second), several other novels including *Mosses from an Old Manse* (1846), *The Marble Faun* (1860), and two children's books, *A Wonder Book* (1852) and *Tanglewood Tales* (1853).

This giant of American literature is better known for his explorations of complex moral and spiritual issues in his great novels than he is for satire. Yet the author of *The Scarlet Letter* and *The House of the Seven Gables* also wrote *The Blithedale Romance*, which takes aim at the follies of life at the Utopian community of Brook Farm, and "The Celestial Railroad," a satirical view of the Transcendentalists, printed here in its entirety.

The Celestial Railroad

Not a great while ago, passing through the gate of dreams, I visited that region of the earth in which lies the famous City of

Destruction. It interested me much to learn that by the public spirit of some of the inhabitants, a railroad has recently been established between this populous and flourishing town and the Celestial City. Having a little time upon my hands, I resolved to gratify a liberal curiosity by making a trip thither. Accordingly, one fine morning after paying my bill at the hotel, and directing the porter to stow my luggage behind a coach, I took my seat in the vehicle and set out for the station house. It was my good fortune to enjoy the company of a gentleman—one Mr. Smooth-it-away—who, though he had never actually visited the Celestial City, yet seemed as well acquainted with its laws, customs, policy, and statistics as with those of the City of Destruction, of which he was a native townsman. Being, moreover, a director of the railroad corporation and one of its largest stockholders, he had it in his power to give me all desirable information respecting that praise-worthy enterprise.

Our coach rattled out of the city, and at a short distance from its outskirts, passed over a bridge of elegant construction, but somewhat too slight, as I imagined, to sustain any considerable weight. On both sides lay an extensive quagmire, which could not have been more disagreeable, either to sight or smell, had all the kennels of the earth emptied their pollution there.

"This," remarked Mr. Smooth-it-away, "is the famous Slough of Despond—a disgrace to all the neighborhood; and the greater that it might so easily be converted into firm ground."

"I have understood," said I, "that efforts have been made for that purpose from time immemorial. Bunyan mentions that above twenty thousand cartloads of wholesome instructions had been thrown in here without effect."

"Very probably! And what effect could be anticipated from such unsubstantial stuff?" cried Mr. Smooth-it-away. "You observe this convenient bridge. We obtained a sufficient foundation for it by throwing into the Slough some editions of books of morality; volumes of French philosophy and German rationalism; tracts, sermons, and essays of modern clergymen; extracts from Plato, Confucius, and various Hindu sages, together with a few ingenious commentaries upon texts of Scripture—all of which, by some scientific process, have been converted into a mass like granite. The whole bog might be filled up with similar matter."

It really seemed to me, however, that the bridge vibrated and heaved up and down in a very formidable manner; and, spite of Mr. Smooth-it-away's testimony to the solidity of its foundation, I should be loath to cross it in a crowded omnibus, especially if each passenger were encumbered with as heavy luggage as that gentleman and myself. Nevertheless, we got over without accident, and soon found ourselves at the station house. This very neat and spacious edifice is erected on the site of the little wicket gate which formerly, as all old pilgrims will recollect, stood directly across the highway, and, by its inconvenient narrowness, was a great obstruction to the traveler of liberal mind and expansive stomach. The reader of John Bunyan will be glad to know that Christian's old friend Evangelist, who was accustomed to supply each pilgrim with a mystic roll, now presides at the ticket office. Some malicious persons, it is true, deny the identity of this reputable character with the Evangelist of old times, and even pretend to bring competent evidence of an imposture. Without involving myself in a dispute, I shall merely observe that, so far as my experience goes, the square pieces of pasteboard now delivered to passengers are much more convenient and useful along the road than the antique roll of parchment. Whether they will be as readily received at the gate of the Celestial City, I decline giving an opinion.

A large number of passengers were already at the station house, awaiting the departure of the cars. By the aspect and demeanor of these persons, it was easy to judge that the feelings of the community had undergone a very favorable change in reference to the celestial pilgrimage. It would have done Bunyan's heart good to see it. Instead of a lonely and ragged man with a huge burden on his back, plodding along sorrowfully on foot while the whole city hooted after him, here were parties of the first gentry and most respectable people in the neighborhood, setting forth towards the Celestial City as cheerfully as if the pilgrimage were merely a summer tour. Among the gentlemen were characters of deserved eminence—magistrates, politicians, and men of wealth, by whose example religion could not but be greatly recommended to their meaner brethren. In the ladies' apartment, too, I rejoiced to distinguish some of those flowers of fashionable society who are so well fitted to adorn the most elevated circles of the Celestial City. There was much pleasant conversation about the news of the day, topics of business and politics, or the lighter matters of amusement; while religion, though indubitably the main thing at heart, was thrown tastefully into the background. Even an infidel would have heard little or nothing to shock his sensibility.

One great convenience of the new method of going on pilgrimage I must not forget to mention. Our enormous burdens, instead of being carried on our shoulders, as had been the custom of old, were all snugly deposited in the baggage car, and, as I was assured, would be delivered to their respective owners at the journey's end. Another thing, likewise, the benevolent reader will be delighted to understand. It may be remembered that there was an ancient feud between Prince Beelzebub and the keeper of the wicket gate, and that the adherents of the former distinguished personage were accustomed to shoot deadly arrows at honest pilgrims while knocking at the door. This dispute, much to the credit as well of the illustrious potentate above mentioned as of the worthy and enlightened directors of the railroad, has been pacifically arranged on the principle of mutual compromise. The prince's subjects are now pretty numerously employed about the station house, some in taking care of the baggage, others in collecting fuel, feeding the engines, and such congenial occupations; and I can conscientiously affirm that persons more attentive to their business, more willing to accommodate, or more generally agreeable to the passengers, are not to be found on any railroad. Every good heart must surely exult at so satisfactory an arrangement of an immemorial difficulty.

"Where is Mr. Greatheart?" inquired I. "Beyond a doubt the directors have engaged that famous old champion to be chief conductor on the railroad?"

"Why, no," said Mr. Smooth-it-away, with a dry cough. "He was offered the situation of brakeman; but, to tell you the truth, our friend Greatheart has grown preposterously stiff and narrow in his old age. He has so often guided pilgrims over the road on foot that he considers it a sin to travel in any other fashion. Besides, the old fellow had entered so heartily into the ancient feud with Prince Beelzebub that he would have been perpetually at blows or ill language with some of the prince's subjects, and thus have embroiled us anew. So, on the whole, we were not sorry when honest Greatheart went off to the Celestial City in a huff and left us at liberty to choose a more suitable and accommodating man. Yonder comes the engineer of the train. You will probably recognize him at once."

The engine at this moment took its station in advance of the cars, looking, I must confess, much more like a sort of mechanical demon that would hurry us to the infernal regions than a laudable contrivance for smoothing our way to the Celestial City. On its top sat a personage almost enveloped in smoke and flame, which, not to startle the reader, appeared to gush from his own mouth and stomach as well as from the engine's brazen abdomen.

"Do my eyes deceive me?" cried I. "What on earth is this! A living creature? If so, he is his own brother to the engine he rides upon!"

"Poh, poh, you are obtuse!" said Mr. Smooth-it-away, with a hearty laugh. "Don't you know Apollyon, Christian's old enemy, with whom he fought so fierce a battle in the Valley of Humiliation? He was the very fellow to manage the engine; and so we have reconciled him to the custom of going on pilgrimage, and engaged him as chief engineer."

"Bravo, bravo!" exclaimed I, with irrepressible enthusiasm. "This shows the liberality of the age; this proves, if anything can, that all musty prejudices are in a fair way to be obliterated. And how will Christian rejoice to hear of this happy transformation of his old antagonist! I promise myself great pleasure in informing him of it when we reach the Celestial City."

The passengers being all comfortably seated, we now rattled away merrily, accomplishing a greater distance in ten minutes than Christian probably trudged over in a day. It was laughable, while we glanced along, as it were, at the tail of a thunderbolt, to observe two dusty foot travelers in the old pilgrim guise, with cockle shell and staff, their mystic rolls of parchment in their hands and their intolerable burdens on their backs. The preposterous obstinacy of these honest people in persisting to groan and stumble along the difficult pathway rather than take advantage of modern improvements excited great mirth among our wiser brotherhood. We greeted the two pilgrims with many pleasant gibes and a roar of laughter; whereupon they gazed at us with such woeful and absurdly compassionate visages that our merriment grew tenfold more obstreperous. Apollyon also entered heartily into the fun, and contrived to flirt the smoke and flame of the engine, or of his own breath, into their faces, and envelop them in an atmosphere of scalding steam. These little practical jokes amused us mightily, and doubtless afforded the pilgrims the gratification of considering themselves martyrs.

At some distance from the railroad, Mr. Smooth-it-away pointed to a large, antique edifice, which, he observed, was a tavern of long standing, and had formerly been a noted stopping place for pilgrims. In Bunyan's road book it is mentioned as the Interpreter's House.

"I have long had a curiosity to visit that old mansion," remarked I.

"It is not one of our stations, as you perceive," said my companion. "The keeper was violently opposed to the railroad; and well he might be, as the track left his house of entertainment on one side, and thus was pretty certain to deprive him of all his reputable customers. But the foot-path still passes his door, and the old gentleman now and then receives a call from some simple traveler, and entertains him with fare as old-fashioned as himself."

Before our talk on this subject came to a conclusion, we were rushing by the place where Christian's burden fell from his shoulders at the sight of the Cross. This served as a theme for Mr. Smooth-it-away, Mr. Live-for-the-world, Mr. Hide-sin-in-the-heart, Mr. Scaly-conscience, and a knot of gentlemen from the town of Shun-repentance, to descant upon the inestimable advantages resulting from the safety of our baggage. Myself, and all the passengers indeed, joined with great unanimity in this view of the matter; for our burdens were rich in many things esteemed precious throughout the world; and, especially, we each of us possessed a great variety of favorite Habits, which we trusted would not be out of fashion even in the polite circles of the Celestial City. It would have been a sad spectacle to see such an assortment of valuable articles tumbling into the sepulcher. Thus pleasantly conversing on the favorable circumstances of our position as compared with those of past pilgrims and of narrow-minded ones at the present day, we soon found ourselves at the foot of the Hill Difficulty. Through the very heart of this rocky mountain, a tunnel had been constructed of most admirable architecture, with a lofty arch and a spacious double track; so that, unless the earth and rocks should chance to crumble down, it will remain an eternal monument of the builder's skill and enterprise. It is a great though incidental advantage that the materials from the heart of the Hill Difficulty have been employed in filling up the Valley of Humiliation, thus obviating the necessity of descending into that disagreeable and unwholesome hollow.

"This is a wonderful improvement, indeed," said I. "Yet I should have been glad of an opportunity to visit the Palace Beautiful and be introduced to the charming young ladies—Miss Prudence, Miss Piety, Miss Charity, and the rest—who have the kindness to entertain pilgrims there."

"Young ladies!" cried Mr. Smooth-it-away, as soon as he could speak for laughing. "And charming young ladies! Why, my dear fellow, they are old maids, every soul of them—prim, starched, dry, and angular; and not one of them, I will venture to say, has altered so much as the fashion of her gown since the days of Christian's pilgrimage."

"Ah, well," said I, much comforted, "then I can very readily dispense with their acquaintance."

The respectable Apollyon was now putting on the steam at a prodigious rate, anxious, perhaps, to get rid of the unpleasant reminiscences connected with the spot where he had so disastrously encountered Christian. Consulting Mr. Bunyan's road book, I perceived that we must now be within a few miles of the Valley of the Shadow of Death, into which doleful region, at our present speed, we should plunge much sooner than seemed at all desirable. In truth, I expected nothing better than to find myself in the ditch on one side or the quag on the other; but on communicating my apprehensions to Mr. Smooth-it-away, he assured me that the difficulties of this passage, even in its worst condition, had been vastly exaggerated, and that, in its present state of improvement, I might consider myself as safe as on any railroad in Christendom.

Even while we were speaking, the train shot into the entrance of this dreaded Valley. Though I plead guilty to some foolish palpitations of the heart during our headlong rush over the causeway here constructed, yet it were unjust to withhold the highest encomiums on the boldness of its original conception and the ingenuity of those who executed it. It was gratifying, likewise, to observe how much care had been taken to dispel the everlasting gloom and supply the defect of cheerful sunshine, not a ray of which has ever penetrated among these awful shadows. For this purpose, the inflammable gas which exudes plentifully from the soil is collected by means of pipes, and thence communicated to a quadruple row of lamps along the whole extent of the passage. Thus a radiance has been created even out of the fiery and sulphurous curse that rests forever upon the valley—a radiance hurtful, however, to the eyes, and somewhat bewildering, as I discovered by the changes which it wrought in the visages of my companions. In this respect, as compared with natural daylight, there is the same difference as between truth and falsehood; but if the reader has ever traveled through the dark Valley, he will have learned to be thankful for any light that he could get—if not from the sky above, then from the blasted soil beneath. Such was the red brilliancy of these lamps that they appeared to build walls of fire on both sides of the track, between which we held our course at lightning speed, while a reverberating thunder filled the Valley with its echoes. Had the engine run off the track—a catastrophe, it is whispered, by no means unprecedented—the bottomless pit, if there be any such place, would undoubtedly have received us. Just as some dismal fooleries of this nature had made my heart quake, there came a tremendous shriek, careering along the valley as if a thousand devils had burst their lungs to utter it, but which proved to be merely the whistle of the engine on arriving at a stopping place.

The spot where we had now paused is the same that our friend Bunyan—a truthful man, but infected with many fantastic notions—had designated, in terms plainer than I like to repeat, as the mouth of the infernal region. This, however, must be a mistake, inasmuch as Mr. Smooth-it-away, while we remained in the smoky and lurid cavern, took occasion to prove that Tophet has not even a metaphorical existence. The place, he assured us, is no other than the crater of a half-extinct volcano, in which the directors had caused forges to be set up for the manufacture of railroad iron. Hence, also, is obtained a plentiful supply of fuel for the use of the engines. Whoever had gazed into the dismal obscurity of the broad cavern mouth, whence ever and anon darted huge tongues of dusky flame, and had seen the strange, half-shaped monsters, and visions of faces horribly grotesque, into which the smoke seemed to wreathe itself, and had heard the awful murmurs, and shrieks, and deep, shuddering whispers of the blast, sometimes forming themselves into words almost articulate, would have seized upon Mr. Smooth-it-away's comfortable explanation as greedily as we did. The inhabitants of the cavern, moreover, were unlovely personages, dark, smoke-begrimed, generally deformed, with misshapen feet, and a glow of dusky redness in their eyes as if their hearts had caught fire and were blazing out of the upper windows. It struck me as a peculiarity that the laborers at the forge and those who brought fuel to the engine, when they began to draw short breath, positively emitted smoke from their mouth and nostrils.

Among the idlers about the train, most of whom were puffing cigars which they had lighted at the flame of the crater, I was perplexed to notice several who, to my certain knowledge, had heretofore set forth by railroad for the Celestial City. They looked dark, wild, and smoky, with a singular resemblance, indeed, to the native inhabitants, like whom, also, they had a disagreeable propensity to ill-natured gibes and sneers, the habit of which had wrought a settled contortion of their visages. Having been on speaking terms with one of these persons—an indolent, good-for-nothing fellow, who went by the name of Take-it-easy—I called him, and inquired what was his business there.

"Did you not start," said I, "for the Celestial City?"

"That's a fact," said Mr. Take-it-easy, carelessly puffing some smoke into my eyes. "But I heard such bad accounts that I never took pains to climb the hill on which the city stands. No business doing, no fun going on, nothing to drink, and no smoking allowed, and a thrumming of church music from morning till night. I would not stay in such a place if they offered me house room and living free."

"But, my good Mr. Take-it-easy," cried I, "why take up your residence here, of all places in the world?"

"Oh," said the loafer, with a grin, "it is very warm hereabouts, and I meet with plenty of old acquaintances, and altogether the place suits me. I hope to see you back again someday soon. A pleasant journey to you."

While he was speaking, the bell of the engine rang, and we dashed away after dropping a few passengers, but receiving no new ones. Rattling onward through the Valley, we were dazzled with the fiercely gleaming gas lamps, as before. But sometimes, in the dark of intense brightness, grim faces, that bore the aspect and expression of individual sins, or evil passions, seemed to thrust themselves through the veil of light, glaring upon us, and stretching forth a great, dusky hand, as if to impede our progress. I almost thought that they were my own sins that appalled me there. These were freaks of imagination—nothing more, certainly—mere delusions, which I ought to be heartily ashamed of; but all through the Dark Valley I was tormented, and pestered, and dolefully bewildered with the same kind of waking dreams. The mephitic gases of that region intoxicate the brain. As the light of natural day, however, began to struggle with the glow of the lanterns, these vain imaginations lost their vividness, and finally vanished with the first ray of sunshine that greeted our escape from the Valley of the Shadow of Death. Ere we had gone a mile beyond it, I could well-nigh have taken my oath that this whole gloomy passage was a dream.

At the end of the valley, as John Bunyan mentions, is a cavern, where, in his days, dwelt two cruel giants, Pope and Pagan, who had strown the ground about their residence with the bones of slaughtered pilgrims. These vile old troglodytes are no longer there; but into their deserted cave another terrible giant has thrust himself, and makes it his business to seize upon honest travelers and fatten them for his table with plentiful meals of smoke, mist, moonshine, raw potatoes, and sawdust. He is a German by birth, and is called Giant Transcendentalist; but as to his form, his features, his substance, and his nature generally, it is the chief peculiarity of this huge miscreant that neither he for himself, nor anybody for him, has ever been able to describe them. As we rushed by the cavern's mouth, we caught a hasty glimpse of him, looking somewhat like an ill-proportioned figure, but considerably more like a heap of fog and duskiness. He shouted after us, but in so strange a phraseology that we knew not what he meant, nor whether to be encouraged or affrighted.

It was late in the day when the train thundered into the ancient city of Vanity, where Vanity Fair is still at the height of prosperity,

and exhibits an epitome of whatever is brilliant, gay, and fasci-
nating beneath the sun. As I purposed to make a considerable
stay here, it gratified me to learn that there is no longer the want
of harmony between the townspeople and pilgrims which im-
pelled the former to such lamentably mistaken measures as the
persecution of Christian and the fiery martyrdom of Faithful. On
the contrary, as the new railroad brings with it great trade and a
constant influx of strangers, the lord of Vanity Fair is its chief
patron, and the capitalists of the city are among the largest stockholders. Many passengers stop to take their pleasure or make their
profit in the Fair, instead of going onward to the Celestial City.
Indeed, such are the charms of the place that people often affirm
it to be the true and only heaven; stoutly contending that there
is no other, that those who seek further are mere dreamers, and
that, if the fabled brightness of the Celestial City lay but a bare
mile beyond the gates of Vanity, they would not be fools enough
to go thither. Without subscribing to these perhaps exaggerated
encomiums, I can truly say that my abode in the city was mainly
agreeable, and my intercourse with the inhabitants productive of
much amusement and instruction.

Being naturally of a serious turn, my attention was directed to
the solid advantages derivable from a residence here, rather than
to the effervescent pleasures which are the grand object with too
many visitants. The Christian reader, if he have had no accounts
of the city later than Bunyan's time, will be surprised to hear that
almost every street has its church, and that the reverend clergy
are nowhere held in higher respect than at Vanity Fair. And well
do they deserve such honorable estimation; for the maxims of
wisdom and virtue which fall from their lips come from as deep
a spiritual source, and tend to as lofty a religious aim, as those of
the sagest philosophers of old. In justification of this high praise
I need only mention the names of the Rev. Mr. Shallow-deep, the
Rev. Mr. Stumble-at-truth, that fine old clerical character the Rev.
Mr. This-today, who expects shortly to resign his pulpit to the Rev.
Mr. That-tomorrow; together with the Rev. Mr. Bewilderment, the
Rev. Mr. Clog-the-spirit, and, last and greatest, the Rev. Dr. Wind-
of-doctrine. The labors of these eminent divines are aided by
those of innumerable lecturers, who diffuse such a various pro-
fundity in all subjects of human or celestial science, that any man

may acquire an omnigenous erudition without the trouble of even learning to read. Thus literature is etherealized by assuming for its medium the human voice; and knowledge, depositing all its heavier particles, except, doubtless, its gold, becomes exhaled into a sound, which forthwith steals into the ever-open ear of the community. These ingenious methods constitute a sort of machinery, by which thought and study are done to every person's hand without his putting himself to the slightest inconvenience in the matter. There is another species of machine for the wholesale manufacture of individual morality. This excellent result is effected by societies for all manner of virtuous purposes, with which a man has merely to connect himself, throwing, as it were, his quota of virtue into the common stock, and the president and directors will take care that the aggregate amount be well applied. All these, and other wonderful improvements in ethics, religion, and literature, being made plain to my comprehension by the ingenious Mr. Smooth-it-away, inspired me with a vast admiration of Vanity Fair.

It would fill a volume, in an age of pamphlets, were I to record all my observations in this great capital of human business and pleasure. There was an unlimited range of society—the powerful, the wise, the witty, and the famous in every walk of life; princes, presidents, poets, generals, artists, actors, and philanthropists— all making their own market at the Fair, and deeming no price too exorbitant for such commodities as hit their fancy. It was well worth one's while, even if he had no idea of buying or selling, to loiter through the bazaars and observe the various sorts of traffic that were going forward.

Some of the purchasers, I thought, made very foolish bargains. For instance, a young man, having inherited a splendid fortune, laid out a considerable portion of it in the purchase of diseases, and finally spent all the rest for a heavy lot of repentance and a suit of rags. A very pretty girl bartered a heart as clear as crystal, and which seemed her most valuable possession, for another jewel of the same kind, but so worn and defaced as to be utterly worthless. In one shop, there were a great many crowns of laurel and myrtle, which soldiers, authors, statesmen, and various other people pressed eagerly to buy; some purchased these paltry wreaths with their lives, others by a toilsome servitude of years, and many

sacrificed whatever was most valuable, yet finally slunk away
without the crown. There was a sort of stock or script, called
Conscience, which seemed to be in great demand, and would
purchase almost anything. Indeed, few rich commodities were to
be obtained without paying a heavy sum in this particular stock,
and a man's business was seldom very lucrative unless he knew
precisely when and how to throw his hoard of conscience into the
market. Yet as this stock was the only thing of permanent value,
whoever parted with it was sure to find himself a loser in the long
run. Several of the speculations were of a questionable character.
Occasionally a member of Congress recruited his pocket by the
sale of his constituents; and I was assured that public officers have
often sold their country at very moderate prices. Thousands sold
their happiness for a whim. Gilded chains were in great demand,
and purchased with almost any sacrifice. In truth, those who desired, according to the old adage, to sell anything valuable for a
song, might find customers all over the Fair; and there were innumerable messes of pottage, piping hot, for such as chose to buy
them with their birthrights. A few articles, however, could not be
found genuine at Vanity Fair. If a customer wished to renew his
stock of youth, the dealers offered him a set of false teeth and an
auburn wig; if he demanded peace of mind, they recommended
opium or a brandy bottle.

Tracts of land and golden mansions, situated in the Celestial
City, were often exchanged, at very disadvantageous rates, for a
few years' lease of small, dismal, inconvenient tenements in Vanity
Fair. Prince Beelzebub himself took great interest in this sort of
traffic, and sometimes condescended to meddle with smaller matters. I once had the pleasure to see him bargaining with a miser
for his soul, which, after much ingenious skirmishing on both
sides, his highness succeeded in obtaining at about the value of
sixpence. The Prince remarked, with a smile, that he was a loser
by the transaction.

Day after day, as I walked the streets of Vanity, my manners and
deportment became more and more like those of the inhabitants.
The place began to seem like home; the idea of pursuing my
travels to the Celestial City was almost obliterated from my mind.
I was reminded of it, however, by the sight of the same pair of
simple pilgrims at whom we had laughed so heartily when Apol-

lyon puffed smoke and steam into their faces at the commence-
ment of our journey. There they stood amidst the densest bustle
of Vanity; the dealers offering them their purple and fine linen
and jewels, the men of wit and humor gibing at them, a pair of
buxom ladies ogling them askance, while the benevolent Mr.
Smooth-it-away whispered some of his wisdom at their elbows, and
pointed to a newly erected temple; but there were these worthy
simpletons, making the scene look wild and monstrous, merely by
their sturdy repudiation of all part in its business or pleasures.

One of them—his name was Stick-to-the-right—perceived in
my face, I suppose, a species of sympathy and almost admiration,
which, to my own great surprise, I could not help feeling for this
pragmatic couple. It prompted him to address me.

"Sir," inquired he, with a sad, yet mild and kindly voice, "do
you call yourself a pilgrim?"

"Yes," I replied, "my right to that appellation is indubitable. I
am merely a sojourner here in Vanity Fair, being bound to the
Celestial City by the new railroad."

"Alas, friend," rejoined Mr. Stick-to-the-right, "I do assure you,
and beseech you to receive the truth of my words, that that whole
concern is a bubble. You may travel on it all your lifetime, were
you to live thousands of years, and yet never get beyond the limits
of Vanity Fair. Yea, though you should deem yourself entering the
gates of the blessed city, it will be nothing but a miserable
delusion."

"The Lord of the Celestial City," began the other pilgrim,
whose name was Mr. Foot-it-to-heaven, "has refused, and will ever
refuse, to grant an act of incorporation for this railroad; and unless that be obtained, no passenger can ever hope to enter his
dominions. Wherefore every man who buys a ticket must lay his
account with losing the purchase money, which is the value of
his own soul."

"Poh, nonsense!" said Mr. Smooth-it-away, taking my arm and
leading me off, "these fellows ought to be indicted for a libel. If
the law stood as it once did in Vanity Fair, we should see them
grinning through the iron bars of the prison window."

This incident made a considerable impression on my mind, and
contributed with other circumstances to indispose me to a permanent residence in the city of Vanity; although, of course, I was

not simple enough to give up my original plan of gliding along easily and commodiously by railroad. Still, I grew anxious to be gone. There was one strange thing that troubled me. Amid the occupations or amusements of the Fair, nothing was more common than for a person—whether at feast, theatre, or church, or trafficking for wealth and honors, or whatever he might be doing, and however unseasonable the interruption—suddenly to vanish like a soap bubble, and be never more seen of his fellows; and so accustomed were the latter to such little accidents that they went on with their business as quietly as if nothing had happened. But it was otherwise with me.

Finally, after a pretty long residence at the Fair, I resumed my journey towards the Celestial City, still with Mr. Smooth-it-away at my side. At a short distance beyond the suburbs of Vanity, we passed the ancient silver mine, of which Demas was the first discoverer, and which is now wrought to great advantage, supplying nearly all the coined currency of the world. A little further onward was the spot where Lot's wife had stood forever under the semblance of a pillar of salt. Curious travelers have long since carried it away piecemeal. Had all regrets been punished as rigorously as this poor dame's were, my yearning for the relinquished delights of Vanity Fair might have produced a similar change in my own corporeal substance, and left me a warning to future pilgrims.

The next remarkable object was a large edifice, constructed of moss-grown stone, but in a modern and airy style of architecture. The engine came to a pause in its vicinity, with the usual tremendous shriek.

"This was formerly the castle of the redoubted giant Despair," observed Mr. Smooth-it-away, "but since his death, Mr. Flimsy-faith has repaired it, and keeps an excellent house of entertainment here. It is one of our stopping places."

"It seems but slightly put together," remarked I, looking at the frail yet ponderous walls. "I do not envy Mr. Flimsy-faith his habitation. Someday it will thunder down upon the heads of the occupants."

"We shall escape at all events," said Mr. Smooth-it-away, "for Apollyon is putting on the steam again."

The road now plunged into a gorge of the Delectable Mountains, and traversed the field where in former ages the blind men wandered and stumbled among the tombs. One of these ancient tombstones had been thrust across the track by some malicious person, and gave the train of cars a terrible jolt. Far up the rugged side of a mountain I perceived a rusty iron door, half overgrown with bushes and creeping plants, but with smoke issuing from its crevices.

"Is that," inquired I, "the very door in the hillside which the shepherds assured Christian was a byway to hell?"

"That was a joke on the part of the shepherds," said Mr. Smooth-it-away, with a smile. "It is neither more nor less than the door of a cavern which they use as a smokehouse for the preparation of mutton hams."

My recollections of the journey are now, for a little space, dim and confused, inasmuch as a singular drowsiness here overcame me, owing to the fact that we were passing over the enchanted ground, the air of which encourages a disposition to sleep. I awoke, however, as soon as we crossed the borders of the pleasant land of Beulah. All the passengers were rubbing their eyes, comparing watches, and congratulating one another on the prospect of arriving so seasonably at the journey's end. The sweet breezes of this happy clime came refreshingly to our nostrils; we beheld the glimmering gush of silver fountains, overhung by trees of beautiful foliage and delicious fruit, which were propagated by grafts from the celestial gardens. Once, as we dashed onward like a hurricane, there was a flutter of wings and the bright appearance of an angel in the air, speeding forth on some heavenly mission. The engine now announced the close vicinity of the final station house by one last and horrible scream, in which there seemed to be distinguishable every kind of wailing and woe, and bitter fierceness of wrath, all mixed up with the wild laughter of a devil or a madman. Throughout our journey, at every stopping place, Apollyon had exercised his ingenuity in screwing the most abominable sounds out of the whistle of the steam engine; but in this closing effort he outdid himself and created an infernal uproar, which, besides disturbing the peaceful inhabitants of Beulah, must have sent its discord even through the celestial gates.

While the horrid clamor was still ringing in our ears, we heard an exulting strain, as if a thousand instruments of music, with height and depth and sweetness in their tones, at once tender and triumphant, were struck in unison, to greet the approach of some illustrious hero, who had fought the good fight and won a glorious victory, and was come to lay aside his battered arms for-ever. Looking to ascertain what might be the occasion of this glad harmony, I perceived, on alighting from the cars, that a multitude of shining ones had assembled on the other side of the river, to welcome two poor pilgrims, who were just emerging from its depths. They were the same whom Apollyon and ourselves had persecuted with taunts, and gibes, and scalding steam, at the com-mencement of our journey—the same whose unworldly aspect and impressive words had stirred my conscience amid the wild revelers of Vanity Fair.

"How amazingly well those men have got on," cried I to Mr. Smooth-it-away. "I wish we were secure of as good a reception."

"Never fear, never fear!" answered my friend. "Come, make haste; the ferryboat will be off directly, and in three minutes you will be on the other side of the river. No doubt you will find coaches to carry you up to the city gates."

A steam ferryboat, the last improvement on this important route, lay at the riverside, puffing, snorting, and emitting all those other disagreeable utterances which betoken the departure to be immediate. I hurried on board with the rest of the passengers, most of whom were in great perturbation: some bawling out for their baggage; some tearing their hair and exclaiming that the boat would explode or sink; some already pale with the heaving of the stream; some gazing affrighted at the ugly aspect of the steersman; and some still dizzy with the slumberous influences of the Enchanted Ground. Looking back to the shore, I was amazed to discern Mr. Smooth-it-away waving his hand in token of fare-well.

"Don't you go over to the Celestial City?" exclaimed I.

"Oh, no!" answered he with a queer smile, and that same dis-agreeable contortion of visage which I had remarked in the in-habitants of the Dark Valley. "Oh, no! I have come thus far only for the sake of your pleasant company. Good-bye! We shall meet again."

And then did my excellent friend Mr. Smooth-it-away laugh out-right, in the midst of which cachinnation a smoke wreath issued from his mouth and nostrils, while a twinkle of lurid flame darted out of either eye, proving indubitably that his heart was all of a red blaze. The impudent fiend! To deny the existence of Tophet, when he felt its fiery tortures raging within his breast. I rushed to the side of the boat, intending to fling myself on shore; but the wheels, as they began their revolutions, threw a dash of spray over me so cold—so deadly cold, with the chill that will never leave those waters until Death be drowned in his own river—that with a shiver and a heartquake I awoke. Thank Heaven it was a dream!

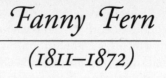

Fanny Fern

(1811–1872)

Under the pseudonym Fanny Fern, Sara Willis Parton (Parton was her third husband's name) wrote an outspoken newspaper column at a time when women writers were supposed to stick to writing "feminine" novels. She was in fact known until recently only as a minor sentimentalist. But her highly popular columns were ferociously funny, sharply satirical, and by nineteenth-century standards extremely "unfeminine." With her "Fanny Fern's Column," first published in 1852, Parton became the first woman newspaper columnist in the modern sense of being paid to write a regularly published essay of social and political opinion. By 1855 the *New York Ledger* was paying her one hundred dollars a column, making her the highest-paid newspaper writer in the country. In addition to her columns, Parton is the author of a satirical novel, *Ruth Hall* (a book that was widely criticized for its depiction of a self-reliant financially independent woman), and of several books for children. Several selections from her newspaper column are printed here.

Have We Any Men Among Us?

WALKING ALONG the street the other day, my eye fell upon this placard,—

MEN WANTED

Well; they have been "wanted" for some time; but the article is not in the market, although there are plenty of spurious imitations. Time was, when a lady could decline writing for a newspaper without subjecting herself to paragraphic attacks from the editor, invading the sanctity of her private life. Time was, when she could decline writing without the editor's revenging himself, by asserting falsely that "he had often refused her offered contributions?" Time was, when if an editor heard a vague rumor affecting a lady's reputation, he did not endorse it by republication, and then meanly screen himself from responsibility by adding, "we presume, however, that this is only an *on dit*!" Time was, when a lady could be a successful authoress, without being obliged to give an account to the dear public of the manner in which she appropriated the proceeds of her honest labors. Time was, when whiskered braggadocios in railroad cars and steamboats did not assert, (in blissful ignorance that they were looking the lady authoress straight in the face!) that they were "on the most intimate terms of friendship with her!" Time was, when *milk-and-water husbands and relatives* did not force a defamed woman to unsex herself in the manner stated in the following paragraph:

"Man Shot by a Young Woman,—One day last week, a young lady of good character, daughter of Col.————, having been calumniated by a young man, called upon him, armed with a revolver. The slanderer could not, or did not deny his allegations; whereupon she fired, inflicting a dangerous if not a fatal wound in his throat."

Yes; it is very true that there are "MEN wanted." Wonder how many 1854 will furnish?

Musical World and Times
Sept. 24, 1853

Tom Pax's Conjugal Soliloquy

MRS. PAX is an authoress. I knew it when I married her. I liked
the idea. I had not tried it then. I had not a clear idea what it
was to have one's wife belong to the public. I thought marriage
was marriage, brains not excepted. I was mistaken. Mrs. Pax is
very kind: I don't wish to say that she is not. Very obliging: I would
not have you think the contrary; but when I put my arm round
Mrs. Pax's waist, and say, "Mary, I love you," she smiles in an
absent, moonlight-kind of a way, and says, "Yes, to-day is Wednesday, is it not? I must write an article for 'The Weekly Monopolizer'
to-day." That dampens my ardor; but presently I say again, being
naturally affectionate, "Mary, I love you;" she replies (still ab-
stractedly), "Thank you, how do you think it will do to call my
next article for 'The Weekly Monopolizer,' 'The Stray Waif?' "

Mrs. Pax sews on all my shirt-buttons with the greatest good
humor: I would not have you think she does not; but with her
thoughts still on "The Weekly Monopolizer," she sews them on
the flaps, instead of the wristbands. This is inconvenient; still Mrs.
Pax is kindness itself; I make no complaint.

I am very fond of walking. After dinner I say to Mrs. Pax, "Mary,
let us take a walk." She says, "Yes, certainly, I must go down town
to read the proof of my article for 'The Monopolizer.' " So, I go
down town with Mrs. Pax. After tea I say, "Mary, let us go to the
theater to-night;" she says, "I would be very happy to go, but the
atmosphere is so bad there, the gas always escapes, and my head
must be clear to-morrow, you know, for I have to write the last
chapter of my forthcoming work, 'Prairie Life.' " So I stay at
home with Mrs. Pax, and as I sit down by her on the sofa, and as
nobody comes in, I think that this, after all, is better, (though I
must say my wife looks well at the Opera, and I like to take her
there). I put my arm around Mrs. Pax. It is a habit I have. In
comes the servant; and brings a handful of letters for her by mail,
directed to "Julia Jesamine!" (that's my wife's *nom-de-plume*). I
remove my arm from her waist, because she says "they are probably business letters which require immediate notice." She sits
down at the table, and breaks the seals. Four of them are from
fellows who want "her autograph." *Mrs. Pax's* autograph! The

fifth is from a gentleman who, delighted with her last book, which he says "mirrored his own soul" (how do you suppose Mrs. Pax found out how to "mirror *his* soul?") requests "permission to correspond with the charming authoress." "Charming!" my wife! "his soul!" Mrs. Pax! The sixth is from a gentleman who desires "the loan of five hundred dollars, as he has been unfortunate in business, and has heard that her works have been very remunerative." Five hundred dollars for John Smith, from my wife! The seventh letter is from a man at the West, offering her her own price to deliver a lecture before the Pigtown Young Men's Institute. *I like that!*

Mrs. Pax opens her writing desk; it is one I gave her; takes some delicate buff note-paper; I gave her that, too; dips her gold pen (my gift) into the inkstand, and writes—writes till eleven o'clock. Eleven! and I, her husband, Tom Pax, sit there and wait for her.

The next morning when I awake, I say, "Mary dear?" She says, "Hush! don't speak, I've just got a capital subject to write about for 'The Weekly Monopolizer.' " Not that I am *complaining* of Mrs. Pax, not at all; not that I don't like my wife to be an authoress; I do. To be sure I can't say that I knew *exactly* what it involved. I did not know, for instance, that the Press in speaking of her by her *nom-de-plume* would call her "OUR Julia," but I would not have you think I object to her being literary. On the contrary, I am not sure that I do not rather like it; but I ask the Editor of "The Weekly Monopolizer," as a man—as a Christian—as a husband —if he thinks it right—if it is doing as he would be done by—to monopolize my wife's thoughts as early as five o'clock in the morning? I merely ask for information. I trust I have no resentful feelings toward the animal.

New York Ledger
Feb. 9, 1856

To Gentlemen

A CALL TO BE A HUSBAND

YES, I did say that "it is not every man who has a call to be a husband;" and I am not going to back out of it.

Has that man a call to be a husband, who, having wasted his youth in excesses, looks around him at the eleventh hour for a "virtuous young girl" (such men have the effrontery to be *very* particular on this point), to nurse up his damaged constitution, and perpetuate it in their offspring?

Has that man a call to be a husband, who, believing that the more the immortal within us is developed in this world, the higher we shall rank with heavenly intelligences in the next, yet deprecates for a wife a woman of thought and intellect, lest a marriage with such should peril the seasoning of his favorite pudding, or lest she might presume in any of her opinions to be aught else than his echo?

Has that man a call to be a husband, who, when the rosy maiden he married is transformed by too early an introduction to the cares and trials of maternity, into a feeble, confirmed invalid, turns impatiently from the restless wife's sick-room, to sun himself in the perfidious smile of one whom he would blush to name in that wife's pure ears?

Has *he* any call to be a husband, who adds to his wife's manifold cares that of selecting and providing the household stores, and inquires of her, at that, how she spent the surplus shilling of yesterday's appropriation?

Has *he* any call to be a husband, who permits his own relatives, in his hearing, to speak disrespectfully or censoriously of his wife?

Has *he* any call to be a husband, who reads the newspaper from beginning to end, giving notice of his presence to the weary wife, who is patiently mending his old coat, only by an occasional "Jupiter!" which may mean, to the harrowed listener, that we have a President worth standing in a driving rain, at the tail of a three-mile procession, to vote for, or—the contrary? and who, after having extracted every particle of news the paper contains, coolly puts it in one of his many mysterious pockets, and goes to sleep in his chair?

Has *he* a call to be a husband, who carries a letter, intended for his wife, in his pocket for six weeks, and expects any thing short of "gunpowder tea" for his supper that night?

Has he a call to be a husband, who leaves his wife to blow out the lamp, and stub her precious little toes while she is navigating for the bed-post?

Has he a call to be a husband, who tells his wife "to walk on a couple of blocks and he will overtake her," and then joins in a hot political discussion with an opponent, after which, in a fit of absence of mind, he walks off home, leaving his wife transformed by his perfidy into "a pillar of salt?"

Has he any call to be a husband, who sits down on his wife's best bonnet, or puts her shawl over her shoulders upside down, or wrong side out at the Opera?

Has he any call to be a husband, who goes "unbeknown" to his wife, to some wretch of a barber, and parts, for twenty-five cents, with a beard which she has coaxed from its first infantile sprout, to luxuriant, full-grown, magnificent, unsurpassable hirsuteness, and then comes home to her horrified vision a pocket edition of Moses?

New York Ledger
November 1, 1856

Has a Mother a Right to Her Children?

MOST UNQUESTIONABLY, law or no law. Let us begin at the beginning. Let us take into consideration the physical prostration of mind and body endured by mothers antecedent to the birth of their off-spring; their extreme nervousness and restlessness, without the ability for locomotion; the great nameless horror which hangs over those who, for the first time, are called upon to endure agonies that no man living would have fortitude to bear more than once, even at their shortest period of duration; and which, to those who have passed through it, is intensified by the vivid recollection (the only verse in the Bible which I call in question being this—"She remembereth no more her pains, for joy that a man-child is born into the world"). Granted that the mother's life is spared through this terrible ordeal, she rises from her sick-bed, after weeks of prostration, with the precious burden in her arms which she carried so long and so patiently beneath her heart. Oh, the continuous, tireless watching necessary to preserve the life and limbs of this fragile little thing! At a time, too, of all times, when the mother most needs relaxation and repose. It is known only to those who have passed through it. Its reward is with Him who seeth in secret.

I speak now only of *good* mothers; mothers who deserve the high and holy name. Mothers who in their unselfish devotion look not at their capacity to endure, but the duties allotted to them (would that husbands and fathers did not so often leave it to the tombstone to call their attention to the former). Mothers, whose fragile hands keep the domestic treadmill in as unerring motion as if no new care was superadded in the feeble wail of the new-born infant. Mothers whose work is literally *never* done; who sleep with one eye open, entrusting to no careless hireling the precious little life. Mothers who can scarce secure to themselves five minutes of the morning hours free from interruption, to ask God's help that a feeble, tried woman may hold evenly the scales of domestic justice amid the conflicting elements of human needs and human frailties. Now I ask you—shall any human law, for any conceivable reason, wrest the child of such a mother from her frenzied clasp?

Shall any human law give into a man's hand, though that man be the child's own father, the sole right to its direction and disposal? Has not she, who suffered, martyr-like, these crucifying pains—these wearisome days and sleepless nights, *earned* this her sweet reward?

Shall any virtuous woman, who is in the full possession of her mental faculties, how poor soever she may be, be *beggared* by robbing her of that which has been, and, thank God! will be the salvation of many a downtrodden wife?

New York Ledger
Apr. 4, 1857

Fresh Leaves

BY FANNY FERN

THIS LITTLE VOLUME has just been laid upon our table. The publishers have done all they could for it, with regard to outward adorning. No doubt it will be welcomed by those who admire this lady's style of writing: we confess ourselves not to be of that number. We have never seen Fanny Fern, nor do we desire to do so. We imagine her, from her writings, to be a muscular, black-browed, grenadier-looking female, who would be more at home in a boxing gallery than in a parlor,—a vociferous, demonstrative, strong-minded horror,—a woman only by virtue of her dress. Bah! the very thought sickens us. We have read, or, rather, tried to read, her halloo-there effusions. When we take up a woman's book we expect to find gentleness, timidity, and that lovely reliance on the patronage of our sex which constitutes a woman's greatest charm. We do not wish to be startled by bold expressions, or disgusted with exhibitions of masculine weaknesses. We do not desire to see a woman wielding the scimitar blade of sarcasm. If she be, unfortunately, endowed with a gift so dangerous, let her —as she values the approbation of our sex—fold it in a napkin. Fanny's strong-minded nose would probably turn up at this inducement. Thank heaven! there are still women who *are* women —who know the place Heaven assigned them, and keep it—who do not waste floods of ink and paper, brow-beating men and stirring up silly women;—who do not teach children that a game of romps is of as much importance as Blair's Philosophy;—who have not the presumption to advise clergymen as to their duties, or lecture doctors, and savants;—who live for something else than to astonish a gaping, idiotic crowd. Thank heaven! there are women writers who do not disturb our complacence or serenity; whose books lull one to sleep like a strain of gentle music; who excite no antagonism, or angry feeling. Woman never was intended for an irritant: she should be oil upon the troubled waters of manhood—soft and amalgamating, a necessary but unobtrusive ingredient;—never challenging attention—never throwing the gauntlet of defiance to a beard, but softly purring beside it lest it bristle and scratch.

The very fact that Fanny Fern has, in the language of her admirers, "elbowed her way through unheard of difficulties," shows that she is an antagonistic, pugilistic female. One must needs, forsooth, get out of her way, or be pushed to one side, or trampled down. How much more womanly to have allowed herself to be doubled up by adversity, and quietly laid away on the shelf of fate, than to have rolled up her sleeves, and gone to fisticuffs with it. Such a woman may conquer, it is true, but her victory will cost her dear; it will neither be forgotten nor forgiven—let her put that in her apron pocket.

As to Fanny Fern's grammar, rhetoric, and punctuation, they are beneath criticism. It is all very well for her to say, those who wish commas, semi-colons and periods, must look for them in the printer's case, or that she who finds ideas must not be expected to find rhetoric or grammar; for our part, we should be gratified if we had even found any ideas!

We regret to be obliged to speak thus of a lady's book: it gives us great pleasure, when we can do so conscientiously, to pat lady writers on the head; but we owe a duty to the public which will not permit us to recommend to their favorable notice an aspirant who has been unwomanly enough so boldly to contest every inch of ground in order to reach them—an aspirant at once so high-stepping and so ignorant, so plausible, yet so pernicious. We have a conservative horror of this pop-gun, torpedo female; we predict for Fanny Fern's "Leaves" only a fleeting autumnal flutter.

New York Ledger
Oct. 10, 1857

A Chapter for Parents

THERE IS one great defect in the present system of family education. Not that there is only one; but we wish to call attention at present to the practice of obliging the *girls* of a family, in almost every instance in which self-denial is involved, to give way to the boys. "Remember he is your brother," is the appeal to tender little hearts, which, though often swelling under a sense of injustice, naturally give way under this argument. This might be all very well, were the boys also taught reciprocity in this matter, but as this unfortunately is not often the case, a monstrous little tyrant is produced whose overbearing exactions and hourly selfishnesses are disgusting to witness. As years roll on, Augustus's handkerchiefs are hemmed at half a wink from his lordship that he wishes it done, and his breakfast kept hot for him, though he change his breakfast hour as often as the disgusted cook leaves her place; while his sister's faintest intimation of her desire for his escort of an evening is met with a yawn, and an allusion to "the fellows" who are always "expecting him." It is easy to see what delightful ideas of reciprocity in mutual good offices Augustus will carry into the conjugal state, if he ever marries. His bride soon finds this out to her dismay, and half a dozen babies, and her wakeful nights and careworn days, are no excuse for not always placing his clean linen on a chair by his bed when needed, "to save him the trouble of opening his bureau drawers." "Before he was married" his handkerchiefs were always laid in a pile in the north-east corner of his drawer, duly perfumed, and with the exquisite word "*Augustus*" embroidered in the corner.—And *now*! "Before he was married" he was always consulted about the number of plums in his pudding.—And *now*! "Before he was married" he was never bothered to wait upon a woman of an evening unless he chose. —And *now*! "Before he was married" he had his breakfast any time between seven in the morning and three in the afternoon. —And *now*!

And so the poor weary woman hears the changes rung upon the newly-discovered virtues and perfections of his family, till she heartily wishes he had never left them. It never once occurs meanwhile to the domestic Nero to look at the *other* side of the question. How should it? when all his life at home was one ovation to his vanity and selfishness. "He could never bear contradiction! dear Augustus couldn't;" so he must never be contradicted. His friends must either agree with him or be silent, "because a contrary course always vexed him." Now we beg all mothers, who are thus educating domestic tyrants in their nurseries, to have some regard for the wife of his future, waiting for him somewhere, all unconscious, poor thing! of her fate; even if they have none on his sisters and themselves.

The most interesting story we read, was one which did *not* end as usual, with the marriage of the children of the family, but followed them into homes of their own, where the results of affectionate and at the same time *judicious* home-training manifested themselves in their beautiful, unselfish lives. It would do no harm, if mothers would sometimes ask themselves, when looking at their boys, what sort of *husband* am I educating for somebody? It is very common to think what sort of *wife* a *daughter* may make. Surely the former question, although so seldom occurring, is no less important.

New York Ledger
Aug. 29, 1863

James Russell Lowell
(1819–1891)

Being born a Lowell in nineteenth-century New England meant becoming a part of a Brahmin caste of writers, ministers, scholars, and industrialists. James's father was pastor of the West Church in Boston, and numerous judges and civic leaders were among his relatives. He himself was a professor of modern languages at Harvard, editor of the *Atlantic Monthly* and the *North American Review,* and finally the American ambassador to London toward the end of his life. What could make a man who would otherwise appear perfectly comfortable with the status quo become first a great reformer and then a great satirist? Only a great evil: slavery. Even though the abolitionist movement had many men of intellectual and social distinction among its adherents, they joined the movement at some risk to their standing among members of their social class. And Lowell's interests in reform went beyond his opposition to slavery in the American South to opposition to tyranny around the world. "Absolute freedom is what I want," he wrote in a letter to a friend in 1845, "for the body first, and then for the mind."

His first published piece of satirical writing, reproduced here as our first selection from *The Biglow Papers,* was a poem inspired by a team of recruiters that had come to Boston to find volunteers for the Mexican War. The "author" of the poem, Hosea Biglow, a New Englander of homely common sense who speaks in a rustic dialect, was to become Lowell's vehicle for expressing strong opinions on a variety of social and political issues. The first poems were published in newspapers, including the weekly *National Anti-*

Slavery Standard, and all were eventually gathered into two books, each a carefully sustained and brilliantly executed satire. Even the books' design—it includes satirical blurbs in the first pages—makes an ironic point.

The Biglow Papers

NO. I. A LETTER

FROM MR. EZEKIEL BIGLOW OF JAALAM
TO THE HON. JOSEPH T. BUCKINGHAM,
EDITOR OF THE BOSTON COURIER,
INCLOSING A POEM OF HIS SON,
MR. HOSEA BIGLOW.

JAYLEM, june 1846.

MISTER EDDYTER:—Our Hosea wuz down to Boston last week, and he see a cruetin Sarjunt a struttin round as popler as a hen with 1 chicking, with 2 fellers a drummin and fifin arter him like all nater. the sarjunt he thout Hosea hedn't gut his i teeth cut cos he looked a kindo's though he'd jest com down, so he cal'lated to hook him in, but Hosy woodn't take none o' his sarse for all he hed much as 20 Rooster's tales stuck onto his hat and eenamost enuf brass a bobbin up and down on his shoulders and figureed onto his coat and trousis, let alone wut nater hed sot in his featers, to make a 6 pounder out on.

wal, Hosea he com home considerabal riled, and arter I'd gone to bed I heern Him a thrashin round like a short-tailed Bull in fli-time. The old Woman ses she to me ses she, Zekle, ses she, our Hosee's gut the chollery or suthin anuther ses she, don't you Bee skeered, ses I, he's oney amakin pottery* ses i, he's ollers on hand at that ere busynes like Da & martin, and shure enuf, cum mornin, Hosy he cum down stares full chizzle, hare on eend and cote tales flyin, and sot rite of to go reed his varses to Parson Wilbur bein he haint aney grate shows o' book larnin himself, bimeby he

* *Aut insanit, aut versos facit.*—H.W.

cum back and sed the parson wuz dreffle tickled with 'em as i hoop you will Be, and said they wuz True grit.

Hosea ses taint hardly fair to call 'em hisn now, cos the parson kind o' slicked off sum o' the last varses, but he told Hosee he didn't want to put his ore in to tetch to the Rest on 'em, bein they wuz verry well As thay wuz, and then Hosy ses he sed suthin a nuther about Simplex Mundishes or sum sech feller, but I guess Hosea kind o' didn't hear him, for I never hearn o' nobody o' that name in this villadge, and I've lived here man and boy 76 year cum next tater diggin, and thair aint no wheres a kitting spryer 'n I be.

If you print 'em I wish you'd jest let folks know who hosy's father is, cos my ant Keziah used to say it's nater to be curus ses she, she aint livin though and he's a likely kind o' lad.

EZEKIEL BIGLOW.

THRASH away, you'll *hev* to rattle
    On them kittle drums o' yourn,—
'Taint a knowin' kind o' cattle
    Thet is ketched with mouldy corn;
Put in stiff, you fifer feller,
    Let folks see how spry you be,—
Guess you'll toot till you are yeller
    'Fore you git ahold o' me!

Thet air flag's a leetle rotten,
    Hope it aint your Sunday's best;—
Fact! it takes a sight o' cotton
    To stuff out a soger's chest:
Sence we farmers hev to pay fer 't,
    Ef you must wear humps like these,
Sposin' you should try salt hay fer 't,
    It would du ez slick ez grease.

'T would n't suit them Southun fellers,
    They're a dreffle graspin' set,
We must ollers blow the bellers
    Wen they want their irons het;
May be it's all right ez preachin',

But *my* narves it kind o' grates,
Wen I see the overreachin'
  O' them nigger-drivin' States.

Them thet rule us, them slave-traders,
  Haint they cut a thunderin' swarth,
(Helped by Yankee renegaders,)
  Thru the vartu o' the North!
We begin to think it's nater
  To take sarse an' not be riled;—
Who'd expect to see a tater
  All on eend at bein' biled?

Ez fer war, I call it murder,—
  There you hev it plain an' flat;
I don't want to go no furder
  Than my Testyment fer that;
God hez sed so plump an' fairly,
  It's ez long ez it is broad,
An' you've gut to git up airly
  Ef you want to take in God.

'Taint your eppyletts an' feathers
  Make the thing a grain more right;
'Taint afollerin' your bell-wethers
  Will excuse ye in His sight;
Ef you take a sword an' dror it,
  An' go stick a feller thru,
Guv'ment aint to answer for it,
  God'll send the bill to you.

Wut's the use o' meetin-goin'
  Every Sabbath, wet or dry,
Ef it's right to go amowin'
  Feller-men like oats an' rye?
I dunno but wut it's pooty
  Trainin' round in bobtail coats,
But it's curus Christian dooty
  This ere cuttin' folks's throats.

They may talk o' Freedom's airy
   Tell they're pupple in the face,—
It's a grand gret cemetary
   Fer the barthrights of our race;
They jest want this Californy
   So's to lug new slave-states in
To abuse ye, an' to scorn ye,
   An' to plunder ye like sin.

Aint it cute to see a Yankee
   Take sech everlastin' pains,
All to git the Devil's thankee,
   Helpin' on 'em weld their chains?
Wy, it's jest ez clear ez figgers,
   Clear ez one an' one make two,
Chaps thet make black slaves o' niggers
   Want to make wite slaves o' you.

Tell ye jest the eend I've come to
   Arter cipherin' plaguy smart,
An' it makes a handy sum, tu,
   Any gump could larn by heart;
Laborin' man an' laborin' woman
   Hev one glory an' one shame,
Ev'y thin' thet's done inhuman
   Injers all on 'em the same.

'Taint by turnin' out to hack folks
   You're agoin' to git your right,
Nor by lookin' down on black folks
   Coz you're put upon by wite;
Slavery aint o' nary color,
   'Taint the hide thet makes it wus,
All it keers fer in a feller
   'S jest to make him fill its pus.

Want to tackle *me* in, du ye?
   I expect you'll hev to wait;
Wen cold lead puts daylight thru ye
   You'll begin to kal'late;

'Spose the crows wun't fall to pickin'
    All the carkiss from your bones.
Coz you helped to give a lickin'
    To them poor half-Spanish drones?

Jest go home an' ask our Nancy
    Wether I'd be sech a goose
Ez to jine ye,—guess you'd fancy
    The etarnal bung wuz loose!
She wants me fer home consumption,
    Let alone the hay's to mow,—
Ef you're arter folks o' gumption,
    You've a darned long row to hoe.

Take them editors thet's crowin'
    Like a cockerel three months old,—
Don't ketch any on 'em goin',
    Though they *be* so blasted bold;
Aint they a prime lot o' fellers?
    'Fore they think on 't guess they'll sprout.
(Like a peach thet's got the yellers.)
    With the meanness bustin' out.

Wal, go 'long to help 'em stealin'
    Bigger pens to cram with slaves,
Help the men thet's ollers dealin'
    Insults on your fathers' graves;
Help the strong to grind the feeble,
    Help the many agin the few,
Help the men thet call your people
    Witewashed slaves an' peddlin' crew!

Massachusetts, God forgive her,
    She's akneelin' with the rest,
She, thet ough' to ha' clung fer ever
    In her grand old eagle-nest;
She thet ough' to stand so fearless
    Wile the wracks are round her hurled,
Holdin' up a beacon peerless
    To the oppressed of all the world!

Haint they sold your colored seamen?
   Haint they made your env'ys wiz?
Wut 'll make ye act like freemen?
   Wut 'll git your dander riz?
Come, I'll tell ye wut I'm thinkin'
   Is our dooty in this fix,
They'd ha' done 't ez quick ez winkin'
   In the days o' seventy-six.

Clang the bells in every steeple,
   Call all true men to disown
The tradoocers of our people,
   The enslavers o' their own;
Let our dear old Bay State proudly
   Put the trumpet to her mouth,
Let her ring this messidge loudly
   In the ears of all the South:—

"I'll return ye good fer evil
   Much ez we frail mortils can,
But I wun't go help the Devil
   Makin' man the cus o' man;
Call me coward, call me traiter,
   Jest ez suits your mean idees,—
Here I stand a tyrant-hater,
   An' the friend o' God an' Peace!"

Ef I'd *my* way I hed ruther
   We should go to work an' part,—
They take one way, we take t'other,—
   Guess it would n't break my heart;
Man hed ough' to put asunder
   Them thet God has noways jined;
An' I should n't gretly wonder
   Ef there's thousands o' my mind.

[The first recruiting sergeant on record I conceive to have been that individual who is mentioned in the Book of Job as *going to and fro in the earth, and walking up and down in it*. Bishop Latimer will have him to have been a bishop, but to me that

other calling would appear more congenial. The sect of Cainites
is not yet extinct, who esteemed the first-born of Adam to be
the most worthy, not only because of that privilege of primogen-
iture, but inasmuch as he was able to overcome and slay his
younger brother. That was a wise saying of the famous Marquis
Pescara to the Papal Legate, that *it was impossible for men to serve
Mars and Christ at the same time.* Yet in time past the profession
of arms was judged to be κατ' εξοχήν that of a gentleman, nor
does this opinion want for strenuous upholders even in our day.
Must we suppose, then, that the profession of Christianity was
only intended for losels, or, at best, to afford an opening for
plebeian ambition? Or shall we hold with that nicely metaphysi-
cal Pomeranian, Captain Vratz, who was Count Königsmark's
chief instrument in the murder of Mr. Thynne, that the Scheme
of Salvation has been arranged with an especial eye to the necessities of the upper classes, and that "God would consider *a
gentleman* and deal with him suitably to the condition and profession he had placed him in"? It may be said of us all, *Exemplo
plus quam ratione vivimus.*—H.W.]

No. III. What Mr. Robinson Thinks.

[A few remarks on the following verses will not be out of place.
The satire in them was not meant to have any personal, but
only a general, application. Of the gentleman upon whose letter
they were intended as a commentary Mr. Biglow had never
heard, till he saw the letter itself. The position of the satirist is
oftentimes one which he would not have chosen, had the election been left to himself. In attacking bad principles, he is
obliged to select some individual who has made himself their
exponent, and in whom they are impersonate, to the end that
what he says may not, through ambiguity, be dissipated *tenues in
auras.* For what says Seneca? *Longum iter per præcepta, breve et effi-
cace per exempla.* A bad principle is comparatively harmless while
it continues to be an abstraction, nor can the general mind
comprehend it fully till it is printed in that large type which all
men can read at sight, namely, the life and character, the say-
ings and doings, of particular persons. It is one of the cunning-

est fetches of Satan, that he never exposes himself directly to our arrows, but, still dodging behind this neighbour or that acquaintance, compels us to wound him through them, if at all. He holds our affections as hostages, the while he patches up a truce with our conscience.

Meanwhile, let us not forget that the aim of the true satirist is not to be severe upon persons, but only upon falsehood, and, as Truth and Falsehood start from the same point, and sometimes even go along together for a little way, his business is to follow the path of the latter after it diverges, and to show her floundering in the bog at the end of it. Truth is quite beyond the reach of satire. There is so brave a simplicity in her, that she can no more be made ridiculous than an oak or a pine. The danger of the satirist is, that continual use may deaden his sensibility to the force of language. He becomes more and more liable to strike harder than he knows or intends. He may be careful to put on his boxing-gloves, and yet forget, that, the older they grow, the more plainly may the knuckles inside be felt. Moreover, in the heat of contest, the eye is insensibly drawn to the crown of victory, whose tawdry tinsel glitters through that dust of the ring which obscures Truth's wreath of simple leaves. I have sometimes thought that my young friend, Mr. Biglow, needed a monitory hand laid on his arm,—*aliquid sufflaminandus erat.* I have never thought it good husbandry to water the tender plants of reform with *aqua fortis*, yet, where so much is to do in the beds, he were a sorry gardener who should wage a whole day's war with an iron scuffle on those ill weeds that make the garden-walks of life unsightly, when a sprinkle of Attic salt will wither them up. *Est ars etiam maledicendi,* says Scaliger, and truly it is a hard thing to say where the graceful gentleness of the lamb merges in downright sheepishness. We may conclude with worthy and wise Dr. Fuller, that "one may be a lamb in private wrongs, but in hearing general affronts to goodness they are asses which are not lions."—H.W.]

GUVENER B. is a sensible man;
  He stays to his home an' looks arter his folks;
He draws his furrer ez straight ez he can,
  An' into nobody's tater-patch pokes;—

But John P.
Robinson he
Sez he wunt vote fer Guvener B.

My! aint it terrible? Wut shall we du?
  We can't never choose him, o' course,—thet's flat;
Guess we shall hev to come round, (don't you?)
  An' go in fer thunder an' guns, an' all that;
        Fer John P.
        Robinson he
  Sez he wunt vote fer Guvener B.

Gineral C. is a dreffle smart man:
  He's ben on all sides thet give places or pelf;
But consistency still wuz a part of his plan,—
  He's ben true to *one* party,—an' thet is himself;—
        So John P.
        Robinson he
  Sez he shall vote fer Gineral C.

Gineral C. he goes in fer the war;
  He don't vally princerple more 'n an old cud;
Wut did God make us raytional creeturs fer,
  But glory an' gunpowder, plunder an' blood?
        So John P.
        Robinson he
  Sez he shall vote fer Gineral C.

We were gittin' on nicely up here to our village,
  With good old idees o' wut's right an' wut aint,
We kind o' thought Christ went agin war an' pillage,
  An' thet eppyletts worn't the best mark of a saint;
        But John P.
        Robinson he
  Sez this kind o' thing's an exploded idee.

The side of our country must ollers be took,
  An' Presidunt Polk, you know, *he* is our country;
An' the angel thet writes all our sins in a book

Puts the *debit* to him, an' to us the *per contry*;
  An' John P.
  Robinson he
 Sez this is his view o' the thing to a T.

Parson Wilbur he calls all these argimunts lies;
 Sez they're nothin' on airth but jest *fee, faw, fum;*
An' thet all this big talk of our destinies
 Is half on it ign'ance, an' t'other half rum;
  But John P.
  Robinson he
 Sez it aint no sech thing; an', of course, so must we.

Parson Wilbur sez *he* never heerd in his life
 Thet th' Apostles rigged out in their swaller-tail coats,
An' marched round in front of a drum an' a fife,
 To git some on 'em office, an' some on 'em votes;
  But John P.
  Robinson he
 Sez they did n't know everythin' down in Judee.

Wal, it's a marcy we've gut folks to tell us
 The rights an' the wrongs o' these matters, I vow,—
God sends country lawyers, an' other wise fellers,
 To start the world's team wen it gits in a slough;
  Fer John P.
  Robinson he
 Sez the world'll go right, ef he hollers out Gee!

[The attentive reader will doubtless have perceived in the fore-going poem an allusion to that pernicious sentiment,—"Our country, right or wrong." It is an abuse of language to call a certain portion of land, much more, certain personages elevated for the time being to high station, our country. I would not sever nor loosen a single one of those ties by which we are united to the spot of our birth, nor minish by a tittle the re-spect due to the Magistrate. I love our own Bay State too well to do the one, and as for the other, I have myself for nigh forty years exercised, however unworthily, the function of Justice of the Peace, having been called thereto by the unsolicited kindness of that most excellent man and upright patriot, Caleb Strong. *Patriæ fumus igne alieno luculentior* is best qualified with this,—*Ubi libertas, ibi patria.* We are inhabitants of two worlds, and owe a double, but not a divided, allegiance. In virtue of our clay, this little ball of earth exacts a certain loyalty of us, while, in our capacity as spirits, we are admitted citizens of an invisible and holier fatherland. There is a patriotism of the soul whose claim absolves us from our other and terrene fealty. Our true country is that ideal realm which we represent to ourselves under the names of religion, duty, and the like. Our terrestrial organizations are but far-off approaches to so fair a model, and all they are verily traitors who resist not any attempt to divert them from this their original intendment. When, therefore, one would have us to fling up our caps and shout with the multitude,—"*Our country, however bounded!*" he demands of us that we sacrifice the larger to the less, the higher to the lower, and that we yield to the imaginary claims of a few acres of soil our duty and privilege as liegemen of Truth. Our true country is bounded on the north and the south, on the east and the west, by Justice, and when she oversteps that invisible boundary-line by so much as a hair's-breadth, she ceases to be our mother, and chooses rather to be looked upon *quasi noverca.* That is a hard choice, when our earthly love of country calls upon us to tread one path and our duty points us to another. We must make as noble and becoming an election as did Penelope between Icarios and Ulysses. Veiling our faces, we must take silently the hand of Duty to follow her.

Shortly after the publication of the foregoing poem, there appeared some comments upon it in one of the public prints which seemed to call for animadversion. I accordingly addressed to Mr. Buckingham, of the Boston Courier, the following letter.

"JAALAM, November 4, 1847.

"*To the Editor of the Courier:*

"RESPECTED SIR,—Calling at the post-office this morning, our worthy and efficient postmaster offered for my perusal a paragraph in the Boston Morning Post of the 3d instant, wherein certain effusions of the pastoral muse are attributed to the pen of Mr. James Russell Lowell. For aught I know or can affirm to the contrary, this Mr. Lowell may be a very deserving person and a youth of parts (though I have seen verses of his which I could never rightly understand); and if he be such, he, I am certain, as well as I, would be free from any proclivity to appropriate to himself whatever of credit (or discredit) may honestly belong to another. I am confident, that, in penning these few lines, I am only forestalling a disclaimer from that young gentleman, whose silence hitherto, when rumor pointed to himward, has excited in my bosom mingled emotions of sorrow and surprise. Well may my young parishioner, Mr. Biglow, exclaim with the poet,

'Sic vos non vobis' &c.;

though, in saying this, I would not convey the impression that he is a proficient in the Latin tongue,—the tongue, I might add, of a Horace and a Tully.

"Mr. B. does not employ his pen, I can safely say, for any lucre of worldly gain, or to be exalted by the carnal plaudits of men, *digito monstrari*, &c. He does not wait upon Providence for mercies, and in his heart mean *merces*. But I should esteem myself as verily deficient in my duty (who am his friend and in some unworthy sort his spiritual *fidus Achates*, &c.), if I did not step forward to claim for him whatever measure of applause might be assigned to him by the judicious.

"If this were a fitting occasion, I might venture here a brief dissertation touching the manner and kind of my young friend's poetry. But I dubitate whether this abstruser sort of speculation (though enlivened by some apposite instances from Aristophanes) would sufficiently interest your oppidan readers. As regards their satirical tone, and their plainness of speech, I will only say, that, in my pastoral experience, I have found that the Arch-Enemy loves nothing better than to be treated as a religious, moral, and intellectual being, and that there is no *apage Sathanas!* so potent as ridicule. But it is a kind of weapon that must have a button of good-nature on the point of it.

"The productions of Mr. B. have been stigmatized in some quarters as unpatriotic; but I can vouch that he loves his native

soil with that hearty, though discriminating, attachment which
springs from an intimate social intercourse of many years' standing. In the ploughing season, no one has a deeper share in the
well-being of the country than he. If Dean Swift were right in
saying that he who makes two blades of grass grow where one
grew before confers a greater benefit on the state than he who
taketh a city, Mr. B. might exhibit a fairer claim to the Presidency
than General Scott himself. I think that some of those disinterested lovers of the hard-handed democracy, whose fingers have
never touched any thing rougher than the dollars of our common
country, would hesitate to compare palms with him. It would do
your heart good, respected Sir, to see that young man mow. He
cuts a cleaner and wider swath than any in this town.

"But it is time for me to be at my Post. It is very clear that my
young friend's shot has struck the lintel, for the Post is shaken
(Amos ix. 1). The editor of that paper is a strenuous advocate of
the Mexican war, and a colonel, as I am given to understand. I
presume, that, being necessarily absent in Mexico, he has left his
journal in some less judicious hands. At any rate, the Post has
been too swift on this occasion. It could hardly have cited a more
incontrovertible line from any poem than that which it has selected for animadversion, namely,—

'We kind o' thought Christ went agin war an' pillage.'

"If the Post maintains the converse of this proposition, it can
hardly be considered as a safe guide-post for the moral and religious portions of its party, however many other excellent qualities
of a post it may be blessed with. There is a sign in London on
which is painted,—'The Green Man.' It would do very well as a
portrait of any individual who should support so unscriptural a
thesis. As regards the language of the line in question, I am bold
to say that He who readeth the hearts of men will not account
any dialect unseemly which conveys a sound and pious sentiment.
I could wish that such sentiments were more common, however
uncouthly expressed. Saint Ambrose affirms, that *veritas a quo-
cunque* (why not, then, *quomodocunque?*) *dicatur, a spiritu sancto est.*
Digest also this of Baxter:—'The plainest words are the most profitable oratory in the weightiest matters.'

"When the paragraph in question was shown to Mr. Biglow, the only part of it which seemed to give him any dissatisfaction was that which classed him with the Whig party. He says, that, if resolutions are a nourishing kind of diet, that party must be in a very hearty and flourishing condition; for that they have quietly eaten more good ones of their own baking than he could have conceived to be possible without repletion. He has been for some years past (I regret to say) an ardent opponent of those sound doctrines of protective policy which form so prominent a portion of the creed of that party. I confess, that, in some discussions which I have had with him on this point in my study, he has displayed a vein of obstinacy which I had not hitherto detected in his composition. He is also (*horresco referens*) infected in no small measure with the peculiar notions of a print called the Liberator, whose heresies I take every proper opportunity of combating, and of which, I thank God, I have never read a single line.

"I did not see Mr. B.'s verses until they appeared in print, and there *is* certainly one thing in them which I consider highly improper. I allude to the personal references to myself by name. To confer notoriety on an humble individual who is laboring quietly in his vocation, and who keeps his cloth as free as he can from the dust of the political arena (though *væ mihi si non evangelizavero*), is no doubt an indecorum. The sentiments which he attributes to me I will not deny to be mine. They were embodied, though in a different form, in a discourse preached upon the last day of public fasting, and were acceptable to my entire people (of whatever political views), except the postmaster, who dissented *ex officio*. I observe that you sometimes devote a portion of your paper to a religious summary. I should be well pleased to furnish a copy of my discourse for insertion in this department of your instructive journal. By omitting the advertisements, it might easily be got within the limits of a single number, and I venture to insure you the sale of some scores of copies in this town. I will cheerfully render myself responsible for ten. It might possibly be advantageous to issue it as an *extra*. But perhaps you will not esteem it an object, and I will not press it. My offer does not spring from any weak desire of seeing my name in print; for I can enjoy this satisfaction at any time by turning to the Triennial Catalogue of the University, where it also possesses that added emphasis of Italics with which those of my calling are distinguished.

"I would simply add, that I continue to fit ingenuous youth for college, and that I have two spacious and airy sleeping apartments at this moment unoccupied. *Ingenuas didicisse,* &c. Terms, which vary according to the circumstances of the parents, may be known on application to me by letter, post paid. In all cases the lad will be expected to fetch his own towels. This rule, Mrs. W. desires me to add, has no exceptions.

"Respectfully, your obedient servant,

"HOMER WILBUR, A. M.

"P.S. Perhaps the last paragraph may look like an attempt to obtain the insertion of my circular gratuitously. If it should appear to you in that light, I desire that you would erase it, or charge for it at the usual rates, and deduct the amount from the proceeds in your hands from the sale of my discourse, when it shall be printed. My circular is much longer and more explicit, and will be forwarded without charge to any who may desire it. It has been very neatly executed on a letter sheet, by a very deserving printer, who attends upon my ministry, and is a creditable specimen of the typographic art. I have one hung over my mantelpiece in a neat frame, where it makes a beautiful and appropriate ornament, and balances the profile of Mrs. W., cut with her toes by the young lady born without arms.

"H.W."

I have in the foregoing letter mentioned General Scott in connection with the Presidency, because I have been given to understand that he has blown to pieces and otherwise caused to be destroyed more Mexicans than any other commander. His claim would therefore be deservedly considered the strongest. Until accurate returns of the Mexican killed, wounded, and maimed be obtained, it will be difficult to settle these nice points of precedence. Should it prove that any other officer has been more meritorious and destructive than General S., and has thereby rendered himself more worthy of the confidence and support of the conservative portion of our community, I shall cheerfully insert his name, instead of that of General S., in a future edition. It may be thought, likewise, that General S. has invalidated his claims by too much attention to the decencies of

apparel, and the habits belonging to a gentleman. These abstruser points of statesmanship are beyond my scope. I wonder
not that successful military achievement should attract the admiration of the multitude. Rather do I rejoice with wonder to behold how rapidly this sentiment is losing its hold upon the
popular mind. It is related of Thomas Warton, the second of
that honored name who held the office of Poetry Professor at
Oxford, that, when one wished to find him, being absconded, as
was his wont, in some obscure alehouse, he was counselled to
traverse the city with a drum and fife, the sound of which inspiring music would be sure to draw the Doctor from his retirement into the street. We are all more or less bitten with this
martial insanity. *Nescio quâ dulcedine. . . . cunctos ducit.* I confess
to some infection of that itch myself. When I see a Brigadier-
General maintaining his insecure elevation in the saddle under
the severe fire of the training-field, and when I remember that
some military enthusiasts, through haste, inexperience, or an
over-desire to lend reality to those fictitious combats, will sometimes discharge their ramrods, I cannot but admire, while I
deplore, the mistaken devotion of those heroic officers. *Semel in-
sanivimus omnes.* I was myself, during the late war with Great
Britain, chaplain of a regiment, which was fortunately never
called to active military duty. I mention this circumstance with
regret rather than pride. Had I been summoned to actual warfare, I trust that I might have been strengthened to bear myself
after the manner of that reverend father in our New England
Israel, Dr. Benjamin Colman, who, as we are told in Turell's
life of him, when the vessel in which he had taken passage for
England was attacked by a French privateer, "fought like a philosopher and a Christian. . . . and prayed all the while he
charged and fired." As this note is already long, I shall not here
enter upon a discussion of the question, whether Christians may
lawfully be soldiers. I think it sufficiently evident, that, during
the first two centuries of the Christian era, at least, the two professions were esteemed incompatible. Consult Jortin on this
head.—H.W.]

Ambrose Bierce

(1842–1914?)

Bierce served in the Civil War, then became a journalist. His first published writings were in literary criticism, but his short stories would assure him a permanent place in the pantheon of American writers. *In the Midst of Life* (1891) and *Can Such Things Be?* (1893) are collections that contain some of the finest American short stories. "An Occurrence at Owl Creek Bridge," for example, is probably one of the most frequently anthologized short stories in all of American literature, and has been the subject of several dramatizations as well. As a satirist, his most important work is *The Devil's Dictionary* (1906), a collection of sharply satirical definitions presented in alphabetical order on a large variety of social and political subjects. A sample follows.

The Devil's Dictionary

Abet, v.t. To encourage in crime, as to aid poverty with pennies.

Ability, n. The natural equipment to accomplish some small part of the meaner ambitions distinguishing able men from dead ones. In the last analysis ability is commonly found to consist mainly in a high degree of solemnity. Perhaps, however, this impressive quality is rightly appraised; it is no easy task to be solemn.

Abnormal, adj. Not conforming to standard. In matters of thought and conduct, to be independent is to be abnormal, to be abnormal is to be detested. Wherefore the lexicographer adviseth a striving toward a straiter resemblance to the Average Man than he hath to himself. Whoso attaineth thereto shall have peace, the prospect of death and the hope of Hell.

Aborigines, *n.* Persons of little worth found cumbering the soil of a newly discovered country. They soon cease to cumber; they fertilize.

Abroad, *adj.* At war with savages and idiots. To be a Frenchman abroad is to be miserable; to be an American abroad is to make others miserable.

Abrupt, *adj.* Sudden, without ceremony, like the arrival of a cannon-shot and the departure of the soldier whose interests are most affected by it. Dr. Samuel Johnson beautifully said of another author's ideas that they were "concatenated without abruption."

Abscond, *v. i.* To "move in a mysterious way," commonly with the property of another.

Absence, *n.* That which "makes the heart grow fonder"—of absence. Absence of mind is the cerebral condition essential to success in popular preaching. It is sometimes termed lack of sense.

Absent, *adj.* Peculiarly exposed to the tooth of detraction; vilified; hopelessly in the wrong; superseded in the consideration and affection of another.

Absentee, *n.* A person with an income who has had the forethought to remove himself from the sphere of exaction.

Absolute, *adj.* Independent, irresponsible. An absolute monarchy is one in which the sovereign does as he pleases so long as he pleases the assassins. Not many absolute monarchies are left, most of them having been replaced by limited monarchies, where the sovereign's power for evil (and for good) is greatly curtailed, and by republics, which are governed by chance.

Abstainer, *n.* A weak person who yields to the temptation of denying himself a pleasure. A total abstainer is one who abstains from everything but abstention, and especially from inactivity in the affairs of others.

Absurdity, *n.* A statement or belief manifestly inconsistent with one's own opinion.

Abuse, *n.* Unanswerable wit.

Academe, n.   An ancient school where morality and philosophy were taught.

Academy, n. (from academe).   A modern school where football is taught.

Accident, n.   An inevitable occurrence due to the action of immutable natural laws.

Accomplice, n.   One associated with another in a crime, having guilty knowledge and complicity, as an attorney who defends a criminal, knowing him guilty. This view of the attorney's position in the matter has not hitherto commanded the assent of attorneys, no one having offered them a fee for assenting.

Accord, n.   Harmony.

Accordion, n.   An instrument in harmony with the sentiments of an assassin.

Accountability, n.   The mother of caution.

Achievement, n.   The death of endeavor and the birth of disgust.

Acknowledge, v. t.   To confess. Acknowledgment of one another's faults is the highest duty imposed by our love of truth.

Acquaintance, n.   A person whom we know well enough to borrow from, but not well enough to lend to. A degree of friendship called slight when its object is poor or obscure, and intimate when he is rich or famous.

Acquit, v. t.   To render judgment in a murder case in San Francisco.

Actually, adv.   Perhaps; possibly.

Adage, n.   Boned wisdom for weak teeth.

Adamant, n.   A mineral frequently found beneath a corset. Soluble in solicitate of gold.

Adder, n.   A species of snake. So called from its habit of adding funeral outlays to the other expenses of living.

Adherent, n.   A follower who has not yet obtained all that he expects to get.

Administration, n.   An ingenious abstraction in politics, designed to receive the kicks and cuffs due to the premier or president. A man of straw, proof against bad-egging and dead-catting.

Admiral, n.   That part of a war-ship which does the talking while the figure-head does the thinking.

Admiration, n.   Our polite recognition of another's resemblance to ourselves.

Adore, v. t.   To venerate expectantly.

Advice, n.   The smallest current coin.

Aesthetics, n.   The most unpleasant ticks afflicting the race. Worse than wood-ticks.

Affection, n.   In morals, a sentiment; in medicine, a disease. To a young woman an affection of the heart means love; to a doctor it may mean fatty degeneration. The difference is one of nomenclature merely.

Affectionate, adj.   Addicted to being a nuisance. The most affectionate creature in the world is a wet dog.

Affianced, pp.   Fitted with an ankle-ring for the ball-and-chain.

Affliction, n.   An acclimatizing process preparing the soul for another and bitter world.

Affirm, v. t.   To declare with suspicious gravity when one is not compelled to wholly discredit himself with an oath.

Age, n.   That period of life in which we compound for the vices that we still cherish by reviling those that we have no longer the enterprise to commit.

Agitator, n.   A statesman who shakes the fruit trees of his neighbors—to dislodge the worms.

Agrarian, n.   A politician who carries his real estate under his nails. A son of the soil who, like Aeneas, carries his father on his person.

Air, n.   A nutritious substance supplied by a bountiful Providence for the fattening of the poor.

Alderman, n.   An ingenious criminal who covers his secret thieving with a pretence of open marauding.

Alien, n.   An American sovereign in his probationary state.

Allegiance, n.   The traditional bond of duty between the taxer and the taxee. It is not reversible.

Alliance, n.   In international politics, the union of two thieves who have their hands so deeply inserted in each other's pocket that they cannot separately plunder a third.

Alone, adj.   In bad company.

Amateur, n.   A public nuisance who mistakes taste for skill, and confounds his ambition with his ability.

Amazon, n.   One of an ancient race who do not appear to have been much concerned about woman's rights and the equality of the sexes. Their thoughtless habit of twisting the necks of the males has unfortunately resulted in the extinction of their kind.

Ambidextrous, *adj.* Able to pick with equal skill a right-hand pocket or a left.

Ambition, *n.* An overmastering desire to be vilified by enemies while living and made ridiculous by friends when dead.

Amnesty, *n.* The state's magnanimity to those offenders whom it would be too expensive to punish.

Anoint, *v. t.* To grease a king or other great functionary already sufficiently slippery.

Antipathy, *n.* The sentiment inspired by one's friend's friend.

Aphorism, *n.* Predigested wisdom.

Apologize, *v. i.* To lay the foundation for a future offence.

Apostate, *n.* A leech who, having penetrated the shell of a turtle only to find that the creature has long been dead, deems it expedient to form a new attachment to a fresh turtle.

Apothecary, *n.* The physician's accomplice, undertaker's benefactor and grave worm's provider.

Appeal, *v. t.* In law, to put the dice into the box for another throw.

Appetite, *n.* An instinct thoughtfully implanted by Providence as a solution to the labor question.

Applause, *n.* The echo of a platitude.

Architect, *n.* One who drafts a plan of your house, and plans a draft of your money.

Ardor, *n.* The quality that distinguishes love without knowledge.

Arena, *n.* In politics, an imaginary rat-pit in which the statesman wrestles with his record.

Aristocracy, *n.* Government by the best men. (In this sense the word is obsolete; so is that kind of government.) Fellows that wear downy hats and clean shirts—guilty of education and suspected of bank accounts.

Armor, *n.* The kind of clothing worn by a man whose tailor is a blacksmith.

Arrayed, *p.p.* Drawn up and given an orderly disposition, as a rioter hanged to a lamppost.

Arrest, *v. t.* Formally to detain one accused of unusualness. God made the world in six days and was arrested on the seventh.— *The Unauthorized Version.*

Arsenic, n. A kind of cosmetic greatly affected by the ladies, whom it greatly affects in turn.

Art, n. This word has no definition. Its origin is related as follows by the ingenious Father Gassalasca Jape, S.J.

> One day a wag—what would the wretch be at?—
> Shifted a letter of the cipher RAT,
> And said it was a god's name! Straight arose
> Fantastic priests and postulants (with shows,
> And mysteries, and mummeries, and hymns,
> And disputations dire that lamed their limbs)
> To serve his temple and maintain the fires,
> Expound the law, manipulate the wires.
> Amazed, the populace the rites attend,
> Believe whate'er they cannot comprehend,
> And, inly edified to learn that two
> Half-hairs joined so and so (as Art can do)
> Have sweeter values and a grace more fit
> Than Nature's hairs that never have been split,
> Bring cates and wines for sacrificial feasts,
> And sell their garments to support the priests.

Artlessness, n. A certain engaging quality to which women attain by long study and severe practice upon the admiring male, who is pleased to fancy it resembles the candid simplicity of his young.

Asperse, v. t. Maliciously to ascribe to another vicious actions which one has not had the temptation and opportunity to commit.

Ass, n. A public singer with a good voice but no ear. In Virginia City, Nevada, he is called the Washoe Canary, in Dakota, the Senator, and everywhere the Donkey. The animal is widely and variously celebrated in the literature, art and religion of every age and country; no other so engages and fires the human imagination as this noble vertebrate. Indeed, it is doubted by some (Ramasilus, *lib. II., De Clem.*, and C. Stantatus, *De Temperamente*) if it is not a god; and as such we know it was worshipped by the Etruscans, and, if we may believe Macrobious, by the Cupasians also. Of the only two animals admitted into the Mahometan Paradise along with the souls of men, the ass that carried Balaam is one, the dog of the Seven Sleepers the other. This is no small distinction. From what has been written about this beast might be compiled a library of great splendor and magnitude, rivaling that of the Shakspearean cult, and that which clusters about the Bible. It may be said, generally, that all literature is more or less Asinine.

Astrology, n.   The science of making the dupe see stars. Astrology is by some held in high respect as the precursor of astronomy. Similarly, the night-howling tomcat has a just claim to reverential consideration as the precursor to the hurtling bootjack.

Attorney, n.   A person legally appointed to mismanage one's affairs which one has not himself the skill to rightly mismanage.

Auctioneer, n.   The man who proclaims with a hammer that he has picked a pocket with his tongue.

Australia, n.   A country lying in the South Sea, whose industrial and commercial development has been unspeakably retarded by an unfortunate dispute among geographers as to whether it is a continent or an island.

Authentic, adj.   Indubitably true—in someone's opinion.

B

Babe or Baby, n.   A misshapen creature of no particular age, sex, or condition, chiefly remarkable for the violence of the sympathies and antipathies it excites in others, itself without sentiment or emotion. There have been famous babes; for example, little Moses, from whose adventure in the bulrushes the Egyptian hierophants of seven centuries before doubtless derived their idle tale of the child Osiris being preserved on a floating lotus leaf.

Bacchus, n.   A convenient deity invented by the ancients as an excuse for getting drunk.

Back, n.   That part of your friend which it is your privilege to contemplate in your adversity.

Backbite, v. t.   To speak of a man as you find him when he can't find you.

Bait, n.   A preparation that renders the hook more palatable. The best kind is beauty.

Bang, *n.* The cry of a gun. That arrangement of a woman's hair which suggests the thought of shooting her; hence the name.

Barometer, *n.* An ingenious instrument which indicates what kind of weather we are having.

Barrack, *n.* A house in which soldiers enjoy a portion of that of which it is their business to deprive others.

Bastinado, *n.* The act of walking on wood without exertion.

Bath, *n.* A kind of mystic ceremony substituted for religious worship, with what spiritual efficacy has not been determined.

Battle, *n.* A method of untying with the teeth a political knot that would not yield to the tongue.

Beard, *n.* The hair that is commonly cut off by those who justly execrate the absurd Chinese custom of shaving the head.

Beauty, *n.* The power by which a woman charms a lover and terrifies a husband.

Befriend, *v. t.* To make an ingrate.

Beg, *v.* To ask for something with an earnestness proportioned to the belief that it will not be given.

Beggar, *n.* One who has relied on the assistance of his friends.

Belladonna, *n.* In Italian a beautiful lady; in English a deadly poison. A striking example of the essential identity of the two tongues.

Benefactor, *n.* One who makes heavy purchases of ingratitude, without, however, materially affecting the price, which is still within the means of all.

Betrothed, *p.p.* The condition of a man and a woman who, pleasing to one another and objectionable to their friends, are anxious to propitiate society by becoming unendurable to each other.

Bigamy, *n.* A mistake in taste for which the wisdom of the future will adjudge a punishment called trigamy.

Bigot, *n.* One who is obstinately and zealously attached to an opinion that you do not entertain.

Billingsgate, *n.* The invective of an opponent.

Birth, *n.* The first and direst of all disasters. As to the nature of it there appears to be no uniformity. Castor and Pollux were born from the egg. Pallas came out of a skull. Galatea was once a block of stone. Peresilis, who wrote in the tenth century, avers that he grew up out of the ground where a priest had spilled

holy water. It is known that Arimaxus was derived from a hole
in the earth, made by a stroke of lightning. Leucomedon was
the son of a cavern in Mount Ætna, and I have myself seen a
man come out of a wine cellar.

Blackguard, *n.*   A man whose qualities, prepared for display like
a box of berries in a market—the fine ones on top—have been
opened on the wrong side. An inverted gentleman.

Blank-verse, *n.*   Unrhymed iambic pentameters—the most difficult kind of English verse to write acceptably; a kind, therefore,
much affected by those who cannot acceptably write any kind.

Body-snatcher, *n.*   A robber of grave-worms. One who supplies the
young physicians with that with which the old physicians have
supplied the undertaker.

Bondsman, *n.*   A fool who, having property of his own, undertakes
to become responsible for that entrusted by another to a third.

  Philippe of Orleans wishing to appoint one of his favorites,
a dissolute nobleman, to a high office, asked him what security
he would be able to give. "I need no bondsmen," he replied,
"for I can give you my word of honor." "And pray what may
be the value of that?" inquired the amused Regent. "Monsieur,
it is worth its weight in gold."

Bore, *n.*   A person who talks when you wish him to listen.

Botany, *n.*   The science of vegetables—those that are not good to
eat, as well as those that are. It deals largely with their flowers,
which are commonly badly designed, inartistic in color, and ill-
smelling.

Bottle-nosed, *adj.*   Having a nose created in the image of its maker.

Boundary, *n.*   In political geography, an imaginary line between
two nations, separating the imaginary rights of one from the
imaginary rights of the other.

Brain, *n.*   An apparatus with which we think that we think. That
which distinguishes the man who is content to *be* something
from the man who wishes to *do* something. A man of great
wealth, or one who has been pitchforked into high station, has
commonly such a headful of brain that his neighbors cannot
keep their hats on. In our civilization, and under our republican form of government, brain is so highly honored that it is
rewarded by exemption from the cares of office.

Brandy, *n.*   A cordial composed of one part thunder-and-lightning, one part remorse, two parts bloody murder, one part death-hell-and-the-grave and four parts clarified Satan. Dose, a headful all the time. Brandy is said by Dr. Johnson to be the drink of heroes. Only a hero will venture to drink it.

Bride, *n.* A woman with a fine prospect of happiness behind her.

Brute, *n.* See HUSBAND.

C

Caaba, *n.* A large stone presented by the archangel Gabriel to the patriarch Abraham, and preserved at Mecca. The patriarch had perhaps asked the archangel for bread.

Cabbage, *n.* A familiar kitchen-garden vegetable about as large and wise as a man's head.

The cabbage is so called from Cabagius, a prince who on ascending the throne issued a decree appointing a High Council of Empire consisting of the members of his predecessor's Ministry and the cabbages in the royal garden. When any of his Majesty's measures of state policy miscarried conspicuously it was gravely announced that several members of the High Council had been beheaded, and his murmuring subjects were appeased.

Calamity, *n.* A more than commonly plain and unmistakable reminder that the affairs of this life are not of our own ordering. Calamities are of two kinds: misfortune to ourselves, and good fortune to others.

Callous, *adj.* Gifted with great fortitude to bear the evils afflicting another.

When Zeno was told that one of his enemies was no more he was observed to be deeply moved. "What!" said one of his disciples, "you weep at the death of an enemy?" "Ah, 'tis true," replied the great Stoic; "but you should see me smile at the death of a friend."

Cannibal, *n.* A gastronome of the old school who preserves the simple tastes and adheres to the natural diet of the pre-pork period.

Cannon, *n.* An instrument employed in the rectification of national boundaries.

Capital, *n.* The seat of misgovernment. That which provides the fire, the pot, the dinner, the table and the knife and fork for the anarchist; the part of the repast that himself supplies is the disgrace before meat. *Capital Punishment,* a penalty regarding the justice and expediency of which many worthy persons—including all the assassins—entertain grave misgivings.

Carnivorous, adj. Addicted to the cruelty of devouring the timorous vegetarian, his heirs and assigns.

Carouse, v. i. To celebrate with appropriate ceremonies the birth of a noble headache.

Cartesian, adj. Relating to Descartes, a famous philosopher, author of the celebrated dictum, *Cogito ero sum*—whereby he was pleased to suppose he demonstrated the reality of human existence. The dictum might be improved, however, thus: *Cogito cogito ergo cogito sum*—"I think that I think, therefore I think that I am;" as close an approach to certainty as any philosopher has yet made.

Cat, n. A soft, indestructible automaton provided by nature to be kicked when things go wrong in the domestic circle.

Caviler, n. A critic of our own work.

Cemetery, n. An isolated suburban spot where mourners match lies, poets write at a target and stone-cutters spell for a wager. The inscription following will serve to illustrate the success attained in these Olympian games:

His virtues were so conspicuous that his enemies, unable to overlook them, denied them, and his friends, to whose loose lives they were a rebuke, represented them as vices. They are here commemorated by his family, who shared them.

Censor, n. An officer of certain governments, employed to suppress the works of genius. Among the Romans the censor was an inspector of public morals, but the public morals of modern nations will not bear inspection.

Cerberus, n. The watch-dog of Hades, whose duty it was to guard the entrance—against whom or what does not clearly appear; everybody, sooner or later, had to go there, and nobody wanted to carry off the entrance.

Childhood, n. The period of human life intermediate between the idiocy of infancy and the folly of youth—two removes from the sin of manhood and three from the remorse of old age.

Chinaman, n. A working man whose faults are docility, skill, industry, frugality and temperance, and whom we clamor to be forbidden by law to employ; whose labor opens countless avenues of employment to the whites and cheapens the necessities of life to the poor; to whom the squalor of poverty is imputed to be a congenial vice, exciting not compassion but resentment.

Chorus, *n.* In opera, a band of howling dervishes who terrify the audience while the singers are taking breath.

Christen, *v. t.* To ceremoniously afflict a helpless child with a name.

Christian, *n.* One who believes that the New Testament is a divinely inspired book admirably suited to the spiritual needs of his neighbor. One who follows the teachings of Christ in so far as they are not inconsistent with a life of sin.

Circumlocution, *n.* A literary trick whereby the writer who has nothing to say breaks it gently to the reader.

Circus, *n.* A place where horses, ponies and elephants are permitted to see men, women and children acting the fool.

Clairvoyant, *n.* A person, commonly a woman, who has the power of seeing that which is invisible to her patron—namely, that he is a blockhead.

Clarionet, *n.* An instrument of torture operated by a person with cotton in his ears. There are two instruments that are worse than a clarionet—two clarionets.

Clergyman, *n.* A man who undertakes the management of our spiritual affairs as a method of bettering his temporal ones.

Clock, *n.* A machine of great moral value to man, allaying his concern for the future by reminding him what a lot of time remains to him.

Close-fisted, *adj.* Unduly desirous of keeping that which many meritorious persons wish to obtain.

Club, *n.* An association of men for purposes of drunkenness, gluttony, unholy hilarity, murder, sacrilege and the slandering of mothers, wives and sisters.

For this definition I am indebted to several estimable ladies who have the best means of information, their husbands being members of several clubs.

Comfort, *n.* A state of mind produced by contemplation of a neighbor's uneasiness.

Commendation, *n.* The tribute that we pay to achievements that resemble, but do not equal, our own.

Commerce, *n.* A kind of transaction in which A plunders from B the goods of C, and for compensation B picks the pocket of D of money belonging to E.

Compromise, n. Such an adjustment of conflicting interests as gives each adversary the satisfaction of thinking he has got what he ought not to have, and is deprived of nothing except what was justly his due.

Compulsion, n. The eloquence of power.

Conceit, n. Self-respect in one whom we dislike.

Confidant, Confidante, n. One entrusted by A with the secrets of B, confided by *him* to C.

Congratulation, n. The civility of envy.

Congress, n. A body of men who meet to repeal laws.

Conjugal, adj. (Latin, *con*, mutual, and *jugum*, a yoke.) Relating to a popular kind of penal servitude—the yoking together of two fools by a parson.

Connoisseur, n. A specialist who knows everything about something and nothing about anything else.

An old wine-bibber having been smashed in a railway collision, some wine was poured upon his lips to revive him. "Pauillac, 1873," he murmured and died.

Conservative, n. A statesman who is enamored of existing evils, as distinguished from the Liberal, who wishes to replace them with others.

Consolation, n. The knowledge that a better man is more unfortunate than yourself.

Consul, n. In American politics, a person who having failed to secure an office from the people is given one by the Administration on condition that he leave the country.

Consult, v. t. To seek another's approval of a course already decided on.

Contempt, n. The feeling of a prudent man for an enemy who is too formidable safely to be opposed.

Controversy, n. A battle in which spittle or ink replaces the injurious cannon-ball and the inconsiderate bayonet.

Convent, n. A place of retirement for women who wish for leisure to meditate upon the vice of idleness.

Conversation, n. A fair for the display of the minor mental commodities, each exhibitor being too intent upon the arrangement of his own wares to observe those of his neighbor.

Coronation, n. The ceremony of investing a sovereign with the outward and visible signs of his divine right to be blown skyhigh with a dynamite bomb.

Corporation, n. An ingenious device for obtaining individual profit without individual responsibility.

Corsair, n. A politician of the seas.

Court Fool, n. The plaintiff.

Courtship, n. The timid sipping of two thirsty souls from a goblet which both can easily drain but neither replenish.

Coward, n. One who in a perilous emergency thinks with his legs.

Cowlick, n. A tuft of hair which persists in lying the wrong way. In the case of a married man it usually points toward the side that his wife commonly walks on.

Creditor, n. One of a tribe of savages dwelling beyond the Financial Straits and dreaded for their desolating incursions.

Critic, n. A person who boasts himself hard to please because nobody tries to please him.

Cunning, n. The faculty that distinguishes a weak animal or person from a strong one. It brings its possessor much mental satisfaction and great material adversity. An Italian proverb says: "The furrier gets the skins of more foxes than asses."

Cupid, n. The so-called god of love. This bastard creation of a barbarous fancy was no doubt inflicted upon mythology for the sins of its deities. Of all unbeautiful and inappropriate conceptions this is the most reasonless and offensive. The notion of symbolizing sexual love by a semisexless babe, and comparing the pains of passion to the wounds of an arrow—of introducing this pudgy homunculus into art grossly to materialize the subtle spirit and suggestion of the work—this is eminently worthy of the age that, giving it birth, laid it on the doorstep of posterity.

Curiosity, n. An objectionable quality of the female mind. The desire to know whether or not a woman is cursed with curiosity is one of the most active and insatiable passions of the masculine soul.

Curse, v. t. Energetically to belabor with a verbal slap-stick. This is an operation which in literature, particularly in the drama, is commonly fatal to the victim. Nevertheless, the liability to a cursing is a risk that cuts but a small figure in fixing the rates of life insurance.

Custard, n.   A detestable substance produced by a malevolent conspiracy of the hen, the cow and the cook.

Cynic, n.   A blackguard whose faulty vision sees things as they are, not as they ought to be. Hence the custom among the Scythians of plucking out a cynic's eyes to improve his vision.

D

Damn, v.   A word formerly much used by the Paphlagonians, the meaning of which is lost. By the learned Dr. Dolabelly Gak it is believed to have been a term of satisfaction, implying the highest possible degree of mental tranquillity. Professor Groke, on the contrary, thinks it expressed an emotion of tumultuous delight, because it so frequently occurs in combination with the word *jod* or *god*, meaning "joy." It would be with great diffidence that I should advance an opinion conflicting with that of either of these formidable authorities.

Dance, v. i.   To leap about to the sound of tittering music, preferably with arms about your neighbor's wife or daughter. There are many kinds of dances, but all those requiring the participation of the two sexes have two characteristics in common: they are conspicuously innocent, and warmly loved by the vicious.

Dawn, n.   The time when men of reason go to bed. Certain old men prefer to rise at about that time, taking a cold bath and a long walk with an empty stomach, and otherwise mortifying the flesh. They then point with pride to these practices as the cause of their sturdy health and ripe years; the truth being that they are hearty and old, not because of their habits, but in spite of them. The reason we find only robust persons doing this thing is that it has killed all the others who have tried it.

Day, n.   A period of twenty-four hours, mostly misspent. This period is divided into two parts, the day proper and the night, or day improper—the former devoted to sins of business, the latter consecrated to the other sort. These two kinds of social activity overlap.

Debauchee, n.   One who has so earnestly pursued pleasure that he has had the misfortune to overtake it.

Debt, n. An ingenious substitute for the chain and whip of the slave-driver.

Decalogue, n. A series of commandments, ten in number—just enough to permit an intelligent selection for observance, but not enough to embarrass the choice. Following is the revised edition of the Decalogue, calculated for this meridian.

Thou shalt no God but me adore:
'Twere too expensive to have more.

No images nor idols make
For Robert Ingersoll to break.

Take not God's name in vain; select
A time when it will have effect.

Work not on Sabbath days at all,
But go to see the teams play ball.

Honor thy parents. That creates
For life insurance lower rates.

Kill not, abet not those who kill;
Thou shalt not pay thy butcher's bill.

Kiss not thy neighbor's wife, unless
Thine own thy neighbor doth caress.

Don't steal; thou'lt never thus compete
Successfully in business. Cheat.

Bear not false witness—that is low—
But "hear 'tis rumored so and so."

Covet thou naught that thou hast not
By hook or crook, or somehow, got.

Decide, v. i. To succumb to the preponderance of one set of influences over another set.

Defame, v. t.   To lie about another. To tell the truth about another.

Defenceless, adj.   Unable to attack.

Defendant, n.   In law, an obliging person who devotes his time and character to preserving property for his lawyer.

Defraud, v. t.   To impart instruction and experience to the confiding.

Degradation, n.   One of the stages of moral and social progress from private station to political preferment.

Delegation, n.   In American politics, an article of merchandise that comes in sets.

Deliberation, n.   The act of examining one's bread to determine which side it is buttered on.

Deluge, n.   A notable first experiment in baptism which washed away the sins (and sinners) of the world.

Delusion, n.   The father of a most respectable family, comprising Enthusiasm, Affection, Self-denial, Faith, Hope, Charity and many other goodly sons and daughters.

Demagogue, n.   A political opponent.

Demure, adj.   Grave and modest-mannered, like a particularly unscrupulous woman.

Dentist, n.   A prestidigitator, who puts metal into your mouth and pulls coins out of your pocket.

Deny, v. t.   See HURL BACK THE ALLEGATION.

Dependent, adj.   Reliant upon another's generosity for the support which you are not in a position to exact from his fears.

Deportment, n.   An invention of the devil, to assist his followers into good society.

Deputy, n.   A male relative of an officeholder, or of his bondsman. The deputy is commonly a beautiful young man, with a red necktie and an intricate system of cobwebs extending from his nose to his desk. When accidentally struck by the janitor's broom, he gives off a cloud of dust.

Desertion, n.   An aversion to fighting, as exhibited by abandoning an army or a wife.

Deshabille, n.   A reception costume for intimate friends varying according to locality, e.g., in Borriboola Gha, a streak of red and yellow paint across the thorax. In San Francisco, pearl earrings and a smile.

Destiny, *n.* A tyrant's authority for crime and a fool's excuse for failure.

Diagnosis, *n.* A physician's forecast of disease by the patient's pulse and purse.

Diaphragm, *n.* A muscular partition separating disorders of the chest from disorders of the bowels.

Diary, *n.* A daily record of that part of one's life, which he can relate to himself without blushing.

Dice, *n.* Small polka-dotted cubes of ivory, constructed like a lawyer to lie on any side, but commonly on the wrong one.

Dictator, *n.* The chief of a nation that prefers the pestilence of despotism to the plague of anarchy.

Dictionary, *n.* A malevolent literary device for cramping the growth of a language and making it hard and inelastic. This dictionary, however, is a most useful work.

Digestion, *n.* The conversion of victuals into virtues. When the process is imperfect, vices are evolved instead—a circumstance from which that wicked writer, Dr. Jeremiah Blenn, infers that the ladies are the greater sufferers from dyspepsia.

Diplomacy, *n.* The patriotic art of lying for one's country.

Disabuse, *v. t.* To present your neighbor with another and better error than the one which he has deemed it advantageous to embrace.

Discriminate, *v. i.* To note the particulars in which one person or thing is, if possible, more objectionable than another.

Discussion, *n.* A method of confirming others in their errors.

Disobedience, *n.* The silver lining to the cloud of servitude.

Disobey, *v. t.* To celebrate with an appropriate ceremony the maturity of a command.

Dissemble, *v. i.* To put a clean shirt upon the character.

Distance, *n.* The only thing that the rich are willing for the poor to call theirs, and keep.

Distress, *n.* A disease incurred by exposure to the prosperity of a friend.

Divination, *n.* The art of nosing out the occult. Divination is of as many kinds as there are fruit-bearing varieties of the flowering dunce and the early fool.

Divine, *n.* A bird of pray.

Divorce, *n.* A resumption of diplomatic relations and rectification of boundaries.

Doctrinaire, n.   One whose doctrine has the demerit of antago-
nizing your own.

Dog, n.   A kind of additional or subsidiary Deity designed to catch
the overflow and surplus of the world's worship. This Divine
Being in some of his smaller and silkier incarnations takes, in
the affection of Woman, the place to which there is no human
male aspirant. The Dog is a survival—an anachronism. He toils
not, neither does he spin, yet Solomon in all his glory never lay
upon a door-mat all day long, sun-soaked and fly-fed and fat,
while his master worked for the means wherewith to purchase
an idle wag of the Solomonic tail, seasoned with a look of tol-
erant recognition.

Dragoon, n.   A soldier who combines dash and steadiness in so
equal measure that he makes his advances on foot and his retreats on horseback.

Dramatist, n.   One who adapts plays from the French.

Drowsy, adj.   Profoundly affected by a play adapted from the
French.

Dullard, n.   A member of the reigning dynasty in letters and life.
The Dullards came in with Adam, and being both numerous
and sturdy have overrun the habitable world. The secret of their
power is their insensibility to blows; tickle them with a bludgeon
and they laugh with a platitude. The Dullards came originally
from Bœotia, whence they were driven by stress of starvation,
their dulness having blighted the crops. For some centuries
they infested Philistia, and many of them are called Philistines
to this day. In the turbulent times of the Crusades they withdrew thence and gradually overspread all Europe, occupying
most of the high places in politics, art, literature, science and
theology. Since a detachment of Dullards came over with the
Pilgrims in the *Mayflower* and made a favorable report of the
country, their increase by birth, immigration, and conversion
has been rapid and steady. According to the most trustworthy
statistics the number of adult Dullards in the United States is
but little short of thirty millions, including the statisticians. The
intellectual centre of the race is somewhere about Peoria, Illinois, but the New England Dullard is the most shockingly
moral.

Duty, n.   That which sternly impels us in the direction of profit,
along the line of desire.

E

Eat, v. i. To perform successively (and successfully) the functions of mastication, humectation, and deglutition.

"I was in the drawing-room, enjoying my dinner," said Brillat-Savarin, beginning an anecdote. "What!" interrupted Rochebriant; "eating dinner in a drawing-room?" "I must beg you to observe, monsieur," explained the great gastronome, "that I did not say I was eating my dinner, but enjoying it. I had dined an hour before."

Eavesdrop, v. i. Secretly to overhear a catalogue of the crimes and vices of another or yourself.

Eccentricity, n. A method of distinction so cheap that fools employ it to accentuate their incapacity.

Economy, n. Purchasing the barrel of whiskey that you do not need for the price of the cow that you cannot afford.

Edible, adj. Good to eat, and wholesome to digest, as a worm to a toad, a toad to a snake, a snake to a pig, a pig to a man, and a man to a worm.

Editor, n. A person who combines the judicial functions of Minos, Rhadamanthus and Æacus, but is placable with an obolus; a severely virtuous censor, but so charitable withal that he tolerates the virtues of others and the vices of himself; who flings about him the splintering lightning and sturdy thunders of admonition till he resembles a bunch of firecrackers petulantly uttering its mind at the tail of a dog; then straightway murmurs a mild, melodious lay, soft as the cooing of a donkey intoning its prayer to the evening star. Master of mysteries and lord of law, high-pinnacled upon the throne of thought, his face suffused with the dim splendors of the Transfiguration, his legs intertwisted and his tongue a-cheek, the editor spills his will along the paper and cuts it off in lengths to suit. And at intervals from behind the veil of the temple is heard the voice of the foreman demanding three inches of wit and six lines of religious meditation, or bidding him turn off the wisdom and whack up some pathos.

Education, n. That which discloses to the wise and disguises from the foolish their lack of understanding.

Effect, n. The second of two phenomena which always occur together in the same order. The first, called a Cause, is said to generate the other—which is no more sensible than it would be for one who has never seen a dog except in pursuit of a rabbit to declare the rabbit the cause of the dog.

Egotist, n.   A person of low taste, more interested in himself than in me.

Ejection, n.   An approved remedy for the disease of garrulity. It is also much used in cases of extreme poverty.

Elector, n.   One who enjoys the sacred privilege of voting for the man of another man's choice.

Elegy, n.   A composition in verse, in which, without employing any of the methods of humor, the writer aims to produce in the reader's mind the dampest kind of dejection. The most famous English example begins somewhat like this:

> The cur foretells the knell of parting day;
>   The loafing herd winds slowly o'er the lea;
> The wise man homeward plods; I only stay
>   To fiddle-faddle in a minor key.

Eloquence, n.   The art of orally persuading fools that white is the color that it appears to be. It includes the gift of making any color appear white.

Elysium, n.   An imaginary delightful country which the ancients foolishly believed to be inhabited by the spirits of the good. This ridiculous and mischievous fable was swept off the face of the earth by the early Christians—may their souls be happy in Heaven!

Emancipation, n.   A bondman's change from the tyranny of another to the despotism of himself.

Embalm, v. t.   To cheat vegetation by locking up the gases upon which it feeds. By embalming their dead and thereby deranging the natural balance between animal and vegetable life, the Egyptians made their once fertile and populous country barren and incapable of supporting more than a meagre crew. The modern metallic burial casket is a step in the same direction, and many a dead man who ought now to be ornamenting his neighbor's lawn as a tree, or enriching his table as a bunch of radishes, is doomed to a long inutility. We shall get him after awhile if we are spared, but in the meantime the violet and rose are languishing for a nibble at his *glutœus maximus.*

Emotion, n. A prostrating disease caused by a determination of the heart to the head. It is sometimes accompanied by a copious discharge of hydrated chloride of sodium from the eyes.

Finley Peter Dunne

(1867–1936)

Finley Peter Dunne became a newspaper reporter at the age of seventeen, after graduating from high school dead last in a class of fifty students. For the first two decades of the twentieth century, he was America's favorite humorous newspaper columnist—this at a time when Chicago, where Dunne lived and wrote, had more than thirty daily newspapers. He worked for more than a half dozen different papers, then settled at the *Evening Post*, where Mr. Dooley was born, modeled on the real-life saloon keeper of a newspapermen's bar on Dearborn Street. He wrote on whatever he found interesting or pertinent—health fads, society, war, poverty, political affairs, social problems, and more, and his Irish bartender, a model of ordinary common sense and human decency, became a daily presence in the lives of readers all over the country. In more than seven hundred essays the fictional Mr. Dooley managed to expose deceit and hypocrisy among the mighty in a good-humored way that made his creator an important advocate for honesty and tolerance in public life.

Mr. Dooley

"Thim was prize fightin' days, Jawn. Sure Murphy'd take this man Corbett be th' hair an' pull him around th' block, he wud so."

"You're an expert," said Mr. McKenna with deference. "Who do you think'll win if they come together?"

"Well," said Mr. Dooley. "If 'tis a long-range fight Corbett ought to win. But I think Fitz'll get th' money if there's much in-fightin'. Corbett'd win over a tiliphone but Fitzsimmons'll smother him through a speakin'-chube." (Nov. 2, 1895)

EDUCATION IN IRELAND AND CHICAGO

"I see here," said Mr. Dooley, laying down his paper, "that there's a man out in th' hootchy-cootchy colledge on th' Midway that believes in corporeal punishment f'r childher."

"I seen that," said Mr. Hennessy, "an' I'd like to have him here. I'd go to th' flure with him. I'll bet he's near-sighted an' is afraid iv cows. I niver knowed a man that wanted to club little childher that wasn't. I had me own share iv hoistin' whin I was a kid an' I swore that if iver a ma-an laid hands on child iv mine I'd inthrojooce mesilf to him be means iv a pickax."

"I was licked good whin I was a kid," said Mr. Dooley solemnly. "I wint to school to an old hedge schoolmasther be th' name iv Larney. There were free schools nearer, but none iv us was sint. Our people paid Larney to polish us off an' he done it. Glory be, he was a rough man, a long-legged, sour-faced ol' man, as hard as his blackthorn stick an' as knotty. He larned us 'A-ah-b-l-e, to be competent' an' 'A-ah-b-e-l, a boy's name.' I can see him now in his knee breeches takin' off his long coat an' callin' out, 'McGuire, give ye'er back to Misther Dooley: I want to teach him th' etiket iv th' house iv larnin'.' He used a hoe-handle, an' whin he got through we were in a way to think betther thin to set down. Lord save us, it's fifty years an' more since I laid eyes on him, an' he's been dead most iv th' time, but to this day I dhream iv him an' wake up in terror, with th' cold chills chasin' each other down me back.

"I don't believe in corporeal punishment ayether for teacher or scholar," Mr. Dooley went on. "In th' ol' days whin we had a little school out here f'r thim that was too pious to go to th' public schools most iv th' throuble come fr'm th' scholars lammin' th' teachers. That was befure th' Christian brothers come. I niver

knowed a boy to lick a Christian brother. Most iv th' mimbers iv
that order wud've gone into th' prize ring if they hadn't landed
where they did. I'd match thim again anny body iv men in th'
wurruld at annything like their weight. There was wan iv thim
wanst, Brother Aloysius, that cleaned out th' whole Hogan fam'ly
in Halsted sthreet with th' 'Lives iv the Saints' tied to a book-
sthrap. But ye raymimber that. 'Twas befure th' Christian brothers
come that we had th' little school. They r-run out teacher afther
teacher. I've seen a whole procession iv thim pass this very dure.

"Well, afther a while a quite, gentlemanly young man from
colledge come along an' offered to take th' school. He was a big
man an' a strhong wan, but he was warned befurehand that he'd
have throuble. 'I guess I can get along all right,' says he, with that
quite, fearless look iv a man that knows his own strength. An' he
took th' school. F'r a time there was no throuble an' he was an
ideel school masther. He inthrested th' childher in their studies,
told thim stories an' learned thim to sing songs. He was a gr-reat
favorite with th' girls an' the parents swore be him. School life
took on a new color an' th' attindance was niver so high.

"But throuble was brewin'. No teacher had iver got away with
that school, an' th' rough la-ads did not propose to let this jood
from colledge do it. Wan day they was an open revolt. Some wan
pegged a lump iv coal at th' school masther an' th' school masther
descinded on Tom Mulhern, who was a quite lad, but had been
pointed out as th' toughest in th' class. 'Mulhern,' said th' teacher
ca'mly, 'come out here,' he says. 'What f'r?' says Mulhern. 'I un-
dherstand ye're quite a fighter,' says the young man in th' same
steady voice. 'I want to teach ye a lesson in boxin',' he says. 'Ye're
a good, strhong la-ad,' he says, 'but ye need insthruction in
boxin',' he says, with a smile on his face. 'I want th' school to see
Tom larn to box,' he says. 'Ivry man sh'd larn th' manly art iv self-
defense,' he says. 'All right,' says Tom Mulhern. 'Me father sint
me here to larn sums, but,' he says, 'if ye can teach me anny other
accomplishments,' he says, 'I'm ye'er gooseberry,' he says.

"Th' school was silent as a church as th' big, hulkin' rowdy
faced th' quite but determined masther. 'Put up ye'er hands,' says
th' masther, 'f'r I'm goin' to hit ye har-rd,' he says. 'Poke away,
ol' spoort,' says th' lout, an' suddenly th' masther's fist shot out
like lightenin'. But just at that moment Tom ducked his head an'

comin' up undher th' masther's high gyard he ripped in a stiff right hand punch in th' wind an' cracked him wan in th' nose with th' left. As th' school masther sunk again a blackboard, with th' quite, confident smile turnin' green, Tom hooked him on th' point iv th' jaw an' put him out. Mike O'Grady pulled out a stop watch an' counted. 'Wan, two, three, four, five, six, siven, eight, nine, tin,' he says. 'Th' fight goes to Mulhern,' he says. Ye see, Tom Mulhern was th' welterweight champeen iv Illinye an' only wint to school whin he was not fightin' f'r $50 a corner.

"Afther that come th' brothers, an' whin wan iv thim wint through th' Christian jooty class with a couplin'-pin th' school become ordherly."

"Well, annyhow, I don't believe in lammin' th' kids," said Mr. Hennessy.

"Nayether do I," said Mr. Dooley. "If a lad don't want to go to school I say lave him stay away. There's too much idyacation annyhow. There's twinty men in this counthry that can write pothry to wan that can dhrive a car or hoop a bar'l." (July 10, 1897)

BRIDGEPORT IN THE CIVIL WAR

"Jawn," said Mr. Dooley the other evening, "did ye see th' p'rade yisterday?"

"Yes," said Mr. McKenna.

"Was it good?"

"Fine."

"Who led th' polis?"

"Mike Brennan, on horseback."

"Be hivins," said Mr. Dooley, "I wisht I'd been there, f'r when I knowed Mike Brennan he couldn't ride a thrunk without houldin' on. But I've made it a rule niver to go out on Dec'ration Day. It turns the hear-rt in me gray f'r to see th' women marchin' to Calv'ry with their veils over their heads an' thim little pots iv gyraniums in their hands. Th' sojers has thim that'll fire salutes over their graves an' la-ads to talk about thim, but there's none but th' widdy f'r to break her hear-rt above th' poor soul that died afther his hands had tur-rned to leather fr'm handlin' a pick. But

thin what's th' odds? Dam'd th' bit iv difference it makes to a
man wanst he's tucked away in Calv'ry whether he died f'r his
counthry or was r-run over be a brewery-wagon. Whin Gavin nails
th' lid on th' crate an' sinds down to th' corner grocery f'r th'
pallbearers we're all akel an' all heroes.

"Ye was a little bit iv a kid, Jawn, durin' th' war and ye raymimber nawthin' about it. But to me th' mim'ry iv it is as fr-resh as
paint. I wint through it all. I mind as well as if it happened yisterday whin Thomas Duggan came up th' r-road wan afternoon
an' says he: 'Barrygard,' says he, 'is firin' on Sumter.' I'd niver
hear-rd iv Barrygard an' says I: 'Is he,' I says; 'whin did he lose
his job on th' Alton?' I says. 'Tut, tut,' says he. 'Barrygard is a
while Jawnny Powers was bein' done up an' purtend he was in on
th' play; I'd get afther him.

"Thin I'd put up a social colony like Hull House down town
near th' banks an' th' boord iv thrade an' th' stock exchange. I'd
have ladin' citizens come in an' larn be contact with poor an'
honest people th' advantage iv a life they've on'y heard iv. I think
th' Hull House idee is right, but I'd apply it diff'rent. A man
wurrukin' in a bank all day thryin' to get money anny way he can,
how's he goin' to know anny diff'rent? What he needs is to be
cheered up, have th' pi-anny played to him be nice-lookin' girls,
an' find out somethin' iv th' beauties iv honest poverty be con-
varsin' with poor an' honest people."

"But where'd ye get th' la-ads to r-run it?" asked Mr. Hennessy.

"That's easy," said Mr. Dooley. "If ye'll get th' bankers I'll get
th' others. I know thousands iv poor but honest men that ar-re
on'y waitin' f'r th' chanst to get wan crack at a banker." (Jan. 15,
1898)

"I am in favor iv th' departmint stores. I riconize thim as a
monsthrous evil, but they are a sign iv th' gr-reat an' growin'
cinthrilization iv thrade an' cannot be stopped so long as they pay
rint an' advertise.

"I denounce th' sale iv opyum as detrimintal to th' morals an'
injooryous to th' complexions iv th' race, but owin' to th' lar-rge
number iv houses in this gr-reat an' growin' city iv ours that ar-re
occupied be opyum j'ints I wud so rigulate th' thraffic that it cud
grow without inflictin' injury on th' people.

"Fin'lly, I denounce as criminal, wasteful, extravagant, damna-

ble, scand'lous an' low th' prisint administhration an' all admin-
isthrations past an' to come, an' on this platform," said Mr.
Dooley, "I appeal to ye, Hinnissy, f'r ye'er suffrages."

"I've on'y wan undher th' Austhrelyan law," said Mr. Hennessy,
"an' that's pledged already."

"Very well," said Mr. Dooley, "go on thin an' vote f'r J. Irving
Pearce, if ye want to." (March 27, 1897)

THE CAMPAIGN OF 1897:
THE CROW IN THE TREE

"Me poor head is achin' with th' turmoil iv th' campaign," said
Mr. Hennessy. "With all th' candydates in th' field I'm crazy. It
usen't to be so. In th' good ol' days whin it was allus Charter H.
Harrison again Jawn M. Smythe's Unknown we niver had no
throuble in pickin' an' choosin'. We ayether voted f'r Charter or
some wan else did. I mind goin' to th' polls about noon wan
iliction day to deposit me vote. 'What's ye'er name?' says th' clerk.
'Hinnissy,' says I. 'Hinnissy, Hinnissy, Timothy Hinnissy, is it?' he
says. 'It is,' says I. 'Well, I'm sorry, Mr. Hinnissy,' says he, 'but
there was a man in here an hour ago that voted f'r ye,' he says.
'Ye'll have to pick a name out iv this list,' he says. An' I voted
undher th' name iv Olson."

"Ye needn't put ye'erself to throuble choosin'," said Mr.
Dooley. "All ye have to do is to vote f'r th' people's choice, th'
boy orator iv Haley's slough—an' that's me. There's nawthin'
wrong with me platform. I'm f'r civil sarvice rayform that doesn't
rayform. I'm f'r compinsation f'r franchises if none iv it iver gets
to th' people that wud spind it in exthravagance. I want th' saloons closed afther midnight—th' saloons iv Schwartzmeister an'
Ahern, rowdy places. I'll close me own whin I get tired. Why ain't
I th' ideel candydate?

"An' I'm f'r th' Sthreet Ca-ar Magnum. I'm th' on'y candydate
that comes out fair an' square an' declares that he's th' creature
iv that gr-reat an' good man. Some iv me opponents is fightin'
him an' some others is sayin' nawthin', but diggin' har-rd into th'
pockets where he keeps his change. But I'm a corporation man,

a sthreet railway tool, an' if ilicted I promise to deliver over a
blanket morgedge on th' town to that saint on earth th' Sthreet
Ca-ar Magnum. What he'll be in th' hereafther I dinnaw, but if
he didn't put up that tillyscope f'r to survey a route f'r a trolley
line in Moodyville I don't know th' frind iv th' people.

"If half th' men on earth did as much good as th' Sthreet
Ca-ar Magnum iviry human bein' 'd be a stockholder. I heard a
fellow say wanst that th' man that made two shares iv stock grow
where on'y wan growed befure was a binifacthor to th' race. Th'
Sthreet Ca-ar Magnum makes eight grow. An' if half th' men on
earth was as honest as th' Sthreet Ca-ar Magnum they'd have th'
other half in th' pinitintiary. They'se no frills on this great an'
good philanthropist. He searches out th' hear-rts iv men an' whin
he finds thim r-rings thim up. Ye can't deceive a lad that meets
Virtue whin it comes f'r a dividend an' that knows where th' rayform ilimint does its bankin'. A man comes along with a fair front
concealin' th' divilish purpose iv givin' th' people iv this city a
chanst f'r their lives—wan chanst in tin thousand f'r to lift their
heads an' thank th' Lord f'r livin'. He wants to make it so a man
can go to th' city hall to pay his taxes without havin' his pocket
picked. He wants to write acrost the page, dark with bloodshed
an' plunder, wan line iv goold that our childher—ye'ers, not
mine, f'r I have none, thank th' Lord—can read without shame.
An' people believe in him, an' crowd to hear him, an' cheer him,
an' bid him good luck. But not th' Sthreet Ca-ar Magnum. Thank
th' saints f'r wan man clear-sighted enough to pinithrate human
motives. Thank th' Lord f'r th' crooked yardstick. Th' Sthreet
Ca-ar Magnum says: 'He's a fraud an' an ass.' A fraud an' an ass!

"An' mebbe he is, too. An ass, annyhow, to think that annything can be done that th' Sthreet Ca-ar Magnum doesn't write
temprematoor" in, like an archbishop in a caddychism. Th' on'y
candydate that has a r-right to live is th' wan that turns in his
platform like a thrip-sheet iv a conductor f'r th' Sthreet Ca-ar
Magnum to approve. An' th' Sthreet Ca-ar Magnum knows his
business. He has what th' pa-apers calls 'th' key iv th' situation.'
I butt up again a man on th' sthreet an' he falls again another
man an' that man reels again you, Hinnissy, walkin' along th'
curb, ca'm an' peaceful, an' out ye go into th' mud. I don't like
Schwartzmeister—an' I don't—an' I heave a rock through his

window, an' lo! an' behold, I hit me cousin Mike standin' at th' ba-ar takin' his quiet drink. I go out to make th' Sthreet Ca-ar Magnum give back part iv what he took, an' th' first thing I know me banker that has his bonds piled up like cordwood in his safe tells me to take th' little account that I'm savin' against license day around th' corner an' lave it in th' ash bar'l. Th' crow is up in th' three, no doubt, black an' ugly, stealin' me potatoes an' makin' me life miserable with his noise, but whin I throw a club at him he's out iv th' way an' it smashes into a nest full iv eggs that some frind of mine has been hatchin' out.

"An' that's why I'm th' sthreetcar candydate. I believe in th' Magnum. I am in favor iv corruption an' bribery, f'r 'tis on'y be means iv thim we can live comfortably, die happy an' dhraw inthrest. Virtue is shovellin' coal at a dollar-an'a-half a day."

"I don't believe it," said Mr. Hennessy, flaring up. "I don't believe wan wur-rud iv it."

"Go wan," said Mr. Dooley. "Ye've been to hear Moody." (April 3, 1897)

The Campaign of 1897:
Post-election Analysis

[In the election of Tuesday, April 6, Carter Harrison, Jr. won a landslide victory, and a safe majority of known boodlers was returned to the city council. These included Bridgeport's Billy O'Brien, who had been serving as a state senator. The Union League Club was the bastion of Chicago's WASP business and community leadership. Here, Mr. Dooley explains the election as a product of the combined stupidity of voters and reformers.]

"That frind iv ye'ers, Dugan, is an intilligent man," said Mr. Dooley. "All he needs is an index an' a few illusthrations to make him a bicyclopedja iv useless information."

"Well," said Mr. Hennessy, judiciously, "he ain't no Soc-rates an' he ain't no answers-to-questions colum; but he's a good man that goes to his jooty, an' as handy with a pick as some people are with a cocktail spoon. What's he been doin' again ye?"

"Nawthin'," said Mr. Dooley, "but he was in her Choosday. 'Did ye vote?' says I. 'I did,' says he. 'Which wan iv th' distin- guished bunko steerers got ye'er invalu'ble suffrage?' says I. 'I didn't have none with me,' says he, 'but I voted f'r Charter Haitch,' says he. 'I've been with him in six ilictions,' says he, 'an' he's a good man,' he says. 'D'ye think ye're votin' f'r th' best?' says I. 'Why, man alive,' I says, 'Charter Haitch was assassinated three years ago,' I says. 'Was he?' says Dugan. 'Ah, well, he's lived that down be this time. He was a good man,' he says.

"Ye see, that's what thim rayform lads wint up again. If I liked rayformers, Hinnissy, an' wanted f'r to see thim win out wanst in their lifetime, I'd buy thim each a suit iv chilled steel, ar-rm him with raypeatin' rifles, an' take thim east iv State Sthreet an' south iv Jackson Bullyvard. At prisint th' opinion that pre-vails in th' ranks iv th' gloryous ar-rmy iv ray-form is that there ain't anny- thing worth seein' in this lar-rge an' commodyous desert but th' pest-house an' the bridewell. Me frind Willum J. O'Brien is no rayformer. But Willum J. undherstands that there's a few hun- dherds iv thousands iv people livin' in a part iv th' town that looks like nawthin' but smoke fr'm th' roof iv th' Onion League Club that have on'y two pleasures in life, to wur-ruk an' to vote, both iv which they do at th' uniform rate iv wan dollar an' a half a day. That's why Willum J. O'Brien is now a sinitor an' will be an al- dherman afther next Thursdah, an' it's why other people are sind- ing him flowers.

"This is th' way a rayform candydate is ilicted. Th' boys down town has heerd that things ain't goin' r-right somehow. Franchises is bein' handed out to none iv thim; an' wanst in a while a mimber iv th' club, comin' home a little late an' thryin' to riconcile a pair iv r-round feet with an embroidered sidewalk, meets a sthrong ar-rm boy that pushes in his face an' takes away all his marbles. It begins to be talked that th' time has come f'r good citizens f'r to brace up an' do somethin', an' they agree to nomynate a can- dydate f'r aldherman. 'Who'll we put up?' says they. 'How's Clar- ence Doolittle?' says wan. 'He's laid up with a coupon thumb, an' can't r-run.' 'An' how about Arthur Doheny?' 'I swore an oath whin I came out iv colledge I'd niver vote f'r a man that wore a made tie.' 'Well, thin, let's thry Willie Boye.' 'Good,' says th' com- ity. 'He's jus' th' man f'r our money.' An' Willie Boye, after thinkin' it over, goes to his tailor an' ordhers three dozen pairs iv pants, an' decides f'r to be th' sthandard-bearer iv th' people. Musin' over his fried eyesthers an' asparagus an' his champagne booze, he bets a polo pony again a box of golf-balls he'll be ili-cited unanimous; an' all th' good citizens make a vow f'r to set th' alar-rm clock f'r half-past three on th' afthernoon iv iliction day, so's to be up in time to vote f'r th' riprisintitive iv pure gover'mint.

" 'Tis some time befure they comprehind that there ar-re other candydates in th' field. But th' other candydates know it. Th' sthrongest iv thim—his name is Flannigan, an' he's a re-tail dealer in wines an' liquors, an' he lives over his establishment. Flannigan was nomynated enthusyastically at a prim'ry held in his bar-rn; an' befure Willie Boye had picked out pants that wud match th' color iv th' Austhreelyan ballot this here Flannigan had put a man on th' day watch, tol' him to speak gently to anny raygistered voter that wint to sleep behind th' sthove, an' was out that night visitin' his frinds. Who was it judged th' cake walk? Flannigan. Who was it carrid th' pall? Flannigan. Who was it sthud up at th' christen-ing? Flannigan. Whose ca-ards did th' grievin' widow, th' blushin' bridegroom, or th' happy father find in th' hack? Flannigan's. Ye bet ye'er life. Ye see Flannigan wasn't out f'r th' good iv th' com-muaity. Flannigan was out f'r Flannigan an' th' stuff.

"Well, iliction day come around; an' all th' imminent frinds iv good gover'mint had special wires sthrung into th' club, an' waited f'r th' returns. Th' first precin't showed 28 votes f'r Willie Boye to 14 f'r Flannigan. 'That's my precin't,' says Willie. 'I won-dher who voted thim fourteen?' 'Coachmen,' says Clarence Doo-little. 'There are thirty-five precin'ts in this ward,' says th' leader iv th' rayform ilimint. 'At this rate, I'm sure iv 440 meejority. Gos-soon,' he says, 'put a keg iv sherry wine on th' ice,' he says. 'Well,' he says, 'at last th' community is relieved fr'm misrule,' he says. 'To-morrah I will start in arrangin' amindmints to th' tariff sche-dool an' th' ar-bitration threety,' he says. 'We must be up an' doin',' he says. 'Hol' on there,' says wan iv th' comity. 'There must be some mistake in this fr'm th' sixth precin't, he says. 'Where's the sixth precin't?' says Clarence. 'Over be th' dumps,' says Willie. 'I told me futman to see to that. He lives at th' cor-ner iv Des-plaines an Bloo Island Av'noo on Goose's Island,' he says. 'What does it show?' 'Flannigan, three hundherd an' eighty-five; Hansen, forty-eight; Schwartz, twinty; O'Malley, sivinteen; Casey, ten; O'Day, eight; Larsen, five; O'Rourke, three; Mulcahy, two; Schmitt, two; Moloney, two; Riordon, two; O'Malley, two; Willie Boye, wan.' 'Gintlemin,' says Willie Boye, arisin' with a stern look in his eyes, 'th' rascal has bethrayed me. Waither, take th' sherry wine off th' ice. They'se no hope f'r sound financial legislation this year. I'm goin' home.'

"An', as he goes down th' sthreet, he hears a band play an' sees a procission headed be a calceem light; an', in a carredge, with his plug hat in his hand an' his di'mond makin' th' calceem look like a piece iv punk in a smoke-house, is Flannigan, payin' his first visit this side iv th' thracks." (April 10, 1897)

Mark Twain

(1835–1910)

Most of Twain's writing contains satire: *Innocents Abroad* (1869) takes American tourists to task, *The Gilded Age* (1873) pokes fun at the hypocrisies of the moneyed classes (and incidentally gave its name to an era), and his masterpiece, *The Adventures of Huckleberry Finn* (1884), makes human weakness of all kinds the object of his biting wit. Twain's fierce desire for social justice and his uncompromising egalitarianism find their highest expression in his satire.

In his later years, Twain was devastated by the deaths of his wife and two daughters, and his satire degenerated into a kind of misanthropic pessimism. *The Man Who Corrupted Hadleyburg* (1899), *What Is Man?* (1905), and *The Mysterious Stranger* (1916) are works from this period. But at his best, Twain produced some of the sharpest, most penetrating, and most durable satire in all of American literature. In shorter pieces, Twain could be devastating, as "The War Prayer" and "Fenimore Cooper's Literary Offenses" here demonstrate. Twain was also a very successful paid lecturer, and "Advice to Youth" was originally delivered as a speech. "A Helpless Situation" is a nice companion to Benjamin Franklin's letter of recommendation written a hundred years earlier.

Fenimore Cooper's Literary Offenses

The Pathfinder and *The Deerslayer* stand at the head of Cooper's novels as artistic creations. There are others of his works which contain parts as perfect as are to be found in these, and scenes even more thrilling. Not one can be compared with either of them as a finished whole.

The defects in both of these tales are comparatively slight. They were pure works of art.—*Prof. Lounsbury.*

The five tales reveal an extraordinary fullness of invention.

. . . One of the very greatest characters in fiction, Natty Bumppo. . . .

The craft of the woodsman, the tricks of the trapper, all the delicate art of the forest, were familiar to Cooper from his youth up.—*Prof. Brander Matthews.*

Cooper is the greatest artist in the domain of romantic fiction yet produced by America.—*Wilkie Collins.*

It seems to me that it was far from right for the Professor of English Literature in Yale, the Professor of English Literature in Columbia, and Wilkie Collins to deliver opinions on Cooper's literature without having read some of it. It would have been much more decorous to keep silent and let persons talk who have read Cooper.

Cooper's art has some defects. In one place in *Deerslayer,* and in the restricted space of two-thirds of a page, Cooper has scored 114 offenses against literary art out of a possible 115. It breaks the record.

There are nineteen rules governing literary art in the domain of romantic fiction—some say twenty-two. In *Deerslayer* Cooper violated eighteen of them. These eighteen require:

1. That a tale shall accomplish something and arrive somewhere. But the *Deerslayer* tale accomplishes nothing and arrives in the air.

2. They require that the episodes of a tale shall be necessary parts of the tale, and shall help to develop it. But as the *Deerslayer* tale is not a tale, and accomplishes nothing and arrives nowhere, the episodes have no rightful place in the work, since there was nothing for them to develop.

3. They require that the personages in a tale shall be alive, except in the case of corpses, and that always the reader shall be

able to tell the corpses from the others. But this detail has often been overlooked in the *Deerslayer* tale.

4. They require that the personages in a tale, both dead and alive, shall exhibit a sufficient excuse for being there. But this detail also has been overlooked in the *Deerslayer* tale.

5. They require that when the personages of a tale deal in conversation, the talk shall sound like human talk, and be talk such as human beings would be likely to talk in the given circumstances, and have a discoverable meaning, also a discoverable purpose, and a show of relevancy, and remain in the neighborhood of the subject in hand, and be interesting to the reader, and help out the tale, and stop when the people cannot think of anything more to say. But this requirement has been ignored from the beginning of the *Deerslayer* tale to the end of it.

6. They require that when the author describes the character of a personage in his tale, the conduct and conversation of that personage shall justify said description. But this law gets little or no attention in the *Deerslayer* tale, as Natty Bumppo's case will amply prove.

7. They require that when a personage talks like an illustrated, gilt-edged, tree-calf, hand-tooled, seven-dollar Friendship's Offering in the beginning of a paragraph, he shall not talk like a negro minstrel in the end of it. But this rule is flung down and danced upon in the *Deerslayer* tale.

8. They require that crass stupidities shall not be played upon the reader as "the craft of the woodsman, the delicate art of the forest," by either the author or the people in the tale. But this rule is persistently violated in the *Deerslayer* tale.

9. They require that the personages of a tale shall confine themselves to possibilities and let miracles alone; or, if they venture a miracle, the author must so plausibly set it forth as to make it look possible and reasonable. But these rules are not respected in the *Deerslayer* tale.

10. They require that the author shall make the reader feel a deep interest in the personages of his tale and in their fate; and that he shall make the reader love the good people in the tale and hate the bad ones. But the reader of the *Deerslayer* tale dislikes the good people in it, is indifferent to the others, and wishes they would all get drowned together.

11. They require that the characters in a tale shall be so clearly

defined that the reader can tell beforehand what each will do in a given emergency. But in the *Deerslayer* tale this rule is vacated.

In addition to these large rules there are some little ones. These require that the author shall

12. *Say* what he is proposing to say, not merely come near it.
13. Use the right word, not its second cousin.
14. Eschew surplusage.
15. Not omit necessary details.
16. Avoid slovenliness of form.
17. Use good grammar.
18. Employ a simple and straightforward style.

Even these seven are coldly and persistently violated in the *Deerslayer* tale.

Cooper's gift in the way of invention was not a rich endowment; but such as it was he liked to work it, he was pleased with the effects, and indeed he did some quite sweet things with it. In his little box of stage-properties he kept six or eight cunning devices, tricks, artifices for his savages and woodsmen to deceive and circumvent each other with, and he was never so happy as when he was working these innocent things and seeing them go. A favorite one was to make a moccasined person tread in the tracks of the moccasined enemy, and thus hide his own trail. Cooper wore out barrels and barrels of moccasins in working that trick. Another stage-property that he pulled out of his box pretty frequently was his broken twig. He prized his broken twig above all the rest of his effects, and worked it the hardest. It is a restful chapter in any book of his when somebody doesn't step on a dry twig and alarm all the reds and whites for two hundred yards around. Every time a Cooper person is in peril, and absolute silence is worth four dollars a minute, he is sure to step on a dry twig. There may be a hundred handier things to step on, but that wouldn't satisfy Cooper. Cooper requires him to turn out and find a dry twig; and if he can't do it, go and borrow one. In fact, the Leatherstocking Series ought to have been called the Broken Twig Series.

I am sorry there is not room to put in a few dozen instances of the delicate art of the forest, as practised by Natty Bumppo and some of the other Cooperian experts. Perhaps we may venture two or three samples. Cooper was a sailor—a naval officer; yet he gravely tells us how a vessel, driving toward a lee shore in a gale, is steered for a particular spot by her skipper because he knows of an *undertow* there which will hold her back against the gale and save her. For just pure woodcraft, or sailorcraft, or whatever it is, isn't that neat? For several years Cooper was daily in the society of artillery, and he ought to have noticed that when a cannon-ball strikes the ground it either buries itself or skips a hundred feet or so; skips again a hundred feet or so—and so on, till finally it gets tired and rolls. Now in one place he loses some "females"—as he always calls women—in the edge of a wood near a plain at night in a fog, on purpose to give Bumppo a chance to show off the delicate art of the forest before the reader. These mislaid people are hunting for a fort. They hear a cannon-blast, and a cannon-ball presently comes rolling into the wood and stops at their feet. To the females this suggests nothing. The case is very different with the admirable Bumppo. I wish I may never know peace again if he doesn't strike out promptly and *follow the track* of that cannon-ball across the plain through the dense fog and find the fort. Isn't it a daisy? If Cooper had any real knowledge of Nature's ways of doing things, he had a most delicate art in concealing the fact. For instance: one of his acute Indian experts, Chingachgook (pronounced Chicago, I think), has lost the trail of a person he is tracking through the forest. Apparently that trail is hopelessly lost. Neither you nor I could ever have guessed out the way to find it. It was very different with Chicago. Chicago was not stumped for long. He turned a running stream out of its course, and there, in the slush in its old bed, were that person's moccasin tracks. The current did not wash them away, as it would have done in all other like cases—no, even the eternal laws of Nature have to vacate when Cooper wants to put up a delicate job of woodcraft on the reader.

We must be a little wary when Brander Matthews tells us that Cooper's books "reveal an extraordinary fullness of invention." As a rule, I am quite willing to accept Brander Matthews's literary judgments and applaud his lucid and graceful phrasing of them; but that particular statement needs to be taken with a few tons of salt. Bless your heart, Cooper hadn't any more invention than a horse; and I don't mean a high-class horse, either; I mean a clothes-horse. It would be very difficult to find a really clever "sit-

uation'' in Cooper's books, and still more difficult to find one of
any kind which he has failed to render absurd by his handling of
it. Look at the episodes of "the caves"; and at the celebrated
scuffle between Maqua and those others on the table-land a few
days later; and at Hurry Harry's queer water-transit from the castle
to the ark; and at Deerslayer's half-hour with his first corpse; and
at the quarrel between Hurry Harry and Deerslayer later; and at
—but choose for yourself; you can't go amiss.

If Cooper had been an observer his inventive faculty would have
worked better; not more interestingly, but more rationally, more
plausibly. Cooper's proudest creations in the way of "situations"
suffer noticeably from the absence of the observer's protecting
gift. Cooper's eye was splendidly inaccurate. Cooper seldom saw
anything correctly. He saw nearly all things as through a glass eye,
darkly. Of course a man who cannot see the commonest little
every-day matters accurately is working at a disadvantage when he
is constructing a "situation." In the *Deerslayer* tale Cooper has a
stream which is fifty feet wide where it flows out of a lake; it
presently narrows to twenty as it meanders along for no given
reason, and yet when a stream acts like that it ought to be required to explain itself. Fourteen pages later the width of the
brook's outlet from the lake has suddenly shrunk thirty feet, and
become "the narrowest part of the stream." This shrinkage is not
accounted for. The stream has bends in it, a sure indication that
it has alluvial banks and cuts them; yet these bends are only thirty
and fifty feet long. If Cooper had been a nice and punctilious
observer he would have noticed that the bends were oftener nine
hundred feet long than short of it.

Cooper made the exit of that stream fifty feet wide, in the first
place, for no particular reason; in the second place, he narrowed
it to less than twenty to accommodate some Indians. He bends a
"sapling" to the form of an arch over this narrow passage, and
conceals six Indians in its foliage. They are "laying" for a settler's
scow or ark which is coming up the stream on its way to the lake;
it is being hauled against the stiff current by a rope whose stationary end is anchored in the lake; its rate of progress cannot be
more than a mile an hour. Cooper describes the ark, but pretty
obscurely. In the matter of dimensions "it was little more than a
modern canal-boat." Let us guess, then, that it was about one

hundred and forty-feet long. It was of "greater breadth than common." Let us guess, then, that it was about sixteen feet wide. This leviathan had been prowling down bends which were but a third as long as itself, and scraping between banks where it had only two feet of space to spare on each side. We cannot too much admire this miracle. A low-roofed log dwelling occupies "two-thirds of the ark's length"—a dwelling ninety feet long and sixteen feet wide, let us say—a kind of vestibule train. The dwelling has two rooms—each forty-five feet long and sixteen feet wide, let us guess. One of them is the bedroom of the Hutter girls, Judith and Hetty; the other is the parlor in the daytime, at night it is papa's bedchamber. The ark is arriving at the stream's exit now, whose width has been reduced to less than twenty feet to accommodate the Indians—say to eighteen. There is a foot to spare on each side of the boat. Did the Indians notice that there was going to be a tight squeeze there? Did they notice that they could make money by climbing down out of that arched sapling and just stepping aboard when the ark scraped by? No, other Indians would have noticed these things, but Cooper's Indians never notice anything. Cooper thinks they are marvelous creatures for noticing, but he was almost always in error about his Indians. There was seldom a sane one among them.

The ark is one hundred and forty-feet long; the dwelling is ninety feet long. The idea of the Indians is to drop softly and secretly from the arched sapling to the dwelling as the ark creeps along under it at the rate of a mile an hour, and butcher the family. It will take the ark a minute and a half to pass under. It will take the ninety-foot dwelling a minute to pass under. Now, then, what did the six Indians do? It would take you thirty years to guess, and even then you would have to give it up, I believe. Therefore, I will tell you what the Indians did. Their chief, a person of quite extraordinary intellect for a Cooper Indian, warily watched the canal-boat as it squeezed along under him, and when he had got his calculations fined down to exactly the right shade, as he judged, he let go and dropped. And *missed the house!* That is actually what he did. He missed the house, and landed in the stern of the scow. It was not much of a fall, yet it knocked him silly. He lay there unconscious. If the house had been ninety-seven feet long he would have made the trip. The fault was Cooper's,

not his. The error lay in the construction of the house. Cooper
was no architect.

There still remained in the roost five Indians. The boat has
passed under and is now out of their reach. Let me explain what
the five did—you would not be able to reason it out for yourself.
No. 1 jumped for the boat, but fell in the water astern of it. Then
No. 2 jumped for the boat, but fell in the water still farther astern
of it. Then No. 3 jumped for the boat, and fell a good way astern
of it. Then No. 4 jumped for the boat, and fell in the water *away*
astern. Then even No. 5 made a jump for the boat—for he was
a Cooper Indian. In the matter of intellect, the difference between a Cooper Indian and the Indian that stands in front of the
cigar-shop is not spacious. The scow episode is really a sublime
burst of invention; but it does not thrill, because the inaccuracy
of the details throws a sort of air of fictitiousness and general
improbability over it. This comes of Cooper's inadequacy as an
observer.

The reader will find some examples of Cooper's high talent for
inaccurate observation in the account of the shooting-match in
The Pathfinder.

A common wrought nail was driven lightly into the target, its
head having been first touched with paint.

The color of the paint is not stated—an important omission,
but Cooper deals freely in important omissions. No, after all, it
was not an important omission; for this nail-head is *a hundred yards
from* the marksmen, and could not be seen by them at that distance, no matter what its color might be. How far can the best
eyes see a common house-fly? A hundred yards? It is quite impossible. Very well; eyes that cannot see a house-fly that is a hundred yards away cannot see an ordinary nail-head at that distance,
for the size of the two objects is the same. It takes a keen eye to
see a fly or a nail-head at fifty yards—one hundred and fifty feet.
Can the reader do it?

The nail was lightly driven, its head painted, and game called.
Then the Cooper miracles began. The bullet of the first marks-
man chipped an edge of the nail-head; the next man's bullet
drove the nail a little way into the target—and removed all the
paint. Haven't the miracles gone far enough now? Not to suit

Cooper; for the purpose of this whole scheme is to show off his prodigy, Deerslayer-Hawkeye-Long-Rifle-Leatherstocking-Path-finder-Bumppo before the ladies.

"Be all ready to clench it, boys!" cried out Pathfinder, stepping into his friend's tracks the instant they were vacant. "Never mind a new nail; I can see that, though the paint is gone, and what I can see I can hit at a hundred yards, though it were only a mosquito's eye. Be ready to clench!"

The rifle cracked, the bullet sped its way, and the head of the nail was buried in the wood, covered by the piece of flattened lead.

There, you see, is a man who could hunt flies with a rifle, and command a ducal salary in a Wild West show to-day if we had him back with us.

The recorded feat is certainly surprising just as it stands; but it is not surprising enough for Cooper. Cooper adds a touch. He has made Pathfinder do this miracle with another man's rifle; and not only that, but Pathfinder did not have even the advantage of loading it himself. He had everything against him, and yet he made that impossible shot; and not only made it, but did it with absolute confidence, saying, "Be ready to clench." Now a person like that would have undertaken that same feat with a brickbat, and with Cooper to help he would have achieved it, too.

Pathfinder showed off handsomely that day before the ladies. His very first feat a thing which no Wild West show can touch. He was standing with the group of marksmen, observing—a hundred yards from the target, mind; one Jasper raised his rifle and drove the center of the bull's-eye. Then the Quartermaster fired. The target exhibited no result this time. There was a laugh. "It's a dead miss," said Major Lundie. Pathfinder waited an impressive moment or two; then said, in that calm, indifferent, know-it-all way of his, "No, Major, he has covered Jasper's bullet, as will be seen if any one will take the trouble to examine the target."

Wasn't it remarkable! How *could* he see that little pellet fly through the air and enter that distant bullet-hole? Yet that is what he did; for nothing is impossible to a Cooper person. Did any of those people have any deep-seated doubts about this thing? No; for that would imply sanity, and these were all Cooper people.

The respect for Pathfinder's skill and for his *quickness and accuracy of sight* [the italics are mine] was so profound and general, that the instant he made this declaration the spectators began to distrust their own opinions, and a dozen rushed to the target in order to ascertain the fact. There, sure enough, it was found that the Quartermaster's bullet had gone through the hole made by Jasper's, and that, too, so accurately as to require a minute examination to be certain of the circumstance, which, however, was soon clearly established by discovering one bullet over the other in the stump against which the target was placed.

They made a "minute" examination; but never mind, how could they know that there were two bullets in that hole without digging the latest one out? for neither probe nor eyesight could prove the presence of any more than one bullet. Did they dig? No; as we shall see. It is the Pathfinder's turn now; he steps out before the ladies, takes aim, and fires.

But, alas! here is a disappointment; an incredible, an unimaginable disappointment—for the target's aspect is unchanged; there is nothing there but that same old bullet-hole!

"If one dared to hint at such a thing," cried Major Duncan, "I should say that the Pathfinder has also missed the target!"

As nobody had missed it yet, the "also" was not necessary; but never mind about that, for the Pathfinder is going to speak.

"No, no, Major," said he, confidently, "that *would* be a risky declaration. I didn't load the piece, and can't say what was in it; but if it was lead, you will find the bullet driving down those of the Quartermaster and Jasper, else is not my name Pathfinder."

A shout from the target announced the truth of this assertion.

Is the miracle sufficient as it stands? Not for Cooper. The Pathfinder speaks again, as he "now slowly advances toward the stage occupied by the females":

"That's not all, boys, that's not all; if you find the target touched at all, I'll own to a miss. The Quartermaster cut the wood, but you'll find no wood cut by that last messenger."

The miracle is at last complete. He knew—doubtless *saw*—at the distance of a hundred yards—that his bullet had passed into the hole *without fraying the edges*. There were now three bullets in that one hole—three bullets embedded processionally in the body of the stump back of the target. Everybody knew this—somehow or other—and yet nobody had dug any of them out to make sure. Cooper is not a close observer, but he is interesting. He is certainly always that, no matter what happens. And he is more interesting when he is not noticing what he is about than when he is. This is a considerable merit.

The conversations in the Cooper books have a curious sound in our modern ears. To believe that such talk really ever came out of people's mouths would be to believe that there was a time when time was of no value to a person who thought he had something to say; when it was the custom to spread a two-minute remark out to ten; when a man's mouth was a rolling-mill, and busied itself all day long in turning four-foot pigs of thought into thirty-foot bars of conversational railroad iron by attenuation; when subjects were seldom faithfully stuck to, but the talk wandered all around and arrived nowhere; when conversations consisted mainly of irrelevancies, with here and there a relevancy, a relevancy with an embarrassed look, as not being able to explain how it got there.

Cooper was certainly not a master in the construction of dialogue. Inaccurate observation defeated him here as it defeated him in so many other enterprises of his. He even failed to notice that the man who talks corrupt English six days in the week must and will talk it on the seventh, and can't help himself. In the *Deerslayer* story he lets Deerslayer talk the showiest kind of book-talk sometimes, and at other times the basest of base dialects. For instance, when some one asks him if he has a sweetheart, and if so, where she abides, this is his majestic answer:

"She's in the forest—hanging from the boughs of the trees, in a soft rain—in the dew on the open grass—the clouds that float about in the blue heavens—the birds that sing in the woods—the sweet springs where I slake my thirst—and in all the other glorious gifts that come from God's Providence!''

And he preceded that, a little before, with this:

"It consarns me as all things that touches a fri'nd consarns a fri'nd."

And this is another of his remarks:

"If I was Injin born, now, I might tell of this, or carry in the scalp and boast of the expl'ite afore the whole tribe; or if my inimy had only been a bear"—[and so on].

We cannot imagine such a thing as a veteran Scotch Commander-in-Chief comporting himself in the field like a windy melodramatic actor, but Cooper could. On one occasion Alice and Cora were being chased by the French through a fog in the neighborhood of their father's fort:

"*Point de quartier aux coquins!*" cried an eager pursuer, who seemed to direct the operations of the enemy.

"Stand firm and be ready, my gallant 60ths!" suddenly exclaimed a voice above them; "wait to see the enemy; fire low, and sweep the glacis."

"Father! father!" exclaimed a piercing cry from out the mist, "it is I! Alice! thy own Elsie! spare, O! save your daughters!"

"Hold!" shouted the former speaker, in the awful tones of parental agony, the sound reaching even to the woods, and rolling back in solemn echo. " 'Tis she! God has restored me my children! Throw open the sally-port; to the field, 60ths, to the field! pull not a trigger, lest ye kill my lambs! Drive off these dogs of France with your steel!"

Cooper's word-sense was singularly dull. When a person has a poor ear for music he will flat and sharp right along without knowing it. He keeps near the tune, but it is *not* the tune. When a person has a poor ear for words, the result is a literary flatting and sharping; you perceive what he is intending to say, but you also perceive that he doesn't *say* it. This is Cooper. He was not a word-musician. His ear was satisfied with the *approximate* word. I will furnish some circumstantial evidence in support of this charge. My instances are gathered from half a dozen pages of the tale called *Deerslayer.* He uses "Verbal" for "oral"; "precision" for "facility"; "phenomena" for "marvels"; "necessary" for "pre-determined"; "unsophisticated" for "primitive"; "preparation" for "expectancy"; "rebuked" for "subdued"; "dependent on" for "resulting from"; "fact" for "condition"; "fact" for "conjec-ture"; "precaution" for "caution"; "explain" for "determine"; "mortified" for "disappointed"; "meretricious" for "factitious"; "materially" for "considerably"; "decreasing" for "deepening"; "increasing" for "disappearing"; "embedded" for "inclosed"; "treacherous" for "hostile"; "stood" for "stooped"; "softened" for "replaced"; "rejoined" for "remarked"; "situation" for "condition"; "different" for "differing"; "insensible" for "un-sentient"; "brevity" for "celerity"; "distrusted" for "suspicious"; "mental imbecility" for "imbecility"; "eyes" for "sight"; "counteracting" for "opposing"; "funeral obsequies" for "obse-quies."

There have been daring people in the world who claimed that Cooper could write English, but they are all dead now—all dead but Lounsbury. I don't remember that Lounsbury makes the claim in so many words, still he makes it, for he says that *Deerslayer* is a "pure work of art." Pure, in that connection, means fault-less—faultless in all details—and language is a detail. If Mr. Lounsbury had only compared Cooper's English with the English which he writes himself—but it is plain that he didn't; and so it is likely that he imagines until this day that Cooper's is as clean and compact as his own. Now I feel sure, deep down in my heart, that Cooper wrote about the poorest English that exists in our language, and that the English of *Deerslayer* is the very worst that even Cooper ever wrote.

I may be mistaken, but it does seem to me that *Deerslayer* is not a work of art in any sense; it does seem to me that it is destitute of every detail that goes to the making of a work of art; in truth, it seems to me that *Deerslayer* is just simply a literary *delirium tremens.*

A work of art? It has no invention; it has no order, system, sequence, or result; it has no lifelikeness, no thrill, no stir, no seeming of reality; its characters are confusedly drawn, and by their acts and words they prove that they are not the sort of people the author claims that they are; its humor is pathetic; its pathos is funny; its conversations are—oh! indescribable; its love-scenes odious; its English a crime against the language.

Counting these out, what is left is Art. I think we must all admit that.

1895

A Helpless Situation

Once or twice a year I get a letter of a certain pattern, a pattern that never materially changes, in form and substance, yet I cannot get used to that letter—it always astonishes me. It affects me as the locomotive always affects me: I say to myself, "I have seen you a thousand times, you always look the same way, yet you are always a wonder, and you are always impossible; to contrive you is clearly beyond human genius—you can't exist, you don't exist, yet here you are!"

I have a letter of that kind by me, a very old one. I yearn to print it, and where is the harm? The writer of it is dead years ago, no doubt, and if I conceal her name and address—her this-world address—I am sure her shade will not mind. And with it I wish to print the answer which I wrote at the time but probably did not send. If it went—which is not likely—it went in the form of a copy, for I find the original still here, pigeonholed with the said letter. To that kind of letters we all write answers which we do not send, fearing to hurt where we have no desire to hurt; I have done it many a time, and this is doubtless a case of the sort.

THE LETTER

X——., CALIFORNIA, *June 3, 1879*

Mr. S. L. Clemens, *Hartford, Conn.*

DEAR SIR,—You will doubtless be surprised to know who has presumed to write and ask a favor of you. Let your memory go back to your days in the Humboldt mines—'62–'63. You will remember, you and Clagett and Oliver and the old blacksmith Tillou lived in a lean-to which was half-way up the gulch, and there were six log cabins in the camp—strung pretty well separated up the gulch from its mouth at the desert to where the last claim was, at the divide. The lean-to you lived in was the one with a canvas roof that the cow fell down through one night, as told about by you in *Roughing It*—my uncle Simmons remembers it very well. He lived in the principal cabin, half-way up the divide, along with Dixon and Parker and Smith. It had two rooms, one for kitchen and the other for bunks, and was the only one that had. You and your party were there on the great night, the time they had dried-apple-pie, Uncle Simmons often speaks of it. It seems curious that dried-apple-pie should have seemed such a great thing, but it was, and it shows how far Humboldt was out of the world and difficult to get to, and how slim the regular bill of fare was. Sixteen years ago—it is a long time. I was a little girl then, only fourteen. I never saw you, I lived in Washoe. But Uncle Simmons ran across you every now and then, all during those weeks that you and party were there working your claim which was like the rest. The camp played out long and long ago, there wasn't silver enough in it to make a button. You never saw my husband, but he was there after you left, *and lived in that very lean-to*, a bachelor then but married to me now. He often wishes there had been a photographer there in those days, he would have taken the lean-to. He got hurt in the old Hal Clayton claim that was abandoned like the others putting in a blast and not climbing out quick enough, though he scrambled the best he could. It landed him clear down on the trail and hit a Piute. For weeks they thought he would not get over it but he did, and is all right, now. Has been ever since. This is a long introduction but it is the only way I can make myself known. The favor I ask I feel assured your generous heart will grant: Give me some advice about a book I have written. I do not claim anything for it only it is mostly true and as interesting as most of the books of the times. I am unknown in the literary world and you know what that means unless one has some one of influence (like yourself) to help you by speaking a good word for you. I would like to place the book on royalty basis plan with any one you would suggest.

This is a secret from my husband and family. I intend it as a surprise in case I get it published.

Feeling you will take an interest in this and if possible write me a letter to some publisher, or, better still, if you could see them for me and then let me hear.

I appeal to you to grant me this favor. With deepest gratitude I thank you for your attention.

One knows, without inquiring, that the twin of that embarrassing letter is forever and ever flying in this and that and the other direction across the continent in the mails, daily, nightly, hourly, unceasingly, unrestingly. It goes to every well-known merchant, and railway official, and manufacturer, and capitalist, and Mayor, and Congressman, and Governor, and editor, and publisher, and author, and broker, and banker—in a word, to every person who is supposed to have "influence." It always follows the one pattern: "You do not know me, *but you once knew a relative of mine*," etc., etc. We should all like to help the applicants, we should all be glad to do it, we should all like to return the sort of answer that is desired, but— Well, there is not a thing we can do that would be a help, for not in any instance does that letter ever come from anyone who *can* be helped. The struggler whom you *could* help does his own helping; it would not occur to him to apply to you, a stranger. He has talent and knows it, and he goes into his fight eagerly and with energy and determination—all alone, preferring to be alone. That pathetic letter which comes to you from the incapable, the unhelpable—how do you who are familiar with it answer it? What do you find to say? You do not want to inflict a wound; you hunt ways to avoid that. What do you find? How do you get out of your hard place with a contented conscience? Do you try to explain? The old reply of mine to such a letter shows that I tried that once. Was I satisfied with the result? Possibly; and possibly not; probably not; almost certainly not. I have long ago forgotten all about it. But, anyway, I append my effort:

THE REPLY

I know Mr. H., and I will go to him, dear madam, if upon reflection you find you still desire it. There will be a conversation. I know the form it will take. It will be like this:

Mr. H. How do her books strike you?

Mr. Clemens. I am not acquainted with them.

H. Who has been her publisher?

C. I don't know.

H. She *has* one, I suppose?

C. I—I think not.

H. Ah. You think this is her first book?

C. Yes—I suppose so. I think so.

H. What is it about? What is the character of it?

C. I believe I do not know.

H. Have you seen it?

C. Well—no, I haven't.

H. Ah-h. How long have you known her?

C. I don't know her.

H. Don't know her?

C. No.

H. Ah-h. How did you come to be interested in her book, then?

C. Well, she—she wrote and asked me to find a publisher for her, and mentioned you.

H. Why should she apply to you instead of to me?

C. She wished me to use my influence.

H. Dear me, what has *influence* to do with such a matter?

C. Well, I think she thought you would be more likely to examine her book if you were influenced.

H. Why, what we are here *for* is to examine books—anybody's book that comes along. It's our *business*. Why should we turn away a book unexamined because it's a stranger's? It would be foolish. No publisher does it. On what ground did she request your influence, since you do not know her? She must have thought you knew her literature and could speak for it. Is that it?

C. No; she knew I didn't.

H. Well, what then? She had a reason of *some* sort for believing you competent to recommend her literature, and also under obligations to do it?

C. Yes, I—I knew her uncle.

H. Knew her *uncle*?

C. Yes.

H. Upon my word! So, you knew her uncle; her uncle knows her literature; he indorses it to you; the chain is complete, nothing further needed; you are satisfied, and therefore—

C. No, that isn't all, there are other ties. I know the cabin her uncle lived in, in the mines; I knew his partners, too; also I came near knowing her husband before she married him, and I *did* know the abandoned shaft where a premature blast went off and he went flying through the air and clear down to the trail and hit an Indian in the back with almost fatal consequences.

H. To *him*, or to the Indian?

C. She didn't say which it was.

H. (*With a sigh*). It certainly beats the band! You don't know *her*, you don't know her literature, you don't know who got hurt when the blast went off, you don't know a single thing for us to build an estimate of her book upon, so far as I—

C. I knew her uncle. You are forgetting her uncle.

H. Oh, what use is *he*? Did you know him long? How long was it?

C. Well, I don't know that I really knew him, but I must have met him, anyway. I think it was that way; you can't tell about these things, you know, except when they are recent.

H. Recent? When was all this?

C. Sixteen years ago.

H. What a basis to judge a book upon! At first you said you knew him, and now you don't know whether you did or not.

C. Oh yes, I knew him; anyway, I think I thought I did; I'm perfectly certain of it.

H. What makes you think you thought you knew him?

C. Why, she says I did, herself.

H. She says so!

C. Yes, she does, and I *did* know him, too, though I don't remember it now.

H. Come—how can you know it when you don't remember it.

C. I don't know. That is, I don't know the process, but I *do* know lots of things that I don't remember, and remember lots of things that I don't know. It's so with every educated person.

H. (*After a pause.*) Is your time valuable?

C. No—well, not very.

H. Mine is.

So I came away then, because he was looking tired. Overwork, I reckon; I never do that; I have seen the evil effects of it. My mother was always afraid I would overwork myself, but I never did.

Dear madam, you see how it would happen if I went there. He would ask me those questions, and I would try to answer them to suit him, and he would hunt me here and there and yonder and get me embarrassed more and more all the time, and at last he would look tired on account of overwork, and there it would end and nothing done. I wish I could be useful to you, but, you see, they do not care for uncles or any of those things; it doesn't move them, it doesn't have the least effect, they don't care for anything but the literature itself, and they as good as despise influence. But they do care for books, and are eager to get them and examine them, no matter whence they come, nor from whose pen. If you will send yours to a publisher—any publisher—he will certainly examine it, I can assure you of that.

1905

Advice to Youth

Being told I would be expected to talk here, I inquired what sort of a talk I ought to make. They said it should be something suitable to youth—something didactic, instructive, or something in the nature of good advice. Very well. I have a few things in my mind which I have often longed to say for the instruction of the young: for it is in one's tender early years that such things will best take root and be most enduring and most valuable. First, then, I will say to you, my young friends—and I say it beseechingly, urgingly——

Always obey your parents, when they are present. This is the best policy in the long run, because if you don't they will make you. Most parents think they know better than you do, and you can generally make more by humoring that superstition than you can by acting on your own better judgment.

Be respectful to your superiors, if you have any, also to strangers, and sometimes to others. If a person offends you, and you are in doubt as to whether it was intentional or not, do not resort to extreme measures; simply watch your chance and hit him with a brick. That will be sufficient. If you shall find that he had not intended any offense, come out frankly and confess yourself in the wrong when you struck him; acknowledge it like a man and say you didn't mean to. Yes, always avoid violence; in this age of charity and kindliness, the time has gone by for such things. Leave dynamite to the low and unrefined.

Go to bed early, get up early—this is wise. Some authorities say get up with the sun; some others say get up with one thing, some with another. But a lark is really the best thing to get up with. It gives you a splendid reputation with everybody to know that you get up with the lark; and if you get the right kind of a lark, and work at him right, you can easily train him to get up at half past nine, every time—it is no trick at all.

Now as to the matter of lying. You want to be very careful about lying; otherwise you are nearly sure to get caught. Once caught, you can never again be, in the eyes of the good and the pure, what you were before. Many a young person has injured himself permanently through a single clumsy and ill-finished lie, the result of carelessness born of incomplete training. Some authorities hold that the young ought not to lie at all. That, of course, is putting it rather stronger than necessary; still, while I cannot go quite so far as that, I do maintain, and I believe I am right, that the young ought to be temperate in the use of this great art until practice and experience shall give them that confidence, elegance, and precision which alone can make the accomplishment graceful and profitable. Patience, diligence, painstaking attention to detail—these are the requirements; these, in time, will make the student perfect; upon these, and upon these only, may he rely as the sure foundation for future eminence. Think what tedious years of study, thought, practice, experience, went to the equipment of that peerless old master who was able to impose upon the whole world the lofty and sounding maxim that "truth is mighty and will prevail"—the most majestic compound fracture of fact which any of woman born has yet achieved. For the history of our race, and each individual's experience, are sown thick with evidence that a truth is not hard to kill and that a lie told well is immortal. There in Boston is a monument of the man who discovered anesthesia; many people are aware, in these latter days, that that man didn't discover it at all, but stole the discovery from another man. Is this truth mighty, and will it prevail? Ah no, my hearers, the monument is made of hardy material, but the lie it tells will outlast it a million years. An awkward, feeble, leaky lie is a thing which you ought to make it your unceasing study to avoid; such a lie as that has no more real permanence than an average truth. Why, you might as well tell the truth at once and be done with it. A feeble, stupid, preposterous lie will not live two years—except it be a slander upon somebody. It is indestructible, then, of course, but that is no merit of yours. A final word: begin your practice of this gracious and beautiful art early—begin now. If I had begun earlier, I could have learned how.

Never handle firearms carelessly. The sorrow and suffering that have been caused through the innocent but heedless handling of firearms by the young! Only four days ago, right in the next farmhouse to the one where I am spending the summer, a grandmother, old and gray and sweet, one of the loveliest spirits in the land, was sitting at her work, when her young grandson crept in and got down an old, battered, rusty gun which had not been touched for many years and was supposed not to be loaded, and pointed it at her, laughing and threatening to shoot. In her fright she ran screaming and pleading toward the door on the other side of the room; but as she passed him he placed the gun almost against her very breast and pulled the trigger! He had supposed it was not loaded. And he was right—it wasn't. So there wasn't any harm done. It is the only case of that kind I ever heard of. Therefore, just the same, don't you meddle with old unloaded firearms; they are the most deadly and unerring things that have ever been created by man. You don't have to take any pains at all with them; you don't have to have a rest, you don't have to have any sights on the gun, you don't have to take aim, even. No, you just pick out a relative and bang away, and you are sure to get him. A youth who can't hit a cathedral at thirty yards with a Gatling gun in three-quarters of an hour, can take up an old empty musket and bag his grandmother every time, at a hundred. Think what Waterloo would have been if one of the armies had been boys armed with old muskets supposed not to be loaded, and the other army had been composed of their female relations. The very thought of it makes one shudder.

There are many sorts of books; but good ones are the sort for the young to read. Remember that. They are a great, an inestimable, an unspeakable means of improvement. Therefore be careful in your selection, my young friends; be very careful; confine yourselves exclusively to Robertson's Sermons, Baxter's *Saint's Rest, The Innocents Abroad*, and works of that kind.

But I have said enough. I hope you will treasure up the instructions which I have given you, and make them a guide to your feet and a light to your understanding. Build your character thoughtfully and painstaking upon these precepts, and by and by, when you have got it built, you will be surprised and gratified to see how nicely and sharply it resembles everybody else's.

The Art of Inhumation

(FROM *LIFE ON THE MISSISSIPPI*)

About the same time, I encountered a man in the street, whom I had not seen for six or seven years; and something like this talk followed. I said,—

"But you used to look sad and oldish; you don't now. Where did you get all this youth and bubbling cheerfulness? Give me the address."

He chuckled blithely, took off his shining tile, pointed to a notched pink circlet of paper pasted into its crown, with something lettered on it, and went on chuckling while I read, "J. B——, UNDERTAKER." Then he clapped his hat on, gave it an irreverent tilt to leeward, and cried out,—

"That's what's the matter! It used to be rough times with me when you knew me—insurance-agency business, you know; mighty irregular. Big fire, all right—brisk trade for ten days while people scared; after that, dull policy-business till next fire. Town like this don't have fires often enough—a fellow strikes so many dull weeks in a row that he gets discouraged. But you bet you, *this* is the business! People don't wait for examples to *die*. No, sir, they drop off right along—there ain't any dull spots in the undertaker line. I just started in with two or three little old coffins and a hired hearse, and *now* look at the thing! I've worked up a business here that would satisfy any man, don't care who he is. Five years ago, lodged in an attic; live in a swell house now, with a mansard roof, and all the modern inconveniences."

"Does a coffin pay so well? Is there much profit on a coffin?"

"*Go*-way! How you talk!" Then, with a confidential wink, a dropping of the voice, and an impressive laying of his hand on my arm; "Look here; there's one thing in this world which is n't ever cheap. That's a coffin. There's one thing in this world which a person don't ever try to jew you down on. That's a coffin. There's one thing in this world which a person don't say,—'I'll look around a little, and if I find I can't do better I'll come back and take it.' That's a coffin. There's one thing in this world which a person won't take in pine if he can go walnut; and won't take in walnut if he can go mahogany; and won't take in mahogany if he can go an iron casket with silver door-plate and bronze handles. That's a coffin. And there's one thing in this world which you don't have to worry around after a person to get him to pay for. And *that's* a coffin. Undertaking?—why it's the dead-surest business in Christendom, and the nobbiest.

"Why, just look at it. A rich man won't have anything but your very best; and you can just pile it on, too—pile it on and sock it to him—he won't ever holler. And you take in a poor man, and if you work him right he'll bust himself on a single lay-out. Or especially a woman. F'r instance: Mrs. O'Flaherty comes in— widow—wiping her eyes and kind of moaning. Unhandkerchiefs one eye, bats it around tearfully over the stock; says,—

" 'And fhat might ye ask for that wan?'

" 'Thirty-nine dollars, madam,' says I.

" 'It's a foine big price, sure, but Pat shall be buried like a gintleman, as he was, if I have to work me fingers off for it. I'll have that wan, sor.'

" 'Yes, madam,' says I, 'and it is a very good one, too; not costly, to be sure, but in this life we must cut our garment to our clothes, as the saying is.' And as she starts out, I heave in, kind of casually, 'This one with the white satin lining is a beauty, but I am afraid —well, sixty-five dollars *is* a rather—rather—but no matter, I felt obliged to say to Mrs. O'Shaughnessy,—'

" 'D'ye mane to soy that Bridget O'Shaughnessy bought the mate to that joo-ul box to ship that dhrunken divil to Purgatory in?'

" 'Yes, madam.'

" 'Then Pat shall go to heaven in the twin to it, if it takes the last rap the O'Flaherties can raise; and moind you, stick on some extras, too, and I'll give ye another dollar.'

"And as I lay-in with the livery stables, of course I don't forget

to mention that Mrs. O'Shaughnessy hired fifty-four dollars' worth
of hacks and flung as much style into Dennis's funeral as if he
had been a duke or an assassin. And of course she sails in and
goes the O'Shaughnessy about four hacks and an omnibus better.
That *used* to be, but that's all played now; that is, in this particular
town. The Irish got to piling up hacks so, on their funerals, that
a funeral left them ragged and hungry for two years afterward; so
the priest pitched in and broke it all up. He don't allow them to
have but two hacks now, and sometimes only one.''

"Well," said I, "if you are so light-hearted and jolly in ordinary
times, what *must* you be in an epidemic?''

He shook his head.

"No, you're off, there. We don't like to see an epidemic. An
epidemic don't pay. Well, of course I don't mean that, exactly;
but it don't pay in proportion to the regular thing. Don't it occur
to you, why?''

"No.''

"Think.''

"I can't imagine. What is it?''

"It's just two things.''

"Well, what *are* they?''

"One's Embamming.''

"And what's the other?''

"Ice.''

"How is that?''

"Well, in ordinary times, a person dies, and we lay him up in
ice; one day, two days, maybe three, to wait for friends to come.
Takes a lot of it—melts fast. We charge jewelry rates for that ice,
and war-prices for attendance. Well, don't you know, when there's
an epidemic, they rush 'em to the cemetery the minute the
breath's out. No market for ice in an epidemic. Same with Embamming. You take a family that's able to embam, and you've got
a soft thing. You can mention sixteen different ways to do it—
though there *ain't* only one or two ways, when you come down to
the bottom facts of it—and they'll take the highest-priced way,
every time. It's human nature—human nature in grief. It don't
reason, you see. 'Time being, it don't care a dam. All it wants is
physical immortality for deceased, and they're willing to pay for
it. All you've got to do is to just be ca'm and stack it up—they'll
stand the racket. Why, man, you can take a defunct that you could

n't *give* away; and get your embamming traps around you and go to work; and in a couple of hours he is worth a cool six hundred—that's what *he's* worth. There ain't anything equal to it but trading rats for di'monds in time of famine. Well, don't you see, when there's an epidemic, people don't wait to embam. No, indeed they don't; and it hurts the business like hellth, as we say— hurts it like hell-th, *health*, see?—Our little joke in the trade. Well, I must be going. Give me a call whenever you need any—I mean, when you're going by, sometime.''

In his joyful high spirits, he did the exaggerating himself, if any has been done. I have not enlarged on him.

With the above brief references to inhumation, let us leave the subject. As for me, I hope to be cremated. I made that remark to my pastor once, who said, with what he seemed to think was an impressive manner,—

"I would n't worry about that, if I had your chances.''

Much he knew about it—the family all so opposed to it.

American in Europe

(FROM *A TRAMP ABROAD*)

One lingers about the Cathedral a good deal, in Venice. There is a strong fascination about it—partly because it is so old, and partly because it is so ugly. Too many of the world's famous buildings fail of one chief virtue—harmony; they are made up of a methodless mixture of the ugly and the beautiful; this is bad; it is confusing, it is unrestful. One has a sense of uneasiness, of distress, without knowing why. But one is calm before St. Mark, one is calm within it, one would be calm on top of it, calm in the cellar; for its details are masterfully ugly, no misplaced and impertinent beauties are intruded anywhere; and the consequent result is a grand harmonious whole, of soothing, entrancing, tranquilizing, soul-satisfying ugliness. One's admiration of a perfect thing always grows, never declines; and this is the surest evidence to him that it *is* perfect. St. Mark is perfect. To me it soon grew to be so nobly, so augustly ugly, that it was difficult to stay away from it, even for a little while. Every time its squat domes disappeared from my view, I had a despondent feeling; whenever they reappeared, I felt an honest rapture—I have not known any happier hours than those I daily spent in front of Florian's, looking across the Great Square at it. Propped on its long row of low thick-legged columns, its back knobbed with domes, it seemed like a vast warty bug taking a meditative walk.

St. Mark is not the oldest building in the world, of course, but it seems the oldest, and looks the oldest—especially inside. When the ancient mosaics in its walls become damaged, they are repaired but not altered; the grotesque old pattern is preserved. Antiquity has a charm of its own, and to smarten it up would only damage it. One day I was sitting on a red marble bench in the vestibule looking up at an ancient piece of apprentice-work, in mosaic, illustrative of the command to "multiply and replenish the earth." The Cathedral itself had seemed very old; but this picture was illustrating a period in history which made the building seem young by comparison. But I presently found an antique which was older than either the battered Cathedral or the date assigned to that piece of history; it was a spiral-shaped fossil as large as the crown of a hat; it was embedded in the marble bench, and had been sat upon by tourists until it was worn smooth. Contrasted with the inconceivable antiquity of this modest fossil, those other things were flippantly modern—jejune—mere matters of day-before-yesterday. The sense of the oldness of the Cathedral vanished away under the influence of this truly venerable presence.

St. Mark's is monumental; it is an imperishable remembrancer of the profound and simple piety of the Middle Ages. Whoever could ravish a column from a pagan temple, did it and contributed his swag to this Christian one. So this fane is upheld by several hundred acquisitions procured in that peculiar way. In our day it would be immoral to go on the highway to get bricks for a church, but it was no sin in the old times. St. Mark's was itself the victim of a curious robbery once. The thing is set down in the history of Venice, but it might be smuggled into the Arabian Nights and not seem out of place there:

Nearly four hundred and fifty years ago, a Candian named Stammato, in the suite of a prince of the house of Este, was allowed to view the riches of St. Mark. His sinful eye was dazzled and he hid himself behind an altar, with an evil purpose in his heart, but a priest discovered him and turned him out. Afterward he got in again—by false keys, this time. He went there, night after night, and worked hard and patiently, all alone, overcoming difficulty after difficulty with his toil, and at last succeeded in removing a great block of the marble paneling which walled the lower part of the treasury; this block he fixed so that he could take it out and put it in at will. After that, for weeks, he spent all his midnights in his magnificent mine, inspecting it in security, gloating over its marvels at his leisure, and always slipping back to his obscure lodgings before dawn, with a duke's ransom under his cloak. He did not need to grab, haphazard, and run—there was no hurry. He could make deliberate and well-considered selections; he could consult his æsthetic tastes. One comprehends how undisturbed he was, and how safe from any danger of interruption, when it is stated that he even carried off a unicorn's horn—a mere curiosity—which would not pass through the egress entire, but had to be sawn in two—a bit of work which cost him hours of tedious labor. He continued to store up his treasures at home until his occupation lost the charm of novelty and became monotonous; then he ceased from it, contented. Well he might be; for his collection, raised to modern values, represented nearly $50,000,000!

He could have gone home much the richest citizen of his country, and it might have been years before the plunder was missed; but he was human—he could not enjoy his delight alone, he must have somebody to talk about it with. So he exacted a solemn oath from a Candian noble named Crioni, then led him to his lodgings and nearly took his breath away with a sight of his glittering hoard. He detected a look in his friend's face which excited his suspicion, and was about to slip a stiletto into him when Crioni saved himself by explaining that that look was only an expression of supreme and happy astonishment. Stammato made Crioni a present of one of the state's principal jewels—a huge carbuncle, which afterward figured in the Ducal cap of state—and the pair parted. Crioni went at once to the palace, denounced the criminal, and handed over the carbuncle as evidence. Stammato was arrested, tried, and condemned, with the old-time Venetian promptness. He was hanged between the two great columns in the Piazza—with a gilded rope, out of compliment to his love of gold, perhaps. He got no good of his booty at all—it was *all* recovered.

In Venice we had a luxury which very seldom fell to our lot on the Continent—a home dinner with a private family. If one could always stop with private families, when traveling, Europe would have a charm which it now lacks. As it is, one must live in the hotels, of course, and that is a sorrowful business. A man accustomed to American food and American domestic cookery would not starve to death suddenly in Europe; but I think he would gradually waste away, and eventually die.

He would have to do without his accustomed morning meal. That is too formidable a change altogether; he would necessarily suffer from it. He could get the shadow, the sham, the base counterfeit of that meal; but that would do him no good, and money could not buy the reality.

To particularize: the average American's simplest and commonest form of breakfast consists of coffee and beefsteak; well, in Europe, coffee is an unknown beverage. You can get what the European hotel-keeper thinks is coffee, but it resembles the real thing as hypocrisy resembles holiness. It is a feeble, characterless, uninspiring sort of stuff, and almost as undrinkable as if it had been made in an American hotel. The milk used for it is what the French call "Christian" milk,—milk which has been baptized.

After a few months' acquaintance with European "coffee," one's mind weakens, and his faith with it, and he begins to wonder if the rich beverage of home, with its clotted layer of yellow cream on top of it, is not a mere dream, after all, and a thing which never existed.

Next comes the European bread,—fair enough, good enough, after a fashion, but cold; cold and tough, and unsympathetic; and never any change, never any variety,—always the same tiresome thing.

Next, the butter,—the sham and tasteless butter; no salt in it, and made of goodness knows what.

Then there is the beefsteak. They have it in Europe, but they don't know how to cook it. Neither will they cut it right. It comes on the table in a small, round, pewter platter. It lies in the center of this platter, in a bordering bed of grease-soaked potatoes; it is the size, shape, and thickness of a man's hand with the thumb and fingers cut off. It is a little overdone, is rather dry, it tastes pretty insipidly, it rouses no enthusiasm.

Imagine a poor exile contemplating that inert thing; and imagine an angel suddenly sweeping down out of a better land and setting before him a mighty porterhouse steak an inch and a half thick, hot and sputtering from the griddle; dusted with fragrant pepper; enriched with little melting bits of butter of the most unimpeachable freshness and genuineness; the precious juices of the meat trickling out and joining the gravy, archipelagoed with mushrooms; a township or two of tender, yellowish fat gracing an outlying district of this ample county of beefsteak; the long white bone which divides the sirloin from the tenderloin still in its place; and imagine that the angel also adds a great cup of American home-made coffee, with the cream a-froth on top, some real butter, firm and yellow and fresh, some smoking-hot biscuits, a plate of hot buckwheat cakes, with transparent syrup,—could words describe the gratitude of this exile?

The European dinner is better than the European breakfast, but it has its faults and inferiorities; it does not satisfy. He comes to the table eager and hungry; he swallows his soup,—there is an undefinable lack about it somewhere; thinks the fish is going to be the thing he wants,—eats it and isn't sure; thinks the next dish is perhaps the one that will hit the hungry place,—tries it, and is conscious that there was a something wanting about it, also. And thus he goes on, from dish to dish, like a boy after a butterfly which just misses getting caught every time it alights, but somehow doesn't get caught after all; and at the end the exile and the boy have fared about alike; the one is full, but grievously unsatisfied, the other has had plenty of exercise, plenty of interest, and a fine lot of hopes, but he hasn't got any butterfly. There is here and there an American who will say he can remember rising from a European table d'hôte perfectly satisfied; but we must not overlook the fact that there is also here and there an American who will lie.

The number of dishes is sufficient; but then it is such a monotonous variety of *unstriking* dishes. It is an inane dead level of "fair-to-middling." There is nothing to *accent* it. Perhaps if the roast of mutton or of beef,—a big, generous one,—were brought on the table and carved in full view of the client, that might give the right sense of earnestness and reality to the thing; but they don't do that, they pass the sliced meat around on a dish, and so you are perfectly calm, it does not stir you in the least. Now a vast roast turkey, stretched on the broad of his back, with his heels in the air and the rich juices oozing from his fat sides . . . but I may as well stop there, for they would not know how to cook him. They can't even cook a chicken respectably; and as for carving it, they do that with a hatchet.

This is about the customary table d'hôte bill in summer:

Soup (characterless).

Fish—sole, salmon, or whiting—usually tolerably good.

Roast—mutton or beef—tasteless—and some last year's potatoes.

A pâté, or some other made dish—usually good—"considering."

One vegetable—brought on in state, and all alone—usually insipid lentils, or string beans, or indifferent asparagus.

Roast chicken, as tasteless as paper.

Lettuce-salad—tolerably good.

Decayed strawberries or cherries.

Sometimes the apricots and figs are fresh, but this is no advantage, as these fruits are of no account anyway.

The grapes are generally good, and sometimes there is a tolerably good peach, by mistake.

The variations of the above bill are trifling. After a fortnight one discovers that the variations are only apparent, not real; in the third week you get what you had the first, and in the fourth week you get what you had the second. Three or four months of this weary sameness will kill the robustest appetite.

It has now been many months, at the present writing, since I have had a nourishing meal, but I shall soon have one,—a modest, private affair, all to myself. I have selected a few dishes, and made out a little bill of fare, which will go home in the steamer that precedes me, and be hot when I arrive—as follows:

Radishes. Baked apples, with cream.

Fried oysters; stewed oysters. Frogs.

American coffee, with real cream.

American butter.

Fried chicken, Southern style.

Porter-house steak.

Saratoga potatoes.

Broiled chicken, American style.

Hot biscuits, Southern style.

Hot wheat-bread, Southern style.

Hot buckwheat cakes.
American toast. Clear maple syrup.
Virginia bacon, broiled.
Blue points, on the half shell.
Cherry-stone clams.
San Francisco mussels, steamed.
Oyster soup. Clam soup.
Philadelphia Terrapin soup.
Oysters roasted in shell— Northern style.
Soft-shell crabs. Connecticut shad.
Baltimore perch.
Brook trout, from Sierra Nevadas.
Lake trout, from Tahoe.
Sheephead and croakers from New Orleans.
Black bass from the Mississippi.
American roast beef.
Roast turkey, Thanksgiving style.
Cranberry sauce. Celery.
Roast wild turkey. Woodcock.
Canvasback-duck, from Baltimore.
Prairie hens, from Illinois.
Missouri partridges, broiled.
'Possum. Coon.
Boston bacon and beans.
Bacon and greens, Southern style.

Hominy. Boiled onions. Turnips.
Pumpkin. Squash. Asparagus.
Butter Beans. Sweet potatoes.
Lettuce. Succotash. String beans.
Mashed potatoes. Catsup.
Boiled potatoes, in their skins.
New potatoes, minus the skins.
Early rose potatoes, roasted in the ashes, Southern style, served hot.
Sliced tomatoes, with sugar or vinegar. Stewed tomatoes.
Green corn, cut from the ear and served with butter and pepper.
Green corn, on the ear.
Hot corn-pone, with chitlings, Southern style.
Hot hoe-cake, Southern style.
Hot egg-bread, Southern style.
Hot light-bread, Southern style.
Buttermilk. Iced sweet milk.
Apple dumplings, with real cream.
Apple pie. Apple fritters.
Apple puffs, Southern style.
Peach cobbler, Southern style.
Peach pie. American mince pie.
Pumpkin pie. Squash pie.
All sorts of American pastry.

Fresh American fruits of all sorts, including strawberries, which are not to be doled out as if they were jewelry, but in a more liberal way.

Ice-water—not prepared in the ineffectual goblet, but in the sincere and capable refrigerator.

Americans intending to spend a year or so in European hotels, will do well to copy this bill and carry it along. They will find it an excellent thing to get up an appetite with, in the dispiriting presence of the squalid table d'hôte.

Foreigners cannot enjoy our food, I suppose, any more than we can enjoy theirs. It is not strange; for tastes are made, not born. I might glorify my bill of fare until I was tired; but after all, the Scotchman would shake his head and say, "Where's your haggis?" and the Fijian would sigh and say, "Where's your missionary?"

I have a neat talent in matters pertaining to nourishment. This has met with professional recognition. I have often furnished recipes for cookbooks. Here are some designs for pies and things, which I recently prepared for a friend's projected cookbook, but as I forgot to furnish diagrams and perspectives, they had to be left out, of course.

Recipe for an Ash-Cake.

Take a lot of water and add to it a lot of coarse Indian meal and about a quarter of a lot of salt. Mix well together, knead into the form of a "pone," and let the pone stand a while,—not on its edge, but the other way. Rake away a place among the embers, lay it there, and cover it an inch deep with hot ashes. When it is done, remove it; blow off all the ashes but one layer; butter that one and eat.

N. B. No household should ever be without this talisman. It has been noticed that tramps never return for another ash-cake.

Recipe for New England Pie.

To make this excellent breakfast dish, proceed as follows: Take a sufficiency of water and a sufficiency of flour, and construct a bullet-proof dough. Work this into the form of a disk, with the edges turned up some three-fourths of an inch. Toughen and kiln-dry it a couple of days in a mild but unvarying temperature. Construct a cover for this redoubt in the same way and of the same material. Fill with stewed dried apples; aggravate with cloves, lemon-peel, and slabs of citron; add two portions of New Orleans sugar, then solder on the lid and set in a safe place till it petrifies. Serve cold at breakfast and invite your enemy.

Recipe for German Coffee.

Take a barrel of water and bring it to a boil; rub a chiccory berry against a coffee berry, then convey the former into the water. Continue the boiling and evaporation until the intensity of the flavor and aroma of the coffee and chiccory has been diminished to a proper degree; then set aside to cool. Now unharness the remains of a once cow from the plow, insert them in a hydraulic press, and when you shall have acquired a teaspoonful of that pale blue juice which a German superstition regards as milk, modify the malignity of its strength in a bucket of tepid water and ring up the breakfast. Mix the beverage in a cold cup, partake with moderation, and keep a wet rag around your head to guard against overexcitement.

To Carve Fowls in the German Fashion.

Use a club, and avoid the joints.

The War Prayer

(DICTATED 1904–05)

It was a time of great and exalting excitement. The country was up in arms, the war was on, in every breast burned the holy fire of patriotism; the drums were beating, the bands playing, the toy pistols popping, the bunched firecrackers hissing and spluttering; on every hand and far down the receding and fading spread of roofs and balconies a fluttering wilderness of flags flashed in the sun; daily the young volunteers marched down the wide avenue gay and fine in their new uniforms, the proud fathers and mothers and sisters and sweethearts cheering them with voices choked with happy emotion as they swung by; nightly the packed mass meetings listened, panting, to patriot oratory which stirred the

deepest deeps of their hearts, and which they interrupted at briefest intervals with cyclones of applause, the tears running down
their cheeks the while; in the churches the pastors preached devotion to flag and country, and invoked the God of Battles, be-
seeching His aid in our good cause in outpouring of fervid
eloquence which moved every listener. It was indeed a glad and
gracious time, and the half dozen rash spirits that ventured to
disapprove of the war and cast a doubt upon its righteousness
straightway got such a stern and angry warning that for their personal safety's sake they quickly shrank out of sight and offended
no more in that way.

Sunday morning came—next day the battalions would leave for
the front; the church was filled; the volunteers were there, their
young faces alight with martial dreams—visions of the stern advance, the gathering momentum, the rushing charge, the flashing
sabers, the flight of the foe, the tumult, the enveloping smoke,
the fierce pursuit, the surrender!—them home from the war,
bronzed heroes, welcomed, adored, submerged in golden seas of
glory! With the volunteers sat their dear ones, proud, happy, and
envied by the neighbors and friends who had no sons and brothers to send forth to the field of honor, there to win for the flag,
or, failing, die the noblest of noble deaths. The service proceeded;
a war chapter from the Old Testament was read; the first prayer
was said; it was followed by an organ burst that shook the building,
and with one impulse the house rose, with glowing eyes and beating hearts, and poured out that tremendous invocation—

> "God the all-terrible! Thou who ordainest,
> Thunder thy clarion and lightning thy sword!"

Then came the "long" prayer. None could remember the like of
it for passionate pleading and moving and beautiful language.
The burden of its supplication was, that an ever-merciful and be-
nignant Father of us all would watch over our noble young soldiers, and aid, comfort, and encourage them in their patriotic
work; bless them, shield them in the day of battle and the hour
of peril, bear them in His mighty hand, make them strong and
confident, invincible in the bloody onset; help them to crush the

foe, grant to them and to their flag and country imperishable
honor and glory—

An aged stranger entered and moved with slow and noiseless
step up the main aisle, his eyes fixed upon the minister, his long
body clothed in a robe that reached to his feet, his head bare, his
white hair descending in a frothy cataract to his shoulders, his
seamy face unnaturally pale, pale even to ghastliness. With all eyes
following him and wondering, he made his silent way; without
pausing, he ascended to the preacher's side and stood there, waiting. With shut lids the preacher, unconscious of his presence,
continued his moving prayer, and at last finished it with the
words, uttered in fervent appeal, "Bless our arms, grant us the
victory, O Lord our God, Father and Protector of our land and
flag!"

The stranger touched his arm, motioned him to step aside—
which the startled minister did—and took his place. During some
moments he surveyed the spellbound audience with solemn eyes,
in which burned an uncanny light; then in a deep voice he said:

"I come from the Throne—bearing a message from Almighty
God!" The words smote the house with a shock; if the stranger
perceived it he gave no attention. "He has heard the prayer of
His servant your shepherd, and will grant it if such shall be your
desire after I, His messenger, shall have explained to you its
import—that is to say, its full import. For it is like unto many of
the prayers of men, in that it asks for more than he who utters it
is aware of—except he pause and think.

"God's servant and yours has prayed his prayer. Has he paused
and taken thought? Is it one prayer? No, it is two—one uttered,
the other not. Both have reached the ear of Him Who heareth
all supplications, the spoken and the unspoken. Ponder this—
keep it in mind. If you would beseech a blessing upon yourself,
beware! lest without intent you invoke a curse upon a neighbor
at the same time. If you pray for the blessing of rain upon your
crop which needs it, by that act you are possibly praying for a
curse upon some neighbor's crop which may not need rain and
can be injured by it.

"You have heard your servant's prayer—the uttered part of it.
I am commissioned of God to put into words the other part of
it—that part which the pastor—and also you in your hearts—

fervently prayed silently. And ignorantly and unthinkingly? God grant that it was so! You heard these words: 'Grant us the victory, O Lord our God!' That is sufficient. The *whole* of the uttered prayer is compact into those pregnant words. Elaborations were not necessary. When you have prayed for victory you have prayed for many unmentioned results which follow victory—*must* follow it, cannot help but follow it. Upon the listening spirit of God the Father fell also the unspoken part of the prayer. He commandeth me to put it into words. Listen!

"O Lord our Father, our young patriots, idols of our hearts, go forth to battle—be Thou near them! With them—in spirit—we also go forth from the sweet peace of our beloved firesides to smite the foe. O Lord our God, help us to tear their soldiers to bloody shreds with our shells; help us to cover their smiling fields with the pale forms of their patriot dead; help us to drown the thunder of the guns with the shrieks of their wounded, writhing in pain; help us to lay waste their humble homes with a hurricane of fire; help us to wring the hearts of their unoffending widows with unavailing grief; help us to turn them out roofless with their little children to wander unfriended the wastes of their desolated land in rags and hunger and thirst, sports of the sun flames of summer and the icy winds of winter, broken in spirit, worn with travail, imploring Thee for the refuge of the grave and denied it—for our sakes who adore Thee, Lord, blast their hopes, blight their lives, protract their bitter pilgrimage, make heavy their steps, water their way with their tears, stain the white snow with the blood of their wounded feet! We ask it, in the spirit of love, of Him Who is the Source of Love, and Who is the ever-faithful refuge and friend of all that are sore beset and seek His aid with humble and contrite hearts. Amen."

(*After a pause.*) "Ye have prayed it; if ye still desire it, speak! The messenger of the Most High waits."

It was believed afterward that the man was a lunatic, because there was no sense in what he said.

George Ade
(1866–1944)

George Ade was born in Kentland, Indiana, the youngest of three sons, and attended Purdue University where he excelled in literary studies. After graduation, he got a job working for the *Chicago News* as a reporter. There he wrote a series of columns that used the whole range of Chicago characters as protagonists —policemen and politicians, prostitutes and shop girls, people from every walk of life and every nationality of Chicago's melting pot. He also wrote short stories, essays, and light verse, but it was his plays that made him both famous and wealthy. His *Sultan of Sulu*, the first act of which is excerpted here, was a comic opera reminiscent of Gilbert and Sullivan, which satirized American imperialistic foreign policy in the Philippines. It was a hit in Chicago and New York, and road companies successfully took the production across the country. Its satirical edge is as sharp today as it was the day the play opened.

The Sultan of Sulu

AN ORIGINAL SATIRE IN TWO ACTS

THE SCENES

ACT I.—*An open place in front of the Sultan's palace, city of Sulu or Jolo, Philippine Islands*, 1899.

ACT II.—*The hanging garden of the Sultan's palace. One day is sup-posed to elapse between the two acts.*

ACT I

Scene: An open place in Sulu. The SULTAN'S *palace, with Sulu flag flying in front of it, at stage right. Suggestion of tropical vegetation at stage left. Beyond, the open sea.*

Time: Early morning. During the opening chorus, the stage gradually becomes lighted with the glow of sunrise. Native men and women on stage, kneeling.

OPENING CHORUS

The darkness breaks! The day's begun!
Hail to the Sultan and the sun!
One cannot rank above the other;
The sun is but the Sultan's brother.
Behold the sun! Majestic sun!
He is the Sultan's brother.

Well may he ride in crimson pride,
He is the Sultan's brother.

With regal sway, the King of day;
And this the reason, we should say,
He is the Sultan's brother!

[*Six of the wives of* KI-RAM *enter, romping. They are:* MAURICIA, SELINA, NATIVIDAD, PEPITA, NATALIA, RAMONA—*young and attractive things.*]

THE SIX WIVES
In early morn, at breakfast-time
It is our wifely duty
To greet the Sultan with a rhyme
And to cheer him with our beauty.
So we come, a sweet sextette
Of most unwilling brides,

To tap upon the castanet
And do our Spanish glides.

[*Dance*]

In early morn, at breakfast-time,
It is our wifely duty
To tap upon the castanet
And do our Spanish glides.

ALL
Behold the sun, etc.

[*At conclusion of the chorus, the natives salaam to wives and retire as* HADJI *comes from the palace, pausing on the upper step to salute the cluster of wives.*]

HADJI. [*Mysterious and sotto voce.*] Oh! oh! Ladies, not so much noise! *Not* so much noise?! Our beloved ruler is now taking his beauty sleep in the inner chamber. Are all of the Sultan's loving and obedient wives present at the morning round-up?

WIVES. [*Ad lib.*] Here! Yes. Present, etc. [HADJI *gesticulates for silence. Wives group about in sitting posture.*]

HADJI. In order to make sure, we shall proceed with the usual roll-call. [*He consults a book containing the official list of wives.*] Mauricia! Mauricia!

MAURICIA. Here!

HADJI. Selina.

SELINA. Here!

HADJI. Daily catechism. Do you love your husband?

SELINA. What is the answer?

HADJI. The answer is, "I adore him."

SELINA. All right; put it down.

HADJI. Such devotion is touching. [*Calling.*] Natividad!

NATIVIDAD. Here!

HADJI. [*Calling.*] Pepita—Pepita—Pete! Where is the Gibson girl of the Philippine Islands?

PEPITA. Here!

HADJI. Pepita—a question from the book. Suppose the Sultan should die—would you remarry?

PEPITA. What is the answer?

HADJI. The answer is, "Never!" Shall I so record it?

PEPITA. *Never!*

HADJI. Oh, how she loves that man! [*From the book again.*] Natalia—naughty little Natty!

NATALIA. Here!

HADJI. Ramona! Ramona! Blithesome creature, where art thou?

RAMONA. Here!

HADJI. Ramona—a question from the book. Do you—

RAMONA. [*Interrupting.*] Yes.

HADJI. I am delighted to hear it. [*Calling.*] Chiquita! Chiquita! Has any one seen the sunny soubrette of the southern seas? [*Cadenza heard outside.*] Aha! Gallivanting as usual. [CHIQUITA *enters and salaams.*]

HADJI. Now that our entire domestic household has assembled, I wish to make an announcement. It has come to the ears of our august ruler that your uncle, the Datto Mandi of Parang, is encamped near the city. [*The wives arise, with various exclamations of surprise. The news appears to please them.* HADJI *invokes silence.*] He has come to recapture you, but never fear. We, editorially speaking, will protect you.

CHIQUITA. But we *wish* to be recaptured. We *want* to go back to dear old Parang.

HADJI. [*Injured tone.*] Oh, Chiquita! Thus do you repay Ki-Ram's single-hearted devotion?

CHIQUITA. [*Confronting* HADJI.] Single-hearted fiddle-sticks! How can a man have a single-hearted devotion for eight different women? We were brought here as captives. When it came to a choice between an ignominious death and Ki-Ram, we hesitated for a while and then chose Ki-Ram.

HADJI. Such impertinence! I shall inform his Majesty. [HADJI *goes into palace.*]

[*Boom of cannon heard in the distance, followed by rattle of musketry. Wives retreat to rear of palace in frightened confusion as* HADJI *comes out and stands on the steps.* DINGBAT, *a native guard, with drawn sword of the kris shape, rushes on from left.*]

DINGBAT. What do you think, sir?

HADJI. I'm a private secretary. I'm not permitted to think.

DINGBAT. A large white ship has come into the harbor.

HADJI. A ship—in the harbor?

DINGBAT. It is crowded with soldiers.

HADJI. Soldiers?

DINGBAT. The flag is one of red, white, and blue, spangled with stars.

HADJI. Never heard of such a flag.

DINGBAT. What's more, sir, they're coming ashore.

HADJI. Soldiers on this side. [*Indicating left.*] Mandi on this. [*Indicating right.*] How glad I am that I am merely a private secretary! [*Distant boom of cannon.*] Aha! That seems friendly. They are firing a salute.

[*Shell, with fuse sputtering, rolls on from left and disappears behind palace. Sound of explosion.* HADJI *disappears headlong into the palace, followed by* DINGBAT. *The broken volleys of musketry become louder and louder. In the incidental music there is a suggestion of "A Hot Time in the Old Town." Sharp yells are heard off left, and then a body of United States Volunteers in khaki and marines in white pours on the stage in pell-mell confusion.* LIEUTENANT WILLIAM HARDY, *in a white uniform of the Regulars, comes down through the center of the charging squad. He has his sword drawn.*]

LIEUTENANT HARDY AND CHORUS OF SOLDIERS

"HIKE"

We haven't the appearance, goodness knows,
    Of plain commercial men:
From a hasty glance, you might suppose
    We are fractious now and then.
But though we come in warlike guise
    And battle-front arrayed,
It's all a business enterprise;
    We're seeking foreign trade.

REFRAIN

We're as mild as any turtle dove
    When we see the foe a-coming,

Our thoughts are set on human love
    When we hear the bullets humming.
We teach the native population
    What the golden rule is like,
And we scatter public education
    On ev'ry blasted hike!

We want to assimilate, if we can,
    Our brother who is brown;
We love our dusky fellow-man
    And we hate to hunt him down.
So, when we perforate his frame,
    We want him to be good.
We shoot at him to make him tame,
    If he but understood.

REFRAIN

We're as mild, etc.

[*During the second verse, the wives and native women return timidly, drawn by curiosity. They gather about the soldiers and study them carefully, more or less frightened but not altogether displeased.* LIEUTENANT HARDY *addresses the company of natives.*]

HARDY. I am here to demand an audience with the Sultan.

CHIQUITA. [*Stepping forth.*] *Indeed!* And who are you that presumes to demand an audience with the Bright Morning Light of the Orient?

HARDY. Why, how do you do? I am Lieutenant Hardy—a modest representative of the U.S.A. [HADJI *cautiously emerges from the palace.*]

HADJI. [*Overhearing.*] The U.S.A.? Where is *that* on the map?

HARDY. Just now it is spread all over the map. Perhaps you don't know it, but we are the owners of this island. We paid twenty millions of dollars for you. [*All whistle.*] At first it did seem a large price, but now that I have seen you [*indicating wives*] I am convinced it was a bargain. [CHIQUITA *has lighted a native cigarette and is serenely puffing it.* LIEUTENANT HARDY *addresses her chidingly.*] You don't mean to say you smoke?

CHIQUITA. Don't the ladies of your country smoke?

HARDY. The *ladies* do—the women *don't*. [HADJI *observes the confidential chat between the officer and the principal wife, and he is disturbed in spirit.*]

HADJI. Lieutenant! [*More loudly.*] *Lieutenant!* Did you come ashore to talk business or to break into the harem?

HARDY. Beg pardon. [*Stepping back into a stiff, military attitude.*] Does the Sultan surrender?

HADJI. He says he will *die* first.

HARDY. *That* can be arranged. We are here as emissaries of peace, but we never object to a skirmish—eh, boys? [*The soldiers respond with a warlike shout, which frightens the native women. The lieutenant reassures them.*]

HARDY. Young ladies, don't be alarmed. We may slaughter all the others, but *you* will be spared. Meet us here after the battle.

HADJI. The *battle!* [*He falls against* DINGBAT. *Then he dejectedly moves over to centre and addresses the wives.*] Mesdames Ki-Ram, his Majesty is about to dictate to me his last will and testament. In one hour you will be widows—all of you. You had better begin picking out your black goods.

CHIQUITA. And I never *did* look well in black. [*Sound of gong heard in palace.*]

HADJI. Excuse me. [*Exit into palace after* DINGBAT.]

[LIEUTENANT HARDY *resumes his confidential relations with wives and native women.*]

HARDY. Young ladies, you never saw a real Yankee girl, did you?

CHIQUITA. What is she like?

HARDY. The American girl? The most remarkable combination of innocence and knowledge, of modesty and boldness, of schoolgirl simplicity and married-woman diplomacy.

[*Native boys, running on from left, call attention to the approach of the American party. All the natives bow with their arms extended in a deferential salaam. Soldiers come to "present arms."*]

WELCOME CHORUS

Welcome, Americanos!
Welcome, in Oriental style!

Welcome, Americanos!
Welcome, in Oriental style!
Sulu bids you welcome!
Sulu bids you welcome!

[COLONEL JEFFERSON BUDD, HENRIETTA BUDD, WAKEFUL M.
JONES, PAMELA FRANCES JACKSON, *and the four school-ma'ams enter,
with smiling acknowledgments of the vocal greeting.* HENRIETTA *is a very
attractive girl, in a stunning summer gown.* COLONEL BUDD *is large
and imposing, somewhat overburdened with conscious dignity. He wears
a colonel's service uniform.* WAKEFUL M. JONES *is a brisk young man
in flannels.* MISS JACKSON *is a sedate and rigid spinster. Her attire
indicates that she has made a partial compromise with the dress-reformers,
but has a lingering fondness for stylish garments that fit. After the entrance,* HENRIETTA *advances from the group and breaks into the
anticipated song.*]

HENRIETTA BUDD AND CHORUS

"PALM BRANCHES WAVING"

Palm branches waving
A welcome to the queen of the day,
While from above the birds seem to join in the lay.
Long have I sought thee,
O charming little tropical isle!
Here let me dwell—let me dwell awhile.
Softly comes the southern breeze—
Land so bright, of pure delight.
Oh, how I have longed for thee!

HENRIETTA AND CHORUS
'Neath the shade of spreading trees—
Ah, Sulu, fair Sulu,
'Tis the land I have longed to see.

HENRIETTA
Long have I sought thee,
O charming little tropical isle!
Here let me dwell—let me dwell awhile.

HARDY. [*Addressing company of natives.*] Ladies and gentlemen, Colonel Budd! [*Pointing out that august personage.*] His daughter, Miss Henrietta Budd! [*Jones calls attention to Miss Jackson.*]

JONES. And this is Miss Pamela Frances Jackson, a lady who knows as much as any man—and then some more.

PAMELA. [*Inquiringly.*] The Sultan?

CHIQUITA. He is within—making his will.

HENRIETTA. His will?

CHIQUITA. He expects to be captured. They are going to do something dreadful to him.

BUDD. [*Impressively.*] We are going to assimilate him.

CHIQUITA. Yes, that's why he's making his will.

JONES. If he really expects to die, now is the time to talk life insurance. [*He starts towards the palace, whereupon the alarmed wives crowd in front of him.*] No! And why not?

CHIQUITA. For entering that majestic presence unheralded, the punishment is death.

ALL. Death!

[*Jones smiles disdainfully and buttons his coat.*]

JONES. Watch me! [*He motions them to right and left and hurriedly enters palace. The natives are amazed at his audacity.*]

CHIQUITA. Poor man!

HARDY. Don't worry about Mr. Jones. He's from Chicago. [*Looking about, sees soldiers warming up to wives.*] I'm afraid my men are in danger. [*MISS JACKSON comes to the rescue.*]

PAMELA. Young ladies! You are rather young to be trifling with soldiers.

CHIQUITA. *Not* so young. We are married—*all* of us.

PAMELA. What, married women flirting! It is an uncivilized country. Gather about me. [*They come to her and she advises them in a patronizing manner.*] When you have become Americanized you won't follow soldiers. You'll compel *them* to follow *you.* [*The expeditious* JONES *comes from the palace, gleefully waving a paper.*]

JONES. I have insured his life for fifty thousand pesos. I convinced him that he would be a dead man in less than fifteen minutes.

BUDD. [*Preparing for an effort.*] Soldiers of the republic!

ALL. Hear! Hear!

BUDD. For the first time you are about to stand in the presence of royalty. Stiffen yourselves for the ordeal, and remember, no deference, for each of you is a sovereign in his own right.

CHORUS TO SULTAN

Sultan! Mighty Sultan!
  Thrice glorious in defeat.
Sultan! Wretched Sultan!
  This great affliction meet.

[*There is a slow thrumming of Oriental music, during which* HADJI
appears on the steps of the palace and makes a mournful announcement.]

HADJI. Ladies and gentlemen, his Majesty is coming prepared to
  die according to contract. He has only one request to make. It
  is that you do not ask him to die a cheap and common death.
  [*The natives prostrate themselves.* KI-RAM *comes from palace, accompanied by his two Nubian slaves,* DIDYMOS *and* RASTOS. *The Sultan
  is attired in funereal black and is the picture of woe.*]

KI-RAM
[*Recitative.*] What do you think? I've got to die;
  My time has come to say good-bye
  To my upholstered Sulu throne
  And all that I can call my own.

[*He comes down and dolefully sings what he believes to be his swan-song.*]

KI-RAM AND CHORUS

"THE SMILING ISLE"

We have no daily papers
To tell of Newport capers,
  No proud four hundred to look down on ordinary folk;
We have no stocks and tickers,
No Scotch imported liquors,
  To start us on the downward path and some day land us broke;
We've not a single college
Where youth may get a knowledge
  Of chorus girls and cigarettes, of poker and the like;
No janitors to sass us,

No bell-boys to harass us,
    And we've never known the pleasure of a labor-union strike.

REFRAIN
And that is why, you'll understand,
I love my own, my native land,
My little isle of Sulu.
    [*Chorus.*] Sulu!
Smiling isle of Sulu!
    [*Chorus.*] Sulu!
I'm not ready to say good-bye,
I'm mighty sorry that I have to die.

We have no prize-fight sluggers,
No vaudevillian muggers,
    No one of us has ever shot the chutes or looped the loop;
No cable-cars or trolleys,
No life-insurance jollies,
    No bank cashiers to take our money 'ere they fly the coop;
No bookies and no races,
No seaside summer places;
    No Bertha Clays and Duchesses to make the females cry;
We have no dairy lunches,
Where they eat their food in bunches,
    And we don't insult our stomachs with the thing they call mincepie.

REFRAIN
And that is why, etc.

We have no short-haired ladies
Who are always raising Hades
    With their finical and funny old reformatory fads;
No ten-cent publications,
Sold at all the railway stations,
    With a page or two of reading and a hundred stuffed with "ads";
We never chew in Sulu
Any pepsin gum or tofu—
    In fact, we're not such savages as some of you might think;
And during intermission
We always crave permission
    Before we walk on other people just to get a drink.

REFRAIN

And that is why, etc.

We have no politicians,
And under no conditions
  Do we tolerate the fraud who cures by laying on of hands;
We have no elocutionists,
No social revolutionists,
  No amateur dramatics, and no upright baby grands;
We don't play golf and tennis,
And we never know the menace
  Of a passing fad or fancy that may turn the nation's head;
I'm proud of my dominion
When I voice the bold opinion
  That we'll never know the tortures of a patent folding-bed.

REFRAIN

And that is why, etc.

[*The song being ended,* KI-RAM *stands apart in an attitude supposed to signify heroic resignation.*]

KI-RAM. Now, then, for a farewell speech that will look well in the school histories. I die—I die that Sulu may—

BUDD. Why, your Majesty, you are not expected to die.

KI-RAM. No? [*With an expression of glad surprise.*]

BUDD. We are your friends. We have come to take possession of the island and teach your benighted people the advantages of free government. We hold that all government derives its just powers from the consent of the governed.

ALL. Hear! Hear!

BUDD. Now, the question is, do you consent to this benevolent plan?

[*The soldiers bring their guns to "charge bayonets."* KI-RAM *looks right and left and finds himself walled in by threatening weapons. He hesitates.*]

KI-RAM. Are all the guns loaded?

BUDD. They *are.*

KI-RAM. I consent.

BUDD. Good! The education of your neglected race will begin at once under the direction of these young ladies.

[*He calls attention to the school-ma'ams standing in the background. When* KI-RAM *sees the luscious quartette he is visibly impressed.*]

KI-RAM. Young ladies? Oh-h-h! Who are they?

BUDD. Four of our most interesting products—four highly culti-vated, dignified, demure New England school-ma'ams. [*The school-ma'ams advance, stepping rather high, and introduce them-selves.*]

THE FOUR SCHOOL-MA'AMS

"FROM THE LAND OF THE CEREBELLUM"

From the land of the cerebellum,
    Where clubs abound and books are plenty,
Where people know before you tell 'em
    As much as any one knows,
We come to teach this new possession
    All that's known to a girl of twenty;
And such a girl, it's our impression,
    Knows more than you might suppose.

You may judge by our proper bearing
    That we're accomplished, proud, and haughty,
Those simple little gowns we're wearing
    Proclaim our innocent style.
You must not think because we're frisky
    That we're *re*-ally bold or naughty;
We never flirt when it seems risky,
    Except for a little while.

KI-RAM. [*Gazing at them with unconcealed admiration.*] Are they go-ing to open school here?

BUDD. This very day.

KI-RAM. I'll be there early with my face washed and a red apple for my dear teacher.

BUDD. We believe that in three weeks or a month we will have you as cultured as the people of my native State.

KI-RAM. And what State is that?

BUDD. The State of Arkansaw! [*On the word "Arkansaw," the Colonel removes his cap reverently, and the soldiers solemnly lift their hats.*]

KI-RAM. Arkansaw? Never heard of it.

BUDD. What! Never heard of Arkansaw? Then permit me to tell you that in Arkansaw they never heard of Sulu. Hereafter, you understand, you are not a Sultan, but a Governor.

KI-RAM. A Governor! Is that a promotion?

BUDD. Most assuredly! A Governor is the noblest work of the campaign committee. Ladies and gentlemen—

ALL. Hear! Hear!

BUDD. [*In oratorical fashion.*] I take pleasure in introducing to you that valiant leader, that incorruptible statesman, that splendid type of perfect manhood, our fellow-citizen, the Honorable Ki-Ram, next Governor of Sulu. [*Cheers.*] He will be inaugurated here in one hour. I request you to prepare for the festivities. [*Another cheer and all exeunt except* KI-RAM, BUDD, *and* CHIQUITA. *The principal wife seems disposed to loiter near the Colonel and admire him.*]

KI-RAM. Chiquita, run along; don't annoy the Colonel. [CHIQUITA *goes into the palace, but before doing so she gives the Colonel a lingering glance, which seems to warm him considerably.* KI-RAM *grasps* BUDD *by the hand.*] Colonel, I want to thank you. It was great! [*Attempting to imitate* BUDD'S *oratorical flight.*] That some-kind-of-a-leader, that umptatallable statesman, that—that—Say, where did you learn that kind of talk?

BUDD. You mustn't mind that. I'm in politics. I say that about every one.

[KI-RAM *blows whistle, which he carries suspended on a cord about his neck.* DIDYMOS *and* RASTOS *bring stools and then exeunt, dancing in unison. As they go into the palace,* KI-RAM *and* BUDD *seat themselves. At the same moment* GALULA *comes from behind the palace carrying a large, long-handled fan of Oriental pattern. She is an elderly female, all of whose native charms have long since disappeared. Think of the homeliest woman you ever saw; multiply her unloveliness by two, and the reader will have* GALULA. *She timorously approaches* KI-RAM *and begins fanning him from behind.*]

KI-RAM. Colonel, you'll excuse me for mentioning it, but you are one of the handsomest men I ever saw. I—I— [*He pauses with an expression of alarm growing on his countenance.* GALULA *continues to fan him.*] Colonel, do you feel a draft? [*Turns and sees* GA-LULA.] Oh-h-h! Galula, I know you love me, and I don't blame you, but you want to remember one thing, "Absence makes the heart grow fonder." [*She exits, looking back at him yearningly.*] That's one of them.

BUDD. One of *what*?

KI-RAM. One of my wives. She is the charter member. I've tried to lose her, but I can't. The other seven were those society buds that you saw here a moment ago. I captured them about a month ago.

BUDD. You *captured* them? [*Eagerly.*] Then the beautiful creature with whom I was chatting—she did not marry you voluntarily?

KI-RAM. Galula is the only one that ever married me voluntarily. The others I— [*Gesture of reaching out, taking hold of something, and pulling it in.*] Did you ever hear of the Datto Mandi of Parang?

BUDD. What is it—some new kind of breakfast food?

KI-RAM. Certainly *not.* The Datto Mandi is a warlike gentleman who holds forth on the other side of the island. About a month ago I needed a new batch of wives. I turned the former assort-ment out to pasture, then I went over to Parang and stampeded seven of Mandi's lovely nieces. This annoyed Mandi.

BUDD. Naturally.

KI-RAM. He is now encamped outside the wall, waiting for a chance to recapture *them,* and incidentally carve *me* into small, red cubes. Now, then, if I'm to be Governor here, I shall expect you to pro-tect *me* against *him.* [COLONEL BUDD *arises and bursts into oratory.*]

BUDD. Most assuredly! Wherever our flag floats there human rights shall be protected, though the heavens fall. Oh—

KI-RAM. Shake out the parachute, Colonel! [*Arises.*] Come down! I understand all that. And just to prove that I appreciate what you have done for me, and what I expect you to do for me in the future, do you know what I am going to do?

BUDD. I can't imagine.

KI-RAM. Well, I'm going to set 'em up.

BUDD. Set 'em up?

KI-RAM. I'm going to set 'em up to the wives. [*Makes a profound*

bow.] Have a wife on me. Take your pick of the eight. Do me
a favor. Choose the one with the fan.

BUDD. What, your Majesty! Take another man's wife? Barbarous!
Barbarous!

KI-RAM. Barbarous, perhaps, but it frequently happens.

BUDD. Besides, I—I—[*hesitating*]—may as well tell you that I have
proposed marriage to Miss Jackson, the Judge Advocate. The
Judge has the matter under advisement.

KI-RAM. That's all right—marry both of them.

BUDD. My *dear* sir, do you realize that under our laws a man is
entitled to only one wife?

KI-RAM. How *could* a man struggle along with only one wife! Suffering Allah! I wonder if they'll try to work that rule on me?
[KI-RAM *starts to enter the palace, when* JONES, *entering at right from
rear of palace, accosts him sharply.*]

JONES. Governor!

KI-RAM. Well?

JONES. Are you ready for the reception?

KI-RAM. What is a reception? Something civilized?

JONES. [*Taking him by the arm.*] A reception, Governor, is a function at which a large number of people assemble in order to
be exclusive. The entire population files past. You shake hands
with each person, and say, "I am happy to meet you."

KI-RAM. That's what I say, but *am* I happy?

JONES. Probably not.

BUDD. However, you must pretend to enjoy these little tortures.

JONES. At least, until the other people are out of hearing distance.

KI-RAM, BUDD, AND JONES

"OH, WHAT A BUMP!"

JONES

At a musicale, a five-o'clock,
    Or social jamboree,
'Tis there the swagger people flock
    For a bite and a sip of tea;
        And this is what you hear:
"It's been a charming afternoon";

"Delighted, don't you know";
"Sorry I have to leave so soon,
  But really I must go."
    But after she's away
    In her coupé,
    What *does* this self-same woman say?

Ki-Ram and Budd

Well, what *does* she say?

Jones

"That was the tackiest time I've had
  In twenty years or more.
The crowd was jay and the tea was bad
  And the whole affair a bore."

Trio

Oh, what a bump! Alackaday!
  'Twould darken her whole career,
Could the hostess know what people say
  When she's not there to hear.

Budd

The bashful youth who's rather slow
  When he has made a call,
Receives a message, soft and low,
  At parting in the hall.
    And this is what she says:
"Now come as often as you can.
  I love these little larks.
It's seldom that I meet a man
  Who makes such bright remarks."
    But when he tears away
    From this fairy fay,
    What does the artful maiden say?

Ki-Ram and Jones

Well, what *does* she say?

BUDD

"Of all the dummies I ever met
　　　　　　He's the limit, and no mistake,
As a touch-me-not and mamma's pet,
　　　　　　That Johnnie takes the cake."

TRIO

Oh, what a bump! Alakaday!
　　　　　　'Twould darken his whole career,
Could Harold know what Mabel says
　　　　　　When he's not there to hear

KI-RAM

Did you ever feel like saying—
　　　　　　When some precocious brat
Recites a piece called "Mary's Lamb"
　　　　　　Or "Little Pussy Cat"?
　　　　　　　　　And this is what you say:
"What marvellous talent she does possess
　　　　　　For one of her tender age.
I think she'd make a great success
　　　　　　If you'd put her on the stage."
　　　　　　　　　But later in the day,
　　　　　　　　　When you get away,
　　　　　　　　　What do you then proceed to say?

BUDD AND JONES

Well, what *do* you say?

KI-RAM

"If that awful kid belonged to me,
　　　　　　I'll tell you what I'd do—
I'd keep *it* under lock and key
　　　　　　And spank it black and blue."

TRIO

Oh, what a bump! Alackaday!
　　　　　　'Twould darken the child's career,
Could parents know what callers say
　　　　　　When they're not there to hear.

JONES

Perhaps the most terrific bump
  Is found in politics.
The campaign speaker on the stump
  Is up to all the tricks,
      And this is what he says:
"Oh, fellow-citizens, I see
  Before me here today
The sovereign voters, pure and free,
  Whom I shall e'er obey."
    But when he's won the race,
    Gets a nice, fat place,
    What does the people's servant say?

KI-RAM AND BUDD

Well, what *does* he say?

JONES

"Well, maybe I didn't con those yaps
  With that patriotic bluff.
Now that I've landed one of the snaps,
  I'm going to get the stuff."

TRIO

Oh, what a bump! Alackaday!
  'Twould darken their whole career
Could voters know what bosses say
  When they're not there to hear.

KI-RAM

Some ladies of the smartest set
  Met on the boulevard.
They shook hands most effusively
  And kissed each other *hard.*
    And this is what one said:
"Why, Alice, dear, what a zippy gown!
  The fit is perfectly fine;
And that dream of a hat! How swell you look!
  Good-bye, dear. Drop me a line."
    But when she said good-day,

And wafted on her way,
What did this gushing lady say?

BUDD AND JONES
Well, what *did* she say?

KI-RAM
"Did you ever see such a fright of a dress?
　It was wrinkled all *up* the back,
And those feathers, too—she's had them dyed:
　They were on her last winter's hat.
　　[*Spoken.*] The *upstart!*"

TRIO
Oh, what a bump! Alackaday!
　'Twould darken her whole career,
Could a woman know what her friends all say
　When she's not there to hear.

[*A dance concludes this number, and the three exeunt into the palace as* HENRIETTA BUDD *enters, followed by* LIEUTENANT HARDY, *who appears to be expostulating and pleading.*]

HENRIETTA. Mr. Hardy, it cannot be. My father objects to you in language which I dare not repeat.

HARDY. He objects to *me*? [*Indignant and surprised.*]

HENRIETTA. He told me only yesterday that I must *never* marry you.

HARDY. But I had not proposed to you yesterday.

HENRIETTA. True, but I knew what was coming. I have been engaged many times, and I notice that the man who intends to propose acts very strangely for a day or two in advance. So I went to father and said: "Lieutenant Hardy is about to propose to me."

HARDY. Whereupon he said—

HENRIETTA. "My child, never marry a Regular. There are no heroes except in the Volunteer service. The Volunteer goes home and is elected to Congress. The Regular keeps right ahead, a plain fighting man."

HARDY. Plain fighting man, perhaps, but even a plain fighting man may love, and I love you, Henrietta—I love you as only a West-Pointer *can* love the one girl in sight. [*Kisses her impetuously.*]

HENRIETTA. [*Retreating the usual number of steps.*] Lieutenant! Is it proper?

HARDY. It is customary among engaged couples. And we *are* engaged, aren't we?

HENRIETTA. Yes, I suppose we are—in a sort of a way.

HENRIETTA AND HARDY

"ENGAGED IN A SORT OF A WAY"

HARDY

Sweetheart, doubt my love no more;
 Believe me sincere.
I love no other on this tropic shore;
 You're the only girl that's here.

HENRIETTA

Lieutenant, I cannot withstand
 A man who pleads like you;
So here's the promise of my heart and hand,
 At least for a month or two.

HARDY

We are engaged in a sort of a way.

HENRIETTA

And we will truly love each other.

HARDY

Though it may chance there will soon come a day
When I can learn to love another.

HENRIETTA

I take this man on probation.

HARDY

And I will take her just the same.

BOTH

For it is simply a slight variation
Of the same little flirting game.

HENRIETTA

Marriage is a doubtful state.
  I think of it with dread.
Still, an engagement need not indicate
  That we really mean to wed.

HARDY

Henrietta, you are quite correct.
  I have been engaged before.
Frankly, I'll tell you, also, I expect
  That *I'll* be engaged some more.

HARDY

We are engaged, etc.

[*The waltz refrain continues.* HARDY *and* HENRIETTA *waltz away as*
KI-RAM *comes out of the palace, followed by* PAMELA FRANCES JACKSON.
KI-RAM *is greatly interested in the waltz. As* HARDY *and* HENRIETTA
disappear he turns and puts his arm around PAMELA, *and they execute
a waltz characterized by activity rather than poetry of motion. At the conclusion,* KI-RAM *is somewhat "blown" but altogether delighted.*]

KI-RAM. Oh, my! Pamela, that is simply hilarious. What do you
  call that?
PAMELA. It is called a waltz, your Majesty.
KI-RAM. Well, it may not be *proper*, but it *is* enjoyable.
PAMELA. It is quite proper, I assure you.
KI-RAM. Is it? I had no idea that anything as pleasant as that could
  be proper. [*He wraps his arm about her.*] Pamela, I suspect that
  we are going to be very jolly playmates.
PAMELA. Your Majesty! [*She is horrified at his presumption.*]
KI-RAM. What is it?
PAMELA. Your arm!
KI-RAM. Yes—what about it?
PAMELA. You have your arm around me.

KI-RAM. I know it. You said it was proper.

PAMELA. It *is* proper, when we are moving about. As a stationary form of amusement, I am afraid it would cause comment.

KI-RAM. *All right!* Let's move about. Anything to be civilized. [*He does a few eccentric dance steps without releasing his hold on* PAMELA.]

PAMELA. Why, your Majesty, how strangely you act! [*Breaking away from him.*]

KI-RAM. Pamela, when I first saw you, do you know, I was not particularly attracted to you. But now—now— [*He approaches her and she retreats. He pauses and reflects.*] I wonder if that cocktail had anything to do with it.

PAMELA. Cocktail? [*Surprised and pained.*]

KI-RAM. When the Colonel took me aside in there he said he was going to make me acquainted with one of the first blessings of civilization. He told me that the constitution and the cocktail followed the flag. Then he gave me an amber-colored beverage with a roguish little cherry nestling at the bottom. And, oh, little friend, when I felt that delicious liquid trickle down the corridors of my inmost being, all the incandescent lights were turned on and the birds began to sing. I felt myself bursting into full bloom, like a timid little flower kissed by the morning sunlight. So I ordered two more.

PAMELA. Three cocktails! Oh!

KI-RAM. I've had three, and I wish I'd made it thirty-three. I believe I'll climb a tree. You pick out any tree around here and I'll climb it. [*Unable to control his joyous emotions, he begins to run around in a circle until stopped short by* PAMELA, *who is determined to be severe with him.*]

PAMELA. Your Majesty, a little bit of advice! Beware of the cocktail. [*She sits on one of the stools.*]

KI-RAM. Beware of nothing! I'm going to drink cocktails all day and waltz all night. I'm going to be so civilized that people will talk about me. Pamela, Pammy [*seats himself beside her*], did you ever think you would like to live in a palace and have Sultana printed on your visiting-cards? [GALULA *comes on and begins to fan from behind.*]

PAMELA. Perhaps I have had my little ambition. Who hasn't?

KI-RAM. Well, I think I can fix it for you. Of course— [*He pauses, full of suspicion. To* PAMELA.] Do you feel a draft? [*Turns and sees* GALULA.] Oh-h! Galula, according to the *Ladies' Home Journal*, it is not considered good form for a wife to hang around when her husband is proposing marriage to another lady. [GALULA *exits, much disheartened.*] Sometimes I am almost sorry I married that one.

PAMELA. [*Aghast.*] Is she your wife?

KI-RAM. You don't think I would be so impolite to a lady who was *not* my wife, do you?

PAMELA. And she *is* your wife?

KI-RAM. She's *one* of them.

PAMELA. *One!*

KI-RAM. I have eight.

PAMELA. *Eight!* [*Rising and shrinking from him.*]

KI-RAM. Eight or nine, I forget which; I have them coming and going all the time.

PAMELA. Eight wives already, and you—[*he arises and retreats*]— you dare to make this scandalous proposition, and to me—to *me!*

KI-RAM. You didn't expect to have me all to yourself, did you?

PAMELA. Colonel! Colonel! [*Calling.*]

KI-RAM. Sh-h! I'll take it back—honestly, I will.

PAMELA. Colonel!

KI-RAM. Say, what's the matter with you? Can't you take a joke? [BUDD *comes from palace.*]

BUDD. My dear Miss Jackson, what *is* the matter?

KI-RAM. Don't believe a word she tells you.

PAMELA. Colonel, this babarian has had the monumental effrontery to ask me to join his harem.

BUDD. Wha-a-a-t!

KI-RAM. It was your fault—you gave it to me with a cherry in it.

PAMELA. [*To* KI-RAM.] Silence! [*To* BUDD.] I know that at one word from me you would run this contemptible foreign person through and through. But I do not ask it. I can execute my own revenge for this hideous insult. Tomorrow I am to be Judge-Advocate. Then shall the law deal with this miscreant. Tomor-row—you—you— [PAMELA *enters palace greatly agitated.*]

BUDD. Your Majesty, why—*why* did you propose marriage to Miss Jackson?

KI-RAM. Do you know—I'm beginning to ask myself that question.

BUDD. Didn't I tell you, sir that *I* intended to marry her?

KI-RAM. That's it! I knew she was engaged to you, and therefore I argued that she could not possibly marry me, so I would not be taking any chances in proposing. What do you suppose she is going to do to me?

BUDD. I suspect, sir, that as Judge-Advocate she is going to compel you to give up those eight wives.

KI-RAM. [*Much pleased.*] I'm going to get rid of Galula at last! Colonel, I want to celebrate. Let's go into the palace and drink three more of those things that follow the flag.

BUDD. You will excuse me if I don't refuse. [*They start towards palace.* HENRIETTA *and* HARDY *stroll on, in loving attitude;* BUDD *sees them; stands on steps watching them.* KI-RAM *enters palace.*] Henrietta, once more I must remind you that you are the daughter of a military hero who expects to go to Congress. Come. [HEN-RIETTA *starts towards him, regretfully. At the palace steps she turns and throws a kiss to* HARDY *and exits after* BUDD.]

HARDY. By George! I thought this being engaged would prove a lark. It's serious business. I wonder if Henrietta really loves me. If I but knew. [HARDY *enters palace. School-ma'ams enter, followed by a flock of wives, natives, and soldiers.*]

ALL

> Give three cheers for education—
>   Hurrah! Hurrah! Hurrah!
> Give three cheers for education—
>   Hurrah! Hurrah! Hurrah!
> A tiger, too, for education.
>   How we love our teachers dear!
> An attractive aggregation
>   From the Western Hemisphere.
> Give three cheers—
>   Hurrah! Hurrah! Hurrah!

[PAMELA *comes from the palace and stands on the top step, regarding the educational movement with a smile of gratification.*]

PAMELA. I am glad to see that the school has opened with so much enthusiasm. I will grant a short recess, as I have something of great importance to communicate to the wives of Ki-Ram.

NATIVE WOMEN AND SOLDIERS

[*Singing as they march away*]
Oh, the knowledge we are gaining
In our little school!
Modern methods they're explaining
In our little school!
We shall learn, from day to day,
What to do and what to say,
In the truly Newport way,
In our little school!

[PAMELA *beckons the wives to her.*]

PAMELA. I have good news for you. Ki-Ram is no longer your husband.
WIVES. No-o-o?
PAMELA. The new law allows a man but one wife. You shall be divorced tomorrow. If the governor objects, he can then be imprisoned for bigamy—or, rather, octagamy. If he consents, then he will have to pay alimony to all of you.
MAURICIA. What is alimony?
PAMELA. Pin-money, my child—plenty of it. You are to be free and have plenty of spending-money. *That* is usually a novelty for a married woman. By the way, Didymos! Rastos! [*The two slaves approach.*] You are slaves no longer, but free citizens of Sulu. Serve the Governor, if you choose, but compel him to pay union wages and tip you liberally. You understand? [*She enters palace.*]
CHIQUITA. Tomorrow we shall be American grass-widows. Now for the soldiers.
PEPITA. We must be careful.
CHIQUITA. Nonsense! We have nothing to fear from these gentle strangers after being courted by Sulu sweethearts.

Chiquita and Wives, Didymos and Rastos

"MY SULU LULU LOO"

In Sulu once there lived a belle
Whose winning ways had cast a spell
Upon a chief of great renown—
 He was smitten sore.
He followed her both night and day:
He tried to steal this girl away:
And underneath her window he
 Repeated o'er and o'er:

Refrain
Lulu, you're my Sulu Lulu Loo!
Lulu, do take pity on me, do!
I want no one else but you!
Lulu, you're my Sulu Lulu Loo!

If she went out to take a stroll,
This palpitating, eager soul
Would wave his snaky knife at her,
 Saying, "Fly with me!"
In jungle deep she thought to hide.
Since she could not become his bride,
When all at once she heard this song
 From out a bamboo-tree:

Refrain.
Lulu, you're my Sulu Lulu Loo, etc.

[Chiquita, Didymos, Rastos, *and wives exeunt with dance as* Ki-Ram *enters with the four school-ma'ams. He has two on each side and is making a sincere effort to embrace all four at the same time.*]

Ki-Ram. Why not? I think you might—to oblige a friend. Young ladies, I have only eight. I need some blondes to help out the color scheme. I've fallen into the habit of marrying nearly all of the ladies I meet.

A School-Ma'am. We didn't come over here to marry. We are interested in education.

Ki-Ram. Married life is an education.

[*A blare of trumpets.* Budd, Hadji, Dingbat, Didymos, *and* Rastos *come from palace. The natives kneel, and one of the slaves advances towards* Ki-Ram *a silken pillow on which is a shaggy silk hat of the kind seen at State conventions.* Ki-Ram *is mystified. He looks at the hat.*]

Ki-Ram. What's that?

Budd. The insignia of your new office.

Ki-Ram. [*Picking it up to examine it.*] My! My! What is it—animal, vegetable, or mineral?

Budd. It is called a hat. This is the kind worn by all Governors.

Ki-Ram. With the fur rubbed the wrong way?

Budd. A true statesman invariably has the fur rubbed the wrong way.

Hadji. [*Announcing.*] They are coming for the inauguration.

Budd. [*To* Ki-Ram.] Did you hear that? Get ready.

Ki-Ram. Colonel, there is only one thing that will get me ready.

Budd. And what is that?

Ki-Ram. You know—it has a cherry in it.

[*They hurriedly enter palace. Volunteers, marines, fife-and-drum corps, wives, natives, and various members of the American party enter from right and left and mass in front of the palace.*]

Chorus

CHORUS TO THE GOVERNOR

Ki-Ram, the new-made chief!
　　Our ruler democratic,
From recent state of grief,
　　Transferred to bliss ecstatic.
Forgetful of his scare
　　And its attendant pallor, he
Accepts this job, so fair—
　　Also the salaree!

[BUDD *comes from palace and takes his place in front of the soldiers.*
KI-RAM *comes to the palace steps, proudly exhibiting the hat.*]

KI-RAM
No crown for me of ordinary gold:
A Governor I'm to be, and I've been told
That this, which the Colonel calls a hat,
Is the proper gear for a democrat.

BUDD
'Tis emblematic, chaste, and pat,
He's proud to wear a hat like that.

[KI-RAM *comes down and faces the assemblage. He puts on the hat,
which falls over his ears.*]

KI-RAM
[*Recitative.*] How do I look?

ALL
Glorious! Wonderful!
What do you think of that?
Could anything excel
The simple beauty of a hat?

[*The boom of a cannon is heard. A sergeant lowers the Sulu flag from
the tall pole in front of the palace.*]

HARDY
Let all at strict attention stand,
The blessed moment's nigh.
When o'er this liberated land
The stars and stripes shall fly.

[*Another gun salute. The stars and stripes break from the top of the
flag-staff to the music of "The Star-Spangled Banner." A roll of drums,
and* HENRIETTA *enters and comes down front.*]

HENRIETTA
If I would be a soldier's bride,
I must not grieve, whate'er betide,

But laugh the tear-drops from my eye,
And cheerily wave the last good-bye.
And every girl who's left behind
   Civilian love will spurn;
For never a one will change her mind
   Till the Volunteers return.

ALL

March, march, hearts are light,
   Step with jaunty pride
To the fight! To the fight!
   Where each may win a bride.
For they know the girls they're leaving behind
   All civilian love will spurn,
And never a one will change her mind
   Till the Volunteers return.

[*During this chorus* KI-RAM, *on the palace steps, consumes many cocktails brought to him by* DIDYMOS *and* RASTOS. *At conclusion of the chorus all turn and salute the flag.*]

CURTAIN

Stephen Crane

(1871–1900)

Stephen Crane dropped out of college to work as an author and part-time newspaper reporter in New York City. His first novel, *Maggie: A Girl of the Streets* (1893), the story of an innocent girl from the slums who descends into prostitution and suicide, brought him only contempt, but his second, *The Red Badge of Courage*, and his first volume of poetry, *The Black Riders*—both published in 1895—made him famous. Even combat veterans were astonished at his ability to imagine and reproduce on the page the feel of battle despite the fact that he had never seen battle himself. His use of realistic techniques in telling the story of a young Civil War soldier, and the decidedly anti-romantic tone of *The Red Badge of Courage*, have made some critics consider him the first truly modern American novelist.

Crane's fame as a writer of fiction about war, and perhaps also his curiosity to discover how accurately he had described combat, led him to a career as a war correspondent. In 1897, while he was reporting on the insurrection in Cuba, his ship was sunk and he wound up rowing a dinghy and finally swimming ashore through the surf. The incident became the material for one of his most famous short stories, "The Open Boat." He also covered the Greco-Turkish war for the *New York Journal,* and the Spanish-American War for the *Journal* and the *New York World.* He died in England, not yet twenty-nine years old, the victim of tuberculosis complicated by malaria that he had caught in Cuba.

Crane's other fiction includes *The Third Violet* (1897) and a satirical novel about a war correspondent, *Active Service* (1899). In addition to his novels and poetry, Crane published several books of short stories. A selection of his darkly satirical verse follows here.

A newspaper is a collection of half-injustices

A newspaper is a collection of half-injustices
Which, bawled by boys from mile to mile,
Spreads its curious opinion
To a million merciful and sneering men,
While families cuddle the joys of the fireside
When spurred by tale of dire lone agony.
A newspaper is a court
Where every one is kindly and unfairly tried
By a squalor of honest men.
A newspaper is a market
Where wisdom sells its freedom
And melons are crowned by the crowd.
A newspaper is a game
Where his error scores the player victory
While another's skill wins death.
A newspaper is a symbol;
It is fetless life's chronicle,
A collection of loud tales
Concentrating eternal stupidities,
That in remote ages lived unhaltered,
Roaming through a fenceless world.

War Is Kind

Do not weep, maiden, for war is kind.
Because your lover threw wild hands toward the sky
And the affrighted steed ran on alone,

Do not weep.
War is kind.

Hoarse, booming drums of the regiment
Little souls who thirst for fight,
These men were born to drill and die
The unexplained glory flies above them
Great is the battle-god, great, and his kingdom——
A field where a thousand corpses lie.

Do not weep, babe, for war is kind.
Because your father tumbled in the yellow trenches,
Raged at his breast, gulped and died,
Do not weep.
War is kind.

Swift, blazing flag of the regiment
Eagle with crest of red and gold,
These men were born to drill and die
Point for them the virtue of slaughter
Make plain to them the excellence of killing
And a field where a thousand corpses lie.

Mother whose heart hung humble as a button
On the bright splendid shroud of your son,
Do not weep.
War is kind.

Guy Wetmore Carryl

(1873–1904)

Carryl joined the staff of *Munsey's* magazine in 1895, the year he graduated from Columbia College. By 1896, he had moved to Paris where he would remain until 1902, first as a representative of Harper and Brothers, and then as a contributor to *Life, Munsey's,* and *Collier's* magazines. He first became known for his light verse—*Fables for the Frivolous* (1898), *Mother Goose for Grownups* (1900), and *Grimm Tales Made Gay* (1902)—but achieved critical success as a novelist with the publication of *The Lieutenant Governor* in 1903 and *The Transgression of Andrew Vane* the following year. He died in 1904 at the age of thirty-two.

How Little Red Riding Hood
Came to be Eaten

Most worthy of praise
Were the virtuous ways
   Of Little Red Riding Hood's Ma,
And no one was ever
More cautious and clever
   Than Little Red Riding Hood's Pa.
They never misled,
For they meant what they said,
   And would frequently say what they meant,

And the way she should go
They were careful to show,
  And the way that they showed her, she went.

It thus is n't strange
That Red Riding Hood's range
  Of virtues so steadily grew,
That soon she won prizes
Of different sizes,
  And golden encomiums, too!
As a general rule
She was head of her school,
  And at six was so notably smart
That they gave her a cheque
For reciting "The Wreck
  of the Hesperus," wholly by heart!
And you all will applaud her the more, I am
      sure,
When I add that this money she gave to the
      poor.

At eleven this lass
Had a Sunday-school class,
  At twelve wrote a volume of verse,
At thirteen was yearning
For glory, and learning
  To be a professional nurse.
To a glorious height
The young paragon might
  Have grown, if not nipped in the bud,
But the following year
Struck her smiling career
  With a dull and a sickening thud!
(I have shed a great tear at the thought of her
      pain,
And must copy my manuscript over again!)
Not dreaming of harm,
One day on her arm
  A basket she hung. It was filled

With jellies, and ices,
And gruel, and spices,
   And chicken-legs, carefully grilled,
And a savory stew,
And a novel or two
   She'd persuaded a neighbor to loan,
And a hot-water can,
And a Japanese fan,
   And a bottle of *eau-de-cologne*,
And the rest of the things that your family fill
Your room with, whenever you chance to be ill!

She expected to find
Her decrepit but kind
   Old Grandmother waiting her call,
But the visage that met her
Completely upset her:
   It was n't familiar at all!
With a whitening cheek
She started to speak,
   But her peril she instantly saw:—
Her Grandma had fled,
And she'd tackled instead
   Four merciless Paws and a Maw!
When the neighbors came running, the wolf to
      subdue,
He was licking his chops, (and Red Riding
      Hood's, too!)
At this terrible tale
Some readers will pale,
   And others with horror grow dumb,
And yet it was better,
I fear, he should get her:
   Just think what she might have become!
For an infant so keen
Might in future have been
   A woman of awful renown,
Who carried on fights
For her feminine rights
   As the Mare of an Arkansas town.

She might have continued the crime of her
     'teens,
And come to write verse for the Big Magazines!
The Moral: There's nothing much glummer
   Than children whose talents appall:
One much prefers those who are dumber,
   But as for the paragons small,
If a swallow cannot make a summer
   It can bring on a summary fall!

How Rudeness and Kindness Were Justly Rewarded

Once on a time, long years ago
   (Just when I quite forget),
Two maidens lived beside the Po,
   One blonde and one brunette.
The blonde one's character was mild,
From morning until night she smiled,
Whereas the one whose hair was brown
Did little else than pine and frown.
   (*I* think one ought to draw the line
   At girls who always frown and pine!)

The blonde one learned to play the harp,
   Like all accomplished dames,
And trained her voice to take *C* sharp
   As well as Emma Eames;
Made baskets out of scented grass,
And paper-weights of hammered brass,
And lots of other odds and ends
For gentlemen and lady friends.
   (*I* think it takes a deal of sense
   To manufacture gifts for gents!)

The dark one wore an air of gloom,
   Proclaimed the world a bore,

And took her breakfast in her room
    Three mornings out of four.
With crankiness she seemed imbued,
And everything she said was rude:
She sniffed, and sneered, and, what is more,
When very much provoked, she swore!
    (*I* think that I could never care
    For any girl who'd learned to swear!)

One day the blonde was striding past
    A forest, all alone,
When all at once her eyes she cast
    Upon a wrinkled crone,
Who tottered near with shaking knees,
And said: "A penny, if you please!"
And you will learn with some surprise
This was a fairy in disguise!
    (*I* think it must be hard to know
    A fairy who's incognito!)

The maiden filled her trembling palms
    With coinage of the realm.
The fairy said: "Take back your alms!
    My heart they overwhelm.
Henceforth at every word shall slip
A pearl or ruby from your lip!"
And, when the girl got home that night,—
She found the fairy's words were right!
    (*I* think there are not many girls
    Whose words are worth their weight in pearls!)

It happened that the cross brunette,
    Ten minutes later, came
Along the self-same road, and met
    That bent and wrinkled dame,
Who asked her humbly for a sou.
The girl replied: "Get out with you!"
The fairy cried: "Each word you drop,
A toad from out your mouth shall hop!"

(*I* think that nothing incommodes
   One's speech like uninvited toads!)

And so it was, the cheerful blonde
   Lived on in joy and bliss,
And grew pecunious, beyond
   The dreams of avarice!
And to a nice young man was wed,
And I have often heard it said
No other man who ever walked
Most loved his wife when most she talked!
   (*I* think this very fact, forsooth,
   Goes far to prove I tell the truth!)

The cross brunette the fairy's joke
   By hook or crook survived,
But still at every word she spoke
   An ugly toad arrived,
Until at last she had to come
To feigning she was wholly dumb,
Whereat the suitors swarmed around,
And soon a wealthy mate she found.
   (*I* think nobody ever knew
   The happier husband of the two!)

The Moral of the tale is: Bah!
Nous avons changé tout celà.
No clear idea I hope to strike
Of what *your* nicest girl is like,
But she whose best young man *I* am
Is not an oyster, nor a clam!

Edith Wharton

(1862–1937)

Edith Wharton is better known for her novels, especially the Pulitzer prize–winning *The Age of Innocence* (1920) and the uncharacteristically dark and tragic *Ethan Frome* (1911), than she is for her other writings that include poetry, travel books, literary criticism, and short stories. It was in fact a novel, *The House of Mirth* (1905), with which she won her first critical and popular success. But her subtle irony and sometimes pointed satire comes across vividly in the stories, two of which follow here. Wharton deals with her favorite subject in each: The pretentions of turn-of-the-century New York society, the world into which she herself was born and in which she functioned as a young hostess before she took up writing full time. Her own struggle against the social conventions of her world is undoubtedly reflected in these stories whose characters are treated sharply but without contempt or cruelty.

Xingu

I

MRS. BALLINGER is one of the ladies who pursue Culture in bands, as though it were dangerous to meet alone. To this end she had founded the Lunch Club, an association composed of herself and several other indomitable huntresses of erudition. The Lunch Club, after three or four winters of lunching and debate, had acquired such local distinction that the entertainment of distinguished strangers became one of its accepted functions; in recognition of which it duly extended to the celebrated Osric Dane, on the day of her arrival in Hillbridge, an invitation to be present at the next meeting.

The club was to meet at Mrs. Ballinger's. The other members, behind her back, were of one voice in deploring her unwillingness to cede her rights in favor of Mrs. Plinth, whose house made a more impressive setting for the entertainment of celebrities; while, as Mrs. Leveret observed, there was always the picture gallery to fall back on.

Mrs. Plinth made no secret of sharing this view. She had always regarded it as one of her obligations to entertain the Lunch Club's distinguished guests. Mrs. Plinth was almost as proud of her obligations as she was of her picture gallery; she was in fact fond of implying that the one possession implied the other, and that only a woman of her wealth could afford to live up to a standard as high as that which she had set herself. An all-round sense of duty, roughly adaptable to various ends, was, in her opinion, all that Providence exacted of the more humbly stationed; but the power which had predestined Mrs. Plinth to keep a footman clearly intended her to maintain an equally specialized staff of responsibilities. It was the more to be regretted that Mrs. Ballinger, whose obligations to society were bounded by the narrow scope of two parlormaids, should have been so tenacious of the right to entertain Osric Dane.

The question of that lady's reception had for a month past profoundly moved the members of the Lunch Club. It was not that they felt themselves unequal to the task, but that their sense of the opportunity plunged them into the agreeable uncertainty of the lady who weighs the alternatives of a well-stocked wardrobe. If such subsidiary members as Mrs. Leveret were fluttered by the thought of exchanging ideas with the author of *The Wings of Death*, no forebodings disturbed the conscious adequacy of Mrs. Plinth, Mrs. Ballinger and Miss Van Vluyck. *The Wings of Death* had, in fact, at Miss Van Vluyck's suggestion, been chosen as the subject of discussion at the last club meeting, and each member had thus been enabled to express her own opinion or to appropriate whatever sounded well in the comments of the others.

Mrs. Roby alone had abstained from profiting by the opportu-

nity but it was now openly recognized that, as a member of the
Lunch Club, Mrs. Roby was a failure. "It all comes," as Miss Van
Vluyck put it, "of accepting a woman on a man's estimation."
Mrs. Roby, returning to Hillbridge from a prolonged sojourn in
exotic lands—the other ladies no longer took the trouble to remember where—had been heralded by the distinguished biolo-
gist, Professor Foreland, as the most agreeable woman he had ever
met; and the members of the Lunch Club, impressed by an en-
comium that carried the weight of a diploma, and rashly assuming
that the Professor's social sympathies would follow the line of his
professional bent, had seized the chance of annexing a biological member. Their disillusionment was complete. At Miss Van
Vluyck's first offhand mention of the pterodactyl Mrs. Roby had
confusedly murmured: "I know so little about meters—" and after that painful betrayal of incompetence she had prudently withdrawn from further participation in the mental gymnastics of the
club.

"I suppose she flattered him," Miss Van Vluyck summed up—
"or else it's the way she does her hair."

The dimensions of Miss Van Vluyck's dining room having restricted the membership of the club to six, the nonconductiveness
of one member was a serious obstacle to the exchange of ideas,
and some wonder had already been expressed that Mrs. Roby
should care to live, as it were, on the intellectual bounty of the
others. This feeling was increased by the discovery that she had
not yet read *The Wings of Death*. She owned to having heard the
name of Osric Dane; but that—incredible as it appeared—was
the extent of her acquaintance with the celebrated novelist. The
ladies could not conceal their surprise; but Mrs. Ballinger, whose
pride in the club made her wish to put even Mrs. Roby in the
best possible light, gently insinuated that, though she had not had
time to acquaint herself with *The Wings of Death*, she must at least
be familiar with its equally remarkable predecessor, *The Supreme
Instant*.

Mrs. Roby wrinkled her sunny brows in a conscientious effort
of memory, as a result of which she recalled that, oh, yes, she *had*
seen the book at her brother's, when she was staying with him in
Brazil, and had even carried it off to read one day on a boating
party; but they had all got to shying things at each other in the

boat, and the book had gone overboard, so she had never had the chance—

The picture evoked by this anecdote did not increase Mrs. Roby's credit with the club, and there was a painful pause, which was broken by Mrs. Plinth's remarking: "I can understand that, with all your other pursuits, you should not find much time for reading; but I should have thought you might at least have *got up The Wings of Death* before Osric Dane's arrival."

Mrs. Roby took this rebuke good-humoredly. She had meant, she owned, to glance through the book; but she had been so absorbed in a novel of Trollope's that—

"No one reads Trollope now," Mrs. Ballinger interrupted.

Mrs. Roby looked pained. "I'm only just beginning," she confessed.

"And does he interest you?" Mrs. Plinth inquired.

"He amuses me."

"Amusement," said Mrs. Plinth, "is hardly what I look for in my choice of books."

"Oh, certainly, *The Wings of Death* is not amusing," ventured Mrs. Leveret, whose manner of putting forth an opinion was like that of an obliging salesman with a variety of other styles to submit if his first selection does not suit.

"Was it *meant* to be?" inquired Mrs. Plinth, who was fond of asking questions that she permitted no one but herself to answer. "Assuredly not."

"Assuredly not—that is what I was going to say," assented Mrs. Leveret, hastily rolling up her opinion and reaching for another. "It was meant to—to elevate."

Miss Van Vluyck adjusted her spectacles as though they were the black cap of condemnation. "I hardly see," she interposed, "how a book steeped in the bitterest pessimism can be said to elevate, however much it may instruct."

"I meant, of course, to instruct," said Mrs. Leveret, flurried by the unexpected distinction between two terms which she had supposed to be synonymous. Mrs. Leveret's enjoyment of the Lunch Club was frequently marred by such surprises; and not knowing her own value to the other ladies as a mirror for their mental complacency she was sometimes troubled by a doubt of her worthiness to join in their debates. It was only the fact of having a

dull sister who thought her clever that saved her from a sense of
hopeless inferiority.

"Do they get married in the end?" Mrs. Roby interposed.

"They—who?" the Lunch Club collectively exclaimed.

"Why, the girl and man. It's a novel, isn't it? I always think
that's the one thing that matters. If they're parted it spoils my
dinner."

Mrs. Plinth and Mrs. Ballinger exchanged scandalized glances,
and the latter said: "I should hardly advise you to read *The Wings
of Death* in that spirit. For my part, when there are so many books
one *has* to read, I wonder how any one can find time for those
that are merely amusing."

"The beautiful part of it," Laura Glyde murmured, "is surely
just this—that no one can tell *how The Wings of Death* ends. Osric
Dane, overcome by the awful significance of her own meaning,
has mercifully veiled it—perhaps even from herself—as Apelles,
in representing the sacrifice of Iphigenia, veiled the face of Aga-
memnon."

"What's that? It is poetry?" whispered Mrs. Leveret to Mrs.
Plinth, who, disdaining a definite reply, said coldly: "You should
look it up. I always make it a point to look things up." Her tone
added—"Though I might easily have it done for me by the
footman."

"I was about to say," Miss Van Vluyck resumed, "that it must
always be a question whether a book *can* instruct unless it ele-
vates."

"Oh—" murmured Mrs. Leveret, now feeling herself hopelessly astray.

"I don't know," said Mrs. Ballinger, scenting in Miss Van
Vluyck's tone a tendency to depreciate the coveted distinction of
entertaining Osric Dane; "I don't know that such a question can
seriously be raised as to a book which has attracted more attention
among thoughtful people than any novel since *Robert Elsmere*."

"Oh, but don't you see," exclaimed Laura Glyde, "that it's just
the dark hopelessness of it all—the wonderful tone scheme of
black on black—that makes it such an artistic achievement? It
reminded me when I read it of Prince Rupert's *manière noire* . . .
the book is etched, not painted, yet one feels the color values so
intensely. . . ."

"Who is *he*?" Mrs. Leveret whispered to her neighbor. "Someone she's met abroad?"

"The wonderful part of the book," Mrs. Ballinger conceded, "is that it may be looked at from so many points of view. I hear that as a study of determinism Professor Lupton ranks it with *The Data of Ethics.*"

"I'm told that Osric Dane spent ten years in preparatory studies before beginning to write it," said Mrs. Plinth. "She looks up everything—verifies everything. It has always been my principle, as you know. Nothing would induce me, now, to put aside a book before I'd finished it, just because I can buy as many more as I want."

"And what do *you* think of *The Wings of Death*?" Mrs. Roby abruptly asked her.

It was the kind of question that might be termed out of order, and the ladies glanced at each other as though disclaiming any share in such a breach of discipline. They all knew there was nothing Mrs. Plinth so much disliked as being asked her opinion of a book. Books were written to read; if one read them what more could be expected? To be questioned in detail regarding the contents of a volume seemed to her as great an outrage as being searched for smuggled laces at the Custom House. The club had always respected this idiosyncrasy of Mrs. Plinth's. Such opinions as she had were imposing and substantial: her mind, like her house, was furnished with monumental "pieces" that were not meant to be disarranged; and it was one of the unwritten rules of the Lunch Club that, within her own province, each member's habits of thought should be respected. The meeting therefore closed with an increased sense, on the part of the other ladies, of Mrs. Roby's hopeless unfitness to be one of them.

II

Mrs. Leveret, on the eventful day, arrived early at Mrs. Ballinger's, her volume of *Appropriate Allusions* in her pocket.

It always flustered Mrs. Leveret to be late at the Lunch Club: she liked to collect her thoughts and gather a hint, as the others assembled, of the turn the conversation was likely to take. Today, however, she felt herself completely at a loss; and even the familiar contact of *Appropriate Allusions*, which stuck into her as she sat down, failed to give her any reassurance. It was an admirable little volume, compiled to meet all the social emergencies; so that, whether on the occasion of Anniversaries, joyful or melancholy (as the classification ran), of Banquets, social or municipal, or of Baptisms, Church of England or sectarian, its student need never be at a loss for a pertinent reference. Mrs. Leveret, though she had for years devoutly conned its pages, valued it, however, rather for its moral support than for its practical services; for though in the privacy of her own room she commanded an army of quotations, these invariably deserted her at the critical moment, and the only phrase she retained—*Canst thou draw out leviathan with a hook?*—was one she had never yet found occasion to apply.

Today she felt that even the complete mastery of the volume would hardly have insured her self-possession; for she thought it probable that, even if she *did*, in some miraculous way, remember an Allusion, it would be only to find that Osric Dane used a different volume (Mrs. Leveret was convinced that literary people always carried them), and would consequently not recognize her quotations.

Mrs. Leveret's sense of being adrift was intensified by the appearance of Mrs. Ballinger's drawing room. To a careless eye its aspect was unchanged; but those acquainted with Mrs. Ballinger's way of arranging her books would instantly have detected the marks of recent perturbation. Mrs. Ballinger's province, as a member of the Lunch Club, was the Book of the Day. On that, whatever it was, from a novel to a treatise on experimental psychology, she was confidently, authoritatively "up." What became of last year's books, or last week's even; what she did with the "subjects" she had previously professed with equal authority; no one had ever yet discovered. Her mind was an hotel where facts came and went like transient lodgers, without leaving their address behind, and frequently without paying for their board. It was Mrs. Ballinger's boast that she was "abreast with the Thought of the Day," and her pride that this advanced position should be expressed by the books on her table. These volumes, frequently renewed, and almost always damp from the press, bore names generally unfamiliar to Mrs. Leveret, and giving her, as she furtively scanned them, a disheartening glimpse of new fields of knowledge to be breathlessly traversed in Mrs. Ballinger's wake. But today a number of maturer-looking volumes were adroitly mingled with the *primeurs* of the press—Karl Marx jostled Professor Bergson, and the *Confessions of St. Augustine* lay beside the last work on "Mendelism"; so that even to Mrs. Leveret's fluttered perceptions it was clear that Mrs. Ballinger didn't in the least know what Osric Dane was likely to talk about, and had taken measures to be prepared for anything. Mrs. Leveret felt like a passenger on an ocean steamer who is told that there is no immediate danger, but that she had better put on her lifebelt.

It was a relief to be roused from these forebodings by Miss Van Vluyck's arrival.

"Well, my dear," the newcomer briskly asked her hostess, "what subjects are we to discuss today?"

Mrs. Ballinger was furtively replacing a volume of Wordsworth by a copy of Verlaine. "I hardly know," she said, somewhat nervously. "Perhaps we had better leave that to circumstances."

"Circumstances?" said Miss Van Vluyck drily. "That means, I suppose, that Laura Glyde will take the floor as usual, and we shall be deluged with literature."

Philanthropy and statistics were Miss Van Vluyck's province, and she resented any tendency to divert their guest's attention from these topics.

Mrs. Plinth at this moment appeared.

"Literature?" she protested in a tone of remonstrance. "But this is perfectly unexpected. I understood we were to talk of Osric Dane's novel."

Mrs. Ballinger winced at the discrimination, but let it pass. "We can hardly make that our chief subject—at least not *too* intentionally," she suggested. "Of course we can let our talk *drift* in that direction; but we ought to have some other topic as an introduction, and that is what I wanted to consult you about. The fact is, we know so little of Osric Dane's taste and interests that it is difficult to make any special preparation."

"It may be difficult," said Mrs. Plinth with decision, "but it is necessary. I know what that happy-go-lucky principle leads to. As I told one of my nieces the other day, there are certain emergencies for which a lady should always be prepared. It's in shocking taste to wear colors when one pays a visit of condolence, or a last year's dress when there are reports that one's husband is on the wrong side of the market; and so it is with conversation. All I ask is that I should know beforehand what is to be talked about; then I feel sure of being able to say the proper thing."

"I quite agree with you," Mrs. Ballinger assented; "but—"

And at that instant, heralded by the fluttered parlormaid, Osric Dane appeared upon the threshold.

Mrs. Leveret told her sister afterward that she had known at a glance what was coming. She saw that Osric Dane was not going to meet them halfway. That distinguished personage had indeed entered with an air of compulsion not calculated to promote the easy exercise of hospitality. She looked as though she were about to be photographed for a new edition of her books.

The desire to propitiate a divinity is generally in inverse ratio to its responsiveness, and the sense of discouragement produced by Osric Dane's entrance visibly increased the Lunch Club's eagerness to please her. Any lingering idea that she might consider herself under an obligation to her entertainers was at once dispelled by her manner: as Mrs. Leveret said afterward to her sister, she had a way of looking at you that made you feel as if there was something wrong with your hat. This evidence of greatness produced such an immediate impression on the ladies that a shudder of awe ran through them when Mrs. Roby, as their hostess, led the great personage into the dining room, turned back to whisper to the others: "What a brute she is!"

The hour about the table did not tend to revise this verdict. It was passed by Osric Dane in the silent deglutition of Mrs. Ballinger's menu, and by the members of the club in the emission of tentative platitudes which their guest seemed to swallow as perfunctorily as the successive courses of the luncheon.

Mrs. Ballinger's reluctance to fix a topic had thrown the club into a mental disarray which increased with the return to the drawing room, where the actual business of discussion was to open. Each lady waited for the other to speak; and there was a general shock of disappointment when their hostess opened the conversation by the painfully commonplace inquiry: "Is this your first visit to Hillbridge?"

Even Mrs. Leveret was conscious that this was a bad beginning;

and a vague impulse of deprecation made Miss Glyde interject: "It is a very small place indeed."

Mrs. Plinth bristled. "We have a great many representative people," she said, in the tone of one who speaks for her order.

Osric Dane turned to her. "What do they represent?" she asked.

Mrs. Plinth's constitutional dislike to being questioned was intensified by her sense of unpreparedness; and her reproachful glance passed the question on to Mrs. Ballinger.

"Why," said the lady, glancing in turn at the other members, "as a community I hope it is not too much to say that we stand for culture."

"For art—" Miss Glyde interjected.

"For art and literature," Mrs. Ballinger amended.

"And for sociology, I trust," snapped Miss Van Vluyck.

"We have a standard," said Mrs. Plinth, feeling herself suddenly secure on the vast expanse of a generalization; and Mrs. Leveret, thinking there must be room for more than one on so broad a statement, took courage to murmur: "Oh, certainly; we have a standard."

"The object of our little club," Mrs. Ballinger continued, "is to concentrate the highest tendencies of Hillbridge—to centralize and focus its intellectual effort."

This was felt to be so happy that the ladies drew an almost audible breath of relief.

"We aspire," the President went on, "to be in touch with whatever is highest in art, literature and ethics."

Osric Dane again turned to her. "What ethics?" she asked.

A tremor of apprehension encircled the room. None of the ladies required any preparation to pronounce on a question of morals; but when they were called ethics it was different. The club, when fresh from the *Encyclopedia Britannica*, the *Reader's Handbook* or Smith's *Classical Dictionary*, could deal confidently with any subject; but when taken unawares it had been known to define agnosticism as a heresy of the Early Church and Professor Froude as a distinguished histologist; and such minor members as Mrs. Leveret still secretly regarded ethics as something vaguely pagan.

Even to Mrs. Ballinger, Osric Dane's question was unsettling, and there was a general sense of gratitude when Laura Glyde leaned forward to say, with her most sympathetic accent: "You must excuse us, Mrs. Dane, for not being able, just at present, to talk of anything but *The Wings of Death.*"

"Yes," said Miss Van Vluyck, with a sudden resolve to carry the war into the enemy's camp. "We are so anxious to know the exact purpose you had in mind in writing your wonderful book."

"You will find," Mrs. Plinth interposed, "that we are not superficial readers."

"We are eager to hear from you," Miss Van Vluyck continued, "if the pessimistic tendency of the book is an expression of your own convictions or—"

"Or merely," Miss Glyde thrust in, "a somber background brushed in to throw your figures into more vivid relief. *Are* you not primarily plastic?"

"*I* have always maintained," Mrs. Ballinger interposed, "that you represent the purely objective method—"

Osric Dane helped herself critically to coffee. "How do you define objective?" she then inquired.

There was a flurried pause before Laura Glyde intensely murmured: "In reading *you* we don't define, we feel."

Osric Dane smiled. "The cerebellum," she remarked, "is not infrequently the seat of the literary emotions." And she took a second lump of sugar.

The sting that this remark was vaguely felt to conceal was almost neutralized by the satisfaction of being addressed in such technical language.

"Ah, the cerebellum," said Mrs. Van Vluyck complacently. "The club took a course in psychology last winter."

"Which psychology?" asked Osric Dane.

There was an agonizing pause, during which each member of the club secretly deplored the distressing inefficiency of the others. Only Mrs. Roby went on placidly sipping her chartreuse. At last Mrs. Ballinger said, with an attempt at a high tone: "Well, really, you know, it was last year that we took psychology, and this winter we have been so absorbed in—"

She broke off, nervously trying to recall some of the club's discussions; but her faculties seemed to be paralyzed by the petrifying stare of Osric Dane. What *had* the club been absorbed in? Mrs. Ballinger, with a vague purpose of gaining time, repeated slowly: "We've been so intensely absorbed in—"

Mrs. Roby put down her liqueur glass and drew near the group with a smile.

"In Xingu?" she gently prompted.

A thrill ran through the other members. They exchanged confused glances, and then, with one accord, turned a gaze of mingled relief and interrogation on their rescuer. The expression of each denoted a different phase of the same emotion. Mrs. Plinth was the first to compose her features to an air of reassurance: after a moment's hasty adjustment her look almost implied that it was she who had given the word to Mrs. Ballinger.

"Xingu, of course!" exclaimed the latter with her accustomed promptness, while Miss Van Vluyck and Laura Glyde seemed to be plumbing the depths of memory, and Mrs. Leveret, feeling apprehensively for *Appropriate Allusions*, was somehow reassured by the uncomfortable pressure of its bulk against her person.

Osric Dane's change of countenance was no less striking than that of her entertainers. She too put down her coffee cup, but with a look of distinct annoyance; she too wore, for a brief moment, what Mrs. Roby afterward described as the look of feeling for something in the back of her head; and before she could dissemble these momentary signs of weakness, Mrs. Roby, turning to her with a deferential smile, had said: "And we've been so hoping that today you would tell us just what you think of it."

Osric Dane received the homage of the smile as a matter of course; but the accompanying question obviously embarrassed her, and it became clear to her observers that she was not quick at shifting her facial scenery. It was as though her countenance had so long been set in an expression of unchallenged superiority that the muscles had stiffened, and refused to obey her orders.

"Xingu—" she said, as if seeking in her turn to gain time.

Mrs. Roby continued to press her. "Knowing how engrossing the subject is, you will understand how it happens that the club has let everything else go to the wall for the moment. Since we took up Xingu I might almost say—were it not for your books— that nothing else seems to us worth remembering."

Osric Dane's stern features were darkened rather than lit up by an uneasy smile. "I am glad to hear that you make one exception," she gave out between narrowed lips.

"Oh, of course," Mrs. Roby said prettily; "but as you have shown us that—so very naturally!—you don't care to talk of your own things, we really can't let you off from telling us exactly what you think about Xingu; especially," she added, with a still more persuasive smile, "as some people say that one of your last books was saturated with it."

It was an *it*, then—the assurance sped like fire through the parched minds of the other members. In their eagerness to gain the least little clue to Xingu they almost forgot the joy of assisting at the discomfiture of Mrs. Dane.

The latter reddened nervously under her antagonist's challenge. "May I ask," she faltered out, "to which of my books you refer?"

Mrs. Roby did not falter. "That's just what I want you to tell us; because, though I was present, I didn't actually take part."

"Present at what?" Mrs. Dane took her up; and for an instant the trembling members of the Lunch Club thought that the champion Providence had raised up for them had lost a point. But Mrs. Roby explained herself gaily: "At the discussion, of course. And so we're dreadfully anxious to know just how it was that you went into the Xingu."

There was a portentous pause, a silence so big with incalculable dangers that the members with one accord checked the words on their lips, like soldiers dropping their arms to watch a single combat between their leaders. Then Mrs. Dane gave expression to their inmost dread by saying sharply: "Ah—you say *the* Xingu, do you?"

Mrs. Roby smiled undauntedly. "It *is* a shade pedantic, isn't it? Personally, I always drop the article: but I don't know how the other members feel about it."

The other members looked as though they would willingly have dispensed with this appeal to their opinion, and Mrs. Roby, after a bright glance about the group, went on: "They probably think, as I do, that nothing really matters except the thing itself—except Xingu."

No immediate reply seemed to occur to Mrs. Dane, and Mrs. Ballinger gathered courage to say: "Surely everyone must feel that about Xingu."

Mrs. Plinth came to her support with a heavy murmur of assent, and Laura Glyde sighed out emotionally: "I have known cases where it has changed a whole life."

"It has done me worlds of good," Mrs. Leveret interjected, seeming to herself to remember that she had either taken it or read it the winter before.

"Of course," Mrs. Roby admitted, "the difficulty is that one must give up so much time to it. It's very long."

"I can't imagine," said Miss Van Vluyck, "grudging the time given to such a subject."

"And deep in places," Mrs. Roby pursued; (so then it was a book!) "And it isn't easy to skip."

"I never skip," said Mrs. Plinth dogmatically.

"Ah, it's dangerous to, in Xingu. Even at the start there are places where one can't. One must just wade through."

"I should hardly call it *wading*," said Mrs. Ballinger sarcastically.

Mrs. Roby sent her a look of interest. "Ah—you always found it went swimmingly?"

Mrs. Ballinger hesitated. "Of course there are difficult passages," she conceded.

"Yes; some are not at all clear—even," Mrs. Roby added, "if one is familiar with the original."

"As I suppose you are?" Osric Dane interposed, suddenly fixing her with a look of challenge.

Mrs. Roby met it by a deprecating gesture. "Oh, it's really not difficult up to a certain point; though some of the branches are very little known, and it's almost impossible to get at the source."

"Have you ever tried?" Mrs. Plinth inquired, still distrustful of Mrs. Roby's thoroughness.

Mrs. Roby was silent for a moment; then she replied with lowered lids: "No—but a friend of mine did; a very brilliant man; and he told me it was best for women—not to. . . ."

A shudder ran around the room. Mrs. Leveret coughed so that the parlormaid, who was handing the cigarettes, should not hear; Miss Van Vluyck's face took on a nauseated expression, and Mrs. Plinth looked as if she were passing someone she did not care to bow to. But the most remarkable result of Mrs. Roby's words was the effect they produced on the Lunch Club's distinguished guest. Osric Dane's impassive features suddenly softened to an expression of the warmest human sympathy, and edging her chair toward Mrs. Roby's she asked: "Did he really? And—did you find he was right?"

Mrs. Ballinger, in whom annoyance at Mrs. Roby's unwonted assumption of prominence was beginning to displace gratitude for the aid she had rendered, could not consent to her being allowed, by such dubious means, to monopolize the attention of their guest. If Osric Dane had not enough self-respect to resent Mrs. Roby's flippancy, at least the Lunch Club would do so in the person of its President.

Mrs. Ballinger laid her hand on Mrs. Roby's arm. "We must not forget," she said with a frigid amiability, "that absorbing as Xingu is to *us*, it may be less interesting to—"

"Oh, no, on the contrary, I assure you," Osric Dane intervened.

"—to others," Mrs. Ballinger finished firmly; "and we must not allow our little meeting to end without persuading Mrs. Dane to say a few words to us on a subject which, today, is much more present in all our thoughts. I refer, of course, to *The Wings of Death*."

The other members, animated by various degrees of the same sentiment, and encouraged by the humanized mien of their redoubtable guest, repeated after Mrs. Ballinger: "Oh, yes, you really *must* talk to us a little about your book."

Osric Dane's expression became as bored, though not as haughty, as when her work had been previously mentioned. But before she could respond to Mrs. Ballinger's request, Mrs. Roby had risen from her seat, and was pulling down her veil over her frivolous nose.

"I'm so sorry," she said, advancing toward her hostess with outstretched hand, "but before Mrs. Dane begins I think I'd better run away. Unluckily, as you know, I haven't read her books, so I should be at a terrible disadvantage among you all, and besides, I've an engagement to play bridge."

If Mrs. Roby had simply pleaded her ignorance of Osric Dane's works as a reason for withdrawing, the Lunch Club, in view of her recent prowess, might have approved such evidence of discretion; but to couple this excuse with the brazen announcement that she was foregoing the privilege for the purpose of joining a bridge party was only one more instance of her deplorable lack of discrimination.

The ladies were disposed, however, to feel that her departure —now that she had performed the sole service she was ever likely to render them—would probably make for greater order and dignity in the impending discussion, besides relieving them of the sense of self-distrust which her presence always mysteriously produced. Mrs. Ballinger therefore restricted herself to a formal murmur of regret, and the other members were just grouping themselves comfortably about Osric Dane when the latter, to their dismay, started up from the sofa on which she had been seated.

"Oh wait—do wait, and I'll go with you!" she called out to Mrs. Roby; and, seizing the hands of the disconcerted members, she administered a series of farewell pressures with the mechanical haste of a railway conductor punching tickets.

"I'm so sorry—I'd quite forgotten—" she flung back at them from the threshold; and as she joined Mrs. Roby, who had turned in surprise at her appeal, the other ladies had the mortification of hearing her say, in a voice which she did not take the pains to lower: "If you'll let me walk a little way with you, I should so like to ask you a few more questions about Xingu. . . ."

III

The incident had been so rapid that the door closed on the departing pair before the other members had time to understand what was happening. Then a sense of the indignity put upon them by Osric Dane's unceremonious desertion began to contend with the confused feeling that they had been cheated out of their due without exactly knowing how or why.

There was a silence, during which Mrs. Ballinger, with a perfunctory hand, rearranged the skillfully grouped literature at which her distinguished guest had not so much as glanced; then Miss Van Vluyck tartly pronounced: "Well, I can't say that I consider Osric Dane's departure a great loss."

This confession crystallized the resentment of the other members, and Mrs. Leveret exclaimed: "I do believe she came on purpose to be nasty!"

It was Mrs. Plinth's private opinion that Osric Dane's attitude toward the Lunch Club might have been very different had it welcomed her in the majestic setting of the Plinth drawing rooms; but not liking to reflect on the inadequacy of Mrs. Ballinger's establishment she sought a round-about satisfaction in deprecating her lack of foresight.

"I said from the first that we ought to have had a subject ready. It's what always happens when you're unprepared. Now if we'd only got up Xingu—"

The slowness of Mrs. Plinth's mental processes was always allowed for by the club; but this instance of it was too much for Mrs. Ballinger's equanimity.

"Xingu!" she scoffed. "Why, it was the fact of our knowing so much more about it than she did—unprepared though we were —that made Osric Dane so furious. I should have thought that was plain enough to everybody!"

This retort impressed even Mrs. Plinth, and Laura Glyde, moved by an impulse of generosity, said: "Yes, we really ought to be grateful to Mrs. Roby for introducing the topic. It may have made Osric Dane furious, but at least it made her civil."

"I am glad we were able to show her," added Miss Van Vluyck, "that a broad and up-to-date culture is not confined to the great intellectual centers."

This increased the satisfaction of the other members, and they began to forget their wrath against Osric Dane in the pleasure of having contributed to her discomfiture.

Miss Van Vluyck thoughtfully rubbed her spectacles. "What surprised me most," she continued, "was that Fanny Roby should be so up on Xingu."

This remark threw a slight chill on the company, but Mrs. Ballinger said with an air of indulgent irony: "Mrs. Roby always has the knack of making a little go a long way; still, we certainly owe her a debt for happening to remember that she'd heard of Xingu." And this was felt by the other members to be a graceful way of canceling once and for all the club's obligation to Mrs. Roby.

Even Mrs. Leveret took courage to speed a timid shaft of irony. "I fancy Osric Dane hardly expected to take a lesson in Xingu at Hillbridge!"

Mrs. Ballinger smiled. "When she asked me what we represented—do you remember?—I wish I'd simply said we represented Xingu!"

All the ladies laughed appreciatively at this sally, except Mrs.

Plinth, who said, after a moment's deliberation: "I'm not sure it would have been wise to do so."

Mrs. Ballinger, who was already beginning to feel as if she had launched at Osric Dane the retort which had just occurred to her, turned ironically on Mrs. Plinth. "May I ask why?" she inquired.

Mrs. Plinth looked grave. "Surely," she said, "I understood from Mrs. Roby herself that the subject was one it was as well not to go into too deeply?"

Miss Van Vluyck rejoined with precision: "I think that applied only to an investigation of the origin of the—of the—"; and suddenly she found that her usually accurate memory had failed her. "It's a part of the subject I never studied myself," she concluded.

"Nor I," said Mrs. Ballinger.

Laura Glyde bent toward them with widened eyes. "And yet it seems—doesn't it—the part that is fullest of an esoteric fascination?"

"I don't know on what you base that," said Miss Van Vluyck argumentatively.

"Well, didn't you notice how intensely interested Osric Dane became as soon as she heard what the brilliant foreigner—he *was* a foreigner, wasn't he—had told Mrs. Roby about the origin—the origin of the rite—or whatever you call it?"

Mrs. Plinth looked disapproving, and Mrs. Ballinger visibly wavered. Then she said: "It may not be desirable to touch on the—on that part of the subject in general conversation; but, from the importance it evidently has to a woman of Osric Dane's distinction, I feel as if we ought not to be afraid to discuss it among ourselves—without gloves—though with closed doors, if necessary."

"I'm quite of your opinion," Miss Van Vluyck came briskly to her support; "on condition, that is, that all grossness of language is avoided."

"Oh, I'm sure we shall understand without that," Mrs. Leveret tittered; and Laura Glyde added significantly: "I fancy we can read between the lines," while Mrs. Ballinger rose to assure herself that the doors were really closed.

Mrs. Plinth had not yet given her adhesion. "I hardly see," she began, "what benefit is to be derived from investigating such peculiar customs—"

But Mrs. Ballinger's patience had reached the extreme limit of tension. "This at least," she returned; "that we shall not be placed again in the humiliating position of finding ourselves less up on our own subjects than Fanny Roby!"

Even to Mrs. Plinth this argument was conclusive. She peered furtively about the room and lowered her commanding tones to ask: "Have you got a copy?"

"A—a copy?" stammered Mrs. Ballinger. She was aware that the other members were looking at her expectantly, and that this answer was inadequate, so she supported it by asking another question. "A copy of what?"

Her companions bent their expectant gaze on Mrs. Plinth, who, in turn, appeared less sure of herself than usual. "Why, of—of— the book," she explained.

"What book?" snapped Miss Van Vluyck, almost as sharply as Osric Dane.

Mrs. Ballinger looked at Laura Glyde, whose eyes were interrogatively fixed on Mrs. Leveret. The fact of being deferred to was so new to the latter that it filled her with an insane temerity. "Why, Xingu, of course!" she exclaimed.

A profound silence followed this challenge to the resources of Mrs. Ballinger's library, and the latter, after glancing nervously toward the Books of the Day, returned with dignity: "It's not a thing one cares to leave about."

"I should think *not!*" exclaimed Mrs. Plinth.

"It *is* a book, then?" said Miss Van Vluyck.

This again threw the company into disarray, and Mrs. Ballinger, with an impatient sigh, rejoined: "Why—there *is* a book—naturally. . . ."

"Then why did Miss Glyde call it a religion?"

Laura Glyde started up. "A religion? I never—"

"Yes, you did," Miss Van Vluyck insisted; "you spoke of rites; and Mrs. Plinth said it was a custom."

Miss Glyde was evidently making a desperate effort to recall her statement; but accuracy of detail was not her strongest point. At length she began in a deep murmur: "Surely they used to do something of the kind at the Eleusinian mysteries—"

"Oh—" said Miss Van Vluyck, on the verge of disapproval; and Mrs. Plinth protested: "I understood there was to be no indelicacy!"

Mrs. Ballinger could not control her irritation. "Really, it is too bad that we should not be able to talk the matter over quietly among ourselves. Personally, I think that if one goes into Xingu at all—"

"Oh, so do I!" cried Miss Glyde.

"And I don't see how one can avoid doing so, if one wishes to keep up with the Thought of the Day—"

Mrs. Leveret uttered an exclamation of relief. "There—that's it!" she interposed.

"What's it?" the President took her up.

"Why—it's a—a Thought: I mean a philosophy."

This seemed to bring a certain relief to Mrs. Ballinger and Laura Glyde, but Miss Van Vluyck said: "Excuse me if I tell you that you're all mistaken. Xingu happens to be a language."

"A language!" the Lunch Club cried.

"Certainly. Don't you remember Fanny Roby's saying that there were several branches, and that some were hard to trace? What could that apply to but dialects?"

Mrs. Ballinger could no longer restrain a contemptuous laugh. "Really, if the Lunch Club has reached such a pass that it has to go to Fanny Roby for instruction on a subject like Xingu, it had almost better cease to exist!"

"It's really her fault for not being clearer," Laura Glyde put in.

"Oh, clearness and Fanny Roby!" Mrs. Ballinger shrugged. "I dare say we shall find she was mistaken on almost every point."

"Why not look it up?" said Mrs. Plinth.

As a rule this recurrent suggestion of Mrs. Plinth's was ignored in the heat of discussion, and only resorted to afterward in the privacy of each member's home. But on the present occasion the desire to ascribe their own confusion of thought to the vague and contradictory nature of Mrs. Roby's statements caused the members of the Lunch Club to utter a collective demand for a book of reference.

At this point the production of her treasured volume gave Mrs. Leveret, for a moment, the unusual experience of occupying the center front; but she was not able to hold it long, for *Appropriate Allusions* contained no mention of Xingu.

"Oh, that's not the kind of thing we want!" exclaimed Miss Van Vluyck. She cast a disparaging glance over Mrs. Ballinger's assortment of literature, and added impatiently: "Haven't you any useful books?"

"Of course I have," replied Mrs. Ballinger indignantly; "I keep them in my husband's dressing room."

From this region, after some difficulty and delay, the parlor-maid produced the W-Z volume of an *Encyclopedia* and, in deference to the fact that the demand for it had come from Miss Van Vluyck, laid the ponderous tome before her.

There was a moment of painful suspense while Miss Van Vluyck rubbed her spectacles, adjusted them, and turned to Z; and a murmur of surprise when she said: "It isn't here."

"I suppose," said Mrs. Plinth, "it's not fit to be put in a book of reference."

"Oh, nonsense!" exclaimed Mrs. Ballinger. "Try X."

Miss Van Vluyck turned back through the volume, peering shortsightedly up and down the pages, till she came to a stop and remained motionless, like a dog on a point.

"Well, have you found it?" Mrs. Ballinger inquired after a considerable delay.

"Yes. I've found it," said Miss Van Vluyck in a queer voice.

Mrs. Plinth hastily interposed: "I beg you won't read it aloud if there's anything offensive."

Miss Van Vluyck, without answering, continued her silent scrutiny.

"Well, what *is* it?" exclaimed Laura Glyde excitedly.

"*Do* tell us!" urged Mrs. Leveret, feeling that she would have something awful to tell her sister.

Miss Van Vluyck pushed the volume aside and turned slowly toward the expectant group.

"It's a river."

"A *river*?"

"Yes: in Brazil. Isn't that where she's been living?"

"Who? Fanny Roby? Oh, but you must be mistaken. You've been reading the wrong thing," Mrs. Ballinger exclaimed, leaning over her to seize the volume.

"It's the only Xingu in the *Encyclopedia*; and she *has* been living in Brazil," Miss Van Vluyck persisted.

"Yes: her brother has a consulship there," Mrs. Leveret interposed.

"But it's too ridiculous! I—we—why we *all* remember studying Xingu last year—or the year before last," Mrs. Ballinger stammered.

"I thought I did when *you* said so," Laura Glyde avowed.

"*I* said so?" cried Mrs. Ballinger.

"Yes. You said it had crowded everything else out of your mind."

"Well *you* said it had changed your whole life!"

"For that matter Miss Van Vluyck said she had never grudged the time she'd given it."

Mrs. Plinth interposed: "I made it clear that I knew nothing whatever of the original."

Mrs. Ballinger broke off the dispute with a groan. "Oh, what does it all matter if she's been making fools of us? I believe Miss Van Vluyck's right—she was talking of the river all the while!"

"How could she? It's too preposterous," Miss Glyde exclaimed.

"Listen." Miss Van Vluyck had repossessed herself of the *Encyclopedia*, and restored her spectacles to a nose reddened by excitement. " 'The Xingu, one of the principal rivers of Brazil, rises on the plateau of Mato Grosso, and flows in a northerly direction for a length of no less than one-thousand one-hundred eighteen miles, entering the Amazon near the mouth of the latter river. The upper course of the Xingu is auriferous and fed by numerous branches. Its source was first discovered in 1884 by the German explorer von den Steinen, after a difficult and dangerous expedition through a region inhabited by tribes still in the Stone Age of culture.' "

The ladies received this communication in a state of stupefied silence from which Mrs. Leveret was the first to rally. "She certainly *did* speak of its having branches."

The word seemed to snap the last thread of their incredulity. "And of its great length," gasped Mrs. Ballinger.

"She said it was awfully deep, and you couldn't skip—you just had to wade through," Miss Glyde added.

The idea worked its way more slowly through Mrs. Plinth's compact resistances. "How could there be anything improper about a river?" she inquired.

"Improper?"

"Why, what she said about the source—that it was corrupt?"

"Not corrupt, but hard to get at," Laura Glyde corrected. "Someone who'd been there had told her so. I dare say it was the explorer himself—doesn't it say the expedition was dangerous?"

" 'Difficult and dangerous,' " read Miss Van Vluyck.

Mrs. Ballinger pressed her hands to her throbbing temples. "There's nothing she said that wouldn't apply to a river—to this river!" She swung about excitedly to the other members. "Why, do you remember her telling us that she hadn't read *The Supreme Instant* because she'd taken it on a boating party while she was staying with her brother, and someone had 'shied' it overboard —'shied' of course was her own expression."

The ladies breathlessly signified that the expression had not escaped them.

"Well—and then didn't she tell Osric Dane that one of her books was simply saturated with Xingu? Of course it was, if one of Mrs. Roby's rowdy friends had thrown it into the river!"

This surprising reconstruction of the scene in which they had just participated left the members of the Lunch Club inarticulate. At length, Mrs. Plinth, after visibly laboring with the problem, said in a heavy tone: "Osric Dane was taken in too."

Mrs. Leveret took courage at this. "Perhaps that's what Mrs. Roby did it for. She said Osric Dane was a brute, and she may have wanted to give her a lesson."

Miss Van Vluyck frowned. "It was hardly worthwhile to do it at our expense."

"At least," said Miss Glyde with a touch of bitterness, "she succeeded in interesting her, which was more than we did."

"What chance had we?" rejoined Mrs. Ballinger. "Mrs. Roby monopolized her from the first. And *that*, I've no doubt, was her purpose—to give Osric Dane a false impression of her own standing in the club. She would hesitate at nothing to attract attention: we all know how she took in poor Professor Foreland."

"She actually makes him give bridge teas every Thursday," Mrs. Leveret piped up.

Laura Glyde struck her hands together. "Why, this is Thursday, and it's *there* she's gone, of course; and taken Osric with her!"

"And they're shrieking over us at this moment," said Mrs. Ballinger between her teeth.

This possibility seemed too preposterous to be admitted. "She would hardly dare," said Miss Van Vluyck, "confess the imposture to Osric Dane."

"I'm not so sure: I thought I saw her make a sign as she left. If she hadn't made a sign, why should Osric Dane have rushed out after her?"

"Well, you know, we'd all been telling her how wonderful Xingu was, and she said she wanted to find out more about it," Mrs. Leveret said, with a tardy impulse of justice to the absent.

This reminder, far from mitigating the wrath of the other members, gave it a stronger impetus.

"Yes—and that's exactly what they're both laughing over now," said Laura Glyde ironically.

Mrs. Plinth stood up and gathered her expensive furs about her monumental form. "I have no wish to criticize," she said; "but unless the Lunch Club can protect its members against the recurrence of such—such unbecoming scenes, I for one—"

"Oh, so do I!" agreed Miss Glyde, rising also.

Miss Van Vluyck closed the *Encyclopedia* and proceeded to button herself into her jacket. "My time is really too valuable—" she began.

"I fancy we are all of one mind," said Mrs. Ballinger, looking searchingly at Mrs. Leveret, who looked at the others.

"I always deprecate anything like a scandal—" Mrs. Plinth continued.

"She has been the cause of one today!" exclaimed Miss Glyde.

Mrs. Leveret moaned: "I don't see how she *could*!" and Miss Van Vluyck said, picking up her notebook: "Some women stop at nothing."

"—But if," Mrs. Plinth took up her argument impressively, "anything of the kind had happened in *my* house" (it never would have, her tone implied), "I should have felt that I owed it to myself either to ask for Mrs. Roby's resignation—or to offer mine."

"Oh, Mrs. Plinth—" gasped the Lunch Club.

"Fortunately for me," Mrs. Plinth continued with an awful magnanimity, "the matter was taken out of my hands by our President's decision that the right to entertain distinguished guests was a privilege vested in her office; and I think the other members will agree that, as she was alone in this opinion, she ought to be alone in deciding on the best way of effacing its—its really deplorable consequences."

A deep silence followed this outbreak of Mrs. Plinth's long-stored resentment.

"I don't see why *I* should be expected to ask her to resign—" Mrs. Ballinger at length began; but Laura Glyde turned back to remind her: "You know she made you say that you'd got on swimmingly in Xingu."

An ill-timed giggle escaped from Mrs. Leveret, and Mrs. Ballinger energetically continued "—But you needn't think for a moment that I'm afraid to!"

The door of the drawing room closed on the retreating backs of the Lunch Club, and the President of that distinguished association, seating herself at her writing table, and pushing away a copy of *The Wings of Death* to make room for her elbow, drew forth a sheet of the club's notepaper, on which she began to write: "My dear Mrs. Roby—"

Expiation

I

"I CAN NEVER," said Mrs. Fetherel, "hear the bell ring without a shudder."

Her unruffled aspect—she was the kind of woman whose emotions never communicate themselves to her clothes—and the conventional background of the New York drawing room, with its pervading implication of an imminent tea tray and of an atmosphere in which the social functions have become purely reflex, lent to her declaration a relief not lost on her cousin Mrs. Clinch, who, from the other side of the fireplace, agreed, with a glance at the clock, that it *was* the hour for bores.

"Bores!" cried Mrs. Fetherel impatiently. "If I shuddered at *them*, I should have a chronic ague!"

She leaned forward and laid a sparkling finger on her cousin's shabby black knee. "I mean the newspaper clippings," she whispered.

Mrs. Clinch returned a glance of intelligence. "They've begun already?"

"Not yet; but they're sure to now, at any minute, my publisher tells me."

Mrs. Fetherel's look of apprehension sat oddly on her small features, which had an air of neat symmetry somehow suggestive of being set in order every morning by the housemaid. Someone (there were rumors that it was her cousin) had once said that Paula Fetherel would have been very pretty if she hadn't looked so like a moral axiom in a copybook hand.

Mrs. Clinch received her confidence with a smile. "Well," she said, "I suppose you were prepared for the consequences of authorship?"

Mrs. Fetherel blushed brightly. "It isn't their coming," she owned—"it's their coming *now*."

"Now?"

"The Bishop's in town."

Mrs. Clinch leaned back and shaped her lips to a whistle which deflected in a laugh. "Well!" she said.

"You see!" Mrs. Fetherel triumphed.

"Well—weren't you prepared for the Bishop?"

"Not now—at least, I hadn't thought of his seeing the clippings."

"And why should he see them?"

"Bella—*won't* you understand? It's John."

"John?"

"Who has taken the most unexpected tone—one might almost say out of perversity."

"Oh, perversity—" Mrs. Clinch murmured, observing her cousin between lids wrinkled by amusement. "What tone has John taken?"

Mrs. Fetherel threw out her answer with the desperate gesture of a woman who lays bare the traces of a marital fist. "The tone of being proud of my book."

The measure of Mrs. Clinch's enjoyment overflowed in laughter.

"Oh, you may laugh," Mrs. Fetherel insisted, "but it's no joke to me. In the first place, John's liking the book is so—so—such a false note—it puts me in such a ridiculous position; and then it has set him watching for the reviews—who would ever have suspected John of knowing that books were *reviewed*? Why, he's actually found out about the clipping bureau, and whenever the postman rings I hear John rush out of the library to see if there are any yellow envelopes. Of course, when they *do* come he'll bring them into the drawing room and read them aloud to everybody who happens to be here—and the Bishop is sure to happen to be here!"

Mrs. Clinch repressed her amusement. "The picture you draw is a lurid one," she conceded, "but your modesty strikes me as abnormal, especially in an author. The chances are that some of the clippings will be rather pleasant reading. The critics are not all union men."

Mrs. Fetherel stared. "Union men?"

"Well, I mean they don't all belong to the well-known Society-for-the-Persecution-of-Rising-Authors. Some of them have even been known to defy its regulations and say a good word for a new writer."

"Oh, I dare say," said Mrs. Fetherel, with the laugh her cousin's epigram exacted. "But you don't quite see my point. I'm not at all nervous about the success of my book—my publisher tells me I have no need to be—but I *am* afraid of its being a *succès de scandale.*"

"Mercy!" said Mrs. Clinch, sitting up.

The butler and footman at this moment appeared with the tea tray and when they had withdrawn, Mrs. Fetherel, bending her brightly rippled head above the kettle, continued in a murmur of avowal, "The title, even, is a kind of challenge."

"*Fast and Loose,*" Mrs. Clinch mused. "Yes, it ought to take."

"I didn't choose it for that reason!" the author protested. "I should have preferred something quieter—less pronounced; but I was determined not to shirk the responsibility of what I had written. I want people to know beforehand exactly what kind of book they are buying."

"Well," said Mrs. Clinch, "that's a degree of conscientiousness that I've never met with before. So few books fulfill the promise of their titles that experienced readers never expect the fare to come up to the menu.''

"*Fast and Loose* will be no disappointment on that score," her cousin significantly returned. "I've handled the subject without gloves. I've called a spade a spade."

"You simply make my mouth water! And to think I haven't been able to read it yet because every spare minute of my time has been given to correcting the proofs of 'How the Birds Keep Christmas'! There's an instance of the hardships of an author's life!"

Mrs. Fetherel's eye clouded. "Don't joke, Bella, please. I suppose to experienced authors there's always something absurd in the nervousness of a new writer, but in my case so much is at stake; I've put so much of myself into this book and I'm so afraid of being misunderstood . . . of being, as it were, in advance of my time . . . like poor Flaubert. . . . I *know* you'll think me ridiculous . . . and if only my own reputation were at stake, I should never give it a thought . . . but the idea of dragging John's name through the mire. . . ."

Mrs. Clinch, who had risen and gathered her cloak about her, stood surveying from her genial height her cousin's agitated countenance.

"Why did you use John's name, then?"

"That's another of my difficulties! I *had* to. There would have been no merit in publishing such a book under an assumed name; it would have been an act of moral cowardice. *Fast and Loose* is not an ordinary novel. A writer who dares to show up the hollowness of social conventions must have the courage of her convictions and be willing to accept the consequences of defying society. Can you imagine Ibsen or Tolstoi writing under a false name?" Mrs. Fetherel lifted a tragic eye to her cousin. "You don't know, Bella, how often I've envied you since I began to write. I used to wonder sometimes—you won't mind my saying so?—why, with all your cleverness, you hadn't taken up some more exciting subject than natural history; but I see now how wise you were. Whatever happens, you will never be denounced by the press!"

"Is that what you're afraid of?" asked Mrs. Clinch, as she grasped the bulging umbrella which rested against her chair. "My dear, if I had ever had the good luck to be denounced by the press, my brougham would be waiting at the door for me at this very moment, and I shouldn't have had to ruin this umbrella by using it in the rain. Why, you innocent, if I'd ever felt the slightest aptitude for showing up social conventions, do you suppose I should waste my time writing 'Nests Ajar' and 'How to Smell the Flowers'? There's a fairly steady demand for pseudo-science and colloquial ornithology, but it's nothing, simply nothing, to the ravenous call for attacks on social institutions—especially by those inside the institutions!''

There was often, to her cousin, a lack of taste in Mrs. Clinch's pleasantries, and on this occasion they seemed more than usually irrelevant.

"*Fast and Loose* was not written with the idea of a large sale."

Mrs. Clinch was unperturbed. "Perhaps that's just as well," she returned, with a philosophic shrug. "The surprise will be all the pleasanter, I mean. For of course it's going to sell tremendously; especially if you can get the press to denounce it."

"Bella, how *can* you? I sometimes think you say such things expressly to tease me; and yet I should think you of all women would understand my purpose in writing such a book. It has always seemed to me that the message I had to deliver was not for myself alone, but for all the other women in the world who have felt the hollowness of our social shams, the ignominy of bowing down to the idols of the market, but have lacked either the courage or the power to proclaim their independence; and I have fancied, Bella dear, that, however severely society might punish me for revealing its weaknesses, I could count on the sympathy of those who, like you"—Mrs. Fetherel's voice sank—"have passed through the deep waters."

Mrs. Clinch gave herself a kind of canine shake, as though to free her ample shoulders from any drop of the element she was supposed to have traversed.

"Oh, call them muddy rather than deep," she returned; "and you'll find, my dear, that women who've had any wading to do are rather shy of stirring up mud. It sticks—especially on white clothes."

Mrs. Fetherel lifted an undaunted brow. "I'm not afraid," she proclaimed; and at the same instant she dropped her teaspoon with a clatter and shrank back into her seat. "There's the bell," she exclaimed, "and I know it's the Bishop!"

It was in fact the Bishop of Ossining, who, impressively announced by Mrs. Fetherel's butler, now made an entry that may best be described as not inadequate to the expectations the announcement raised. The Bishop always entered a room well; but, when unannounced, or preceded by a low church butler who gave him his surname, his appearance lacked the impressiveness conferred on it by the due specification of his diocesan dignity. The Bishop was very fond of his niece, Mrs. Fetherel, and one of the traits he most valued in her was the possession of a butler who knew how to announce a bishop.

Mrs. Clinch was also his niece; but, aside from the fact that she possessed no butler at all, she had laid herself open to her uncle's criticism by writing insignificant little books which had a way of going into five or ten editions, while the fruits of his own episcopal leisure—"The Wail of Jonah" (twenty cantos in blank verse), and "Through a Glass Brightly"; or, "How to Raise Funds for a Memorial Window"—inexplicably languished on the back shelves of a publisher noted for his dexterity in pushing "devotional goods." Even this indiscretion the Bishop might, however, have condoned, had his niece thought fit to turn to him for support and advice at the painful juncture of her history when, in her own words, it became necessary for her to invite Mr. Clinch to look out for another situation. Mr. Clinch's misconduct was of the kind especially designed by Providence to test the fortitude of a Christian wife and mother, and the Bishop was absolutely distended with seasonable advice and edification; so that when Bella met his tentative exhortations with the curt remark that she preferred to do her own house cleaning unassisted, her uncle's grief at her ingratitude was not untempered with sympathy for Mr. Clinch.

It is not surprising, therefore, that the Bishop's warmest greetings were always reserved for Mrs. Fetherel; and on this occasion Mrs. Clinch thought she detected, in the salutation which fell to her share, a pronounced suggestion that her own presence was superfluous—a hint which she took with her usual imperturbable good humor.

II

Left alone with the bishop, Mrs. Fetherel sought the nearest refuge from conversation by offering him a cup of tea. The Bishop accepted with the preoccupied air of a man to whom, for the moment, tea is but a subordinate incident. Mrs. Fetherel's nervousness increased; and knowing that the surest way of distracting attention from one's own affairs is to affect an interest in those of one's companion, she hastily asked if her uncle had come to town on business.

"On business—yes—" said the Bishop in an impressive tone. "I had to see my publisher, who has been behaving rather unsatisfactorily in regard to my last book."

"Ah—your last book?" faltered Mrs. Fetherel, with a sickening sense of her inability to recall the name or nature of the work in question, and a mental vow never again to be caught in such ignorance of a colleague's productions.

" 'Through a Glass Brightly,' " the Bishop explained, with an emphasis which revealed his detection of her predicament. "You may remember that I sent you a copy last Christmas?"

"Of course I do!" Mrs. Fetherel brightened. "It was that delightful story of the poor consumptive girl who had no money, and two little brothers to support—"

"Sisters—idiot sisters—" the Bishop gloomily corrected.

"I mean sisters; and who managed to collect money enough to put up a beautiful memorial window to her—her grandfather, whom she had never seen—"

"But whose sermons had been her chief consolation and support during her long struggle with poverty and disease." The Bishop gave the satisfied sigh of the workman who reviews his completed task. "A touching subject, surely; and I believe I did it justice; at least so my friends assured me."

"Why, yes—I remember there was a splendid review of it in the *Reredos*!" cried Mrs. Fetherel, moved by the incipient instinct of reciprocity.

"Yes—by my dear friend Mrs. Gollinger, whose husband, the late Dean Gollinger, was under very particular obligations to me. Mrs. Gollinger is a woman of rare literary acumen, and her praise of my book was unqualified; but the public wants more highly seasoned fare, and the approval of a thoughtful churchwoman carries less weight than the sensational comments of an illiterate journalist." The Bishop bent a meditative eye on his spotless gaiters. "At the risk of horrifying you, my dear," he added, with a slight laugh, "I will confide to you that my best chance of a popular success would be to have my book denounced by the press."

"Denounced?" gasped Mrs. Fetherel. "On what ground?"

"On the ground of immorality." The Bishop evaded her startled gaze, "Such a thing is inconceivable to you, of course; but I am only repeating what my publisher tells me. If, for instance, a critic could be induced—I mean, if a critic were to be found, who called in question the morality of my heroine in sacrificing her own health and that of her idiot sisters in order to put up a memorial window to her grandfather, it would probably raise a general controversy in the newspapers, and I might count on a sale of ten or fifteen thousand within the next year. If he described her as morbid or decadent, it might even run to twenty thousand; but that is more than I permit myself to hope. In fact I should be satisfied with any general charge of immorality." The Bishop sighed again, "I need hardly tell you that I am actuated by no mere literary ambition. Those whose opinion I most value have assured me that the book is not without merit; but, though it does not become me to dispute their verdict, I can truly say that my vanity as an author is not at stake. I have, however, a special reason for wishing to increase the circulation of 'Through a Glass Brightly'; it was written for a purpose—a purpose I have greatly at heart—"

"I know," cried his niece sympathetically. "The chantry window—?"

"Is still empty, alas! and I had great hopes that, under Providence, my little book might be the means of filling it. All our wealthy parishioners have given lavishly to the cathedral, and it was for this reason that, in writing 'Through a Glass,' I addressed my appeal more especially to the less well-endowed, hoping by the example of my heroine to stimulate the collection of small sums throughout the entire diocese, and perhaps beyond it. I am sure," the Bishop feelingly concluded, "the book would have a widespread influence if people could only be induced to read it!"

His conclusion touched a fresh threat of association in Mrs.

Fetherel's vibrating nerve centers. "I never thought of that!" she cried.

The Bishop looked at her inquiringly.

"That one's books may not be read at all! How dreadful!" she exclaimed.

He smiled faintly. "I had not forgotten that I was addressing an authoress," he said. "Indeed, I should not have dared to inflict my troubles on anyone not of the craft."

Mrs. Fetherel was quivering with the consciousness of her involuntary self-betrayal. "Oh, Uncle!" she murmured.

"In fact," the Bishop continued, with a gesture which seemed to brush away her scruples, "I came here partly to speak to you about your novel. 'Fast and Loose,' I think you call it?"

Mrs. Fetherel blushed assentingly.

"And is it out yet?" the Bishop continued.

"It came out about a week ago. But you haven't touched your tea and it must be quite cold. Let me give you another cup."

"My reason for asking," the Bishop went on, with the bland inexorableness with which, in his younger days, he had been known to continue a sermon after the senior warden had looked four times at his watch, "—my reason for asking is, that I hoped I might not be too late to induce you to change the title."

Mrs. Fetherel set down the cup she had filled. "The title?" she faltered.

The Bishop raised a reassuring hand. "Don't misunderstand me, dear child; don't for a moment imagine that I take it to be in any way indicative of the contents of the book. I know you too well for that. My first idea was that it had probably been forced on you by an unscrupulous publisher. I know too well to what ignoble compromises one may be driven in such cases!" He paused, as though to give her the opportunity of confirming this conjecture, but she preserved an apprehensive silence, and he went on, as though taking up the second point in his sermon: "Or, again, the name may have taken your fancy without your realizing all that it implies to minds more alive than yours to offensive innuendoes. It is—ahem—excessively suggestive, and I hope I am not too late to warn you of the false impression it is likely to produce on the very readers whose approbation you would most value. My friend Mrs. Gollinger, for instance—"

Mrs. Fetherel, as the publication of her novel testified, was in theory a woman of independent views; and if in practice she sometimes failed to live up to her standard, it was rather from an irresistible tendency to adapt herself to her environment than from any conscious lack of moral courage. The Bishop's exordium had excited in her that sense of opposition which such admonitions are apt to provoke; but as he went on she felt herself gradually enclosed in an atmosphere in which her theories vainly gasped for breath. The Bishop had the immense dialectical advantage of invalidating any conclusions at variance with his own by always assuming that his premises were among the necessary laws of thought. This method, combined with the habit of ignoring any classifications but his own, created an element in which the first condition of existence was the immediate adoption of his standpoint; so that his niece, as she listened, seemed to feel Mrs. Gollinger's Mechlin cap spreading its conventual shadow over her rebellious brow and the *Revue de Paris* at her elbow turning into a copy of the *Reredos*. She had meant to assure her uncle that she was quite aware of the significance of the title she had chosen, that it had been deliberately selected as indicating the subject of her novel, and that the book itself had been written in direct defiance of the class of readers for whose susceptibilities he was alarmed. The words were almost on her lips when the irresistible suggestion conveyed by the Bishop's tone and language deflected them into the apologetic murmur, "Oh, Uncle, you mustn't think—I never meant—" How much farther this current of reaction might have carried her the historian is unable to compute, for at this point the door opened and her husband entered the room.

"The first review of your book!" he cried, flourishing a yellow envelope. "My dear Bishop, how lucky you're here!"

Though the trials of married life have been classified and catalogued with exhaustive accuracy, there is one form of conjugal misery which has perhaps received inadequate attention; and that is the suffering of the versatile woman whose husband is not equally adapted to all her moods. Every woman feels for the sister who is compelled to wear a bonnet which does not "go" with her gown; but how much sympathy is given to her whose husband refuses to harmonize with the pose of the moment? Scant justice has, for instance, been done to the misunderstood wife whose husband persists in understanding her; to the submissive help-mate whose taskmaster shuns every opportunity of browbeating her, and to the generous and impulsive being whose bills are paid with philosophic calm. Mrs. Fetherel, as wives go, had been fairly exempt from trials of this nature, for her husband, if undistinguished by pronounced brutality or indifference, had at least the negative merit of being her intellectual inferior. Landscape gardeners, who are aware of the usefulness of a valley in emphasizing the height of a hill, can form an idea of the account to which an accomplished woman may turn such deficiencies; and it need scarcely be said that Mrs. Fetherel had made the most of her opportunities. It was agreeably obvious to everyone, Fetherel included, that he was not the man to appreciate such a woman; but there are no limits to man's perversity, and he did his best to invalidate this advantage by admiring her without pretending to understand her. What she most suffered from was this fatuous approval; the maddening sense that, however she conducted herself, he would always admire her. Had he belonged to the class whose conversational supplies are drawn from the domestic circle, his wife's name would never have been off his lips; and to Mrs. Fetherel's sensitive perceptions his frequent silences were indicative of the fact that she was his one topic.

It was, in part, the attempt to escape this persistent approbation that had driven Mrs. Fetherel to authorship. She had fancied that even the most infatuated husband might be counted on to resent, at least negatively, an attack on the sanctity of the hearth; and her anticipations were heightened by a sense of the unpardonableness of her act. Mrs. Fetherel's relations with her husband were in fact complicated by an irrepressible tendency to be fond of him; and there was a certain pleasure in the prospect of a situation that justified the most explicit expiation.

These hopes Fetherel's attitude had already defeated. He read the book with enthusiasm, he pressed it on his friends, he sent a copy to his mother; and his very soul now hung on the verdict of the reviewers. It was perhaps this proof of his general inaptitude that made his wife doubly alive to his special defects; so that his inopportune entrance was aggravated by the very sound of his voice and the hopeless aberration of his smile. Nothing, to the observant, is more indicative of a man's character and circumstances than his way of entering a room. The Bishop of Ossining, for instance, brought with him not only an atmosphere of episcopal authority, but an implied opinion on the verbal inspiration of the Scriptures and on the attitude of the Church toward divorce; while the appearance of Mrs. Fetherel's husband produced an immediate impression of domestic felicity. His mere aspect implied that there was a well-filled nursery upstairs; that his wife, if she did not sew on his buttons, at least superintended the performance of that task; that they both went to church regularly, and that they dined with his mother every Sunday evening punctually at seven o'clock.

All this and more was expressed in the affectionate gesture with which he now raised the yellow envelope above Mrs. Fetherel's clutch; and knowing the uselessness of begging him not to be silly, she said, with a dry despair, "You're boring the Bishop horribly."

Fetherel turned a radiant eye on that dignitary. "She bores us all horribly, doesn't she, sir?" he exulted.

"Have you read it?" said his wife, uncontrollably.

"Read it? Of course not—it's just this minute come. I say, Bishop, you're not going—?"

"Not till I've heard this," said the Bishop, settling himself in his chair with an indulgent smile.

His niece glanced at him despairingly, "Don't let John's nonsense detain you," she entreated.

"Detain him? That's good," guffawed Fetherel. "It isn't as long as one of his sermons—won't take me five minutes to read. Here, listen to this, ladies and gentlemen: 'In this age of festering pessimism and decadent depravity, it is no surprise to the nauseated reviewer to open one more volume saturated with the fetid emanations of the sewer—' "

Fetherel, who was not in the habit of reading aloud, paused with a gasp, and the Bishop glanced sharply at his niece, who kept her gaze fixed on the teacup she had not yet succeeded in transferring to his hand.

" 'Of the sewer,' " her husband resumed; " 'but his wonder is proportionately great when he lights on a novel as sweetly inoffensive as Paula Fetherel's *Fast and Loose*. Mrs. Fetherel is, we believe, a new hand at fiction, and her work reveals frequent traces of inexperience; but these are more than atoned for by her pure fresh view of life and her altogether unfashionable regard for the reader's moral susceptibilities. Let no one be induced by its distinctly misleading title to forego the enjoyment of this pleasant picture of domestic life, which, in spite of a total lack of force in character drawing and of consecutiveness in incident, may be described as a distinctly pretty story.' "

III

It was several weeks later that Mrs. Clinch once more brought the plebeian aroma of heated tramcars and muddy street crossings into the violet-scented atmosphere of her cousin's drawing room.

"Well," she said, tossing a damp bundle of proofs into the corner of a silk-cushioned bergère, "I've read it at last and I'm not so awfully shocked!"

Mrs. Fetherel, who sat near the fire with her head propped on a languid hand, looked up without speaking.

"Mercy, Paula," said her visitor, "you're ill."

Mrs. Fetherel shook her head. "I was never better," she said, mournfully.

"Then may I help myself to tea? Thanks."

Mrs. Clinch carefully removed her mended glove before taking a buttered tea cake; then she glanced again at her cousin.

"It's not what I said just now—?" she ventured.

"Just now?"

"About *Fast and Loose*? I came to talk it over."

Mrs. Fetherel sprang to her feet. "I never," she cried dramatically, "want to hear it mentioned again!"

"Paula!" exclaimed Mrs. Clinch, setting down her cup.

Mrs. Fetherel slowly turned on her an eye brimming with the incommunicable; then, dropping into her seat again, she added, with a tragic laugh: "There's nothing left to say."

"Nothing—?" faltered Mrs. Clinch, longing for another tea cake, but feeling the inappropriateness of the impulse in an atmosphere so charged with the portentous. "Do you mean that everything *has* been said?'' She looked tentatively at her cousin. "Haven't they been nice?''

"They've been odious—odious—'' Mrs. Fetherel burst out, with an ineffectual clutch at her handkerchief. "It's been perfectly intolerable!''

Mrs. Clinch, philosophically resigning herself to the propriety of taking no more tea, crossed over to her cousin and laid a sympathizing hand on that lady's agitated shoulder.

"It *is* a bore at first,'' she conceded; "but you'll be surprised to see how soon one gets used to it.''

"I shall—never—get—used to it—'' Mrs. Fetherel brokenly declared.

"Have they been so very nasty—all of them?''

"Every one of them!'' the novelist sobbed.

"I'm so sorry, dear; it *does* hurt, I know—but hadn't you rather expected it?''

"Expected it?'' cried Mrs. Fetherel, sitting up.

Mrs. Clinch felt her way warily. "I only mean, dear, that I fancied from what you said before the book came out that you rather expected—that you'd rather discounted—''

"Their recommending it to everybody as a perfectly harmless story?''

"Good gracious! Is *that* what they've done?''

Mrs. Fetherel speechlessly nodded.

"Every one of them?''

"Every one.''

"Phew!'' said Mrs. Clinch, with an incipient whistle.

"Why, you've just said it yourself!'' her cousin suddenly reproached her.

"Said what?''

"That you weren't so *awfully* shocked—''

"I? Oh, well—you see, you'd keyed me up to such a pitch that it wasn't quite as bad as I expected—''

Mrs. Fetherel lifted a smile steeled for the worst. "Why not say at once,'' she suggested, "that it's a distinctly pretty story?''

"They haven't said *that*?''

"They've all said it.''

"My poor Paula!''

"Even the Bishop—''

"The Bishop called it a pretty story?"

"He wrote me—I've his letter somewhere. The title rather
scared him—he wanted me to change it; but when he'd read the
book he wrote that it was all right and that he'd sent several copies
to his friends."

"The old hypocrite!" cried Mrs. Clinch. "That was nothing but
professional jealousy."

"Do you think so?" cried her cousin, brightening.

"Sure of it, my dear. His own books don't sell, and he knew
the quickest way to kill yours was to distribute it through the diocese with his blessing."

"Then you don't really think it's a pretty story?"

"Dear me, no! Not nearly as bad as that—"

"You're so good, Bella—but the reviewers?"

"Oh, the reviewers," Mrs. Clinch jeered. She gazed meditatively
at the cold remains of her tea cake. "Let me see," she said, suddenly; "do you happen to remember if the first review came out
in an important paper?"

"Yes—the *Radiator.*"

"That's it! I thought so. Then the others simply followed suit:
they often do if a big paper sets the pace. Saves a lot of trouble. Now if you could only have got the *Radiator* to denounce
you—"

"That's what the Bishop said!" cried Mrs. Fetherel.

"He did?"

"He said his only chance of selling 'Through a Glass Brightly'
was to have it denounced on the ground of immorality."

"H'm," said Mrs. Clinch, "I thought he knew a trick or two."
She turned an illuminated eye on her cousin. "You ought to get
him to denounce *Fast and Loose*!" she cried.

Mrs. Fetherel looked at her suspiciously. "I suppose every book
must stand or fall on its own merits," she said in an unconvinced
tone.

"Bosh! That view is as extinct as the post chaise and the packet
ship—it belongs to the time when people read books. Nobody
does that now; the reviewer was the first to set the example, and
the public was only too thankful to follow it. At first people read
the reviews; now they read only the publishers' extracts from
them. Even these are rapidly being replaced by paragraphs bor-

rowed from the vocabulary of commerce. I often have to look twice before I am sure if I am reading a department store advertisement or the announcement of a new batch of literature. The publishers will soon be having their 'fall and spring openings' and their 'special importations for Horse Show Week.' But the Bishop is right, of course—nothing helps a book like a rousing attack on its morals; and as the publishers can't exactly proclaim the impropriety of their own wares, the task has to be left to the press or the pulpit.''

"The pulpit?'' Mrs. Fetherel mused.

"Why, yes. Look at those two novels in England last year.''

Mrs. Fetherel shook her head hopelessly. "There is so much more interest in literature in England than here.''

"Well, we've got to make the supply create the demand. The Bishop could run your novel up into the hundred thousands in no time.''

"But if he can't make his own sell—''

"My dear, a man can't very well preach against his own writings!''

Mrs. Clinch rose and picked up her proofs.

"I'm awfully sorry for you, Paula dear,'' she concluded, "but I can't help being thankful that there's no demand for pessimism in the field of natural history. Fancy having to write 'The Fall of a Sparrow,' or 'How the Plants Misbehave'!''

IV

Mrs. Fetherel, driving up to the Grand Central Station one morning about five months later, caught sight of the distinguished novelist, Archer Hynes, hurrying into the waiting room ahead of her. Hynes, on his side, recognizing her brougham, turned back to greet her as the footman opened the carriage door.

"My dear colleague! Is it possible that we are traveling together?''

Mrs. Fetherel blushed with pleasure. Hynes had given her two columns of praise in the *Sunday Meteor,* and she had not yet learned to disguise her gratitude.

"I am going to Ossining," she said smilingly.

"So am I. Why, this is almost as good as an elopement."

"And it will end where elopements ought to—in church."

"In church? You're not going to Ossining to go to church?"

"Why not? There's a special ceremony in the cathedral—the chantry window is to be unveiled."

"The chantry window? How picturesque! What *is* a chantry? And why do you want to see it unveiled? Are you after copy— doing something in the Huysmans manner? 'La Cathédrale,' eh?"

"Oh, no," Mrs. Fetherel hesitated. "I'm going simply to please my uncle," she said, at last.

"Your uncle?"

"The Bishop, you know." She smiled.

"The Bishop—the Bishop of Ossining? Why, wasn't he the chap who made that ridiculous attack on your book? Is that prehistoric ass your uncle? Upon my soul, I think you're mighty forgiving to travel all the way to Ossining for one of his stained-glass sociables!"

Mrs. Fetherel's smile flowed into a gentle laugh. "Oh, I've never allowed that to interfere with our friendship. My uncle felt dreadfully about having to speak publicly against my book—it was a great deal harder for him than for me—but he thought it his duty to do so. He has the very highest sense of duty."

"Well," said Hynes, with a shrug. "I don't know that he didn't do you a good turn. Look at that!"

They were standing near the bookstall and he pointed to a placard surmounting the counter and emblazoned with the conspicuous announcement: "*Fast and Loose.* New Edition with Author's Portrait. Hundred and Fiftieth Thousand."

Mrs. Fetherel frowned impatiently. "How absurd! They've no right to use my picture as a poster!"

"There's our train," said Hynes; and they began to push their way through the crowd surging toward one of the inner doors.

As they stood wedged between circumferent shoulders, Mrs. Fetherel became conscious of the fixed stare of a pretty girl who whispered eagerly to her companion. "Look, Myrtle! That's Paula Fetherel right behind us—I knew her in a minute!"

"Gracious—where?" cried the other girl, giving her head a twist which swept her Gainsborough plumes across Mrs. Fetherel's face.

The first speaker's words had carried beyond her companion's ear, and a lemon-colored woman in spectacles, who clutched a copy of the "Journal of Psychology" in one drab cotton-gloved hand, stretched her disengaged hand across the intervening barrier of humanity.

"Have I the privilege of addressing the distinguished author of *Fast and Loose?* If so, let me thank you in the name of the Woman's Psychological League of Peoria for your magnificent courage in raising the standard of revolt against—"

"You can tell us the rest in the car," said a fat man, pressing his good-humored bulk against the speaker's arm.

Mrs. Fetherel, blushing, embarrassed and happy, slipped into the space produced by this displacement, and a few moments later had taken her seat in the train.

She was a little late, and the other chairs were already filled by a company of elderly ladies and clergymen who seemed to belong to the same party, and were still busy exchanging greetings and settling themselves in their places.

One of the ladies, at Mrs. Fetherel's approach, uttered an exclamation of pleasure and advanced with outstretched hand. "My dear Mrs. Fetherel! I am so delighted to see you here. May I hope you are going to the unveiling of the chantry window? The dear Bishop so hoped that you would do so! But perhaps I ought to introduce myself. I am Mrs. Gollinger"—she lowered her voice expressively—"one of your uncle's oldest friends, one who has stood close to him through all this sad business, and who knows what he suffered when he felt obliged to sacrifice family affection to the call of duty."

Mrs. Fetherel, who had smiled and colored slightly at the beginning of this speech, received its close with a deprecating gesture.

"Oh, pray don't mention it," she murmured. "I quite understood how my uncle was placed—I bore him no ill will for feeling obliged to preach against my book."

"He understood that, and was so touched by it! He has often told me that it was the hardest task he was ever called upon to perform—and, do you know, he quite feels that this unexpected gift of the chantry window is in some way a return for his courage in preaching that sermon."

Mrs. Fetherel smiled faintly. "Does he feel that?"

"Yes; he really does. When the funds for the window were so mysteriously placed at his disposal, just as he had begun to despair of raising them, he assured me that he could not help connecting the fact with his denunciation of your book."

"Dear Uncle!" sighed Mrs. Fetherel. "Did he say that?"

"And now," continued Mrs. Gollinger, with cumulative rapture—"now that you are about to show, by appearing at the ceremony today, that there has been no break in your friendly relations, the dear Bishop's happiness will be complete. He was so longing to have you come to the unveiling!"

"He might have counted on me," said Mrs. Fetherel, still smiling.

"Ah, that is so beautifully forgiving of you!" cried Mrs. Gollinger enthusiastically. "But then, the Bishop has always assured me that your real nature was very different from that which—if you will pardon my saying so—seems to be revealed by your brilliant but—er—rather subversive book. 'If you only knew my niece, dear Mrs. Gollinger,' he always said, 'you would see that her novel was written in all innocence of heart'; and to tell you the truth, when I first read the book I didn't think it so very, *very* shocking. It wasn't till the dear Bishop had explained to me—but, dear me, I mustn't take up your time in this way when so many others are anxious to have a word with you."

Mrs. Fetherel glanced at her in surprise, and Mrs. Gollinger continued with a playful smile: "You forget that your face is familiar to thousands whom you have never seen. We all recognized you the moment you entered the train, and my friends here are so eager to make your acquaintance—even those"—her smile deepened—"who thought the dear Bishop not *quite unjustified* in his attack on your remarkable novel."

V

A religious light filled the chantry of Ossining Cathedral, filtering through the linen curtain which veiled the central window and mingling with the blaze of tapers on the richly adorned altar.

In this devout atmosphere, agreeably laden with the incense-like aroma of Easter lilies and forced lilacs, Mrs. Fetherel knelt with a sense of luxurious satisfaction. Beside her sat Archer Hynes, who had remembered that there was to be a church scene in his next novel and that his impressions of the devotional environment needed refreshing. Mrs. Fetherel was very happy. She was conscious that her entrance had sent a thrill through the female devotees who packed the chantry, and she had humor enough to enjoy the thought that, but for the good Bishop's denunciation of her book, the heads of his flock would not have been turned so eagerly in her direction. Moreover, as she entered she had caught sight of a society reporter, and she knew that her presence, and the fact that she was accompanied by Hynes, would be conspicuously proclaimed in the morning papers. All these evidences of the success of her handiwork might have turned a calmer head than Mrs. Fetherel's and though she had now learned to dissemble her gratification, it still filled her inwardly with a delightful glow.

The Bishop was somewhat late in appearing, and she employed the interval in meditating on the plot of her next novel, which was already partly sketched out, but for which she had been unable to find a satisfactory dénouement. By a not uncommon process of ratiocination, Mrs. Fetherel's success had convinced her of her vocation. She was sure now that it was her duty to lay bare the secret plague spots of society, and she was resolved that there should be no doubt as to the purpose of her new book. Experience had shown her that where she had fancied she was calling a spade a spade she had in fact been alluding in guarded terms to the drawing-room shovel. She was determined not to repeat the same mistake, and she flattered herself that her coming novel would not need an episcopal denunciation to insure its sale, however likely it was to receive this crowning evidence of success.

She had reached this point in her meditations when the choir burst into song and the ceremony of the unveiling began. The Bishop, almost always felicitous in his addresses to the fair sex, was never more so than when he was celebrating the triumph of one of his cherished purposes. There was a peculiar mixture of Christian humility and episcopal exultation in the manner with which he called attention to the Creator's promptness in responding to his demand for funds, and he had never been more happily inspired than in eulogizing the mysterious gift of the chantry window.

Though no hint of the donor's identity had been allowed to

escape him, it was generally understood that the Bishop knew who had given the window, and the congregation awaited in a flutter of suspense the possible announcement of a name. None came, however, though the Bishop deliciously titillated the curiosity of his flock by circling ever closer about the interesting secret. He would not disguise from them, he said, that the heart which had divined his inmost wish had been a woman's—is it not to woman's intuitions that more than half the happiness of earth is owing? What man is obliged to learn by the laborious process of experience, woman's wondrous instinct tells her at a glance; and so it had been with this cherished scheme, this unhoped-for completion of their beautiful chantry. So much, at least, he was allowed to reveal; and indeed, had he not done so, the window itself would have spoken for him, since the first glance at its touching subject and exquisite design would show it to have originated in a woman's heart. This tribute to the sex was received with an audible sigh of contentment, and the Bishop, always stimulated by such evidence of his sway over his hearers, took up his theme with gathering eloquence.

Yes—a woman's heart had planned the gift, a woman's hand had executed it, and, might he add, without too far withdrawing the veil in which Christian beneficence ever loved to drape its acts—might he add that, under Providence, a book, a simple book, a mere tale, in fact, had had its share in the good work for which they were assembled to give thanks?

At this unexpected announcement, a ripple of excitement ran through the assemblage, and more than one head was abruptly turned in the direction of Mrs. Fetherel, who sat listening in an agony of wonder and confusion. It did not escape the observant novelist at her side that she drew down her veil to conceal an uncontrollable blush, and this evidence of dismay caused him to fix an attentive gaze on her, while from her seat across the aisle Mrs. Gollinger sent a smile of unctuous approval.

"A book—a simple book—" the Bishop's voice went on above this flutter of mingled emotions. "What is a book? Only a few pages and a little ink—and yet one of the mightiest instruments which Providence has devised for shaping the destinies of man . . . one of the most powerful influences for good or evil which the Creator has placed in the hands of his creatures. . . ."

The air seemed intolerably close to Mrs. Fetherel, and she drew out her scent bottle, and then thrust it hurriedly away, conscious that she was still the center of unenviable attention. And all the while the Bishop's voice droned on. . . .

"And of all forms of literature, fiction is doubtless that which has exercised the greatest sway, for good or ill, over the passions and imagination of the masses. Yes, my friends, I am the first to acknowledge it—no sermon, however eloquent, no theological treatise, however learned and convincing, has ever inflamed the heart and imagination like a novel—a simple novel. Incalculable is the power exercised over humanity by the great magicians of the pen—a power ever enlarging its boundaries and increasing its responsibilities as popular education multiplies the number of readers. . . . Yes, it is the novelist's hand which can pour balm on countless human sufferings, or inoculate mankind with the festering poison of a corrupt imagination. . . ."

Mrs. Fetherel had turned white, and her eyes were fixed with a blind stare of anger on the large-sleeved figure in the center of the chancel.

"And too often, alas, it is the poison and not the balm which the unscrupulous hand of genius proffers to its unsuspecting readers. But, my friends, why should I continue? None know better than an assemblage of Christian women, such as I am now addressing, the beneficent or baleful influences of modern fiction; and so, when I say that this beautiful chantry window of ours owes its existence in part to the romancer's pen"—the Bishop paused, and bending forward, seemed to seek a certain face among the countenances eagerly addressed to his—"when I say that this pen, which for personal reasons it does not become me to celebrate unduly—"

Mrs. Fetherel at this point half-rose, pushing back her chair, which scraped loudly over the marble floor; but Hynes involuntarily laid a warning hand on her arm, and she sank down with a confused murmur about the heat.

"When I confess that this pen, which for once at least has proved itself so much mightier than the sword, is that which was inspired to trace the simple narrative of 'Through a Glass Brightly'"—Mrs. Fetherel looked up with a gasp of mingled relief and anger—"when I tell you, my dear friends, that it was your

Bishop's own work which first roused the mind of one of his flock to the crying need of a chantry window, I think you will admit that I am justified in celebrating the triumphs of the pen, even though it be the modest instrument which your own Bishop wields.''

The Bishop paused impressively, and a faint gasp of surprise and disappointment was audible throughout the chantry. Something very different from this conclusion had been expected, and even Mrs. Gollinger's lips curled with a slightly ironic smile. But Archer Hynes's attention was chiefly reserved for Mrs. Fetherel, whose face had changed with astonishing rapidity from surprise to annoyance, from annoyance to relief, and then back again to something very like indignation.

The address concluded, the actual ceremony of the unveiling was about to take place, and the attention of the congregation soon reverted to the chancel, where the choir had grouped themselves beneath the veiled window, prepared to burst into a chant of praise as the Bishop drew back the hanging. The moment was an impressive one, and every eye was fixed on the curtain. Even Hynes's gaze strayed to it for a moment, but soon returned to his neighbor's face; and then he perceived that Mrs. Fetherel, alone of all the persons present, was not looking at the window. Her eyes were fixed in an indignant stare on the Bishop; a flush of anger burned becomingly under her veil, and her hands nervously crumpled the beautifully printed program of the ceremony.

Hynes broke into a smile of comprehension. He glanced at the Bishop, and back at the Bishop's niece; then, as the episcopal hand was solemnly raised to draw back the curtain, he bent and whispered in Mrs. Fetherel's ear:

"Why, you gave it yourself! You wonderful woman, of course you gave it yourself!''

Mrs. Fetherel raised her eyes to his with a start. Her blush deepened and her lips shaped a hasty "No"; but the denial was deflected into the indignant murmur—"It wasn't *his* silly book that did it, anyhow!''

H. L. Mencken
(1880–1956)

Henry Louis Mencken was born and raised in Baltimore, where, beginning in 1899, he began writing for newspapers. First he was on the staff of the *Morning Herald*, and later that of the *Baltimore Sun*. He started and edited two magazines with George Jean Nathan, *The Smart Set*, a witty and sophisticated journal influential in literary matters that endured for ten years until 1923, and then in 1924 *The American Mercury*, which Mencken and Nathan edited through the early 1930s. At the same time, Mencken was publishing and more or less continuously revising a great work of philology, *The American Language*, the first work of its kind to describe American English as distinct from the British, and a project on which he worked on and off for the rest of his life.

But the times would pass Mencken by. By the 1930s, few people would find the Depression or Franklin Roosevelt's New Deal fit subjects for satire—but Mencken did. When Hitler came to power in Germany, Mencken, always fond of German culture, failed to recognize the dangers Nazism posed to the rest of the world. His influence declined sharply, and his reputation never completely recovered.

Mencken was perhaps first of all a literary critic, but it is his social criticism, much of it in the form of biting satire, that endures. In reviews and essays that have been collected into six volumes entitled *Prejudices* (1919–1927), he skewered the American middle class—the people that he contemptuously, and now famously, referred to as the "booboisie"—for what he viewed as their hypocrisy, pretension, and prudery. A selection from *Prejudices* is offered here.

Rondo on an Ancient Theme

It is the economic emancipation of woman, I suppose, that must be blamed for the present wholesale discussion of the sex question, so offensive to the romantic. Eminent authorities have full often described, and with the utmost heat and eloquence, her state before she was delivered from her fetters and turned loose to root or die. Almost her only feasible trade, in those dark days, was that of wife. True enough, she might also become a servant girl, or go to work in a factory, or offer herself upon the streets, but all of those vocations were so revolting that no rational woman followed them if she could help it: she would leave any one of them at a moment's notice at the call of a man, for the call of a man meant promotion for her, economically and socially. The males of the time, knowing what a boon they had to proffer, drove hard bargains. They demanded a long list of high qualities in the woman they summoned to their seraglios, but most of all they demanded what they called virtue. It was not sufficient that a candidate should be anatomically undefiled; she must also be pure in mind. There was, of course, but one way to keep her so pure, and that was by building a high wall around her mind, and hitting her with a club every time she ventured to peer over it. It was as dangerous, in that Christian era, for a woman to show any interest in or knowledge of the great physiological farce of sex as it would be to-day for a presidential candidate to reveal himself in his cups on the hustings. Everyone knew, to be sure, that as a mammal she had sex, and that as a potential wife and mother she probably had some secret interest in its phenomena, but it was felt, perhaps wisely, that even the most academic theorizing had within it the deadly germs of the experimental method, and so she was forbidden to think about the matter at all, and whatever information she acquired at all she had to acquire by a method of bootlegging.

The generation still on its legs has seen the almost total collapse of that naïve and constabulary system, and of the economic structure supporting it. Beginning with the eighties of the last century, there rose up a harem rebellion which quickly knocked both to pieces. The women of the Western World not only began to plunge heroically into all of the old professions, hitherto sacred to men; they also began to invent a lot of new professions, many of them unimagined by men. Worse, they began to succeed in them. The working woman of the old days worked only until she could snare a man; any man was better than her work. But the working woman of the new days was under no such pressure; her work made her a living and sometimes more than a living; when a man appeared in her net she took two looks at him, one of them usually very searching, before landing him. The result was an enormous augmentation of her feeling of self-sufficiency, her spirit of independence, her natural inclination to get two sides into the bargaining. The result, secondarily, was a revolt against all the old taboos that had surrounded her, all the childish incapacities and ignorances that had been forced upon her. The result, tertiarily, was a vast running amok in the field that, above all others, had been forbidden to her: that of sexual knowledge and experiment.

We now suffer from the effects of that running amok. It is women, not men, who are doing all the current gabbling about sex, and proposing all the new-fangled modifications of the rules and regulations ordained by God, and they are hard at it very largely, I suppose, because being at it at all is a privilege that is still new to them. The whole order of human females, in other words, is passing through a sort of intellectual adolescence, and it is disturbed as greatly as biological adolescents are by the spouting of the hormones. The attitude of men toward the sex question, it seems to me, has not changed greatly in my time. Barring a few earnest men whose mental processes, here as elsewhere, are essentially womanish, they still view it somewhat jocosely. Taking one with another, they believe that they know all about it that is worth knowing, and so it does not challenge their curiosity, and they do not put in much time discussing it, save mockingly. But among the women, if a bachelor may presume to judge, interest in it is intense. They want to know all that is known about it, all that has been guessed and theorized about it; they bristle with ideas of their own about it. It is hard to find a reflective woman, in these days, who is not harboring some new and startling scheme for curing the evils of monogamous marriage; it is impossible to find any woman who has not given ear to such schemes. Women, not men, read the endless books upon the subject that now rise mountain-high in all the book-stores, and women, not men, discuss and rediscuss the notions in them. An acquaintance of mine, a distinguished critic, owns a copy of one of the most revolutionary of these books, by title "The Art of Love," that was suppressed on the day of its publication by the alert Comstocks. He tells me that he has already lent it to twenty-six women and that he has more than fifty applications for it on file. Yet he has never read it himself!

As a professional fanatic for free thought and free speech, I can only view all this uproar in the *Frauenzimmer* with high satisfaction. It gives me delight to see a taboo violated, and that delight is doubled when the taboo is one that is wholly senseless. Sex is more important to women than to men, and so they ought to be free to discuss it as they please, and to hatch and propagate whatever ideas about it occur to them. Moreover, I can see nothing but nonsense in the doctrine that their concern with such matters damages their charm. So far as I am concerned, a woman who knows precisely what a Graafian follicle is is just as charming as one who doesn't—just as charming, and far less dangerous. Charm in women, indeed, is a variable star, and shows different colors at different times. When their chief mark was ignorance, then the most ignorant was the most charming; now that they begin to think deeply and indignantly there is charm in their singular astuteness. But I am inclined to believe that they have not yet attained to a genuine astuteness in the new field of sex. To the contrary, it seems to me that a fundamental error contaminates their whole dealing with the subject, and that is the error of assuming that sexual questions, whether social, physiological, or pathological, are of vast and even paramount importance to mankind in general—in brief, that sex is really a first-rate matter.

I doubt it. I believe that in this department men show better judgment than women, if only because their information is older and their experience wider. Their tendency is to dismiss the whole thing lightly, to reduce sex to the lowly estate of an afterthought and a recreation, and under that tendency there is a sound instinct. I do not believe that the lives of normal men are much colored or conditioned, either directly or indirectly, by purely sexual considerations. I believe that nine-tenths of them would carry on all the activities which engage them now, and with precisely the same humorless diligence, if there were not a woman in the world. The notion that man would not work if he lacked an audience, and that the audience must be a woman, seems to me to be a hollow sentimentality. Men work because they want to eat, because they want to feel secure, because they long to shine among their fellows, and for no other reason. A man may crave his wife's approbation, or some other woman's approbation, of his social graces, of his taste, of his generosity and courage, of his general dignity in the world, but long before he ever gives thought to such things and long after he has forgotten them he craves the approbation of his fellow men. Above all, he craves the approbation of his fellow craftsmen—the men who understand exactly what he is trying to do, and are expertly competent to judge his doing of it. Can you imagine a surgeon putting the good opinion of his wife above the good opinion of other surgeons? If you can, then you can do something that I cannot.

Here, of course, I do not argue absurdly that the good opinion of his wife is nothing to him. Obviously, it is a lot, for if it does not constitute the principal reward of his work, then it at least constitutes the principal joy of his hours of ease, when his work is done. He wants his wife to respect and admire him; to be able to make her do it is also a talent. But if he is intelligent he must discover very early that her respect and admiration do not necessarily run in direct ratio to his intrinsic worth, that the qualities and acts that please her are not always the qualities and acts that are most satisfactory to the censor within him—in brief, that the relation between man and woman, however intimate they may seem, must always remain a bit casual and superficial—that sex, at bottom, belongs to comedy and the cool of the evening and not to the sober business that goes on in the heat of the day. That sober business, as I have said, would still go on if woman were abolished and heirs and assigns were manufactured in rolling-mills. Men would not only work as hard as they do to-day; they would also get almost as much satisfaction out of their work. For of all the men that I know on this earth, ranging from poets to ambassadors and from bishops to statisticians, I know none who labors primarily because he wants to please a woman. They are all hard at it because they want to impress other men and so please themselves.

Woman, plainly enough, are in a far different case. Their emancipation has not yet gone to the length of making them genuinely
free. They have rid themselves, very largely, of the absolute need
to please men, but they have not yet rid themselves of the impulse
to please men. Perhaps they never will: one might easily devise a
plausible argument to that effect on biological grounds. But sufficient unto the day is the phenomenon before us: they have got
rid of the old taboo which forbade them to think and talk about
sex, and they still labor under the old superstition that sex is a
matter of paramount importance. The result, in my judgment, is
an absurd emission of piffle. In every division there is vast and
often ludicrous exaggeration. The campaign for birth control
takes on the colossal proportions of the war for democracy. The
venereal diseases are represented to be as widespread, at least in
men, as colds in the head, and as lethal as apoplexy or cancer.
Great hordes of viragoes patrol the country, instructing school-
girls in the mechanics of reproduction and their mothers in ob-
stetrics. The light-hearted monogamy which produced all of us is
denounced as an infamy comparable to cannibalism. Laws are
passed regulating the mating of human beings as if they were
horned cattle and converting marriage into a sort of coroner's
inquest. Over all sounds the battle-cry of quacks and zealots at all
times and everywhere: *Veritas liberabit vos!*

The truth? How much of this new gospel is actually truth? Perhaps two per cent. The rest is idle theorizing, doctrinaire nonsense, mere scandalous rubbish. All that is worth knowing about
sex—all, that is, that is solidly established and of sound utility—
can be taught to any intelligent boy of sixteen in two hours. Is it
taught in the current books, so enormously circulated? I doubt it.
Absolutely without exception these books admonish the poor ap-
prentice to renounce sex altogether—to sublimate it, as the favorite phrase is, into a passion for free verse, Rotary or the League
of Nations. This admonition is silly, and, I believe, dangerous. It
is as much a folly to lock up sex in the hold as it is to put it in
command on the bridge. Its proper place is in the social hall. As
a substitute for all such nonsense I drop a pearl of wisdom, and
pass on. To wit: the strict monogamist never gets into trouble.

Sinclair Lewis

(1885–1951)

In a series of highly popular satirical novels, Sinclair Lewis took on the provincialism of small-town life (*Main Street*, 1920), the complacency and conformity of American businessmen (*Babbitt*, 1922), the failed ideals of the medical profession (*Arrowsmith*, 1925), and the hypocrisy of leaders of the Protestant church (*Elmer Gantry*, 1927). So well known were these books, and so vivid their protagonists, that "Babbitt" and "Elmer Gantry" are now words of general American usage, and even those who have never read the novels know perfectly well what they refer to.

Lewis graduated from Yale in 1907, then worked as a reporter and editor for various publishers. He wrote for *The Saturday Evening Post* and *Cosmopolitan*, among other magazines, but it was as a novelist that he would achieve his greatest critical and financial success. During the 1920s, in addition to the four novels mentioned above, Lewis published *Dodsworth* (1929), a story of a retired American businessman and his wife on a European tour. By the 1930s, although he continued to produce many novels, his reputation had declined. Among the better known of the later books are *It Can't Happen Here* (1935) about the possibility of the establishment of an American fascist state, and *Kingsblood Royal* (1947) about race relations.

Lewis's short stories are less read now than his novels, but he honed his skills as a satirist with these tales, some of which have an enduring interest today. The one that follows is exemplary.

A Letter from the Queen

Doctor Selig was an adventurer. He did not look it, certainly. He was an amiable young bachelor with thin hair. He was instructor in history and economics in Erasmus College, and he had to sit on a foolish little platform and try to coax some fifty young men and women, who were interested only in cuddling and four-door sedans, to become hysterical about the law of diminishing returns.

But at night, in his decorous boarding house, he sometimes smoked a pipe, which was viewed as obscene in the religious shades of Erasmus, and he was boldly writing a book which was to make him famous.

Of course everyone is writing a book. But Selig's was different. It was profound. How good it was can be seen from the fact that with only three quarters of it done, it already had fifteen hundred footnotes—such lively comments as "*Vid.* J.A.S.H.S. VIII, 234 *et seq.*" A real book, nothing flippant or commercialized.

It was called *The Influence of American Diplomacy on the Internal Policies of Paneuropa.*

"Paneuropa," Selig felt, was a nice and scholarly way of saying "Europe."

It would really have been an interesting book if Doctor Selig had not believed that all literature is excellent in proportion as it is hard to read. He had touched a world romantic and little known. Hidden in old documents, like discovering in a desert an oasis where girls laugh and fountains chatter and the market place is noisy, he found the story of Franklin, who in his mousy fur cap was the Don Juan of Paris, of Adams fighting the British Government to prevent their recognizing the Confederacy, of Benjamin Thompson, the Massachusetts Yankee who in 1791 was chief counselor of Bavaria, with the title of Count Rumford.

Selig was moved by these men who made the young America more admired than she is today. And he was moved and, in a most unscholarly way, he became a little angry as he reviewed the story of Senator Ryder.

He knew, of course, that Lafayette Ryder had prevented war between England and America in the first reign of Grover Cleveland; he knew that Ryder had been Secretary of State, and Ambassador to France, courted by Paris for his wisdom, his manners, his wit; that as Senator he had fathered (and mothered and wet-nursed) the Ryder-Hanklin Bill, which had saved our wheat markets; and that his two books, *Possibilities of Disarmament* and *The Anglo-American Empire*, were not merely glib propaganda for peace, but such inspired documents as would have prevented the Boer War, the Spanish-American War, the Great War, if there had been in his Victorian world a dozen men with minds like his. This Selig knew, but he could not remember when Ryder had died.

Then he discovered with aghast astonishment that Senator Ryder was not dead, but still alive at ninety-two, forgotten by the country he had helped to build.

Yes, Selig felt bitterly, we honor our great men in America—sometimes for as much as two months after the particular act of greatness that tickles us. But this is a democracy. We mustn't let anyone suppose that because we have given him an (undesired) parade up Broadway and a (furiously resented) soaking of publicity on March first, he may expect to be taken seriously on May second.

The Admiral Dewey whom the press for a week labeled as a combination of Nelson, Napoleon, and Chevalier Bayard, they later nagged to his grave. If a dramatist has a success one season, then may the gods help him, because for the rest of his life everyone will attend his plays only in the hope that he will fail.

But sometimes the great glad-hearted hordes of boosters do not drag down the idol in the hope of finding clay feet, but just forget him with the vast, contemptuous, heavy indifference of a hundred and twenty million people.

So felt Doctor Selig, angrily, and he planned for the end of his book a passionate resurrection of Senator Ryder. He had a shy hope that his book would appear before the Senator's death, to make him happy.

Reading the Senator's speeches, studying his pictures in magazine files, he felt that he knew him intimately. He could see, as though the Senator were in the room, that tall ease, the contrast of long thin nose, gay eyes, and vast globular brow that made Ryder seem a combination of Puritan, clown, and benevolent scholar.

Selig longed to write to him and ask—oh, a thousand things that only he could explain; the proposals of Lionel Sackville-West regarding Colombia; what Queen Victoria really had said in that famous but unpublished letter to President Harrison about the Newfoundland fisheries. Why couldn't he write to him?

No! The man was ninety-two, and Selig had too much reverence to disturb him, along with a wholesome suspicion that his letter would be kicked out by the man who had once told Gladstone to go to the devil.

So forgotten was the Senator that Selig could not, at first, find where he lived. Who's Who gave no address. Selig's superior, Professor Munk, who was believed to know everything in the world except the whereabouts of his last-season's straw hat, bleated, "My dear chap, Ryder is dwelling in some cemetery! He passed beyond, if I remember, in 1901."

The mild Doctor Selig almost did homicide upon a venerable midwestern historian.

At last, in a bulletin issued by the Anti-Prohibition League, Selig found among the list of directors: "Lafayette Ryder (form. U. S. Sen., Sec'y State), West Wickley, Vermont." Though the Senator's residence could make no difference to him, that night Selig was so excited that he smoked an extra pipe of tobacco.

He was planning his coming summer vacation, during which he hoped to finish his book. The presence of the Senator drew him toward Vermont, and in an educational magazine he found the advertisement: "Sky Peaks, near Wickley, Vt., woodland nook with peace and a library—congenial and intellectual company and writers—tennis, handball, riding—nightly Sing round Old-time Bonfire—fur. bung. low rates."

That was what he wanted: a nook and a library and lots of low rates, along with nearness to his idol. He booked a fur. bung. for the summer, and he carried his suitcase to the station on the beautiful day when the young fiends who through the year had tormented him with unanswerable questions streaked off to all parts of the world and for three tremendous months permitted him to be a private human being.

When he reached Vermont, Selig found Sky Peaks an old farm, redecorated in a distressingly tea-roomy fashion. His single bungalow, formerly an honest corncrib, was now painted robin's-egg blue with yellow trimmings and christened "Shelley." But the camp was on an upland, and air sweet from hayfield and spruce grove healed his lungs, spotted with classroom dust.

At his first dinner at Sky Peaks, he demanded of the host, one Mr. Iddle, "Doesn't Senator Ryder live somewhere near here?"

"Oh, yes, up on the mountain, about four miles south."

"Hope I catch a glimpse of him some day."

"I'll run you over to see him any time you'd like."

"Oh, I couldn't do that! Couldn't intrude!"

"Nonsense! Of course he's old, but he takes quite an interest in the countryside. Fact, I bought this place from him and—— Don't forget the Sing tonight."

At eight that evening Iddle came to drag Selig from the security of his corncrib just as he was getting the relations of the Locarno Pact and the Versailles Treaty beautifully coördinated.

It was that kind of Sing. "The Long, Long Trail," and "All God's Chillun Got Shoes." (God's Chillun also possessed coats, pants, vests, flivvers, and watermelons, interminably.) Beside Selig at the campfire sat a young woman with eyes, a nose, a sweater, and an athletic skirt, none of them very good or particularly bad. He would not have noticed her, but she picked on him:

"They tell me you're in Erasmus, Doctor Selig."

"Um."

"Real attention to character. And after all, what benefit is there in developing the intellect if the character isn't developed to keep pace with it? You see, I'm in educational work myself—oh, of course nothing like being on a college faculty, but I teach history in the Lincoln High School at Schenectady—my name is Selma Swanson. We must have some good talks about teaching history, mustn't we!"

"Um!" said Selig, and escaped, though it was not till he was safely in his corncrib that he said aloud, "We must *not!*"

For three months he was not going to be a teacher, or heed the horrors of character-building. He was going to be a great scholar. Even Senator Ryder might be excited to know how powerful an intellect was soothing itself to sleep in a corncrib four miles away!

He was grinding hard next afternoon when his host, Iddle, stormed in with: "I've got to run in to Wickley Center. Go right near old Ryder's. Come on. I'll introduce you to him."

"Oh, no, honestly!"

"Don't be silly: I imagine he's lonely. Come on!"

Before Selig could make up his mind to get out of Iddle's tempestuous flivver and walk back, they were driving up a mountain road and past marble gateposts into an estate. Through a damp grove of birches and maples they came out on meadows dominated by an old brick house with a huge porch facing the checkered valley. They stopped with a dash at the porch, and on it Selig saw an old man sunk in a canvas deck chair and covered with a shawl. In the shadow the light seemed to concentrate on his bald head, like a sphere of polished vellum, and on long bloodless hands lying as in death on shawl-draped knees. In his eyes there was no life nor desire for it.

Iddle leaped out, bellowing, "Afternoon, Senator! Lovely day, isn't it? I've brought a man to call on you. This is Mr. Selig of— uh—one of our colleges. I'll be back in an hour."

He seized Selig's arm—he was abominably strong—and almost pulled him out of the car. Selig's mind was one wretched puddle of confusion. Before he could dredge any definite thought out of it, Iddle had rattled away, and Selig stood below the porch, hypnotized by the stare of Senator Ryder—too old for hate or anger, but not too old for slow contempt.

Not one word Ryder said.

Selig cried, like a schoolboy unjustly accused:

"Honestly, Senator, the last thing I wanted to do was to intrude on you. I thought Iddle would just introduce us and take me away. I suppose he meant well. And perhaps subconsciously I did want to intrude! I know your *Possibilities of Disarmament* and *Anglo-American Empire* so well——"

The Senator stirred like an antediluvian owl awakening at twilight. His eyes came to life. One expected him to croak, like a cynical old bird, but his still voice was fastidious:

"I didn't suppose anyone had looked into my books since 1910." Painful yet gracious was the gesture with which he waved Selig to a chair. "You are a teacher?"

"Instructor in a small Ohio college. Economics and history. I'm writing a monograph on our diplomacy, and naturally—— There are so many things that only you could explain!"

"Because I'm so old?"

"No! Because you've had so much knowledge and courage—

perhaps they're the same thing! Every day, literally, in working on my book I've wished I could consult you. For instance—— Tell me, sir, didn't Secretary of State Olney really want war with England over Venezuela? Wasn't he trying to be a tin hero?"

"No!" The old man threw off his shawl. It was somehow a little shocking to find him not in an ancient robe laced with gold, but in a crisp linen summer suit with a smart bow tie. He sat up, alert, his voice harsher. "No! He was a patriot. Sturdy. Honest. Willing to be conciliatory but not flinching. Miss Tully!"

At the Senator's cry, out of the wide fanlighted door of the house slid a trained nurse. Her uniform was so starched that it almost clattered, but she was a peony sort of young woman, the sort who would insist on brightly mothering any male, of any age, whether or not he desired to be mothered. She glared at the intruding Selig; she shook her finger at Senator Ryder, and simpered:

"Now I do hope you aren't tiring yourself, else I shall have to be ever so stern and make you go to bed. The doctor said——"

"Damn the doctor! Tell Mrs. Tinkham to bring me down the file of letters from Richard Olney, Washington, for 1895— O-l-n-e-y—and hustle it!"

Miss Tully gone, the Senator growled, "Got no more use for a nurse than a cat for two tails! It's that mutton-headed doctor, the old fool! He's seventy-five years old, and he hasn't had a thought since 1888. Doctors!"

He delivered an address on the art of medicine with such vigorous blasphemy that Selig shrank in horrified admiration. And the Senator didn't abate the blazing crimson of his oration at the entrance of his secretary, Mrs. Tinkham, a small, narrow, bleached, virginal widow.

Selig expected her to leap off the porch and commit suicide in terror. She didn't. She waited, she yawned gently, she handed the Senator a manila envelope, and gently she vanished.

The Senator grinned. "She'll pray at me tonight! She daren't while you're here. There! I feel better. Good cussing is a therapeutic agent that has been forgotten in these degenerate days. I could teach you more about cussing than about diplomacy—to which cussing is a most valuable aid. Now here is a letter that

Secretary Olney wrote me about the significance of his correspondence with England."

It was a page of history. Selig handled it with more reverence than he had given to any material object in his life.

He exclaimed, "Oh, yes, you used—of course I've never seen the rest of this letter, and I can't tell you, sir, how excited I am to see it. But didn't you use this first paragraph—it must be about on page 276 of your *Anglo-American Empire?*"

"I believe I did. It's not my favorite reading!"

"You know, of course, that it was reprinted from your book in the *Journal of the American Society of Historical Sources* last year?"

"Was it?" The old man seemed vastly pleased. He beamed at Selig as at a young but tested friend. He chuckled, "Well, I suppose I appreciate now how King Tut felt when they remembered him and dug him up. . . . Miss Tully! Hey! Miss Tully, will you be so good as to tell Martens to bring us whisky and soda, with two glasses? Eh? Now you look here, young woman; we'll fight out the whole question of my senile viciousness after our guest has gone. Two glasses, I said! . . . Now about Secretary Olney. The fact of the case was . . ."

Two hours later, Senator Ryder was still talking and in that two hours he had given Selig such unrecorded information as the researcher could not have found in two years of study.

Selig had for two hours walked with presidents and ambassadors; he had the dinner conversation of foreign ministers, conversations so private, so world-affecting, that they never had been set down, even in letters. The Senator had revealed his friendship with King Edward, and the predictions about the future World War the King had made over a glass of mineral water.

The mild college instructor, who till this afternoon had never spoken to anyone more important than the president of a prairie college, was exalted with a feeling that he had become the confidant of kings and field marshals, of Anatole France and Lord Haldane, of Sarah Bernhardt and George Meredith.

He had always known but till now he had never understood that in private these great personages were plain human beings, like Doctor Wilbur Selig of Erasmus. It made him feel close to King Edward to hear (though the Senator may have exaggerated) that the King could not pronounce his own name without a

German accent; it made him feel a man of the world to learn the details of a certain not very elevating party at which an English duke and a German prince and a Portuguese king, accompanied by questionable ladies, had in bibulous intimacy sung to Senator Ryder's leadership the lyric, "How Dry I Am."

During that two hours, there had been ten minutes when he had been entirely off in a Conan Doyle spirit world. His notion of prodigious alcoholic dissipation was a bottle of home-brewed beer once a month. He had tried to mix himself a light whisky and soda—he noted, with some anxiety about the proper drinking-manners in diplomatic society, that he took approximately one third as much whisky as the Senator.

But while the old man rolled his drink in his mouth and shook his bald head rapturously and showed no effect, Selig was suddenly lifted six million miles above the earth, through pink-gray clouds shot with lightning, and at that altitude he floated dizzily while below him the Senator discoursed on the relations of Cuban sugar to Colorado beets.

And once Iddle blatted into sight, in his dirty flivver, suggested taking him away, and was blessedly dismissed by the Senator's curt, "Doctor Selig is staying here for dinner. I'll send him back in my car."

Dinner . . . Selig, though he rarely read fiction, had read in some novel about "candle-flames, stilled in the twilight and reflected in the long stretch of waxed mahogany as in a clouded mirror—candles and roses and old silver." He had read, too, about stag horns and heraldic shields and the swords of old warriors.

Now, actually, the Senator's dining room had neither stag horn nor heraldic shield nor sword, and if there were still candle-flames, there was no mahogany to reflect them, but instead a silver stretch of damask. It was a long room, simple, with old portraits against white panels. Yet Selig felt that he was transported into all the romance he had ever read.

The dinner was countrylike. By now, Selig expected peacocks' tongues and caviar; he got steak and cantaloupe and corn pudding. But there were four glasses at each plate, and along with water, which was the familiar drink at Erasmus, he had, and timidly, tasted sherry, Burgundy, and champagne.

If Wilbur Selig of Iowa and Erasmus had known anything, it was that champagne was peculiarly wicked, associated with light ladies, lewd talk, and losses at roulette invariably terminating in suicide. Yet it was just as he was nibbling at his very first glass of champagne that Senator Ryder began to talk of his delight in the rise of Anglo-Catholicism.

No. It was none of it real.

If he was exhilarated that he had been kept for dinner, he was ecstatic when the Senator said, "Would you care to come for dinner again day after tomorrow? Good. I'll send Martens for you at seven-thirty. Don't dress."

In a dream phantasmagoria he started home, driven by Martens, the Senator's chauffeur-butler, with unnumbered things that had puzzled him in writing his book made clear.

When he arrived at the Sky Peaks camp, the guests were still sitting about the dull campfire.

"My!" said Miss Selma Swanson, teacher of history. "Mr. Iddle says you've spent the whole evening with Senator Ryder. Mr. Iddle says he's a grand person—used to be a great politician."

"Oh, he was kind enough to help me about some confused problems," murmured Selig.

But as he went to bed—in a reformed corncrib—he exulted, "I bet I could become quite a good friend of the Senator! Wouldn't that be wonderful!"

Lafayette Ryder, when his visitor—a man named Selig or Selim—was gone, sat at the long dining table with a cigarette and a distressingly empty cognac glass. He was meditating, "Nice eager young chap. Provincial. But mannerly. I wonder if there really are a few people who know that Lafe Ryder once existed?"

He rang, and the crisply coy Miss Tully, the nurse, waltzed into the dining room, bubbling, "So we're all ready to go to bed now, Senator!"

"We are not! I didn't ring for you; I rang for Martens."

"He's driving your guest."

"Humph! Send in cook. I want some more brandy."

"Oh, now, Daddy Ryder! You aren't going to be naughty, are you?"

"I am! And who the deuce ever told you to call me 'Daddy'? Daddy!"

"You did. Last year."

"I don't—this year. Bring me the brandy bottle."

"If I do, will you go to bed then?"

"I will not!"

"But the doctor——"

"The doctor is a misbegotten hound with a face like a fish. And other things. I feel cheerful tonight. I shall sit up late. Till All Hours."

They compromised on eleven-thirty instead of All Hours, and one glass of brandy instead of the bottle. But, vexed at having thus compromised—as so often, in ninety-odd years, he had been vexed at having compromised with Empires—the Senator was (said Miss Tully) very naughty in his bath.

"I swear," said Miss Tully afterward, to Mrs. Tinkham, the secretary, "if he didn't pay so well, I'd leave that horrid old man tomorrow. Just because he was a politician or something, once, to think he can sass a trained nurse!"

"You would not!" said Mrs. Tinkham. "But he *is* naughty."

And they did not know that, supposedly safe in his four-poster bed, the old man was lying awake, smoking a cigarette and reflecting:

"The gods have always been much better to me than I have deserved. Just when I thought I was submerged in a flood of women and doctors, along comes a man for companion, a young man who seems to be a potential scholar, and who might preserve for the world what I tried to do. Oh, stop pitying yourself, Lafe Ryder! . . . I wish I could sleep."

Senator Ryder reflected, the next morning, that he had probably counted too much on young Selig. But when Selig came again for dinner, the Senator was gratified to see how quickly he was already fitting into a house probably more elaborate than any he had known. And quite easily he told of what the Senator accounted his uncivilized farm boyhood, his life in a state university.

"So much the better that he is naïve, not one of these third-secretary cubs who think they're cosmopolitan because they went to Groton," considered the Senator. "I must do something for him."

Again he lay awake that night, and suddenly he had what seemed to him an inspired idea.

"I'll give young Selig a lift. All this money and no one but hang-

jawed relatives to give it to! Give him a year of freedom. Pay
him—he probably earns twenty-five hundred a year; pay him five
thousand and expenses to arrange my files. If he makes good, I'd
let him publish my papers after I pass out. The letters from John
Hay, from Blaine, from Choate! No set of unpublished documents
like it in America! It would *make* the boy!"

Mrs. Tinkham would object. Be jealous. She might quit. Splendid! Lafe, you arrant old coward, you've been trying to get rid of
that woman without hurting her feelings for three years! At that,
she'll probably marry you on your dying bed!"

He chuckled, a wicked, low, delighted sound, the old man
alone in darkness.

"Yes, and if he shows the quality I think he has, leave him a
little money to carry on with while he edits the letters. Leave
him—let's see."

It was supposed among Senator Ryder's lip-licking relatives and
necessitous hangers-on that he had left of the Ryder fortune perhaps two hundred thousand dollars. Only his broker and he knew
that he had by secret investment increased it to a million, these
ten years of dark, invalid life.

He lay planning a new will. The present one left half his fortune
to his university, a quarter to the town of Wickley for a community
center, the rest to nephews and nieces, with ten thousand each
for the Tully, the Tinkham, Martens, and the much-badgered doctor, with a grave proviso that the doctor should never again dictate
to any patient how much he should smoke.

Now to Doctor Selig, asleep and not even dream-warned in his
absurd corncrib, was presented the sum of twenty-five thousand
dollars, the blessings of an old man, and a store of historical documents which could not be priced in coin.

In the morning, with a headache, and very strong with Miss
Tully about the taste of the aspirin—he suggested that she had
dipped it in arsenic—the Senator reduced Selig to five thousand,
but that night it went back to twenty-five.

How pleased the young man would be.

Doctor Wilbur Selig, on the first night when he had unexpect-
edly been bidden to stay for dinner with Senator Ryder, was as
stirred as by—— What *would* most stir Doctor Wilbur Selig? A
great play? A raise in salary? An Erasmus football victory?

At the second dinner, with the house and the hero less novel to him, he was calmly happy, and zealous about getting information. The third dinner, a week after, was agreeable enough, but he paid rather more attention to the squab in casserole than to the Senator's revelations about the Baring panic, and he was a little annoyed that the Senator insisted (so selfishly) on his staying till midnight, instead of going home to bed at a reasonable hour like ten—with, perhaps, before retiring, a few minutes of chat with that awfully nice bright girl, Miss Selma Swanson.

And through that third dinner he found himself reluctantly critical of the Senator's morals.

Hang it, here was a man of good family, who had had a chance to see all that was noblest and best in the world, and why did he feel he had to use such bad language, why did he drink so much? Selig wasn't (he proudly reminded himself) the least bit narrow-minded. But an old man like this ought to be thinking of making his peace; ought to be ashamed of cursing like a stableboy.

He reproved himself next morning, "He's been mighty nice to me. He's a good old coot—at heart. And of course a great statesman."

But he snapped back to irritation when he had a telephone call from Martens, the chauffeur: "Senator Ryder would like you to come over for tea this afternoon. He has something to show you."

"All right, I'll be over."

Selig was curt about it, and he raged, "Now, by thunder, of all the thoughtless, selfish old codgers! As if I didn't have anything to do but dance attendance on him and amuse him! And here I'd planned to finish a chapter this afternoon! 'Course he does give me some inside information, but still—as if I needed all the tittle-tattle of embassies for my book! Got all the stuff I need now. And how am I to get over there? The selfish old hound never thinks of that! Does he suppose I can afford a car to go over? I'll have to walk! Got half a mind not to go!"

The sulkiness with which he came to tea softened when the Senator began to talk about the Queen Victoria letter.

Historians knew that during the presidency of Benjamin Harrison, when there was hostility between America and Britain over the seizure by both sides of fishing boats, Queen Victoria had written in her own hand to President Harrison. It was believed that she deplored her royal inability to appeal directly to Parliament, and suggested his first taking the difficulty up with Congress. But precisely what was in this unofficial letter, apparently no one knew.

This afternoon Senator Ryder said placidly, "I happen to have the original of the letter in my possession."

"*What?*"

"Perhaps some day I'll give you a glimpse of it. I think I have the right to let you quote it."

Selig was electrified. It would be a sensation—*he* would be a sensation! He could see his book, and himself, on the front pages. But the Senator passed on to a trivial, quite improper anecdote about a certain Brazilian ambassador and a Washington milliner, and Selig was irritable again. Darn it, it was indecent for a man of over ninety to think of such things! And why the deuce was he so skittish and secretive about his old letter? If he was going to show it, why not do it?

So perhaps Doctor Selig of Erasmus was not quite so gracious as a Doctor Selig of Erasmus should have been when, at parting, the old man drew from under his shawl a worn blue-gray pamphlet, and piped:

"I'm going to give you this, if you'd like it. There's only six copies left in the world, I believe. It's the third one of my books —privately printed and not ordinarily listed with the others. It has, I imagine, a few things in it the historians don't know; the real story of the Paris commune."

"Oh, thanks," Selig said brusquely and, to himself, in the Senator's car, he pointed out that it showed what an egotistic old codger Ryder was to suppose that just because he'd written something, it must be a blooming treasure!

He glanced into the book. It seemed to have information. But he wasn't stirred, for it was out of line with what he had decided were the subjects of value to Doctor Selig and, therefore, of general interest.

After tea, now, it was too late for work before dinner, and he had Ryder's chauffeur set him down at Tredwell's General Store, which had become for members of the Sky Peaks camp a combination of department store, post office and café, where they drank wild toasts in lemon pop.

Miss Selma Swanson was there, and Selig laughingly treated her to chewing gum, Attaboy Peanut Candy Rolls, and seven fishhooks. They had such a lively time discussing that funny Miss Elkington up at the camp.

When he started off, with Miss Swanson, he left the Senator's book behind him in the store. He did not miss it till he had gone to bed.

Two days afterward, the Senator's chauffeur again telephoned an invitation to tea for that afternoon, but this time Selig snapped, "Sorry! Tell the Senator I unfortunately shan't be able to come!"

"Just a moment, please," said the chauffeur. "The Senator wishes to know if you care to come to dinner tomorrow evening —eight—he'll send for you."

"Well—— Yes, tell him I'll be glad to come."

After all, dinner here at Sky Peaks was pretty bad, and he'd get away early in the evening.

He rejoiced in having his afternoon free for work. But the confounded insistence of the Senator had so bothered him that he banged a book on his table and strolled outside.

The members of the camp were playing One Old Cat, with Selma Swanson, very jolly in knickerbockers, as cheer leader. They yelped at Selig to join them and, after a stately refusal or two, he did. He had a good time. Afterward he pretended to wrestle with Miss Swanson—she had the supplest waist and, seen close up, the moistest eyes. So he was glad that he had not wasted his afternoon listening to that old bore.

The next afternoon, at six, a splendid chapter done, he went off for a climb up Mount Poverty with Miss Swanson. The late sun was so rich on pasture, pine clumps, and distant meadows, and Miss Swanson was so lively in tweed skirt and brogues—but the stockings were silk—that he regretted having promised to be at the Senator's at eight.

"But of course I always keep my promises," he reflected proudly.

They sat on a flat rock perched above the valley, and he observed in rather a classroom tone, "How remarkable that light is—the way it picks out that farmhouse roof, and then the shadow of those maples on the grass. Did you ever realize that it's less the shape of things than the light that gives a landscape beauty?"

"No, I don't think I ever did. That's so. It's the light! My, how observant you are!"

"Oh, no, I'm not. I'm afraid I'm just a bookworm."

"Oh, you are not! Of course you're tremendously scholarly—my, I've learned so much about study from you—but then, you're so active—you were just a circus playing One Old Cat yesterday. I do admire an all-round man."

At seven-thirty, holding her firm hand, he was saying, "But really, there's so much that I lack that—— But you do think I'm right about it's being so much manlier not to drink like that old man? By the way, we must start back."

At a quarter to eight, after he had kissed her and apologized and kissed her, he remarked, "Still, he can wait a while—won't make any difference."

At eight: "Golly, it's so late! Had no idea. Well, I better not go at all now. I'll just phone him this evening and say I got balled up on the date. Look! Let's go down to the lake and dine on the wharf at the boathouse, just you and I."

"Oh, that would be grand!" said Miss Selma Swanson.

Lafayette Ryder sat on the porch that, along with his dining room and bedroom, had become his entire world, and waited for the kind young friend who was giving back to him the world he had once known. His lawyer was coming from New York in three days, and there was the matter of the codicil to his will. But—the Senator stirred impatiently—this money matter was grubby; he had for Selig something rarer than money—a gift for a scholar.

He looked at it and smiled. It was a double sheet of thick bond, with "Windsor Castle" engraved at the top. Above this address was written in a thin hand: "To my friend L. Ryder, to use if he ever sees fit. Benj. Harrison."

The letter began, "To His Excellency, the President," and it was signed, "Victoria R." In a few lines between inscription and signature there was a new history of the great Victoria and of the Nineteenth Century. . . . Dynamite does not come in large packages.

The old man tucked the letter into a pocket down beneath the rosy shawl that reached up to his gray face.

Miss Tully rustled out, to beg, "Daddy, you won't take more than one cocktail tonight? The doctor says it's so bad for you!"

"Heh! Maybe I will and maybe I won't! What time is it?"

"A quarter to eight."

"Doctor Selig will be here at eight. If Martens doesn't have the cocktails out on the porch three minutes after he gets back, I'll skin him. And you needn't go looking for the cigarettes in my room, either! I've hidden them in a brand-new place, and I'll probably sit up and smoke till dawn. Fact; doubt if I shall go to bed at all. Doubt if I'll take my bath."

He chuckled as Miss Tully wailed, "You're so naughty!"

The Senator need not have asked the time. He had groped down under the shawl and looked at his watch every five minutes since seven. He inwardly glared at himself for his foolishness in anticipating his young friend, but—all the old ones were gone.

That was the devilishness of living so many years. Gone, so long. People wrote idiotic letters to him, still, begging for his autograph, for money, but who save this fine young Selig had come to him? . . . So long now!

At eight, he stirred, not this time like a drowsy old owl, but like an eagle, its lean head thrusting forth from its pile of hunched feathers, ready to soar. He listened for the car.

At ten minutes past, he swore, competently. Confound that Martens!

At twenty past, the car swept up the driveway. Out of it stepped only Martens, touching his cap, murmuring, "Very sorry, sir. Mr. Selig was not at the camp."

"Then why the devil didn't you wait?"

"I did, sir, as long as I dared."

"Poor fellow! He may have been lost on the mountain. We must start a search!"

"Very sorry, sir, but if I may say so, as I was driving back past the foot of the Mount Poverty trail, I saw Mr. Selig with a young woman, sir, and they were talking and laughing and going away from the camp, sir. I'm afraid——"

"Very well. That will do."

"I'll serve dinner at once, sir. Do you wish your cocktail out here?"

"I won't have one. Send Miss Tully."

When the nurse had fluttered to him, she cried out with alarm. Senator Ryder was sunk down into his shawl. She bent over him to hear his whisper:

"If it doesn't keep you from your dinner, my dear, I think I'd like to be helped up to bed. I don't care for anything to eat. I feel tired.''

While she was anxiously stripping the shawl from him, he looked long, as one seeing it for the last time, at the darkening valley. But as she helped him up, he suddenly became active. He snatched from his pocket a stiff double sheet of paper and tore it into fragments which he fiercely scattered over the porch with one sweep of his long arm.

Then he collapsed over her shoulder.

Will Rogers
(1879–1935)

Will Rogers was born in Oolagh, Indian Territory, now part of Oklahoma. He began his career as a cowboy performer in vaudeville, doing rope tricks accompanied by humorous patter, but he grew into an acute observer of the political scene, a homespun philosopher, and commonsensical social critic whose signature phrase, "All I know is what I read in the papers," was familiar to everyone across the country. He starred in movies, wrote newspaper columns, and published books filled with down-to-earth wisdom that gained him an immense popular audience, and the attention of many politicians, even including the president of the United States. The entire nation mourned his death in an airplane crash in 1935. His political satire was as gentle in its form as it was acute in its perceptions, and a sample is presented here.

A Day at the Republican Convention

They just played the National Anthem, and when they finished, they asked the band leader to play something else while the chairman was trying to think of something to say. They are still playing.

The whole show has degenerated into nothing but a dog fight for Vice President. If you are interested in Vice Presidents and such things, you will perhaps be interested in this convention.

Nobody in the history of conventions ever saw a convention start out and end so quick. The "allies" stopped Hoover. Yea, they stopped him from being Secretary of Commerce.

Anyhow, the convention opened with a prayer, a very fervent prayer that Al Smith not be nominated. It was a keynote prayer. If the Lord can see his way clear to bless the Republican Party the way it's been carrying on, then the rest of us ought to get it without even asking for it.

Then they brought on Senator Simeon D. Fess, he delivered what is called the keynote speech. The crowd couldn't hear him and shouted for him to speak louder. Then, when he did speak louder and they did hear him, why, they got sorer than a boil and wanted him to speak low again.

He brought up Nicaragua, but he left our Marines down there. He said that he would protect American lives down there, even if we had to send some there to protect.

Now you all know that a keynote speech is just press notices by a party, written by its own members. Here are just a few things that I bet you didn't know the Republicans were responsible for: radio, telephone, baths, automobiles, savings accounts, law enforcement, workmen living in houses, and a living wage for Senators.

The Democrats had brought war, pestilence, debts, disease, boll weevil, gold teeth, need of farm relief, suspenders, floods, famines.

He told of so much money that we had saved, that I think if he had talked another hour, he would have paid us dividends.

When he got to Coolidge, I thought sure he was referring to Our Saviour, till they told me, "no, it was Coolidge." The way he rated 'em was, Coolidge, The Lord, and then Lincoln.

It was an impromptu address that he had been working on for only six months. He made no attempt at oratory. He just shouted. He dramatized figures. When he told how many millions we had saved, his voice raised, but when our savings had reached the billions, why, his voice reached a crescendo. All expenditures were spoken in an undertone.

Men who yesterday wouldn't allow their names to be even associated with the Vice Presidency, are today announcing they would consider being drafted. In fact, men who two days ago wouldn't even speak to a Vice President, are now trying to get to be one.

They have weeded the Vice Presidential candidates down now to just the following: ninety-six Senators, 435 Congressmen and forty-eight Governors.

If you haven't a room to stay in while here, you can get one now. There is six candidate headquarters that are to be sublet.

All we have done today is listen to Senator Fess explain what he forgot to say yesterday. It seems he left out Teddy Roosevelt's name yesterday, and it took him all day to alibi for it. I don't know who he forgot today that he will have to bring up tomorrow.

They had quite a time seating the Texas delegation, as there was no law in Texas to apply to a Republican primary. Texas never thought they would come to a point where there would ever be any Republicans there. They also have no law against the shooting out of season of reindeer or musk ox.

They adjourned till tomorrow for the sake of the hotels. They could have finished this convention in ten minutes today.

At the Democratic Convention

Ah! They was Democrats today, and we was all proud of 'em. They fought, they fit, they split and adjourned in a dandy wave of dissention. That's the old Democratic spirit! A whole day wasted and nothing done. I tell you, they are getting back to normal.

A whole day fighting over what? A President? No. A platform? No. Well, then, what did they take up eleven hundred delegates' and twelve thousand spectators' time for? Why, to see whether Huey Long, the Louisiana porcupine, was to sit on the floor or in the gallery. And the other four hours was fighting over who would be chairman of a convention that's already a week old.

The Democrats are the only known race of people that give a dinner and then won't decide who will be toastmaster till they all get to the dinner, and fight over it.

But to Huey Long goes the credit of being the first to split the party and get 'em acting like Democrats. I'll bet when Judgement

Day comes, things will go along unusually quiet till all at once
there will be the blamedest fight and it will be over what to do
with Huey. But, by golly, he made a good speech today.

Now comes Senator Barkley with the keynote. What do you
mean "note"? This was no note. This was in three volumes. Barkley leaves from here to go to the Olympic Games, to run in the
marathon. He will win it, too, for that race only lasts three hours.

But it had to be a long speech, for when you start enumerating
the things that the Republicans have got away with in the last
years, you have cut yourself out a job. He touched on the high-
lights of their devilment. He did not have time to go into detail.
This is one keynote speech you can forgive the length, for when
you jot down our ills, you got to have a lot of paper. He had it
all over the Republican keynoter, for this fellow was reading facts,
while the other fellow had to read alibis.

That was yesterday. Nobody was asked to vote on anything today, so there was no fights. Half the Iowa delegation was still in
the hospital from trying to count their own votes yesterday.

This is the third day of the convention. This is the day the
Republicans adjourned. Adjourned! Why, the Democrats haven't
done anything but meet and pray yet. How can you tell when a
Democratic convention is adjourned, and when it's not? A Democrat never adjourns. He is born, becomes of voting age and starts
right in arguing over something, and his first political adjourn-
ment is his date with the undertaker. Politics is business with the
Democrat. He don't work at it, but he tells what he would do if
he was working at it.

I am still trying to get the floor to nominate Coolidge at this
Democratic convention. I know he was a Republican but Democrats did better with him than anybody we ever had in.

Politics ain't on the level. I was only in 'em for an hour but in
that short space of time somebody stole 22 votes from me. I was
sitting there in the press stand asleep—it was way past midnight
—and I wasn't bothering a soul when they woke me up and said
Oklahoma had started me on the way to the White House with
22 votes.

I thought to myself, well, there is no use going there this late
in the night, so I dropped off to sleep again, and that's when
somebody touched me for my whole roll, took the whole 22 votes,
didn't even leave me a vote to get breakfast on.

Course I realize now that I should have stayed awake and protected my interest, but it was the only time I had ever entered national politics and I didn't look for the boys to nick me so quick. Course I should have had a manager, but the whole thing came on me so sudden and I was so sleepy. No man can listen to thirty-five nominating speeches and hold his head up. And I am sure some of these that did the nominating can never hold theirs up again.

Now I don't want you to think that I am belittling the importance of those 22 votes. They was worth something there at the time. Not in money, mind you, for there is not $2.80 in the whole convention. But they buy 'em with promises of offices.

I expect at that minute Franklin D. Roosevelt's bunch would have given me Secretary of State for that 22. And I could have sold them to Al Smith for maybe Mayor of New York. Governor Ritchie would have given me the whole state of Maryland, with the Vice Presidency thrown in just for amusement. Why, I could have taken those 22 votes and run Andy Mellon out of the embassy in England with 'em. I could have got that job with only 10 of the votes.

And what do I do—go to sleep and wake up without even the support of the Virgin Islands. They not only took my votes, but they got my hat and my typewriter. I not only lost my 22 delegates, but I woke up without even as much as an alternate. Now what am I? Just another ex-Democratic Presidential candidate. There's thousands of 'em. Well, the whole thing has been a terrible lesson to me and nothing to do but start in and live it down.

Say, did you ever parade at 6 o'clock in the morning? Course not, nobody ever did but the Democrats. I have been in circus parades and Wild West parades, but I had never entered a political parade. I had laughed at many a one, but I had never become looney enough to participate.

But this morning as dawn was breaking over the machine gun nests of Chicago, and you could just see the early peep of light down early-rising gangsters' rifle barrels, one of Oklahoma's ex-Governors arose and started to put in nomination a fellow ex-Governor. His melodious voice aroused me from my slumbers. It was a friend, Henry Johnston nominating my old friend Bill Murray. When he finished, the heavens broke loose, noise accompanied by bedlam, and what dashes into the arena, not as you would expect at that hour of the morning, a milk wagon, but a band of beautiful little girls, all dressed in kilts, and thank goodness not playing bagpipes, but musical instruments. They had come all the way from Oklahoma City to help "Our" Bill Murray's parade. Was I going to get in it? If I could get woke up, I was. I had no hat. Arthur Brisbane, the great newspaperman, had been sleeping on mine during the nominating speeches. So Amon G. Carter, Texas' sole surviving dirt farmer whose farm is on the principal street of Dallas, acted as my unmounted outrider. He handed me a straw hat with the word "Texas" on the band, and for no reason at all—like Democrats do everything—somebody handed me a cane. I waved it till I almost hit Mrs. Woodrow Wilson in the eye.

Along the route of march, we picked up a couple of girls who had been stranded by some earlier demonstration. They evidently was just "thumbing" their way around the hall. I was against taking them on. But Amon thought perhaps they were maybe F.F.V.'s [First Families of Virginia] from the old Commonwealth of Virginia and were trying to make their way back to Governor Byrd's headquarters in the Culpeper corner of the hall.

Then as if by magic, the rising sun started creeping in through the stained glass windows of this great cathedral of liberty and justice, and I got the first real look at our traveling companions. The heels of their shoes were much run down, which we knew at a glance was the badge of the Republican Party. And then we realized that they were left-overs from the late Hoover uprising in the same hall a few weeks ago.

Some kindly soul that had temporarily escaped depression, handed me a box of popcorn, so I had rations through the biggest part of the pilgrimage. The hall runs about three miles to the lap. The journey got us no votes, but like all these half-witted convention parades, it kept anyone else from getting any votes, or rest, either, until every marcher has become thoroughly disgusted with himself.

I am glad Chicago's children didn't come by on their way to school this morning and see how this wonderful system of choosing our country's leaders was conducted. They would never again have asked: "What's the matter with the country?"

Dorothy Parker

(1893–1967)

The editor of *Vanity Fair* fired Dorothy Parker in 1920 because her drama reviews were too wickedly and sarcastically critical. The editors of a new magazine, *The New Yorker*, were not so decorous as those at *Vanity Fair*, and her wisecracks from her drama reviews in that magazine are legendary. She immortalized an otherwise completely forgettable turkey called *The House Beautiful* with a one-line review: "The House Beautiful," she wrote, "is a play lousy." Katharine Hepburn has no doubt recovered from Parker's remark about her performance in a 1934 play in which, she said, Hepburn "ran the gamut of emotions from A to B." In addition to her theater criticism, she wrote light verse, book reviews, and short stories, all published regularly in *The New Yorker*. In 1929 her short story "Big Blonde" won the O. Henry Award.

Parker's reviews were printed under the pseudonym "Constant Reader," which figures in the famously quotable final line of her review of A. A. Milne's *The House at Pooh Corner*, printed here. She is also the author of light verse, collected in *Enough Rope* (1926), *Sunset Gun* (1928), and *Death and Taxes* (1931), and of two collections of short stories, *Laments for the Living* (1930) and *Here Lies* (1939).

Words, Words, Words

There are times when images blow to fluff, and comparisons stiffen and shrivel. Such an occasion is surely at hand when one is confronted by Dreiser's latest museum piece, *Dawn.* One can but revise a none-too-hot dialectic of childhood; ask, in rhetorical aggressiveness, "What writes worse than a Theodore Dreiser?"— loudly crow the answer, *Two* "Theodore Dreisers"; and, according to temperament, rejoice at the merciful absurdity of the conception, or shudder away from the thought.

The reading of *Dawn* is a strain upon many parts, but the worst wear and tear fall on the forearms. After holding the massive volume for the half-day necessary to its perusal (well, look at that, would you? "massive volume" and "perusal," one right after the other! You see how contagious Mr. D.'s manner is?), my arms ached with a slow, mean persistence beyond the services of aspirin or of liniment. I must file this distress, I suppose, under the head of "Occupational Diseases"; for I could not honestly chalk up such a result against "Pleasure" or even "Improvement." And I can't truly feel that *Dawn* was worth it. If I must have aches, I had rather gain them in the first tennis of the season, and get my back into it.

This present Dreiser book is the record of its author's first twenty years. It requires five hundred and eighty-nine long, wide, and closely printed pages. Nearly six hundred sheets to the title of *Dawn;* God help us one and all if Mr. Dreiser ever elects to write anything called "June Twenty-first"!

The actual account of the writer's early life, and of the lives of his mother, his father, and his nine brothers and sisters which colored and crossed it, is wholly absorbing; but, if I may say so, without that lightning bolt coming barging in the window, what honest setting-down of anyone's first years would not be? And Mr. Dreiser had, in addition, the purely literary good fortune to be a child of poverty—for when, in print, was the shanty not more glamorous than the salon?

Nor should I cavil at the length, and hence the weight, of the book, were it all given over to memories, since if a man were to write down his remembrances and his impressions up to the age of five, much less of twenty, six hundred pages could not begin to contain them. But I do fret, through *Dawn*, at the great desert patches of Mr. Dreiser's moralizing, I do chafe at such monstrous bad writing as that with which he pads out his tale. I have read reviews of this book, written by those whose days are dedicated to literature. "Of course," each one says airily, "Dreiser writes badly," and thus they dismiss that tiny fact, and go off into their waltz-dream. This book, they cry, ranks well beside the *Confessions* of Rousseau; and I, diverted, as is ever the layman, by any plump red herring, mutter, "Oh, Rousseau, my eye," and am preoccupied with that.

But on second thinking, I dare to differ more specifically from the booksie-wooksies. It is of not such small importance to me that Theodore Dreiser writes in so abominable a style. He is regarded, and I wish you could gainsay me, as one of our finest contemporary authors; it is the first job of a writer who demands rating among the great, or even among the good, to write well. If he fails that, as Mr. Dreiser, by any standard, so widely muffs it, he is, I think, unequipped to stand among the big.

For years, you see, I have been crouching in corners hissing small and ladylike anathema of Theodore Dreiser. I dared not yip it out loud, much less offer it up in print. But now, what with a series of events that have made me callous to anything that may later occur, I have become locally known as the What-the-Hell Girl of 1931. In that, my character, I may say that to me Dreiser is a dull, pompous, dated, and darned near ridiculous writer. All right. Go on and bring on your lightning bolts.

Of the earlier Dreiser, the author of *Sister Carrie* and *Jennie Gerhardt*, the portrayer of Muldoon and of Paul Dresser, in *Twelve Men*, you don't think I could be so far gone as to withhold all the reverent praise that is in me, do you? But then I read all those hundreds of thousands of words that made up *An American Tragedy* and, though I hung upon some of them, I later read the newspaper accounts of the Snyder-Gray case, and still later, of the cornering by a hundred or so of New York's finest of the nineteen-year-old "Shorty" Crowley. And I realized, slowly and sadly, that any reporter writes better and more vividly than the man who has been proclaimed the great reporter. It is a quite fair comparison. Mr. Dreiser, with the Chester Gillette case, had a great story; the unnamed men of the daily and the evening papers with the tales of the unhappy Ruth Snyder and the bewildered Judd Gray, and the little Crowley boy who never had a prayer—they had fine stories, too. But they would have lost their jobs, had they written too much.

The booksy ones, with that butterfly touch of theirs, flutter away from Dreiser's bad writing and but brush their wings over the admission that he possesses no humor. Now I know that the term "sense of humor" is dangerous (there's a novel idea!) and that humor is snooted upon, in a dignified manner, by the lofty-minded. Thus Professor Paul Elmer More raises a thin and querulous pipe in his essay on Longfellow—I think it is—to say that there were those who claimed that Longfellow had no humor—of whom I am the first ten. All right, suppose he hadn't, he says, in effect; humor may be all very well for those that like it ("Only fools care to see," said the blind man), but there's no good making a fetish of it. I wouldn't for the world go around making fetishes; yet I am unable to feel that a writer can be complete without humor. And I don't mean by that, and you know it perfectly well, the creation or the appreciation of things comic. I mean that the possession of a sense of humor entails the sense of selection, the civilized fear of going too far. A little humor leavens the lump, surely, but it does more than that. It keeps you, from your respect for the humor of others, from making a dull jackass of yourself. Humor, imagination, and manners are pretty fairly interchangeably interwoven.

Mr. Theodore Dreiser has no humor.

I know that Mr. Dreiser is sincere, or rather I have been told it enough to impress me. So, I am assured, is Mrs. Kathleen Norris sincere; so, I am informed, is Mr. Zane Grey sincere; so, I am convinced, was Mr. Horatio Alger—whose work, to me, that of Mr. Dreiser nearest approximates—sincere. But I will not—oh, come on with your lightning again!—admit that sincerity is the only thing. A good thing, a high thing, an admirable thing; but not the only thing in letters.

The thing that most distressed me in *Dawn* was the philosophizing of its author. His is a sort of pre-war bitterness, a sort of road-company anger at conditions. Once does Mr. Dreiser quote a youthful sister: "When men proposed marriage, I found I didn't like them well enough to marry them, but when they told me I was beautiful and wanted to give me things and take me places, it was a different matter. Where I liked a man, it was easy enough to go with him—it was fun—there wasn't really anything wrong with it that I could see. Aside from the social scheme as people seem to want it, I don't even now see that it was."

On this the author comments: "At this point I am sure any self-respecting moralist will close this book once and for all!" But, you know, I must differ. I don't think that's enough to warrant the closing of a book by even the most self-respecting of moralists. I think that Mr. Dreiser believes that the world is backward, hypocritical, and mean, and so, I suppose, it is; but times have changed and Mr. D. is not now the only advanced one. I think the self-respecting moralists are much less apt to close the book "at this point" than are those that get a bit squeamish over the authenticity of a woman who says, "Aside from the social scheme as people seem to want it—"

Early in this little dandy, you saw that I had been affected by the Dreiser style. That, maybe, is responsible for this plethora of words. I could have checked all this torrent, and given you a true idea of Theodore Dreiser's *Dawn,* had I but succumbed to the influence of the present-day Nash and the sweeter-day Bentley, and had written:

Theodore Dreiser
Should ought to write nicer.

May 30, 1931

Far from Well

The more it
SNOWS-tiddely-pom,
The more it
GOES-tiddely-pom
The more it
GOES-tiddely-pom
On
Snowing.

And nobody
KNOWS-tiddely-pom,
How cold my
TOES-tiddely-pom

How cold my
TOES-tiddely-pom
Are
Growing.

The above lyric is culled from the fifth page of Mr. A. A. Milne's new book, *The House at Pooh Corner*, for, although the work is in prose, there are frequent droppings into more cadenced whimsy. This one is designated as a "Hum," that pops into the head of Winnie-the-Pooh as he is standing outside Piglet's house in the snow, jumping up and down to keep warm. It "seemed to him a Good Hum, such as is Hummed Hopefully to Others." In fact, so Good a Hum did it seem that he and Piglet started right out through the snow to Hum It Hopefully to Eeyore. Oh, darn—there I've gone and given away the plot. Oh, I could bite my tongue out.

As they are trotting along against the flakes, Piglet begins to weaken a bit.

" 'Pooh,' he said at last and a little timidly, because he didn't want Pooh to think he was Giving In, 'I was just wondering. How would it be if we went home now and *practised* your song, and then sang it to Eeyore tomorrow—or—or the next day, when we happen to see him.'

" 'That's a very good idea, Piglet,' said Pooh. 'We'll practise it now as we go along. But it's no good going home to practise it, because it's a special Outdoor Song which Has To Be Sung In The Snow.'

" 'Are you sure?' asked Piglet anxiously.

" 'Well, you'll see, Piglet, when you listen. Because this is how it begins. *The more it snows, tiddely-pom—*'

" 'Tiddely what?' said Piglet." (He took, as you might say, the very words out of your correspondent's mouth.)

" 'Pom,' said Pooh. 'I put that in to make it more hummy.' "

And it is that word "hummy," my darlings, that marks the first place in *The House at Pooh Corner* at which Tonstant Weader Fwowed up.

October 20, 1928

Comment

Oh, life is a glorious cycle of song,
A medley of extemporanea;
And love is a thing that can never go wrong;
And I am Marie of Roumania.

One Perfect Rose

A single flow'r he sent me, since we met.
    All tenderly his messenger he chose;
Deep-hearted, pure, with scented dew still wet—
    One perfect rose.

I knew the language of the floweret;
    "My fragile leaves," it said, "his heart enclose."
Love long has taken for his amulet
    One perfect rose.

Why is it no one ever sent me yet
    One perfect limousine, do you suppose?
Ah no, it's always just my luck to get
    One perfect rose.

James Thurber

(1894–1961)

James Thurber had been a newspaper reporter in his native Ohio for several years after dropping out of college; he moved to New York to work for the *Evening Post*. In 1927 he became managing editor and staff writer for *The New Yorker*, where he worked on staff until 1933 and for the rest of his life as a contributor. Those who know Thurber's classic drawings and cartoons may be surprised to learn that he considered himself a writer first, and only secondarily an artist and cartoonist. In any case, Thurber's cartoon characters—the domineering wife, the submissive husband, the menagerie of animals—are now familiar parts of the American landscape, and a character from one of his short stories, Walter Mitty, has become an eponym for timidity accompanied by grandiose fantasies. His books include two collections of autobiographical essays, *My Life and Hard Times* (1933) and *The Thurber Album* (1952); *Fables for Our Time* (1940); *The Male Animal* (1941), a play; and two classic children's books, *The 13 Clocks* (1950) and *The Wonderful O* (1957). He was the gentlest of satirists, as demonstrated by the piece that follows.

Tom the Young Kidnapper, or, Pay Up and Live

A KIND OF HORATIO ALGER STORY BASED
ON THE SUCCESSFUL $30,000 KIDNAPPING
IN KANSAS CITY OF MISS MARY MCELROY,
WHO HAD A LOVELY TIME, WHOSE
ABDUCTORS GAVE HER ROSES AND WEPT
WHEN SHE LEFT, AND WHOSE FATHER
SAID HE DID NOT WANT THE YOUNG MEN
TO GO TO THE PENITENTIARY

"I would admire to walk with youse to a small, dark cellar and manacle you to a damp wall."

The speaker was a young American, of perhaps twenty-five years, with a frank, open countenance. Betty Spencer, daughter of old Joab Spencer, the irate banker and the richest man in town, flushed prettily. Her would-be abductor flushed, too, and stood twisting his hat in his hands. He was neatly, if flashily, dressed.

"I am sorry," she said, in a voice which was sweet and low, an excellent thing in woman, "I am sorry, but I am on my way to church, for my faith is as that of a little child."

"But I must have sixty or a hundred thousand dollars from your irate father tonight—or tomorrow night at the latest," said Tom McGirt, for it was he. "It is not so much for me as for the 'gang.'"

"Do you belong to a gang?" cried Betty, flushing prettily, a look of admiration in her eyes. In his adoring embarrassment, the young kidnapper tore his hat into five pieces and ate them.

"My, but you must have a strong stomach!" cried the young lady.

"That was nothing," said Tom, modestly. "Anybody would of done the same thing. You know what I wisht? I wisht it had been me stopping a horse which was running away with you at the risk of my life instead of eating a hat." He looked so forlorn and unhappy because no horse was running away with her that she pitied him.

"Does your gang really need the money?" she cried. "For if it really does, I should be proud to have you kidnap me and subject me to a most humiliating but broadening experience."

"The gang don't work, see?" said the young man, haltingly, for he hated to make this confession. "They're too young and strong to work—I mean there is so much to see and do and drink, and if they was working in a factory, say, or an old stuffy office all day, why—" She began to cry, tears welling up into her eyes.

"I shall come with you," she said, "for I believe that young men should be given hundreds of thousands of dollars that they may enjoy life. I wear a five-and-a-half glove, so I hope your manacles fit me, else I could easily escape from those which were too large."

"If we ain't got ones your size," he said, earnestly, drawing himself up to his full height, "I'll go through smoke and flame to git some for you. Because I—well, you see, I—"

"Yes?" she encouraged him, gently.

"Aw, I won't tell youse now," he said. "Some day when I have made myself worthy, I'll tell youse."

"I have faith in you," she said, softly. "I know you will pull this job off. You can do it, and you *will* do it."

"Thanks, Betty," he said. "I appreciate your interest in me. You shall be proud some day of Tom the Young Kidnapper, or Pay Up and Live." He spoke the subtitle proudly.

"I'll go with you," she said. "No matter where."

"It ain't much of a basement," he said, reddening, and twisting an automatic between his fingers. "It's dark and the walls are damp, but me old mother ain't there, and that's something. She's no good," he added.

"I know," she said, softly. They walked on slowly down the street to a nasty part of town where an automobile drew up alongside the curb, and they got in. Four young men with frank, open countenances were inside, their faces freshly scrubbed, their dark hair moistened and slicked down. Tom introduced them all, and they put away their automatics, and took off their hats, and grinned and were very polite. "I am quite happy," Betty told them.

The cellar in which the young gang manacled Betty to a wall was, as Tom had promised, dark and damp, but the chains which fitted around her wrists were very nice and new and quite snug, so she was quite content. Two of the boys played tiddlywinks with her, while the others went out to mail a letter which she had written at the gang's dictation. It read: "Dear Father—Put a hundred thousand berries in an old tin box and drop it out of your car when you see a red light on the old Post Road tonight, or your daughter will never come home. If you tell the police we will bite her ears off." "That's nice," said Betty, reading it over, "for it will afford Father an opportunity, now that I am in mortal danger, to realize how much he loves me and of how little worth money is, and it will show him also that the young men of this town are out to win!"

Betty was kept in the cellar all night, but in the morning Tom brought her chocolate and marmalade on an ivory-colored breakfast tray, and also a copy of Keats' poems, and a fluffy little kitty with a pink ribbon around its neck. One of the other boys brought her a table badminton set, and a third, named Thad the Slasher, or Knife Them and Run, brought her a swell Welsh pony named Rowdy. "Oh," said Betty, "I am so happy I could cry," and she jangled her manacles. Several of the boys did cry, she looked so uncomfortable and so happy, and then Betty cried, and then they all laughed, and put a record on the Victrola.

That night, Betty was still chained to the wall because her old father had not "come through." "He's holding out for only forty grand," explained Tom, reluctantly, for he did not wish her to know that her father was stingy. "I don't guess your father realizes that we really will make away with you if he don't kick in. He thinks mebbe it's a bluff, but we mean business!" His eyes flashed darkly, and Betty's eyes snapped brightly.

"I know you do!" she cried. "Why, it's been worth forty thousand just the experience I've had. I *do* hope he gives you the hundred, for I should like to go back alive and tell everybody how sweet you have been and how lovely it is to be kidnapped!"

On the second morning, Betty was sitting on the damp cellar floor playing Guess Where I Am with Tom and Ned and Dick and Sluggy, when Thad came in, toying with his frank, open clasp knife, his genial countenance clouded by a frown.

"What is wrong, Thad," asked Betty, "for I perceive that something is wrong?" Thad stood silent, kicking the moist dirt of the floor with the toe of his shoe. He rubbed a sleeve against his eye.

"The old man come across with all the dough," he said. "We —we gotta let you go now." He began to cry openly. Tom paled. One of the boys took Betty's chains off. Betty gathered up her presents, the kitty, and the table badminton set, and the poems. "Rowdy is saddled an' waitin' outside," said Thad, brokenly, handing tens and twenties, one at a time, to his pals.

"Goodbyeee," said Betty. She turned to Tom. "Goodbyeee, Tom," she said.

"Goo—" said Tom, and stopped, all choked up.

When Betty arrived at her house, it was full of policemen and relatives. She dropped her presents and ran up to her father, kindly old Judge Spencer, for he had become a kindly old judge while she was in the cellar, and was no longer the irate old banker and no longer, indeed, the town's richest man, for he only had about seven hundred dollars left.

"My child!" he cried. "I wish to reward those young men for teaching us all a lesson. I have become a poorer but a less irate man, and even Chief of Police Jenkins here has profited by this abduction, for he has been unable to apprehend the culprits and it has taken some of the cockiness out of him, I'll be bound."

"That is true, Joab," said the Chief of Police, wiping away a tear. "Those young fellows have shown us all the error of our ways."

"Have they skipped out, Betty?" asked her father.

"Yes, Father," said Betty, and a tear welled up into her eye.

"Ha, ha!" said old Judge Spencer. "I'll wager there was one young man whom you liked better than the rest, eh, my chick? Well, I should like to give him a position and invite him to Sunday dinner. His rescuing you from the flames of that burning shack for only a hundred thous—"

"I didn't do *that*, sir," said a modest voice, and they all turned and looked at the speaker, Tom the Kidnapper, for it was he. "I simply left her loose from the cellar after we got the dough."

"It's the same thing," said her father, in mock sternness. "Young man, we have all been watching you these past two days —that is to say, we have been wondering where you were. You have outwitted us all and been charming to my daughter. You deserve your fondest wish. What will you have?"

"I'll have Scotch-and-soda, sir," said Tom. "And your daughter's hand."

"Ha, ha!" said the kindly old Judge. "There's enterprise for you, Jenkins!" He nudged Jenkins in the ribs and the Chief nudged back, and laughed. So they all had a Scotch-and-soda and then the Judge married his blushing daughter, right then and there, to Tom the Young Kidnapper, or If You Yell We'll Cut Your Throat.

Langston Hughes

(1902–1967)

Langston Hughes was a young graduate of Columbia University and already a published poet when, working as a busboy in a Washington, D.C., hotel, he put three of his poems next to the dinner plate of Vachel Lindsay. It took no more than a day for newspapers to proclaim that Vachel Lindsay had discovered a black busboy poet. Soon two books of Hughes's poems, *The Weary Blues* (1926) and *Fine Clothes to the Jew* (1927) had been published and well received. Hughes became interested in political militancy in the 1930s (he was a newspaper correspondent in the Spanish Civil War, and traveled widely in the Soviet Union and Asia) and his interest in radical politics lasted into the 1960s. His last book of poems, *The Panther and the Lash*, published posthumously, reflects his interest in black militancy. In addition to poetry, Hughes wrote *A Pictorial History of the Negro in America* (1956), some children's books, several novels, and many works for the stage, including the libretto for *Street Scene*, a Kurt Weill opera.

Ballad of the Landlord

Landlord, landlord,
My roof has sprung a leak.
Don't you 'member I told you about it
Way last week?

Landlord, landlord,
These steps is broken down.
When you come up yourself
It's a wonder you don't fall down.

Ten Bucks you say I owe you?
Ten Bucks you say is due?
Well, that's Ten Bucks more'n I'll pay you
Till you fix this house up new.

What? You gonna get eviction orders?
You gonna cut off my heat?
You gonna take my furniture and
Throw it in the street?

Um-huh! You talking high and mighty.
Talk on—till you get through.
You ain't gonna be able to say a word
If I land my fist on you.

Police! Police!
Come and get this man!
He's trying to ruin the government
And overturn the land!

Copper's whistle!
Patrol bell!
Arrest.

Precinct Station.
Iron cell.
Headlines in press:

MAN THREATENS LANDLORD

TENANT HELD NO BAIL

JUDGE GIVES NEGRO 90 DAYS IN COUNTY JAIL

Ku Klux

They took me out
To some lonesome place.
They said, "Do you believe
In the great white race?"

I said, "Mister,
To tell you the truth,
I'd believe in anything
If you'd just turn me loose."

The white man said, "Boy,
Can it be
You're a-standin' there
A-sassin' me?"

They hit me in the head
And knocked me down.
And then they kicked me
On the ground.

A klansman said, "Nigger,
Look me in the face—
And tell me you believe in
The great white race."

American Heartbreak

I am the American heartbreak—
Rock on which Freedom
Stumps its toe—
The great mistake
That Jamestown
Made long ago.

Kurt Vonnegut

(1922–   )

Kurt Vonnegut attended Cornell University, then served in the Army Air Corps during World War II. He was captured by the Germans, and survived the firebombing of Dresden in 1945, a setting he used in his novel *Slaughterhouse Five* (1969). Vonnegut is also the author of *Player Piano* (1952), *The Sirens of Titan* (1959), *Cat's Cradle* (1963), *Breakfast of Champions* (1973), *Galapagos* (1985), and *Hocus Pocus* (1990) as well as several other novels, collections of short stories, plays, and works of nonfiction. The plots of his novels often look like those of conventional science fiction, but Vonnegut's dark humor, grim satire, and deep pessimism set him apart from other practitioners of the genre. The piece reprinted here, presenting Vonnegut's dim view of the 1972 Republican Convention, is representative.

In a Manner That Must Shame God Himself

If I were a visitor from another planet, I would say things like this about the people of the United States in 1972:

"These are ferocious creatures who imagine that they are gentle. They have experimented in very recent times with slavery and genocide." I would call the robbing and killing of American Indians *genocide*.

I would say, "The two real political parties in America are the *Winners* and the *Losers*. The people do not acknowledge this. They claim membership in two imaginary parties, the *Republicans* and the *Democrats*, instead.

"Both imaginary parties are bossed by Winners. When Republicans battle Democrats, this much is certain: Winners will win.

"The Democrats have been the larger party in the past—because their leaders have not been as openly contemptuous of Losers as the Republicans have been.

"Losers can join imaginary parties. Losers can vote."

"Losers have thousands of religions, often of the *bleeding heart* variety," I would go on. "The single religion of the Winners is a harsh interpretation of *Darwinism*, which argues that it is the will of the universe that only the fittest should survive.

"The most pitiless Darwinists are attracted to the Republican party, which regularly purges itself of suspected *bleeding hearts*. It is in the process now of isolating and ejecting Representative Paul N. McCloskey, for instance, who has openly raged and even wept about the killing and maiming of Vietnamese.

"The Vietnamese are impoverished farmers, far, far away. The Winners in America have had them bombed and shot day in and day out, for years on end. This is not madness or foolishness, as some people have suggested. It is a way for the Winners to learn how to be pitiless. They understand that the material resources of the planet are almost exhausted, and that pity will soon be a form of suicide.

"The Winners are rehearsing for *Things to Come*."

"There is a witty winner, a millionaire named William F. Buckley, Jr.," I would go on, "who appears regularly in newspapers and on television. He bickers amusingly with people who think that Winners should help the Losers more than they do.

"He has a nearly permanent and always patronizing rictus when debating."

As a visitor from another planet, I would have nothing to lose socially in supposing that Buckley himself did not know the secret message of his smile. I would then guess at the message: "Yes, oh yes, my dear man—I understand what you have said so clumsily.

But you know in your heart what every Winner knows: that one must behave heartlessly toward Losers, if one hopes to survive."

That may not really be the message in the Buckley smile. But I guarantee you that it was the monolithic belief that underlay the Republican National Convention in Miami Beach, Florida, in 1972.

All the rest was hokum.

Listen: I went to a private luncheon for Winners in Miami Beach, while the convention was farting around several miles away. Nelson Rockefeller was there. John Kenneth Galbraith was there. William F. Buckley, Jr., was there. Arthur O. Sulzberger was there. Jacob Javits was there. Clare Boothe Luce was there. Art Buchwald was there. Barbara Walters was there. Everybody was there. Whether one was a Republican or a Democrat was a hilarious accident, which nobody was required to explain.

I asked Dr. Galbraith what he was doing at a Republican convention. He replied that he had been offered an *indecent* amount of money to banter with Buckley in the morning on NBC.

Barbara Walters invited me to appear on the *Today* show. I told her that I had nothing to say. The convention had left me speechless. It was so heavily guarded, spiritually and physically, that I hadn't been able to see or hear anything that wasn't already available in an official press release. "It's Disneyland under martial law," I said.

"You don't have to say much," she said.

"I'd have to say *something*," I said.

"Just say, 'hello,' " she said.

Hello.

Art Buchwald said he came to the convention in order to see his pals, mostly other news people. He told our table about a column he had just written. The comical premise was that the Republican party had attracted so many campaign contributions that it found itself with two billion dollars it couldn't spend. It decided to buy something nice for the American people. Here was the gift: a free week's bombing of Vietnam.

I asked Clare Boothe Luce what she thought of some young people's efforts to stimulate pity for the people of Vietnam. They had been dressing as Vietnamese there in Miami Beach, and carrying dolls that were painted to look as though they had been disemboweled and burned alive and so on.

Mrs. Luce wished the young people would take an automobile and fill it with something resembling blood. She said she had lost two members of her family in automobile accidents. Automobiles were easily the most terrible killers of our times, she said. Young people should protest about them.

As for the Nixon versus McGovern thing: Everybody was sure that Nixon would win. McGovern, I gathered, though nobody said so out loud, was the butt of a rather elegant practical joke. He was a Winner who had been encouraged by other Winners to identify himself with Losers, to bury himself up to his neck in the horseshit of Populism, so to speak.

Losers hate to vote for Losers. They know what Losers are.

So Nixon would win.

What remained to be discovered at the convention was, among other things, how much pity Republicans as individuals felt for the Vietnamese, and for Americans who were badly housed and badly nourished and so on.

The scientific conclusion is that there was a satisfactory level of pity when the delegates were ordinary social creatures, more or less in isolation and at rest, when majestic policies were not being promulgated in thundering meetings, when the delegates were not threatened by hostile crowds.

But there was a Pavlovian thing going on, and it has been going on for many years now: The wishes of the hostile crowds were invariably humanitarian, and the crowds weren't even hostile most of the time. But wherever they went, armies of policemen went too—to protect nice people from them.

So a Pavlovian connection has been made in the minds of people who are really awfully nice: When more than two people show up with a humanitarian idea, the police should be called.

If the police don't act immediately, and if the humanitarians behave in a manner that is dignified or beautiful or heartbreaking, there is still something nice people can do.

They can ignore the humanitarians.

This is what the nice people did when one of the most honorable military reviews in American history took place on the af-ternoon of August 22, 1972, in front of the Hotel Fontainebleau. This date will not go down in history, because nice people do not want it there.

Several hundred American gunfighters, killers from the war in Vietnam, formed themselves into platoons, with the proper in-tervals between the platoons. Many wore the raffish, spooky rags of modern jungle warfare. They marched silently, in the slope-shouldered route step of tired, hungry veterans—which they were. Their hair was often long, which gave them the cavalier beauty of Indian killers from another time.

Some were in wheelchairs. Many had wounds. John Wayne, the gunfighter's gunfighter, was in Miami Beach somewhere. But he was nowhere to be seen when these real gunfighters came to town. Here was Billy the Kid, multiplied by a thousand—not even whispering, and formed into platoons before the Fontainebleau.

They sat down silently, which was a crime. They were block-ing a public thoroughfare. Some sighed. Some scratched them-selves.

Their message was this: "Let the killing stop."

They went home again.

How many nice people came out of the hotel or came to hotel windows to watch them? None—almost none. It was a police affair.

As for the nonsensical business to be performed by run-of-the-mill delegates: It was mostly listening to speeches composed of glittering half-truths, of listening to eminent theologians pray, of getting autographs, of recoiling from hostile crowds. Saul Stein-berg, the most intelligent artist of our time, should have covered it for *The New Yorker*, along with Renata Adler and Richard Rovere.

It was all clouds and curlicues.

As for the prayers: I heard a lot of famous Republicans and eminent theologians pray at a Worship Service on the Sunday before the convention began. That is another date I would like to see go into American history books: August 20, 1972. In a mo-ment, I will explain why it belongs there.

I listened closely to all the preaching and praying. I wanted to learn, if I could, what the Republican God was shaped like. I came away with this impression: He was about the size of Mount Washington, and very slow to anger.

There were a lot of little sermons, but the main one was delivered, at the request of Richard M. Nixon himself, by Dr. D. Elton Trueblood, a Quaker philosopher, Professor at Large of Earlham College in Richmond, Indiana. Earlham, like Whittier College where Mr. Nixon went to school, is a Quaker school.

Dr. Trueblood's sermon surprised me at one point, because I thought I heard him say that the sovereignty exercised by American politicians came directly from God. Some other reporters there got the same impression. He was speaking extemporaneously, so no copies of the sermon were made available for a detailed check.

But I interviewed him afterward, and recorded our conversation, which went like this:

"After your sermon this morning," I said, "I heard someone say that you had traced sovereignty from the President directly to God. We are usually taught that the sovereignty of the President resides in the people. I was wondering, since you are a theologian—"

"I said nothing about the President," said Trueblood. "I said the sovereignty is God's, not ours, that all we do is under Judgment. This is a way to have a nonidolatrous patriotism."

"So the circuitry would go like this," I said, "if we were to lay it out like a wiring diagram: The President draws his sovereignty from the people, and the people draw it from God. Is that it?"

"No," he said. "I would put it another way: that God alone is sovereign. I accept Luther's doctrine of the two kingdoms of the Church and State, both under God. So that everything we do as a state is under Judgment, therefore derivative."

"So the President is simultaneously responsible to the people and to God?"

"But even more to God than to the people, of course," Dr. Trueblood replied.

I set this down so meticulously and without elisions because I think it proves my claim that on August 20, 1972, the Republican National Convention was opened with a sermon on the *Divine Right of Presidents.*

Of water commissioners too.

I told Dr. Trueblood that I thought Quakers were pacifists and that I was startled by the energy with which Richard M. Nixon, who had a Quaker background, could prosecute a war.

He said I had a simplistic notion about what Quakerism was, that a lot of Americans did. "Why," he said, "when I go around on speaking engagements, they all expect me to look like the man on the box of Quaker Oats."

"So, at this stage of American history, Quakers are an awful lot like everybody else?" I suggested.

Dr. Trueblood agreed heartily. "And we are just as mixed up as everybody else," he assured me. "And anybody that believes in a single pattern of Quaker, he is just plain stupid."

I said to him that many peace-loving people must know that he had the ear of the President and that they must have told him, "My God, Dr. Trueblood, tell him to stop the war."

"Yes," he said, "and often in a most nasty mood, very judgmental sometimes. And I say to them, 'Look here, he is trying to stop it. Don't hinder him in your self-righteousness.' I don't take any lip off them, you understand."

And this Quaker philosopher had even heavier news than that for the bleeding hearts. He was about to send to the President a little-known quotation from Abraham Lincoln, with whom Mr. Nixon in his wartime anguish identifies.

This was it:

We are indeed going through a great trial, a fiery trial. In the very responsible position in which I happen to be placed, being an humble instrument in the hands of our Heavenly Father, as I am and as we all are, to work out His great purposes I have decided that all my works and acts may be according to His Will. VERY DEAR TO ME AND MILLIONS OF OTHER AMERICANS OF ALL CREEDS, COLORS, AND RACES. SO APPROPRIATE IT IS THAT ON THIS SABBATH DAY WE COMMENCE OUR CONVENTION ACTIVITIES WITH THIS WORSHIP SERVICE.

I now accosted one of the hundreds of nubile girls who had flown to Miami at their own expense. They were living proof that young people were crazy about Mr. Nixon. I had heard them cry out their admiration for Ethel Merman at a party for celebrities and youth on the afternoon before.

"I am from *Harper's* magazine," I said, "and I would like to ask you if you think an atheist could possibly be a good President of the United States."

"I don't see how," she said.

"Why not?" I said.

"Well—" she said, "this whole country is founded on God."

"Could a Jew be a good President?" I asked.

"I don't know enough about that to say," she replied.

This was a beautiful white child. I tore my eyes away from her reluctantly, and what did I see? I saw ten American Indians sitting all by themselves on overstuffed furniture in the lobby. Nine were big male Indians.

One was an Indian boy.

Those Indians seemed to have turned to redwood. They did not talk. They did not swivel their heads around to see who was who.

They had a coffee table all to themselves. On it were mimeographed copies of a message they had come great distances to deliver. They were from many tribes.

As I would later discover, the message was addressed as follows: "Att'n: Richard M. Nixon, President U.S.A."

The message said this in part:

We come today in such a manner that must shame God himself. For a country which allows a complete body of people to exist in conditions which are at variance with the ideals of this country, conditions which daily commit injustices and inhumanity, must surely be filled with hate, greed, and unconcern.

I did not go directly to the Indians. I chatted first with a reporter friend. He told me a thing that Dr. Daniel Ellsberg, who had made the Pentagon Papers public, had said about Dr. Henry Kissinger, the President's strikingly happy adviser on foreign affairs. This was it: "Henry has the best deal Faust ever made with Mephistopheles."

I thought that was a ravishing remark. Ellsberg was at the convention, incidentally. Nobody seemed to notice him, even though he stood for everything good Republicans considered treacherous and vile. This was because he looked so much like just another security man.

I told my friend that I had watched Dr. Kissinger on television, while he made gifts of Dutch uncle smiles and autographs to a pair of little girls in white organdy. I was glad that Ellsberg brought up the subject of Mephistopheles, because the scene had seemed definitely evil to me.

Little girls represent life at its most playful and promising, I said. And anybody in Dr. Kissinger's job had a lot to do with random, pointless deaths in Vietnam these days—even deaths of little girls in white on our side. So evil came with the job. Under the circumstances, I found it ugly that a man in such a job would give out Dutch uncle smiles and autographs.

I now glimpsed Abbie Hoffman, the clowning revolutionary. He had been stopped for perhaps the dozenth time that day by security men, who looked just like Dr. Ellsberg. He was a weary clown by now. His press credentials were in order. He was gathering material for a book.

"Who you representing?" he was asked.

"*Field and Stream,*" he said.

I had the feeling he wasn't going to be clowning much more. A lot of naturally funny people who want to help Losers aren't going to clown anymore. They have caught on that clowning doesn't throw off the timing or slow down cruel social machinery. In fact, it usually serves as a lubricant.

Every so often somebody tells me that it is a delicious fact of history that clowns have often been the most effective revolutionaries. That isn't true. Cruel social machines in the past have needed clowns for lubrication so much that they have often manufactured them. Consider the Spanish Inquisition.

When the Inquisition was about to burn somebody alive in a public square, it shaved that person from head to foot. It tortured the person to the point of babbling idiocy, fitted him out with a dunce cap and a lurid paper cloak. His or her face was painted or masked.

Hey presto! A clown!

The idea, of course, was to make the victim comical rather than pitiful. Pity is like rust to a cruel social machine.

I do not say that America's Winners are about to burn America's Losers in public squares—although, if they did, it would be nothing new. I say that the Winners are avid to *neglect* the Losers, which is cruelty too.

And neglecting becomes easier, if only the victims or people who seem to represent them will look like clowns. If clownish-looking people hadn't come to Miami Beach to raise hell with the convention, there still would have been plenty of clowns in the cartoons and prose in campaign literature floating around—jackbooted lesbians, mincing male homosexuals, drug-crazed hippies, prostitutes on their way to the unemployment office in Cadillacs, big fat black mamas with thirteen children and no papa around.

News item from *First Monday*, an official party publication:

Yippie leader Jerry Rubin, a backer of Sen. George McGovern, "no longer" believes that people should kill their parents to demonstrate their dedication to change.

And so on.

And those Indians in the lobby of the Fontainebleau were moving so little, were saying so little because their people were dying of neglect, and they knew damn well that even if they sneezed, this would allow some people to dismiss them as clowning redskins.

So now they were in danger of becoming comical because of their petrified dignity.

These Indians had been harrowingly defeated by white men in greedy, unjust wars. They had been offered death or unconditional surrender—death, or life under hideous conditions. Those who had chosen life, which some people think is a holy thing, asked for mercy now. Their average life expectancy was only forty-six years. Their babies died with sickening regularity. Their water rights had been stolen. Some of their best men were woozy with tuberculosis and narcotics and booze. Their government-run schools were indifferent to Indian ideas of holiness, and so were the white man's laws of the land. One of the things the Indians had come to beg from President Nixon, who never begged anything from anybody, was that their religions be recognized as respectable religions under law.

As the law now stands, they told me, their religions are negligible superstitions deserving no respect.

I'll say this: Their religions couldn't possibly be more chaotic than the Christianity reinvented every day by Dr. D. Elton Trueblood, Professor at Large.

The Indian I talked to most was Ron Petite, a Chippewa. He said that he and the others had come from all over the country to Flamingo Park in Miami Beach, where Losers and friends of Losers had caused a tent city to be built. They moved right out again, disgusted and frightened by clowns.

They went to the Hollywood Indian Reservation, a few miles north of Miami, where Indian notions of sacredness and dignity were respected. They would not be represented there by some hairy white youth who was willing to set a flag on fire and piss on it as a surrogate for oppressed people everywhere.

Ron Petite told a very funny Indian story without cracking a smile. He and the others came into the Fontainebleau with their message to Mr. Nixon, and nobody of any importance would take it from them. They were ignored.

But then they saw people forming into lines. The President's daughters were going to give out autographs. So the Indians got into line too, and patiently waited their turn. Indians are legendary for patience.

When they arrived at last before Patricia or Julie—they weren't sure which—they gave her a message for Dad.

And her dad would say in his acceptance speech that night, among other things, "We covet no one else's territory. We seek no dominion over any other people. We seek peace not only for ourselves but for all the peoples in the world." This was what he had said on Russian television in May.

As a visitor from another planet, I would have to say that this

was only kind of true. I think of all the Winners at that private
party for Winners I went to, and how they like to live, and what
good care they take of their financial affairs. They want to go
anywhere on the planet and live however they please, buy whatever they please.

What could be more human than that?

They want to be planetary aristocrats, welcomed everywhere.
Again: What could be more human than that?

What seems to charm them as much as anything about the rap-
prochement with China is that they may soon be able to travel
there again. That charms *me* too.

If we really liked some part of China, we might want to put up
a little house there, or a motel—or a Colonel Sanders Kentucky
Fried Chicken franchise.

We don't covet anybody's territory. We would just like to buy
or rent some of it, if we can—and then everybody can get rich.

If I were a visitor from another planet, radioing home about
Earth, I wouldn't call Americans *Americans*. I would give them a
name that told a lot about them immediately: I would call them
Realtors.

I would call the Republicans *Super Realtors*. I would call the
Democrats *Inferior Realtors*. And one thing that fascinated me
about the Super Realtors' Worship Service on Sunday was that
Colonel Frank Borman was on the bill. He looked as tired of space
opera as Abbie Hoffman was of clowning. He did his bit, which
was to read about the Creation from *Genesis*, and that was that.

At no point in the Super Realtors' Convention was there any
Kennedy-style boosterism about the glorious opportunities for
Americans in outer space.

Since there were plenty of Republicans at the convention who
were dumb enough to believe that McGovern was really an en-
thusiast for acid, amnesty, and abortion, I am free to think that
they were dumb enough at one point to hope that nice properties
might be had for a song on the Moon.

They had sent some good Republicans up there to have a look
around, to cancel some stamps, to pray and hit a few golf balls,
and they knew better now. Not even Losers, with all their lazy
resourcefulness, could survive on the Moon.

So it was time to think hardheaded thoughts about efficient use of the surface of the Earth again.

And why not make friends again with our old friends the Chinese?

It was perhaps unkind of me to associate Dr. Kissinger with evil. That is no casual thing to do in a country as deeply religious as ours is.

As the mayor of Birmingham told us about our nation on Sunday,

WITH ALL OUR LABORS, SUCCESS OR FAILURE, NOW AND IN THE YEARS AHEAD IT WILL, GOD WILLING, ALWAYS BE "ONE NATION UNDER GOD."

Dr. Kissinger, after all, has been a healer of terrible wounds between the mightiest nations of all. But the Administration he serves is bad news for those nations that are feeble, or what the King James version of the Bible calls "the meek."

The Super Realtors, with Dr. Kissinger as their representative, have worked out crude agreements with the few other truly terrifying powers of the planet as to what can be done and what must not be done with the real estate of the meek.

The Nixon-Kissinger scheme, the Winners' scheme, the neo-Metternichian scheme for lasting world peace is simple. Its basic axiom is to be followed by individuals as well as great nations, by Losers and Winners alike. We have demonstrated the workability of the axiom in Vietnam, in Bangladesh, in Biafra, in Palestinian refugee camps, in our own ghettos, in our migrant labor camps, on our Indian reservations, in our institutions for the defective and the deformed and the aged.

This is it: *Ignore agony.*

I might, with justice and no irony, call Americans *Healers* instead of *Realtors.* I spoke to Art Linkletter at the convention, and he is profoundly bent on healing, and he is as typical an American as one could find.

He had visited South Korea recently, he said, where he had worked years ago to heal children hurt by warfare. They were healthy, happy men and women now. And he had gone to Vietnam too, to help the children with fresher wounds.

(And I must digress at this point to coin an acronym that can serve me now, which is "JACFU." A similar acronym, "JANFU," was coined during the Second World War, along with "SNAFU." It meant "Joint Army-Navy Fuck-Up." I would like "JACFU" to mean "Joint American-Communist Fuck-Up.")

And the children Art Linkletter and so many other Americans are mending or want to mend are surely victims of JACFU.

The walking wounded within our own boundaries, our undeserving poor, are not by any stretch of the imagination victims of JACFU. We creamed them ourselves. Money is tight. We can only afford to heal them a little bit; and even that little bit hurts Winners like bloody murder.

My close friend Dexter Leen, who is a shoe merchant in Hyannis on Cape Cod, used to read *The New York Times* every Sunday, and then come over to my house and tell me that, on the basis of what he had read in there, things were slowly but surely getting better all the time. I remember talking to him one time too, about awful automobile drivers we had known. He knew one woman, back in the days when all cars had radiator ornaments, who never took her eyes off her radiator ornament, he said.

And looking at one day's news or a few days' news or a few years' news is a lot like staring at the radiator ornament of a Stutz Bearcat, it seems to me. Which is why so many of us would love to have a visitor from another planet, who might have a larger view of our day-to-day enterprises, who might be able to give us some clue as to what is really going on.

He would tell us, I think, that no real Winner fears God or believes in a punitive afterlife. He might say that Earthlings put such emphasis on truthfulness in order to be believed when they lie. President Nixon, for instance, was free to lie during his acceptance speech at the convention, if he wanted to, because of his famous love for the truth. And the name of the game was "Survival." Everything else was hokum.

He might congratulate us for learning so much about healing the planet, and warn us against wounding the planet so horribly during our real estate dealings, that it might never heal.

The visitor might say by way of farewell what Charles Darwin seemed to say to us, and we might write his words in stone, all in capital letters, like the words of the mayor of Birmingham:

> THE WINNERS
> ARE AT WAR
> WITH THE LOSERS,
> AND THE FIX
> IS ON.
> THE PROSPECTS
> FOR PEACE ARE
> AWFUL.

Russell Baker

(1925–)

Russell Baker was born in 1853 aboard a schooner in the Maylay Straits, served as a bagman for the railroad during the administration of Ulysses S. Grant, and graduated eight years later from the University of Heidelberg. At least that's what it says on one of his book jackets. Further research reveals that in fact Baker served as a navy flyer in World War II, graduated from Johns Hopkins University in 1947, worked for the *Baltimore Sun* in Baltimore and in London, and moved to the *New York Times* in 1954, where he has worked ever since. His columns have been collected in, among several other volumes, *All Things Considered* (1965) and *The Rescue of Miss Yaskell and Other Pipe Dreams* (1983). He is the author of two memoirs, *Growing Up* (1982) and *The Good Times* (1989), and the editor of *The Norton Book of Light Verse* (1986) and *Russell Baker's Book of American Humor* (1993). Baker's "Observer" column on the *Times* op-ed page was printed three times a week from 1962 through 1988, and has appeared twice a week since then.

Universal Military Motion

The idea behind the MX missile system is sound enough. Place bomb-bearing missiles on wheels and keep them moving constantly through thousands of miles of desert so enemy bombers will not have a fixed target. To confuse things further, move decoy missiles over the same routes so the enemy cannot distinguish between false missiles and the real thing.

As my strategic thinkers immediately pointed out, however, the MX missile system makes very little sense unless matched by an MX Pentagon system. What is the point, they asked, of installing a highly mobile missile system if its command center, the Pentagon, remains anchored like a moose with four broken legs on the bank of the Potomac River?

This is why we propose building 250 moveable structures so precisely like the Pentagon that no one can tell our fake Pentagons from the real thing and to keep all of them, plus the real Pentagon, in constant motion through the country.

Our first plan was to move only the real Pentagon, which would be placed on a large flat-bottom truck bed and driven about the countryside on the existing highway system. We immediately realized, however, that this would not provide sufficient protection against nuclear attack. The Pentagon is very big and easily noticeable. When it is driven along at 55 miles per hour, people can see it coming from miles away. It attracts attention. In short, it is a fat, easily detected target.

With 250 fake Pentagons constantly cruising the roads, the problem is solved. Now, trying to distinguish the real Pentagon from the fake Pentagons, enemy attackers will face the maddening problem of finding a needle in a haystack. With 251 Pentagons in circulation, the sight of a Pentagon on the highway will attract no more attention than a politician's indictment. Thus we foil the enemy's spies.

Still, to add another margin of security we will confuse matters further by building 1,500 Pentagon-shaped fast-food restaurants along the nation's highways.

Each will be an exact replica of the real Pentagon, at least as seen from the outside. Inside, of course, they will be equipped to provide all the necessities for producing acute indigestion, thus providing the wherewithal of highway travel and, in the process, earning the Government a little return on its investment.

Occasionally, when generals and admirals tire of touring and yearn for a little stability, the real Pentagon will be parked alongside the road to masquerade as a fast-food Pentagon. The danger of highway travelers wandering in for a quick hot dog and making trouble while the authentic Pentagon is in the "parked" or "fast-food" mode has also been considered.

These interlopers will simply be told by receptionists that hot dogs are in the back of the building and directed to walk the long route around the Pentagon's outer ring. As they drop from exhaustion they will be removed by military police, carried to their cars, given free hot dogs and advised that next time they should enter their Pentagon fast-food dispensary through the rear door.

There are problems to be ironed out in the MX Pentagon, but we are too busy at the moment perfecting our MX Congress system to trifle with details. With 850 United States Capitols on the highway, we have an extremely touchy problem in deciding whether a Capitol or a Pentagon should have the right of way when they meet at an intersection.

Our proposal to build the MX Pentagon has created serious opposition among highway-safety advocates. Because of its great size and weight, they say, a Pentagon being hauled along the highway at 55 miles per hour is a serious threat to other vehicles.

Unfortunately, this is correct. We tested our first prototype of the fake Pentagon in New Jersey Wednesday with sobering results. The driver had to apply his brakes violently when a van tried to cut him off in traffic, and the Pentagon flew off the truck bed and dented Ho-Ho-Kus.

Our engineers say this problem can be solved by reducing the weight. They propose to do so by eliminating several acres of reserved parking lots attached to the Pentagon.

Opposition from generals and admirals is intense, but our political advisers believe we can work out a happy compromise by eliminating just the enlisted men's parking lots.

Another serious difficulty is posed by the tight clearances on highway tunnels and bridges. Whoever designed the Lincoln Tunnel, for example, apparently cared not a fig about national security.

At present, as we discovered when taking our prototype out for road tests, the Lincoln Tunnel is utterly inadequate to handle Pentagons. Fortunately, since ours was a fake we were able to dismantle it and haul it through in sections. When the system is operational, however, the real Pentagon will also be on the road and it will surely want to enjoy a drive on the Manhattan Westway.

We are already in conference with agents of the Army Corps of Engineers about constructing tunnels under the Hudson generous enough to accommodate the MX Pentagon. Their mouths are watering at the prospects of Congressional appropriations that will be necessary to do the job.

The Navy is pressing us to accept an even more bankruptive solution. It wants to fit every Pentagon with an immense retractable steel hull. With this added feature, each Pentagon could approach the Hudson River ready to steam across.

And not only the Hudson River, as the Navy points out. Imagine an enemy bomber's confusion when, sighting a Pentagon steaming from Weehawken to 34th Street, he adjusts his bomb sights only to discover the Pentagon suddenly sailing down the harbor and out to Martha's Vineyard for the weekend.

Having encouraged the Navy to submit estimates, we were not surprised when the Air Force approached us with a proposal to make all Pentagons airworthy. Because of its air-resistant five-sided configuration, this plan would require wings more than 40 miles long.

Our engineers dislike the idea, because even with wings twice that length a Pentagon would be unable to achieve altitudes greater than 75 feet. The Air Force contends, however, that a low-flying Pentagon would make an impossible target for today's high-speed bombers.

Moreover, if equipped with .50-caliber machine guns and small rockets it would make a devastating weapon for strafing any Congressmen trying to attack the Pentagon's budget, they note.

Our strategic thinkers are reluctant to undertake such radical modifications. It would do our reputation for high-class strategic thinking no good at all if a fake Pentagon had engine trouble and crashed on a medium-size city. As Hermann Pflugelgasser, one of our most brilliant strategic thinkers, observed while we were watching the Yankees game on television the other night, "We've already got the real Pentagon on our backs, who needs a fake Pentagon on the head?"

Life has become a constant burden, thanks to the recent surge of skepticism about the accuracy of what is written in the newspapers.

Last night, for example, my garage was invaded by investigators

looking for evidence that fictions have been published in this column. Imagine my rage. That anyone should think I might stoop
to publishing fiction in the newspaper. . . .

What had aroused these busybodies was my series of reports
about the MX Pentagon. These articles, in case you missed them,
outlined my program for building 250 fake Pentagons and keeping them constantly moving around the American highways on
trucks, along with the real Pentagon, to confuse enemy bombers.

As I have patiently explained time and again, the MX Pentagon
system is an essential companion piece to the MX missile system,
which will keep several hundred missiles moving constantly
around the Southwestern desert to confuse Russian targeters
about where our H-bombs might be coming from. What's the
point of keeping the Russians confused about the whereabouts of
our H-bombs if we don't confuse them about the Pentagon too?

Anyhow, these snoopers suspected my MX Pentagon program
was a fiction. Such is the cynicism of the modern newspaper
reader.

"Your last article said you'd already built three prototype models of the fake Pentagon in this garage," the chief investigator
said. "I don't see any Pentagons in this garage."

Of course he didn't. As I explained, all three were then being
driven around the continent to test whether motorists passing
them on the highway could tell them from the real Pentagon.

One of his lieutenants, obviously hoping to impress the boss
investigator with his brain power, said, "Chief, there isn't room
in this garage to build three Pentagons."

"That's right," said the chief. "In fact, this garage isn't even
big enough to hold one Pentagon."

"Of course not," I noted. "If you observe closely, you will see
it isn't even big enough to contain all of my 1969 Buick Electra."

"So you published fiction in the newspaper, eh?" (Cries of "Resign! Resign!")

It was easy to calm them. "Do you really want me to notify the
Russians where our fake Pentagons are built?"

They agreed I had a point there, and one or two even con-
gratulated me on not being "one of those freedom-of-information
freaks."

"Nevertheless," said the chief investigator, "you'll have to reveal—strictly in confidence, mind you—where the fake Pentagons are being built, or we'll nail you for trying to hornswoggle the American newspaper reader."

So I confided the secret to him. "I build them in the cellar."

"Nobody can build a Pentagon in the cellar," he said. "You'd never get it up the steps."

"Are you accusing me of fictionalizing?"

He was. "In that case, Mr. Doubting Thomas, let's go inside and have a look."

We went to the cellar.

"Just as I suspected," he said. "There's no Pentagon construction going on in here."

"Of course not," I said. "Do you take me for an idiot? For all I know, you could be an agent of the K.G.B. One word from you, and Moscow could be lobbing in one of the big babies and there goes my cellar, not to mention the center of American fake-Pentagon construction."

He looked skeptical. These people are very good at looking skeptical, but not at much else. Apparently, it rarely occurs to them to think.

Since he was obviously baffled, I explained. "Before undertaking construction of the MX Pentagon, I built 2,500 MX cellars which are now located in scattered excavations all over the continent. In one of these cellars, whose location is known only to me, fake Pentagons are now being produced at a prodigious pace. If the Russians decided to take out our fake-Pentagon production capability, their chances of hitting the right one would be practically nil."

"Who's paying for this MX cellar program?" he asked.

"That's not the question," I explained. "The question is, are you, as a patriotic American citizen, willing to pay for a program that will counter the Russians' MX Kremlin system?"

He was astonished to hear about the MX Kremlin. "Oh yes," I confided, "the Russians are building 5,000 fake Kremlins to be kept constantly on the move in order to confuse our bombers. I have the intelligence from captured documents."

Naturally he wanted to see the captured documents. "Impossible," I explained. "They have already been fed into my MX captured-document-shredder system, which consists of 10,000

paper shredders kept in constant circulation between Tallahassee
and Syracuse.''

"You're trying to put me on, aren't you?" he said. It was painful
to see a man so far beyond the healthy reach of truth.

Having managed to convey the impression that they are against
mother's milk, down on orphans and fairly relaxed about torture
conducted by friends of American foreign policy, the Reagan people are now trying to restore bribery's good name.

Like most Reagan enterprises, this one aims to unshackle American business. Because bribery is an ancient tradition in many
foreign lands, Americans are said to be at a competitive disadvantage in foreign markets since they are legally prohibited from
coughing up the baksheesh.

The Administration is now pressing Congress to do something
about it; namely, to decriminalize payoffs to foreign parasites. Naturally, American parasites are outraged. I speak with authority
here. As designer and prime contractor of the MX Pentagon, I
recently retained a highly patriotic parasite to survey the possibilities of enlarging our revenues.

The MX Pentagon program, as I have made clear in the past,
is a vast undertaking. Its aim is to strengthen national security by
building 250 fake Pentagons and keeping them constantly moving
about the country, along with the real Pentagon, to confuse enemy bombers.

A project of this size naturally creates many lucrative opportu-
nities. To cite a small example, in order to give our fake Pen-
tagons absolute authenticity we will need 250 fake Caspar
Weinbergers capable of rising from their desks in our 250 fake
Secretary of Defense offices to shake hands with 250 fake Ronald
Reagans.

Our plant, which is located in my cellar, can produce an excellent fake Weinberger, but lacks the special technology necessary to turn out a good fake Reagan.

Soviet spies seeing our own fake Reagans shaking hands with
our fake Weinbergers would instantly spot the Reagans as nothing
more than foam-filled Naugahyde dummies and signal their
bombers not to waste their time. For this reason we plan to sub-
contract the fake Reagan construction job to another company.

This will be worth a sweet pile of cash once we get our appropriation money from Congress. We are already beset by manufacturers watering at the mouth over prospects of cost overruns. Naturally, I retained a parasite.

His task was to discover which fake-Reagan manufacturer would pay the most to get the contract. I was astonished, as he was, when he returned with news that not a single bidder was willing to slip a sawbuck under the table, much less the $50 million we had anticipated might be available to help me finance a much-needed vacation at Asbury Park and enable him to buy a one-bedroom apartment in Manhattan.

Under existing law, such payments were prohibited as criminal bribes, the companies told him. Well, here was a fine how-de-do.

The man who conceived, planned and was preparing to create the nation's MX Pentagon system was expected to risk everything, yet his nation treated him like a common criminal if he tried to reap the fruits of his venture. What had happened to the American tradition of rewarding initiative?

At this moment the Administration moved toward the rescue, and I discovered that Congress was considering legalizing "bribery," as certain bleeding hearts called it, abroad.

Intense research by our foreign-development staff turned up 15 companies in sundry Asian backwaters and sandy ovens around the Mediterranean littoral that could produce quite a decent fake Reagan. All were willing to honor their ancient tradition by paying satchels of moolah for the contract, but none would pay it to my personal parasite.

Each country had its own domestic agent for collecting, skimming and transmitting the residue of the corporate payoff. Companies that make payoffs to American parasites are apparently closed down next day by their governments.

As a result, I am now in touch with assorted princes, sheiks, beys, interior ministers, kings, queens and jacks. All are prepared to collect plenty from the company that wins the fake-Reagan contract, and to remit enough for two weeks in Asbury Park.

Naturally, I have dismissed my domestic parasite, and he is furious. In fact, he has gone to Washington to lobby against the Administration's scheme. He says it is a conspiracy to deprive American parasites of their livelihood and will only increase the

flow of capital out of the United States at a time when the balance
of payments is already against us.

These political arguments do not interest us here at the command center of the MX Pentagon program. Our concern is the
national security. We are already searching for a subcontractor in
desert or jungle who can produce a fake Pentagon V.I.P. mess so
realistic that Russian bombers can't tell it from the real thing.

If this search and Congressional action go well, I anticipate not
only two weeks in Asbury Park, but also the convenience of a
rental car for the entire stay.

Art Buchwald

(1925–   )

Art Buchwald was born in Mt. Vernon, New York, and grew up in New York City. He served in the marines in World War II, then went to the University of California, but never graduated. Instead he moved to Paris, where he went to work as a columnist for the *International Herald Tribune*. In 1952 the *New York Herald Tribune* syndicated his column, which, although it dealt primarily with French and European matters, was extremely popular in the U.S. By 1962 he had moved to Washington, D.C., where he has written his column ever since. It is now syndicated by the *Los Angeles Times* and appears in more than 550 newspapers around the world. Buchwald is the author of twenty-eight books, including collections of columns, two children's books, and a novel. His autobiography, *Leaving Home*, was published in 1994. Buchwald received the Pulitzer prize for outstanding commentary in 1982.

Pictures From Vietnam

The President was sitting in his Oval Office when Henry Kissinger walked in.

"Say, Henry, these photographs of the moon are fantastic."

"They're not photographs of the moon, Mr. President, they're the latest aerial pictures from South Vietnam."

"Vietnam?"

"Yes, sir. There are now fifty-two million craters in South Vietnam. By the end of the year we should go over the one hundred million mark.''

"That's great, Henry. But I don't see any towns in the photographs.''

"Here. You see this series of rock outcroppings? That was a town. And over here, this bleak, flat, open space—that was a town. And here where this giant hole is—that's a provincial capital.''

"Well, you could have fooled me. There doesn't seem to be much green in the photographs.''

"No, sir, Mr. President. The defoliation program took care of the green. But you notice there's lots of gray.''

"What does that signify, Henry?''

"Our B-52 pacification program is working. Green means cover for the North Vietnamese. Gray means they have to fight in the open. The more gray on the photographs, the better chance we have of turning back naked aggression.''

"What are these brown streaks here?''

"They used to be roads, Mr. President. But you can't call them that anymore.''

"I guess you can't. Where are the hamlets where we have won the hearts and minds of the people?''

"Most of them are in these blue areas, underwater. We had to bomb the dams so the enemy couldn't capture the rice.''

"Uh-huh. I see there are a lot of black areas in the photos. Does that signify anything?''

"Yes, sir. It means our scorched earth policy is working. Every black area on this photograph means the North Vietnamese have been deprived of supplies and shelter. We've left them nothing.''

"Good thinking, Henry. Where are the people?''

"What people, Mr. President?''

"The people we're defending against an imposed Communist government.''

"You can't see them in the photographs. They're hiding in the craters.''

"And the South Vietnamese army?''

"They're hiding in these craters over here.''

"I see. I wish these photographs could be printed in Hanoi. It would certainly give the North Vietnamese something to think about.''

"So do I, Mr. President. Now, this area over here by the sea still has some green in it."

"I was going to ask you about that, Henry."

"The Navy assures me that it should be gray and black in three weeks. It's the type of terrain that lends itself better to shelling than to bombing."

"Well, Henry, I want you to know I believe these are excellent photographs, and I want you to send a 'well done' cable to everyone responsible. The only thing that worries me is what happens if we get a cease fire? Isn't it going to be awfully expensive to make everything green again?"

"Don't worry, Mr. President, we've thought of that. We've asked for bids from the companies who make artificial turf. Once the shooting stops, we're going to carpet South Vietnam from wall to wall."

Telling the Truth

The Pentagon is seriously considering the use of lie detectors to test the veracity of its three million employees, as well as defense contractors and government workers in other departments. They say they want to use the polygraph tests for security reasons.

I have no objection to Defense resorting to lie detector tests providing that the top people take them, too, particularly when testifying on the Hill concerning the military budget.

It doesn't seem too much to ask Secretary Weinberger, his top assistants, and the high-level brass to put on electrodes when they face a House or Senate Armed Services Committee. With the help of this equipment, all of us might be better informed as to what a weapons system will really cost.

"The congressional committee will come to order. General, are you comfortable? Let's just test the polygraph machine to see if it is working. What branch of the service are you in, sir?"

"Nothing can stop the United States Air Force."

"The lie detector checks out fine. We'll now proceed with the questioning. Could you give us some idea what the B-one bomber will cost?"

"Two hundred million dollars."

"Hmmm, the polygraph seems to indicate that is the wrong answer."

"I'm sorry, sir. I didn't understand the question. Do you mean with wings and wheels on it?"

"I'm afraid I wasn't specific. Yes, I do."

"To get it in the air it will cost $234,567,891.50."

"Good. Now this would only be the bare plane and not include such items as radar, communications, bomb racks, cruise missile launcher, and parking lights?"

"That's correct, sir. We might add on another forty million dollars for the equipment, give or take five million."

"The polygraph is acting up again, General. How much did you say?"

"Sixty-five million dollars."

"Very good, General. Now may I ask you about the tests the Air Force has made on the B-one? Are your people satisfied that the contractor will bring in the plane at that price without serious overruns?"

"We're certain of it, sir. They should deliver it on schedule without any bugs in it."

"The needle seems to be flying all over the place. Are you sure of this?"

"No, sir. We're not. But we need the plane."

"We're going to give you the plane, General. We just want to know what we're getting for our money."

"Every plane has bugs in it."

"Don't pout. We know that. Which brings us to the question of the C-five-A cargo plane. We understand a lot of cracks are showing up in the wings. How much will it cost to put on new wings?"

"Half a billion dollars."

"Would you like to try that again?"

"I meant to say a billion dollars. These electrodes are giving me a headache."

"We're sorry about that, General. But actually the idea for introducing the lie detector came out of the Defense Department. Since you people have been using it so successfully we decided to use it, too."

"We're only using it to find out who the whistle-blowers are in the department, and who is leaking detrimental stuff to the press. We would never use it on someone discussing the Defense Department budget."

"Why not, General?"

"Because when it comes to military spending testimony, we consider ourselves officers and gentlemen."

Gore Vidal
(1925–   )

Gore Vidal's father was the first aviation instructor at the United States Military Academy (where the writer was born), and later director of the Bureau of Air Commerce in the Roosevelt administration. His maternal grandfather, T. P. Gore, was a U.S. Senator. Vidal graduated from Exeter, joined the army at the age of seventeen, and served during World War II. He sailed on an army ship, and while on night watch in port wrote his first novel, *Williwaw*, which was published in 1946. He is the author of short stories, television and stage plays, and screenplays, and is perhaps best known for his multivolume fictional chronicle of American history, which Gabriel García Márquez called "historical novels or novelized histories." His essays on literature and politics, one of which is printed here, are famous both for their insight and their mordant wit.

Ronnie and Nancy:
A Life in Pictures

1

I first saw Ronnie and Nancy Reagan at the Republican convention of 1964 in San Francisco's Cow Palace. Ronnie and Nancy (they are called by these names throughout Laurence Leamer's

book *Make-Believe: The Story of Nancy and Ronald Reagan*) were
seated in a box to one side of the central area where the cows—
the delegates, that is—were whooping it up. Barry Goldwater
was about to be nominated for president. Nelson Rockefeller
was being booed not only for his communism but for his inde-
cently uncloseted heterosexuality. Who present that famous day
can ever forget those women with blue-rinsed hair and leathery
faces and large costume jewelry and pastel-tinted dresses with
tasteful matching accessories as they screamed "Lover!" at Nelson? It was like a TV rerun of *The Bacchae*, with Nelson as
Pentheus.

I felt sorry for Nelson. I felt sorry for David Brinkley when a
number of seriously overweight Sunbelt Goldwaterites chased him
through the kitchens of the Mark Hopkins Hotel. I felt sorry for
myself when I, too, had to ward off their righteous wrath: I was
there as a television commentator for Westinghouse. I felt sorry
for the entire media that day as fists were actually shaken at the
anchorpersons high up in the eaves of the hall. I felt particularly
sorry for the media when a former president named Eisenhower,
reading a speech with his usual sense of discovery, attacked the
press, and the convention hall went mad. At last Ike was giving it
to those commie-weirdo-Jew-fags who did not believe in the real
America of humming electric chairs, well-packed prisons, and
kitchens filled with every electrical device that a small brown person of extranational provenance might successfully operate at a
fraction of the legal minimum wage.

As luck would have it, I stood leaning on the metal railing that
enclosed the boxed-in open place where, side by side, Ronnie and
Nancy were seated watching Ike. Suddenly, I was fascinated by
them. First, there was her furious glare when someone created a
diversion during Ike's aria. She turned, lip curled with Bacchan-
tish rage, huge unblinking eyes afire with a passion to kill the
enemy so palpably at hand—or so it looked to me. For all I know
she might have been trying out new contact lenses. In any case, I
had barely heard of Nancy then. Even so, I said to myself: There
is a lot of rage in this little lady. I turned then to Ronnie. I had
seen him in the flesh for a decade or so as each of us earned his
mite in the Hollyjungle. Ronnie was already notorious for his

speeches for General Electric, excoriating communists who were, apparently, everywhere. I had never actually spoken to him at a party because I knew—as who did not?—that although he was the soul of amiability when not excoriating the international mono- lithic menace of atheistic godless communism, he was, far and away, Hollywood's most grinding bore—Chester Chatterbox, in fact. Ronnie never stopped talking, even though he never had anything to say except what he had just read in the *Reader's Digest*, which he studied the way that Jefferson did Montesquieu. He also told show-biz stories of the sort that overexcites civilians in awe of old movie stars, but causes other toilers in the industry to stampede.

I had heard that Reagan might be involved in the coming cam- paign. So I studied him with some care. He was slumped in a folding chair, one hand holding up his chins; he was totally con- centrated on Eisenhower. I remember thinking that I had made the right choice in 1959 when we were casting *The Best Man*, a play that I had written about a presidential convention. An agent had suggested Ronald Reagan for the lead. We all had a good laugh. He is by no means a bad actor, but he would hardly be convincing, I said with that eerie prescience which has earned me the title the American Nostradamus, as a presidential candidate. So I cast Melvyn Douglas, who could have made a splendid pres- ident in real life had his career not been rejuvenated by the play's success, while the actor whom I had rejected had no choice but to get himself elected president. I do remember being struck by the intensity with which Reagan studied Eisenhower. I had seen that sort of concentration a thousand times in half-darkened the- atres during rehearsals or Saturday matinees: The understudy ex- amines the star's performance and tries to figure how it is done. An actor prepares, I said to myself: Mr. Reagan is planning to go into politics. With his crude charm, I was reasonably certain that he could be elected mayor of Beverly Hills.

In time all things converge. The campaign biography and the movie star's biography are now interchangeable. The carefully packaged persona of the old-time movie star resembles nothing so much as the carefully packaged persona of today's politician. Was it not inevitable that the two would at last coincide in one person? That that person should have been Ronald Reagan is a

curiosity of more than minor interest. George Murphy had broken the ice, as it were, by getting elected to the Senate from
California. Years earlier Orson Welles had been approached
about a race for the Senate. Welles is highly political; he is also
uncommonly intelligent. "I was tempted, but then I was talked
out of it," he said over lunch—cups of hot butter with marrow
cubes at Pat's Fish House in Hollywood. "Everyone agreed I could
never win because I was an actor and divorced." He boomed his
delight.

Since Mr. Leamer is as little interested in politics and history
as his two subjects, he is in some ways an ideal chronicler. He
loves the kind of gossip that ordinary folks—his subjects and their
friends—love. He takes an O'Haran delight in brand names while
the "proper" names that are most often seen in syndicated columns ravish him. On the other hand, he is not very interested in
the actual way politics, even as practiced by Ronnie, works. Although Reagan's eight years as governor of California are of some
interest, Leamer gets through the-time-in-Sacramento as quickly
as possible, with only one reference to Bob Moretti, the Democratic speaker of the assembly who, in effect, ran the state while
Ronnie made his speeches around state, country, world on the
dangers of communism. When in town, Ronnie played with his
electric trains (something omitted by Mr. Leamer). On the other
hand, there are twenty-four references to "wardrobe" in the index. So, perhaps, Mr. Leamer has got his priorities right after all.
In any case, he never promised us a Rosebud.

Leamer begins with the inaugural of the fortieth president. First
sentence: "On a gilded California day, Ronald and Nancy Reagan
left their home for the last time." That is *echt Photoplay* and there
is much, much more to come. Such lines as: "She had begun
dating him when he thought he would never love again." You
know, I think I will have some of those Hydrox cookies after all.
"Unlike many of his backers, Ronnie was no snob. He believed
that everybody should have his shot at this great golden honeypot
of American free enterprise." The Golden Horde now arrives in
Washington for the inaugural. "Ostentatious," growled that old
meanie Barry Goldwater, nose out of joint because the man who
got started in politics by giving The Speech for him in 1964 kept

on giving The Speech for himself, and so, sixteen years and four wonderful presidents later, got elected Numero Uno.

Leamer tells us about their wardrobes for the great day. Also, "as a teenager and a young woman, [Nancy] had had her weight problems, but now at fifty-nine [Leamer finks on Nancy: Long ago she sliced two years off her age] she was a perfect size six. Her high cheekbones, huge eyes, delicate features and extraordinary attention to appearance made her lovelier than she had ever been." According to the testimony of the numerous ill-reproduced photographs in the book, this is quite true. The adventures simply of Nancy's nose down the years is an odyssey that we *Photoplay* fans would like to know a lot more about. At first there is a bulb on the tip; then the bulb vanishes but there is a certain thickness around the bridge; then, suddenly, retroussé triumph!

The inaugural turns out to be a long and beautiful commercial to Adolfo, Blass, Saint Laurent, Galanos, de la Renta, and Halston. At one point, Ronnie reads a poem his mother had written; there were "tears in his eyes." During the ceremonies, Ronnie said later, "It was so hard not to cry during the whole thing." But then Ronnie had been discovered, groomed, and coiffed, by the brothers Warner, who knew how to produce tears on cue with Max Steiner's ineffable musical scores. So overwhelming was Maestro Steiner that at one point, halfway up the stairs to die nobly in *Dark Victory*, Bette Davis suddenly stopped and looked down at the weeping director and crew and said, "Tell me now. Just who is going up these goddamned stairs to die? Me or Max Steiner?" She thought the teary music a bit hard on her thespian talents. No, I don't like the Oreos as much as the Hydrox but if that's all there is. . . .

"As her husband spoke . . . her eyes gleamed with tears," while "the Mormon Tabernacle choir brought tears to his eyes." Tears, size sixes, Edwards-Lowell furs, Jimmy and Gloria Stewart, Roy Rogers and Dale Evans, new noses and old ideas, with charity toward none . . . then a final phone call to one of Nancy's oldest friends who says: "Oh, Nancy, you aren't a movie star now, not the biggest movie star. You're the star of the whole world. The biggest star of all." To which Nancy answers, "Yes, I know, and it scares me to death." To which, halfway around the world, at

Windsor Castle, an erect small woman of a certain age somewhat less than that of Nancy is heard to mutter, "What is all this shit?"

Mr. Leamer's book is nicely organized. After "A Gilded Dawn," he flashes back to tell us Nancy's story up until she meets Ronnie (who thought he would never love again); then Mr. Leamer flashes back and tells us Ronnie's story up until that momentous meeting. Then it is side by side into history. Curiously enough Nancy's story is more interesting than Ronnie's because she is more explicable and Mr. Leamer can get a grip on her. Ronnie is as mysterious a figure as ever appeared on the American political stage.

Nancy's mother was Edith Luckett, an actress from Washington, D.C. She worked in films and on the stage: "Edith's just been divorced from a rich playboy who's not worth the powder to blow him up." There is a lot of fine period dialogue in *Make-Believe*. Edith's father was a Virginian who worked for the old Adams Express Company where, thirty-one years earlier, John Surratt had worked; as you will recall, Surratt was one of the conspirators in the Abraham Lincoln murder case. Mr. Leamer tactfully omits this ominous detail.

Edith's marriage to Ken Robbins, "a handsome stage-door johnny . . . from a far better family than Edith's," is skimpily, even mysteriously, described by Mr. Leamer. Where did they meet? When and where were they married? Where did they live? All we are told is that "when Ken entered the service in 1917, he and Edith were newlyweds. But he had his duties and she had her career. . . . Ken had been released from the army in January 1919. Edith had tried to keep the marriage going with her twenty-three-year-old husband [with her career? his duties?], but all she had to show for it was a baby, born on July 6, 1921, in New York City. Ken hadn't even been there." After two years of dragging Nancy around with her ("using trunks as cradles," what else?) Edith parked baby with her older sister, Virginia, in Maryland, while Ken went to live with his mother in New Jersey. So when were Edith and Ken divorced? It does not help that Mr. Leamer constantly refers to Ken as Nancy's "natural father."

Nancy was well looked after by her aunt; she was sent to Sidwell Friends School in Washington, some four years before I went

there. Mr. Sidwell was an ancient Quaker whose elephantine ears
were filled with hair while numerous liver spots made piebald his
kindly bald head. I used to talk to him occasionally: *Never once did
he mention Nancy Robbins.*

Meanwhile, Edith had found Mr. Right, Loyal Davis, M.D.,
F.A.C.S., a brain surgeon of pronounced reactionary politics and
a loathing of the lesser breeds, particularly those of a dusky hue.
The marriage of Edith and Loyal (I feel I know them, thanks to
Mr. Leamer) seems to have been happy and, at fourteen, Nancy
got herself adopted by Mr. Davis and took his name. Nancy Davis
now "traveled at the top of Chicago's social world." She was a
school leader. Yearbook: "Nancy's social perfection is a constant
source of amazement. She is invariably becomingly and suitably
dressed. She can talk, and even better listen intelligently . . ."
Thus was child begetter of the woman and First Lady-to-be. Destiny was to unite her with a man who has not stopped talking,
according to his associates and relatives, for threescore years at
least.

Nancy went to Smith and to deb parties. She herself had a tea-
dance debut in Chicago. She had beaux. She was a bit overweight,
while her nose was still a Platonic essence waiting to happen. A
friend of her mother's, ZaSu Pitts, gave Nancy a small part in a
play that she was bringing to Broadway. From an early age, Nancy
had greasepaint in her eyes. The play opened on Broadway un-
successfully but Nancy stayed on. She modeled, looked for work
(found it in *Lute Song*), dated famous family friends, among them
Clark Gable, who after a few drinks would loosen his false teeth,
which were on some sort of peg and then shake his head until
they rattled like dice. I wonder if he ever did that for Nancy. Can
we ever really and truly know *anyone*? The Oreos are stale.

Hollywood came Nancy's way in the form of Benny Thau, a vice
president of MGM. Nancy had a "blind date" with him. In 1949
Thau was a great power at the greatest studio. He got Nancy a
screen test, and a contract. By now Nancy was, as Mr. Leamer puts
it,

dating Benny Thau. Barbara, the pretty teen-age receptionist, saw
Nancy frequently. Many years later she remembered that she had
orders that on Sunday morning Nancy was to be sent directly into

Benny Thau's suite. Barbara nodded to Miss Davis as she walked into the vice-president's office; nodded again when she left later.

No wonder Nancy thinks the ERA is just plain silly.

Now Mr. Leamer cuts to the career of Ronnie ("Dutch") Reagan. This story has been told so much that it now makes no sense at all. Dixon, Illinois. Father drank (Irish Catholic). Mother stern (Protestant Scots-Irish); also, a fundamentalist Christian, a Disciple of Christ. Brother Neil is Catholic. Ronnie is Protestant. Sunday School teacher. Lifeguard. Eureka College. Drama department. Debating society. Lousy grades. Lousy football player but eager to be a successful jock (like Nixon and Ike *et al.* . . . What would happen if someone who could really play football got elected president?). Imitates radio sportscasters. Incessantly. Told to stop. Gets on everyone's nerves. Has the last laugh. Got a job as . . . sportscaster. At twenty-two. Midst of depression. Gets better job. Goes west. Meets agent. Gets hired by Warner Brothers as an actor. Becomes, in his own words, "the Errol Flynn of the B's."

Mr. Leamer bats out this stuff rather the way the studio press departments used to do. He seems to have done no firsthand research. Dutch is a dreamer, quiet (except that he talks all the time, from puberty on), unread and incurious about the world beyond the road ahead, which was in his case a thrilling one for a boy at that time: sportscaster at twenty-two and then film actor and movie star.

Mr. Leamer might have done well to talk to some of the California journalists who covered Reagan as governor. I was chatting with one last year, backstage in an Orange County auditorium. When I said something to the effect how odd it was that a klutz like Reagan should ever have been elected president, the journalist then proceeded to give an analysis of Reagan that was far more interesting than Mr. Leamer's mosaic of *Photoplay* tidbits. "He's not stupid at all. He's ignorant, which is another thing. He's also lazy, so what he doesn't know by now, which is a lot, he'll never know. That's the way he is. But he's a perfect politician. He knows exactly how to make the thing work for him."

I made some objections, pointed to errors along the way, not to mention the storms now gathering over the republic. "You

can't look at it like that. You see, he's not interested in politics as
such. He's only interested in himself. Consider this. Here is a
fairly handsome ordinary young man with a pleasant speaking
voice who first gets to be what he wants to be and everybody else
then wanted to be, a radio announcer [equivalent to an anchor-
person nowadays]. Then he gets to be a movie star in the Golden
Age of the movies. Then he gets credit for being in the Second
World War while never leaving L.A. Then he gets in at the start
of television as an actor and host. Then he picks up a lot of rich
friends who underwrite him politically and personally and get him
elected governor twice of the biggest state in the union and then
they get him elected president, and if he survives he'll be re-
elected. The point is that here is the only man I've ever heard of
who got everything that he ever wanted. That's no accident."

I must say that as I stepped out on to the stage to make my
speech, I could not help but think that though there may not be
a God there is quite possibly a devil, and we are now trapped in
the era of the Dixon, Illinois, Faust.

One thing that Mr. Leamer quickly picks up on is Ronnie's
freedom with facts. Apparently this began quite early. "Dutch had
been brought up to tell the truth; but to him, facts had become
flat little balloons that had to be blown up if they were to be seen
and sufficiently appreciated." In Hollywood he began a lifelong
habit of exaggerating not only his own past but those stories that
he read in the *Reader's Digest* and other right-wing publications.
No wonder his aides worry every time he opens his mouth without
a script on the TelePrompTer to be read through those contact
lenses that he used, idly, to take out at dinner parties and suck
on.

By 1938 Ronnie was a featured player in *Brother Rat*. He was and
still is an excellent film actor. The notion that he was just another
Jon Hall is nonsense. For a time he was, in popularity with the
fans, one of the top five actors in the country. If his range is
limited that is because what he was called on to do was limited.
You were a type in those days, and you didn't change your type
if you wanted to be a star. But he did marry an actress who was
an exception to the rule. Jane Wyman did graduate from brash
blonde wisecracker to "dramatic" actress (as Mr. Leamer would

say). After the war, she was the bigger star. The marriage fell apart. Natural daughter Maureen and adopted son Michael could not hold them together. Plainly, Jane could not follow Ronnie's sage advice. "We'll lead an ideal life if you'll just avoid doing one thing: Don't think." Never has there been such a perfect prescription for success in late-twentieth-century American political life.

But war clouds were now gathering over the Hollywood Hills. Five months after Pearl Harbor was attacked, Ronnie, though extremely nearsighted, was available for "limited service." To much weeping and gorge-rising, Ronnie went not overseas but over to Culver City where he made training films for the rest of the war. *Modern Screen* headline: BUT WHEN RONNIE WENT RIDING OFF TO BATTLE, HE LEFT HIS HEART BEHIND HIM! *Photoplay*: I WON'T BE DOING THESE PICTURES. UNCLE SAM HAS CALLED ME . . . AND I'M OFF TO THE WAR.

Ronnie was now known for two important roles, one as the doomed "Gipper" in *Knute Rockne, All American* and the other as the playboy whose legs are sawed off ("Where's the rest of me?") in *King's Row*. As Ronnie's films moved once again B-ward, he moved toward politics. Originally, he had been a New Deal liberal, or something. Actually his real political activity was with the Screen Actors Guild where, by and large, in those days at least, first-rate working actors were seldom to be found giving much time to meetings, much less to becoming its president, as Reagan did.

When the McCarthy era broke upon America, Ronnie took a stern anticommie line within his own union. In 1951 in *Fortnight*, he wrote that "several members of Congress are known Communists" and as one whose reviews had not been so good lately, he went on to add that though good American newspapers were attacking "dirty Reds" their publishers didn't know that they were employing "drama and book critics who . . . were praising the creative efforts of their little 'Red Brothers' while panning the work of all non-Communists."

Ronnie then went to work vetting (or, as it was called then, "clearing") people in the movies who might be tainted with communism. This was done through the Motion Picture Industry Council. The witch hunt was on, and many careers were duly ruined. Ronnie believed that no commie should be allowed to work

in the movies and that anyone who did not cooperate with his
council or the House Committee on Un-American Activities (in
other words, refused to allow the committee to ask impertinent
questions about political beliefs) should walk the plank. To this
day, he takes the line that there was never a blacklist in Hollywood
except for the one that commies within the industry drew up in
order to exclude good Americans from jobs. Ronnie has always
been a very sincere sort of liar.

As luck would have it, Nancy Davis cropped up on one of the
nonexistent blacklists. Apparently there were other possibly
pinker actresses named Nancy Davis in lotusland. She asked a
producer what to do; he said that Reagan could clear her. Thus,
they met . . . not so cute, as the Wise Hack would say. It was the
end of 1949. They "dated" for two years. Plainly, she loved this
bona fide movie star who never stopped talking just as she could
never stop appearing to listen (what her stepfather Dr. Davis must
have been like at the breakfast table can only be imagined). But
the woman who had launched the marriage of Ronnie and Janie,
Louella Parsons, the Saint Simon of San Simeon as well as of all
movieland, could not understand why that idyllic couple had split
up. She described in her column how "one of the lovely girls
Ronnie seemed interested in for a while told me he recently said
to her, 'Sure, I like you. I like you fine. But I think I've forgotten
how to fall in love.' I wonder—do those embers of the once perfect love they shared still burn deep with haunting memories that
won't let them forget?" If the popcorn isn't too old, we can pop
it. But no salt and use oleomargarine.

Apparently, the embers had turned to ash. After two years,
thirty-year-old Nancy married the forty-one-year-old Ronnie in the
company of glamorous Mr. and Mrs. William Holden who posed,
beaming, beside their new best friends at a time when they were
their own new worst friends for, according to Mr. Leamer, as they
posed side by side with the Reagans, "The Holdens weren't even
talking to one another."

Nancy's career is now one of wifedom and motherhood and, of
course, listening. Also, in due course, social climbing. She was
born with a silver ladder in her hand, just like the rest of us who
went to Sidwell Friends School. Naturally, there were problems
with Ronnie's first set of children. Ronnie seems not to have been

a particularly attentive father, while Nancy was an overattentive mother to her own two children. But she took a dim view of Ronnie's first litter. The Reagans settled on Pacific Palisades. Ronnie's movie career was grinding to an end; he was obliged to go to Las Vegas to be a gambling casino "emcee." As there were no commies working for the trade papers by then, the reviews were good.

2

The year 1952 is crucial in Reagan's life. The Hollywood unions had always taken the position that no talent agency could go into production on a regular basis since the resulting conflict of interest would screw agency clients. Eventually, federal law forbade this anomaly. But thirty years ago there was a tacit agreement between agencies and unions that, on a case-by-case basis, an occasional movie might be produced by an agency. The Music Corporation of America represented actor Ronald Reagan. Within that vast agency, one Taft Schreiber looked after Ronald Reagan's declining career. At the end of Reagan's term as president of the Screen Actors Guild, he did something unprecedented.

On July 3, 1952, after a series of meetings, Ronnie sent a letter to MCA granting the agency the blanket right to produce films.

Within a few years, MCA was a dominant force in show business. In television, the forty or so shows that Revue Productions produced each week far surpassed the output of other programming suppliers.

Now for the payoff:

Later that year [1954], Taft Schreiber . . . told Ronnie about a possible role introducing a new weekly television anthology series, "The GE Theater" . . . Schreiber owed his position as head of MCA's new Revue Productions to a SAG decision in which Ronnie played an instrumental role,

and so on.

For eight years, Ronnie was GE's host and occasional actor; he also became the corporate voice for General Electric's conservative viewpoint. During Reagan's tours of the country, he gave The

Speech in the name of General Electric in particular and free
enterprise in general. Gradually, Reagan became more and more
right wing. But then if his principal reading matter told him that
the Russians were not only coming but that their little Red brothers were entrenched in Congress and the school libraries and
the reservoirs (fluoride at the ready), he must speak out. Finally,
all this nonsense began to alarm even GE. When he started to
attack socialism's masterpiece, the TVA (a GE client worth 50
million a year to the firm), he was told to start cooling it, which
he did. Then, "In 1962, pleading bad ratings, GE canceled the
program."

During this period, Reagan was not only getting deeper and
deeper into the politics of the far right, but he and Nancy were
getting to know some of the new-rich Hollywood folk outside show
biz. Car dealers such as Holmes Tuttle and other wheeler-dealers
became friends. The wives were into conspicuous consumption
while the husbands were into money and, marginally, conservative
politics which would enable them to make more money, pay less
tax, and punish the poor. Thanks to Ronnie's brother Neil, then
with an advertising agency that peddled Borax, the future leader
of Righteous Christendom became host to Borax's television series, "Death Valley Days." That same year Ronnie attended the
Cow Palace investiture of Barry Goldwater.

"In late October, Goldwater was unable to speak at the big
$1,000-a-plate fund raiser at the Ambassador Hotel in Los Ange-
les. . . . Holmes Tuttle asked Ronnie to pinch-hit." Tuttle sat next
to wealthy Henry Salvatori, Goldwater's finance chairman. Tuttle
suggested that they run Ronnie for governor of California in 1966.
Salvatori didn't think you could run an actor against an old political pro like the Democratic incumbent Pat Brown. But when
Ronnie went national with The Speech on television, Ronnie was
in business as a politician, and his friends decided to finance a
Reagan race. To these new-rich Sunbelters, "Politicians and candidates, even Ronnie, were an inferior breed. 'Reagan doesn't
have great depth,' Salvatori admits, 'but I don't know any politician who does. He's not the most intelligent man who ever was,
but I've never met a politician with great depth. I don't know of
any politician who would be smart enough to run my business,
but Reagan just might.' " There it all is in one nut's shell.

The rest is beginning now to be history. "In the spring of 1965, forty-one rich businessmen formed 'The Friends of Ronald Reagan.'" For fifty thousand dollars a year, they hired a public-relations firm that specialized in political campaigns to groom Ronnie. California politics were carefully explained to him and he was given a crash course in the state's geography, which he may have flunked. He often had no idea where he was, or, as a supporter remarked to Leamer, "once, he didn't know a goddamn canal and where it went. Another time, he was standing in the Eagle River and didn't know where the hell he was," etc. But he had his dream of the city on the hill and he had The Speech and he had such insights as: the graduated income tax was "spawned by Marx as the prime essential of the socialistic state."

Alas, Mr. Leamer is not interested in Reagan's two terms as governor. He is more interested in Nancy's good grooming and circle of "best dressed" friends; also, in the way her past was falsified: "Nancy Davis Reagan was born in Chicago, the only daughter of Dr. and Mrs. Loyal Davis," said a campaign biography. Although Nancy had denied seeing her "natural" father after her adoption, she had indeed kept in touch for a time; but when he was dying in 1972 and her natural cousin tried to get through to her, there was no response. Mr. Leamer goes on rather too much about Nancy's wealthy girlfriends and their clothes as well as her wealthy *cavaliere servente* Jerome Zipkin who has known everyone from my mother to W. Somerset Maugham. "Maugham's biographer, Ted Morgan, thinks the British author may have patterned Elliot Templeton, a snobbish character in *The Razor's Edge*, on his American friend." Since *The Razor's Edge* was published in 1944, when Mr. Zipkin was still under thirty, it is most unlikely that that exquisite Anglophile American snob (and anti-Semite) could have been based on the charming Mr. Zipkin. Actually, for those interested in such trivia, the character was based on Henry de Courcey May, a monocled figure of my youth, much visible at Bailey's Beach in Newport, Rhode Island; although this exquisite was adored by our mothers, we little lads were under orders never to be alone with nice Mr. May—or not-so-nice Mr. Maugham for that matter. But once, on the train from Providence, Mr. May . . . But that is for Mr. Leamer's next book.

In a bored way, Mr. Leamer rushes through the governorship,

using familiar Reagan boiler plate: the highest taxes in the state's history, and so on. He skirts around the most interesting caper of all, the ranch that Reagan was able to acquire through the good offices of MCA. When some details of this transaction were reported in the press, I was at a health spa near San Diego where Jules Stein and his wife (lifelong friends, as Mr. Leamer would say) were also taking the waters. When I asked Jules about the ranch caper, he got very nervous indeed. "What exactly did they print?" he asked. I told him. "Well," he said, "I didn't know anything about that. It was Schreiber who looked after Ronnie." By then Schreiber was dead.

Mr. Leamer tells us more than we want to know about the Reagan children. There seems to be a good deal of bitterness in a family that is closer to that of the Louds than to Judge Hardy's. But this is par for the course in the families of celebrities in general, and of politicians in particular. A ballet-dancer son with his mother's nose did not go down well. A daughter who decided to run for the Senate (and support the ERA) did not go down well either. So in 1982 Ronnie and his brother, Neil, helped to defeat Maureen, which was a pity since she would have been a more honorable public servant than her father. Apparently he has now had second thoughts or something; he has appointed her consultant "to improve his image among women." The family seems a lot creepier than it probably is simply because Reagan, a divorced man, has always put himself forward as the champion of prayer in the schools, and monogamy, and God, and a foe of abortion and smut and pot and the poor.

Mr. Leamer races through the political life: Ronnie sets out to replace Ford as president but instead is defeated in the primaries of 1976. Mr. Leamer finds Ronnie a pretty cold fish despite the professional appearance of warmth. When one of Ronnie's aides, Mike Deaver, lost out in a power struggle within the Reagan campaign, he was banished; and Ronnie never even telephoned him to say, "How are tricks?"

As he did in his own family, Ronnie stood above the squabble. Indeed four years before, when Ronnie had been choking on a peanut, Deaver had saved his life.

For God's sake, Leamer, dramatize! as Henry James always told us to do. When and how did that peanut get into his windpipe? Where were they? Was it the Heimlich maneuver Deaver used?

In 1980 Reagan took the nomination from Bush, whom he genuinely dislikes, if Mr. Leamer is correct. Reagan then wins the presidency though it might be more accurate to say that Carter lost it. Nancy woos Washington's old guard, the Bright Old Things as they are dubbed, who were at first mildly charmed and then more and more bemused by this curious couple who have no interest at all in talking about what Washington's BOT have always talked about: power and politics and history and even, shades of Henry Adams and John Hay, literature and art. Henry James was not entirely ironic when he called Washington "the city of conversation." Ronnie simply bends their ears with stories about Jack Warner while Nancy discusses pretty things.

Mr. Leamer gets quickly through the politics to the drama: the shooting of Ronnie, who was more gravely injured than anyone admitted at the time. By now, Mr. Leamer is racing along: "Unknown to [Nancy's] staff . . . she was accepting dresses and gowns from major designers as well as jewels from Bulgari and Harry Winston." Seven pages later: "Unknown to Nancy's staff, much of this jewelry didn't belong to her; it had been 'borrowed' for an unspecified period from the exclusive jeweler to be part of a White House collection." Nancy wriggled out of all this as best she could, proposing to give her dresses to a museum while suggesting a permanent White House collection of crown jewels for future first ladies. Conspicuous consumption at the White House has not been so visible since Mrs. Lincoln's day. But at least old Abe paid out of his own pocket for his wife's "flub dubs."

The most disturbing aspect of *Make-Believe* is that Ronnie not only is still the president but could probably be reelected. Almost as an afterthought, Mr. Leamer suddenly reveals, in the last pages of his book, the true Reagan problem, which is now a world problem:

What was so extraordinary was Ronnie's apparent psychic distance from the burden of the presidency. He sat in cabinet meetings doodling. Unless held to a rigid agenda, he would start telling Hol-

lywood stories or talk about football in Dixon. Often in one-on-one
conversations Ronnie seemed distracted or withdrawn. "He has a
habit now," his brother, Neil, said. "You might be talking to him,
and it's like he's picking his fingernails, but he's not. And you know
then he's talking to himself."

"If people knew about him living in his own reality, they
wouldn't believe it," said one White House aide. "There are only
ten to fifteen people who know the extent, and until they leave
and begin talking, no one will believe it."

Of all our presidents, Reagan most resembles Warren Harding.
He is handsome, amiable, ignorant; he has an ambitious wife
(Mrs. Harding was known as the Duchess). But in the year 1983
who keeps what brooch from Bulgari is supremely unimportant.
What is important is that in a dangerous world, the United States,
thanks to a worn-out political system, has not a president but an
indolent cue-card reader, whose writers seem eager for us to be,
as soon as possible, at war. To the extent that Reagan is aware of
what is happening, he probably concurs. But then what actor, no
matter how old, could resist playing the part of a wartime president? Even though war is now the last worst hope of earth; and
hardly make-believe.

Mr. Leamer's *Make-Believe* will be criticized because it is largely
a compendium of trivia about personalities. Unfortunately, there
is no other book for him to write—unless it be an updated version
of *Who Owns America?*

Calvin Trillin

(1935–   )

Trillin graduated from Yale in 1957 and worked as a writer and reporter before joining the staff of *The New Yorker* in 1963. His articles for that magazine, published under the heading "U.S. Journal" and published every third week, provided whimsical reportage on American life, eccentric people, and unusual events that somehow escaped the attention of more conventional journalists. Trillin writes often about food, but he is the kind of food writer who calls himself an "eater" rather than a "gourmet." His subject usually turns out to be barbecued ribs or some other equally reliable dish, and his report almost invariably includes a portrait of an eccentric chef or inside information on a restaurant with odd hours or an inaccessible location. His wife Alice and his two daughters are often included in his reporting, and among his several books about food is one called *Alice, Let's Eat: Further Adventures of a Happy Eater* (1978). He is also the author of two novels, *Runestruck* (1977) and *Floater* (1980). His columns are periodically published as books, including, among several others, *Uncivil Liberties* (1982), *Killings* (1984), *Travels With Alice* (1989), and *Too Soon to Tell* (1995). He has also written a memoir, *Remembering Denny* (1993) and a collection of light verse, *Deadline Poet* (1994). With Will Rogers and James Thurber, Trillin takes his place as one of America's kindest satirists.

Old Marrieds

AUGUST 3, 1985

I figured the big question about our twentieth wedding anniversary might be whether the local newspaper would send a reporter out to interview us, the way reporters always used to interview those old codgers who managed to hit one hundred. ("Mr. Scroggins offers no formula for longevity, although he acknowledged that he has polished off a quart of Jim Beam whiskey every day of his adult life.") I figured that might be the big question even though the local newspaper is the *Village Voice.* Or maybe I figured that might be the big question *because* the local newspaper is the *Village Voice.* In Greenwich Village, after all, we are known rather widely for being married. We enjoy a mild collateral renown for having children. Several years ago, in fact, I expressed concern that we might be put on the Gray Line tour of Greenwich Village as a nuclear family.

It occurred to me that all this might be vaguely embarrassing; in recent years it has become common to hear people all over the country speak of long-term marriage in a tone of voice that assumes it to be inextricably intertwined with the music of Lawrence Welk. In the presence of someone who has been married a long time to the same person, a lot of people seem to feel the way they might feel in the presence of a Methodist clergyman or an IRS examiner. When I asked a friend of mine recently how his twenty-fifth college reunion had gone—he had attended with the very same attractive and pleasant woman he married shortly after graduation—he said, "Well, after the first day I decided to start introducing Marge as my second wife, and that seemed to make everyone a lot more comfortable."

This awkwardness in the presence of marriage has, of course, been particularly intense in the Village, a neighborhood so hip that it is no longer unusual to see people wearing their entire supply of earrings on one ear. (" 'I don't hold with jewelry or none of them geegaws,' Mr. Scroggins said, 'although over the long haul I've found that a single gold stud in one ear can set off a spring ensemble to good advantage.' ") In the Village, a lot of people don't get married, and a lot of those who do seem to get unmarried pretty much on the way back from the ceremony. In other words, the institution has been leaking from both ends.

When our older daughter was in first grade at P.S. 3, one of the romantically named grade schools in the Village, I happened to be among the parents escorting the class on a lizard-buying expedition to a local purveyor called Exotic Aquatics. As we crossed Seventh Avenue, the little boy I had by the hand looked up at me and said, "Are you divorced yet?" When I said that I wasn't, he didn't make fun of me or anything like that—they teach tolerance at P.S. 3, along with a smattering of spelling—but I could sense his discomfort in having to cross a major artery in the company of someone who was a little bit behind.

Reaching a twentieth anniversary might just increase such discomfort among our neighbors. I could imagine what would be said if that little boy's parents happened to meet by chance now and our names came up. (As I envision the sort of lives they lead, she has just quit living with her psychotherapist in New Jersey to join a radical feminist woodcutting collective; her former husband is in the process of breaking up with a waitress who has decided that what she really wants to do is direct.) "Oh, them!" the wood-cutter would say. "Why, they've been married for *decades*!"

The more I considered it, the more I thought that if a reporter in our neighborhood came out to interview people on the twentieth anniversary of their marriage, the questions might be less like the ones he'd ask a citizen who had reached the age of one hundred than the ones he'd ask someone who has chosen to construct a replica of the 1939 World's Fair out of multicolored toothpicks in his recreation room. ("Tell me, Mr. McVeeter, is this some sort of nutso fixation, or what?")

Then I happened to run into an old college classmate called Martin G. Kashfleau. In both investments and social trends, Kashfleau prides himself on having just got out of what other people are about to get into and having just got in on the ground floor of what other people haven't yet heard about. After Kashfleau filled me in on his recent activities—he had just got out of whelk-farming tax shelters and into chewing of hallucinogenic kudzu—he asked what I'd been up to.

"Twentieth anniversary," I mumbled.

"Terrific!" Kashfleau said. He looked at me as if I had just revealed that I was in on the ground floor of a hot electronics issue. At least, I think that's the way he looked at me. I really don't have much experience at being looked at as if I had just revealed that I was in on the ground floor of a hot electronics issue.

Kashfleau told me that among people in their twenties marriage has come back into fashion. As he explained the way things have been going, marriage is part of a sort of fifties revival package that includes neckties and naked ambition. "Best thing you ever did," Kashfleau said. "They're all doing it now, but look at the equity you've got built up."

I shrugged modestly. You don't brag about that sort of thing. Then I went home and told my wife that we were in fashion.

"Not while you're wearing that jacket we're not," she said.

I told her about the fifties package that people in their twenties were bringing back into vogue. She said that if the alternative was to be identified with those little strivers, she would prefer to be thought of as inextricably intertwined with the music of Lawrence Welk.

I could see her point, but I still looked forward to an interview with the local paper. I would be modest, almost to a fault. I would not mention Jim Beam whiskey. The reporter would try to be objective, but he wouldn't be able to hide his admiration for my equity.

P. J. O'Rourke
(1947–   )

P. J. O'Rourke, a correspondent for *Rolling Stone* magazine, is the author of *Parliament of Whores* and *Give War a Chance*, as well as *Holidays in Hell*, from which the following piece is excerpted.

The Innocents Abroad, Updated

On Saturday, June 8, 1867, the steamship *Quaker City* left New York harbor. On board was a group of Americans making the world's first package tour. Also on board was Mark Twain making the world's first fun of package tourism.

In its day *The Innocents Abroad* itinerary was considered exhaustive. It included Paris, Marseilles, the Rock of Gibraltar, Lake Como, some Alps, the Czar, the pyramids and the Holy Land plus the glory that was Greece, the grandeur that was Rome and the pile of volcanic ash that was Pompeii.

When these prototypical tourists went home they could count themselves traveled. They had shivered with thoughts of lions in the Colosseum, "done" the Louvre, ogled Mont Blanc, stumbled through the ruins of the Parthenon by moonlight and pondered that eternal riddle—where'd its nose go?—of the Sphinx. They had seen the world.

But what if Mark Twain had to come back from the dead and

escort 1980's tourists on a 1980's tour? Would it be the same? No. I'm afraid Mr. Twain would find there are worse things than innocents abroad in the world today.

In 1988 every country with a middle class to export has gotten into the traveling act. We Yanks, with our hula shirts and funny Kodaks, are no longer in the fore. The earth's travel destinations are jam-full of littering Venezuelans, peevish Swiss, smelly Norwegian backpackers yodeling in restaurant booths, Saudi Arabian businessmen getting their dresses caught in revolving doors and Bengali remittance men in their twenty-fifth year of graduate school pestering fat blonde Belgian *au pair* girls.

At least we American tourists understand English when it's spoken loudly and clearly enough. Australians don't. Once you've been on a plane full of drunken Australians doing wallaby imitations up and down the aisles, you'll never make fun of Americans visiting the Wailing Wall in short shorts again.

The Japanese don't wear short shorts (a good thing, considering their legs), but they do wear three-piece suits in the full range of tenement-hall paint colors, with fit to match. The trouser cuffs drag like bridal trains; the jacket collars have an ox yoke drape; and the vests leave six inches of polyester shirt snapping in the breeze. If the Japanese want to be taken seriously as world financial powers, they'd better quit using the same tailor as variety-show chimps.

The Japanese also travel in packs at a jog trot and get up at six A.M. and sing their company song under your hotel window. They are extraordinary shoplifters. They eschew the usual clothes and trinkets, but automobile plants, steel mills and electronics factories seem to be missing from everywhere they go. And Japs take snapshots of everything, not just everything famous but *everything*. Back in Tokyo there must be a billion color slides of street corners, turnpike off-ramps, pedestrian crosswalks, phone booths, fire hydrants, manhole covers and overhead electrical wires. What are the Japanese doing with these pictures? It's probably a question we should have asked before Pearl Harbor.

Worse than the Japanese, at least worse looking, are the Germans, especially at pool-side. The larger the German body, the smaller the German bathing suit and the louder the German voice issuing German demands and German orders to everybody who doesn't speak German. For this, and several other reasons,

Germany is known as "the land where Israelis learned their manners."

And Germans in a pool cabana (or even Israelis at a discotheque) are nothing compared with French on a tropical shore. A middle-aged, heterosexual, college-educated male wearing a Mickey Mouse T-shirt and a string-bikini bottom and carrying a purse—what else could it be but a vacationing Frenchman? No tropical shore is too stupid for the French. They turn up on the coasts of Angola, Eritrea, Bangladesh and Sri Lanka. For one day they glory in *l'atmosphère très primitif* then spend two weeks in an ear-splitting snit because the natives won't make a *steak frite* out of the family water buffalo.

Also present in Angola, Eritrea and God-Knows-Where are the new breed of yuppie "experience travelers." You'll be pinned down by mortar fire in the middle of a genocide atrocity in the Sudan, and right through it all come six law partners and their wives, in Banana Republic bush jackets, taking an inflatable raft trip down the White Nile and having an "experience."

Mortar fire is to be preferred, of course, to British sports fans. Has anyone checked the passenger list on *The Spirit of Free Enterprise*? Were there any Liverpool United supporters on board? That channel ferry may have been tipped over for fun. (Fortunately the Brits have to be back at their place of unemployment on Monday so they never get further than Spain.)

Then there are the involuntary tourists. Back in 1867, what with the suppression of the slave trade and all, they probably thought they'd conquered the involuntary tourism problem. Alas, no. Witness the African exchange students—miserable, cold, shivering, grumpy and selling cheap wrist watches from the top of cardboard boxes worldwide. (Moscow's Patrice Lumumba University has a particularly disgruntled bunch.) And the Pakistani family with twelve children who've been camped out in every airport on the globe since 1970—will somebody please do something for these people? Their toddler has got my copy of the *Asian Wall Street Journal*, and I won't be responsible if he tries to stuff it down the barrel of the El Al security guard's Uzi again.

Where will Mr. Clemens take these folks? What is the 1980's equivalent of the Grand Tour? What are the travel "musts" of today?

All the famous old monuments are still there, of course, but they're surrounded by scaffolds and green nets and signs saying, "Il pardonne la restoration bitte please." I don't know two people who've ever seen the same famous old monument. I've seen Big Ben. A friend of mine has seen half of the Sistine Chapel ceiling. No one has seen Notre Dame Cathedral for years. It's probably been sold to a shopping mall developer in Phoenix.

We've all, however, seen Dr. Meuller's Sex Shop in the Frankfurt airport. Dr. Meuller's has cozy booths where, for one deutsche mark a minute, we modern tourists can watch things hardly thought of in 1867. And there's nothing on the outside of the booths to indicate whether you're in there viewing basically healthy Swedish nude volleyball films or videos of naked Dobermans cavorting in food. Dr. Meuller's is also a reliable way to meet your boss, old Sunday School teacher or ex-wife's new husband, one of whom is always walking by when you emerge.

Dr. Meuller's is definitely a "must" of modern travel, as is the Frankfurt airport itself. If Christ came back tomorrow, He'd have to change planes in Frankfurt. Modern air travel means less time spent in transit. That time is now spent in transit lounges.

What else? There are "local points of interest" available until the real monuments are restored. These are small piles of stones about which someone will tell you extravagant lies for five dollars. ("And here, please, the Tomb of the Infant Jesus.") And there are the great mini-bars of Europe—three paper cartons of anise-flavored soda pop, two bottles of beer with suspended vegetable matter, a triangular candy bar made of chocolate-covered edelweiss and a pack of Marlboros manufactured locally under license. (*N.B.*: Open that split of Mumm's ½-star in there, and $200 goes on your hotel bill faster than you can say "service non compris.")

In place of celebrated palaces, our era has celebrated parking spots, most of them in Rome. Romans will back a Fiat into the middle of your linguine al pesto if you're sitting too close to the restaurant window.

Instead of cathedrals, mosques and ancient temples, we have duty-free shops—at their best in Kuwait. I never knew there was so much stuff I didn't want. I assumed I wanted most stuff. But that was before I saw a $110,000 crêpe de chine Givenchy chador and a solid-gold camel saddle with twelve Rolex watches embedded in the seat.

The "sermons in stone" these days are all sung with cement. Cement is the granite, the marble, the porphyry of our time. Someday, no doubt, there will be "Elgin Cements" in the British Museum. Meanwhile, we tour the Warsaw Pact countries—cement everywhere, including, at the official level, quite a bit of cement in their heads.

Every modern tourist has seen *Mannix* dubbed in forty languages and the amazing watch adjustments of Newfoundland, Malaysia and Nepal (where time zones are, yes, half an hour off), and France in August when you can travel through the entire country without encountering a single pesky Frenchman or being bothered with anything that's open for business—though, somehow, the fresh dog crap is still a foot deep on the streets of Paris.

Astonishing toilets for humans are also a staple of up-to-date foreign adventure. Anyone who thinks international culture has become bland and uniform hasn't been to the bathroom, especially not in Yugoslavia where it's a hole in the floor with a scary old lady with a mop standing next to it. And, for astonishing toilet paper, there's India where there isn't any.

No present-day traveler, even an extra-odoriferous Central European one, can say he's done it all if he hasn't been on a smell tour of Asia. Maybe what seems pungent to the locals only becomes alarming when sniffed through a giant Western proboscis, but there are some odors in China that make a visit to Bhopal seem like a picnic downwind from the Arpege factory. Hark to the cry of the tourist in the East: "Is it dead or is it dinner?"

Nothing beats the Orient for grand vistas, however, particularly of go-go girls. True, they can't Boogaloo and have no interest in learning. But Thai exotic dancers are the one people left who prefer American-made to Japanese. And they come and sit on your lap between sets, something the girls at the Crazy Horse never do. Now, where'd my wallet go?

Many contemporary tourist attractions are not located in one special place the way tourist attractions used to be. Now they pop up everywhere—that villainous cab driver with the all-consonant last name, for instance. He's waiting outside hotels from Sun City to the Seward Peninsula. He can't speak five languages and can't understand another ten. Hey! Hey! Hey, you! This isn't the way to the Frankfurt airport! Nein! Non! Nyet! Ixnay!

American embassies, too, are all over the map and always breathtaking. In the middle of London, on beautiful Grosvenor Square, there's one that looks like a bronzed Oldsmobile dashboard. And rising from the slums of Manila is another that resembles the Margarine of the Future Pavilion at the 1959 Brussels World Fair. I assume this is all the work of one architect, and I assume he's on drugs. Each American embassy comes with two permanent features—a giant anti-American demonstration and a giant line for American visas. Most demonstrators spend half their time burning Old Glory and the other half waiting for green cards.

Other ubiquitous spectacles of our time include various panics—AIDS, PLO terror and owning U.S. dollars predominate at the moment—and postcards of the Pope kissing the ground. There's little ground left unkissed by this pontiff, though he might think twice about kissing anything in some of the places he visits. (Stay away from Haiti, San Francisco and Mykonos, J.P., please.)

Then there's the squalor. This hasn't changed since 1867, but tourists once tried to avoid it. Now they seek it out. Modern tourists have to see the squalor so they can tell everyone back home how it changed their perspective on life. Describing squalor, if done with sufficient indignation, makes friends and relatives morally obligated to listen to your boring vacation stories. (Squalor is conveniently available, at reasonable prices, in Latin America.)

No, the Grand Tour is no longer a stately procession of like-minded individuals through half a dozen of the world's major principalities. And it's probably just as well if Mark Twain doesn't come back from the dead. He'd have to lead a huge slew of multinational lunatics through hundreds of horrible countries with disgusting border formalities. And 1980's customs agents are the only thing worse than 1980's tourists. Damn it, give that back! You know perfectly well that it's legal to bring clean socks into Tanzania. Ow! Ouch! Where are you taking me!?

Of course you don't have to go to Africa to get that kind of treatment. You can have your possessions stolen right on the Piccadilly Line if you want. In fact, in 1987, you can experience most of the indignities and discomforts of travel in your own hometown, wherever you live. Americans flock in seething masses to any dim-wit local attraction—tall ships making a landing, short actors making a move, Andrew Wyeth making a nude Helga fracas—just as if they were actually going somewhere. The briefest commuter flight is filled with businessmen dragging mountainous garment bags and whole computers on board. They are worse pests than mainland Chinese taking Frigidaires home on the plane. And no modern business gal goes to lunch without a steamer trunk-size tote full of shoe changes, Sony Walkman tapes and tennis rackets. When she makes her way down a restaurant aisle, she'll crack the back of your head with this exactly the same way a Mexican will with a crate of chickens on a Yucatán bus ride.

The tourism ethic seems to have spread like one of the new sexual diseases. It now infects every aspect of daily life. People carry backpacks to work and out on dates. People dress like tourists at the office, the theater and church. People are as rude to their fellow countrymen as ever they are to foreigners.

Maybe the right thing to do is stay home in a comfy armchair and read about travel as it should be—in Samuel Clemens's *Huckleberry Finn.*

Molly Ivins

(1944–)

Molly Ivins has been a newspaper reporter for the *Houston Chronicle*, the *Minneapolis Star Tribune*, *The New York Times*, and other newspapers. She contributes essays and reports to *The Nation*, *The New York Times Book Review*, and *The Progressive*, among other periodicals, and has appeared as an occasional columnist on National Public Radio. Her two collections of pieces, *Molly Ivins Can't Say That, Can She?* and *Nothin' But Good Times Ahead*, were published in 1991 and 1993. She presently writes for the *Fort Worth Star Telegram*.

H. Ross Went Seven Bubbles Off Plumb (and Other Tales)

Well, our attorney general is under indictment. He ran as "the people's lawyer"; now we call him "the people's felon." But it's just a commercial bribery charge; he should get shed of it. We all know there's nothing wrong with Jim Mattox but rotten personality. Meantime, over in the Legislature, the latest incumbent indicted was Senator Carl Parker of Port Arthur, brought up two weeks ago on charges of pushing pornography, running prostitutes, and perjury. We feel this is the best indictment of a sitting legislator since last year, when Representative Bubba London of Bonham got sent up for cattle rustling. It's rare to find a good case of cattle rustling in the Lege anymore, so we're real proud of London. Happily, Senator Parker is unopposed, so we expect this to be the finest case of reelection-despite-trying-circumstances since 1982, when Senator John Wilson of LaGrange was reelected although seriously dead. Several distinguished former members have been indicted of late on charges ranging from misappropriation of funds to child abuse. We're running about normal on that front.

On matters cultural, when the World's Fair in New Orleans had Texas Week recently, they invited two of our biggest stars, Willie Nelson and Ralph the Diving Pig from San Marcos. Willie has been galaxy-famous for years now, but this was Ralph's first shot at international exposure, so we were all real thrilled for him. Ralph's the Greg Louganis of porkerdom.

We're having another bingo crackdown: we are big on busting grannies for bingo. If you bingo bad enough in this state, they'll put you in the Texas Department of Corrections, the Lone Star Gulag. Texas and California are running about even to see which state can put the most human beings in Stripe City. We got a three-strikes law here—three felonies and it's life—so we got guys doing terminal stretches for passing two bad checks and aggravated mopery.

T.D.C. is so overcrowded they were like berserk rats in there in the vicious summer heat. There have been more than 270 stabbings in T.D.C. this year. Judge William Wayne Justice, who, in my opinion, is a great American hero and, in everybody's opinion, is the most hated man in Texas, has declared the conditions in the system unconstitutional. Judge Justice continues to labor under the illusion that the U.S. Constitution applies in Texas. Just last year he de-segged a public housing project in Clarksville— almost twenty years after the Civil Rights Act—so the citizens started threatening to kill him again. Anyway, the prisons are being worked on; the Legislature passed some reforms because they knew if they didn't, Judge Justice would. He already made them clean up the whole juvenile corrections system. So now it's just a question of whether the reforms can beat the riot in under the wire.

We have also had educational reform, and it come a gully-washer. First off, our new governor, Mark White, shows signs of intelligence above vegetable level, which means he will never make the list of truly great governors, such as Dolph Briscoe, the living Pet Rock. So Marko Blanco appointed H. Ross Perot to head up this committee to figure out what's wrong with the public schools. H. Ross took off like an unguided missile. I keep having to explain to foreigners that some loopy right-wing Dallas billionaires are a lot better than others, and H. Ross happens to be one of our better right-wing billionaires. This is assuming you don't make him so mad that he goes out and buys an army and invades your country with it. But he mostly does that to no-account countries full of tacky ragheads, so no one minds. Anyway, H. Ross decided everything was wrong with the schools—teachers, courses, books. The Board of Education had ruled that no one could teach evolution as fact in Texas schools, and H. Ross said it was making us look dumber than the Luzbuddy debate team. Actually, he said "laughingstock." Then H. Ross went seven bubbles off plumb, crazy as a peach-orchard boar, and announced the trouble with the schools is *too much football.* That's when we all realized H. Ross Perot is secretly an agent of the Kremlin; yes, a commie, out to destroy the foundation of the entire Texan way of life.

The Legislature had a fit of creeping socialism and passed nearly every one of H. Ross's reforms, so now a kid can't play football unless he's passing *all* his courses, and he has to take stuff like math and English. Probably means the end of the world is close at hand. The Legislature even raised some taxes to pay for all this school stuff; first time they've raised taxes in thirteen years, so you see how serious it is.

Economically speaking, Texas is a very big state. (It's real embarrassing to have to say that, but they make us learn it in school here.) Most economists break it into six zones to report on what's going on. It's not unusual for Texas to be declared a disaster area for drought and flood simultaneously, and our economy is like that, too. In the Metroplex, which was called Dallas/Fort Worth back before chairs became "ergonomically designed seating systems," there is just a flat-out boom. The area has technically achieved full employment, 3.5 percent un-. Its building boom should crap out before long, but its economy is almost recessionproof—insurance, banking, merchandising, and defense contracts. The Centex Corridor (a.k.a. Austin and San Antone) is also Fat City; lot of high-tech firms coming in, supposed to be the new Silicon Valley. But Austin and San Antone are both mellow ol' towns, never wanted to be like Dallas or Houston. Fair amount of no-growth sentiment there, for Texas. But we reckon it's too late: both towns about ruint; gonna need separate books for the White Pages and Yellow Pages before long. The land sharks are in a greed frenzy, turning over sections every couple months for another $1 million, building all over the aquifer. There never was much around Houston or Dallas to crud up, but the limestone hills and fast rivers of Central Texas—that's a shame.

Contrarywise, the Rio Grande Valley's a disaster area. It's truck-farming country, mainly citrus, and also the most Third World place you can find in the U.S. of A. In fact, it's still feudal in some ways. The Valley was already reeling from the peso devaluation last year—we're talking as high as 50 percent unemployment in some Valley counties—when the big freeze hit right after Christmas and just wiped out the whole crop. Now the question's not how widespread unemployment is; it's how widespread hunger is, how bad malnutrition is. A real mess. The governor and the churches have been great; the Reagan administration, zero.

Also hurting real bad is most of West Texas. This drought has cut so deep the ranchers have even had to sell off their starter herds. Just nothing left. The Panhandle, the Plains, even in Central Texas, there's no pasture. A goddamn drought is just the sorriest kind of calamity. A flood, a hurricane, or a tornado hits and then it's over, but a drought takes a long, long time to kill your cattle and your spirit, and gives you so many, many chances to get your hopes up again—in vain. You folks back East, your beef's going up considerable; we got nothing to start over with when this does break. Our farmers are bleeding to death. Mark White carried every rural (we pronounce that *rule*) area in this state in 1982 against a Republican incumbent with more money than God. But one of the laws of politics is It Ain't a Trend Till You've Seen It Twice. The polls show Reagan winning Texas with 75 percent of the vote.

Politically, we've got more talent in statewide office now than in living memory: not a certified Neanderthal in the bunch, and the treasurer, Ann Richards, is one of the smartest, funniest peo-

ple in politics anywhere. Our populist Ag Commish, Jim Hightower, keeps us amused with his observations: "Why would I want
to be a middle-of-the-road politician? Ain't nothin' in the middle
of the road but yellow stripes and dead armadillos." (Tell the
truth, I also had a great fondness for Hightower's predecessor, an
entertaining linthead named Reagan V. Brown, who wanted to
nuke the fire ants. Brown probably lost because he called Booker
T. Washington a nigger, but there were extenuating circumstances: he called him a *great* nigger.)

Our congressional delegation still boasts enough wood to start
a lumberyard. We've got a helluva U.S. Senate race. In one corner
is Phil Gramm, the former Boll Weevil Democrat, now a full-
fledged Republican, named the most right-wing member of
Congress by the *National Journal.* And in the other corner, a thirty-
eight-year-old liberal State Senator from Austin named Lloyd Doggett: smart, clean, hard-working Mr. Integrity, actually looks like
the young Abe Lincoln. If you could jack up Doggett and run a
sense of humor in under him, he'd be about perfect.

Doggett's a long shot because there is an ungodly amount of
right-wing money in this state, and no decent newspapers, except
for the *Dallas Times Herald.* (I'd say that even if I didn't work for
it.) Gramm is running a charming campaign, accusing Doggett of
being soft on queers and commies. That usually sells well down
here. Doggett can get pretty nasty his own self, in down-populist
fashion. Right now he seems to be concentrating on convincing
the corporate types that Gramm's so far gone in ideology he
doesn't have enough sense to protect the state's economic interests. We used to have a congressman like that from Dallas named
Jim Collins. The rest of the guys would be trying to sneak gas
deregulation past the Yankees, and Collins would go into a dia-
tribe about school busing. He didn't just miss the play; he never
understood what *game* it was.

People always try to tell you how much Texas is changing.
Hordes of Yankee yuppies have moved in, and we have herpes
bars, roller discos, and other symptoms of civilization. I think,
though, maybe Texas is in a permanent state of *plus ça change.*
While it is true that there are Texans who play polo and eat pasta
salad, the place is still reactionary, cantankerous, and hilarious.

The Nation, October 14, 1984

New Heights of Piffle

It just gets better and better, doesn't it? The Los Angeles riots may have been a tragedy for L.A., and are indeed indicative of a larger tragedy in this country, but they have inspired our only presidential candidates to new heights of piffle.

Immediately after the verdict in the Rodney King case was announced, George Bush was inspired to say, "The court system has worked. What we need now is calm and respect for the law while we wait for the appeals process to work." No one had bothered to explain to the president that you cannot appeal an acquittal.

Then Dan Quayle contributed his mite by blaming the situation on declining values, for which he fingered sitcom character Murphy Brown. We live in a great nation.

It's now clear that the flag-and-Willie-Horton of the 1992 campaign will be values—a shame, since it used to be a perfectly good word. A trifle amorphous, to be sure, but when you added some modifier—Christian values, humanistic values, family values—at least we were all in the same ballpark as to what we were talking about. Going back to Puritan days, Americans have been fond of sitting around disparaging other people's morals. We could continue to do this for the rest of this political campaign, or we might start talking about how to fix what's wrong with the country.

Meantime, my man H. Ross is stronger than Tabasco, surging into the lead in the polls on the strength of not having proposed one damn thing about how to fix anything. I was enchanted by H. Ross's 1955 letter to the secretary of the navy explaining why he, Ross Perot, did not want to finish his four-year hitch. He was shocked, *shocked*, to find that men in the United States Navy took the Lord's name in vain. Gadzooks! We are shocked, too, of course. What a shattering surprise.

"I have found the Navy to be a fairly Godless organization," wrote Perot. "I do not enjoy the prospect of continuing to stand on the quarterdeck as Officer of the Deck in foreign ports, being subjected to drunken tales of moral emptiness, passing out penicillin pills, and seeing promiscuity on the part of married men.

"I constantly hear the Lord's name taken in vain at all levels. I find it unsatisfying to live, work, and be directed in an atmosphere where taking God's name in vain is a part of the everyday vocab-

ulary. I have observed little in the way of a direct effort to improve
a man morally while he is in the Navy or even hold him at his
present moral level.''

Well, poop, I always counted on the navy for moral uplift myself. Doesn't everyone enlist in the navy for corrective spiritual
enlightenment? Where's Mr. Roberts when you need him?

What we have here is a Portrait of the Young Man as a Prig.
Comparing the letter Bill Clinton wrote at age twenty-one to the
letter Ross Perot wrote at twenty-five is an exercise in the difference between pietistic piffle and genuine moral agony. Young Bill
Clinton was clearly tortured by the war in Vietnam—not so much
by the prospect of being killed as of having to kill on behalf of a
corrupt regime that did not even have the support of its own
people. Ross Perot, as he later admitted, did not get along with
his commanding officer.

Perot's interest in other people's marital fidelity is beginning
to seem more than a little wiggy. He often lectured his employees
on the subject in the early days of EDS. In some ways, he did try
to help strengthen the families of those who worked for him—
he gave stock to wives in their names, took couples out to dinner,
held family picnics for employees. But he also demanded total
loyalty of his employees and worked them to a point where they
almost never saw their families. The definition of an absentee
father was someone working for EDS. An absentee father who
never took the Lord's name in vain.

While we're all engaged in these weighty debates about Murphy
Brown and cursing in the navy, the country continues to unravel,
and a good place for serious students of government to watch it
do so is at Dan Quayle's very own Council on Competitiveness.
Here we see, unobscured by smoke screens of rhetoric, what's
wrong with the country. This is where the special interests who
have given huge contributions to the Republican party get their
payoffs. And what a festive sight it is. Relax the regulations, bend
the rules, grant exceptions, pay off the contributors. No shame,
no bull.

These are the people bringing you a campaign the centerpiece
of which is moral values. Don't you think we should know better
than to listen to politicians prating about values?